✻ LAURA ✻
Shepherd-Robinson

DAUGHTERS
of
NIGHT

PAN BOOKS

First published 2021 by Mantle

This paperback edition first published 2022 by Pan Books
an imprint of Pan Macmillan
The Smithson, 6 Briset Street, London ECIM 5NR
EU representative: Macmillan Publishers Ireland Ltd, 1st Floor,
The Liffey Trust Centre, 117–126 Sheriff Street Upper,
Dublin 1, DOI YC43
Associated companies throughout the world
www.panmacmillan.com

ISBN 978-1-5098-8084-3

1 3 5 7 9 8 6 4 2

A CIP catalogue record for this book is available from the British Library.

Map artwork by Neil Gower

Typeset in Adobe Caslon by Jouve (UK), Milton Keynes
Printed and bound by CPI Group (UK) Ltd, Croydon, CRO 4YY

Visit **www.panmacmillan.com** to read more about all our books
and to buy them. You will also find features, author interviews and
news of any author events, and you can sign up for e-newsletters
so that you're always first to hear about our new releases.

DAUGHTERS *of* NIGHT

Laura Shepherd-Robinson worked in politics for nearly twenty years before re-entering normal life to complete an MA in Creative Writing at City University. *Blood & Sugar*, her first novel, won the Historical Writers' Association Debut Crown and the Specsavers/CrimeFest Best Debut Novel prize; was a Waterstones Thriller of the Month; and was a *Guardian* and *Telegraph* novel of the year. It was also shortlisted for the Crime Writers' Association John Creasey (New Blood) Dagger, the Sapere Books Historical Dagger, the Goldsboro Glass Bell and the Amazon Publishing/ Capital Crime Best Debut Novel award, as well as being longlisted for the Theakston's Old Peculier Crime Novel of the Year prize. *Daughters of Night* is her second novel.

Also by Laura Shepherd-Robinson

Blood & Sugar

To my dad, for the Oresteia *and so much else*

'Vice, in its true light, is so deformed, that it shocks us at first sight; and would hardly ever seduce us, if it did not at first wear the mask of some virtue.'

Lord Chesterfield, *Letters to His Son on the Art of Becoming a Man of the World and a Gentleman*, 1748

In Attendance

The Corsham Household

Caroline Corsham (Caro) – *'Known for her opinions'*
Captain Henry Corsham (Harry) – *her husband, a Member
of Parliament, presently in France*
Gabriel Corsham – *Harry and Caro's infant son*
Miles – *a footman*

Peregrine Child's Lodgings

Peregrine Child – *a thief-taker, formerly magistrate of
Deptford*
Sophie Hardcastle – *a sailor's wife, mother of two children,
sometimes shares Child's bed*

The Beau Monde

Octavius, Lord March – *heir to the Earl of Amberley, a poet*
Lieutenant Edward Dodd-Bellingham (Neddy) – *a war hero*
Simon Dodd-Bellingham – *the lieutenant's half-brother, an
antiquarian and dealer in classical artefacts*
Jonathan Stone – *moneylender to the beau monde*
Nicholas Cavill-Lawrence – *Under-Secretary of State for the
Home Office*

In Attendance

THE WHORES' CLUB

Lucy Loveless – *a five-guinea prostitute*
Kitty Carefree – *a ten-guinea prostitute, friend of Lucy Loveless*
Hector – *a link-boy, Secretary to the Whores' Club*

THE AGNETTI HOUSEHOLD

Jacobus Agnetti – *a painter of portraits and classical scenes*
Theresa Agnetti – *his estranged wife*
Cassandra Willoughby – *his assistant*

THE TABLEAUX HOUSE ON COMPTON STREET

Maria Havilland – *the owner*
Pamela – *'The Virtuous Maid'*
Cecily – *'Artemis, Goddess of Virgins'*

THE CRAVEN HOUSEHOLD

Mordechai Craven – *Caro's younger brother, a banker*
Louisa Craven – *his wife, mother of his children*
Ambrose Craven – *Caro's elder brother, a banker*

BOW STREET

Sir Amos Fox – *the Bow Street magistrate*
Orin Black – *a Bow Street Runner, friend of Peregrine Child*

THE STREET

Jenny Wren – *a prostitute and thief, an informant of Peregrine Child*
Finn Daley – *a moneylender*

Nelly Diver, formerly known as Annie Yearley – *a prostitute and thief, a friend of Lucy Loveless from the old days*

Misc.

Ezra Von Siegel – *a lamplighter at the Vauxhall Pleasure Gardens*
Solomon Loredo – *a jeweller in the Jewish Quarter*
Erasmus Knox – *Jonathan Stone's man of business*
Richmond Baird – *agent of the Home Office*
Hester Rainwood – *matron of the Magdalen Hospital for Penitent Prostitutes*
Ansell Ward – *a merchant and alderman of the City of London, a former client of Simon Dodd-Bellingham*
Humphrey Sillerton – *a Clapham merchant*

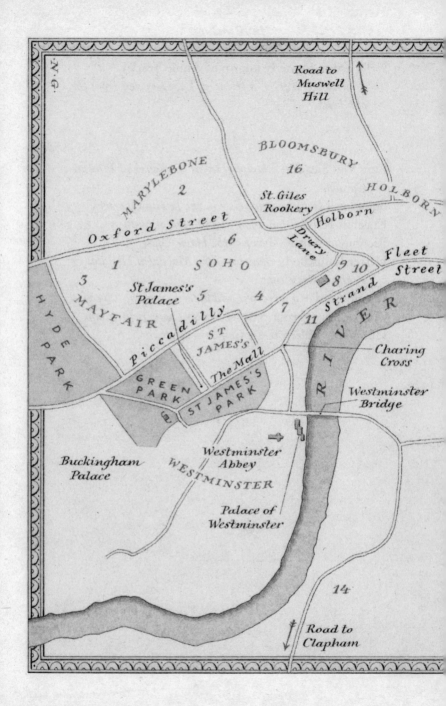

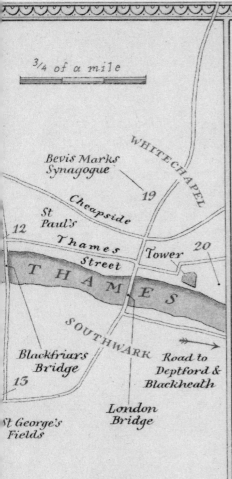

3/4 of a mile

Bevis Marks
Synagogue

WHITECHAPEL

Cheapside

19

St
Paul's

12

Thames

Street

Tower

20

THAMES

SOUTHWARK

Blackfriars
Bridge

Road to
Deptford &
Blackheath

13

London
Bridge

St George's
Fields

1 Caro's house
2 Lucy Loveless's lodgings
3 Craven House
4 Mrs Havilland's tableaux
   house & The Golden Pear-Tree
5 Kitty Carefree's
   lodgings
6 Carlisle House
   Assembly Rooms
7 Jacobus Agnetti's house
8 Covent Garden
9 Sir Amos Fox's house & the
   Brown Bear Tavern
10 Theatre Royal
11 Amberley House
12 Bridewell House
   of Correction
13 Magdalen Hospital
   for Penitent Prostitutes
14 Vauxhall Pleasure
   Gardens
15 Nellie Diver's lodgings,
   Winchester Palace
16 The Dodd-Bellingham
   residence
17 Peregrine Child's
   lodgings
18 Ansell Ward's house
19 Solomon Loredo's shop
20 The Rag Fair

LONDON
— 1782 —

BOOK ONE

*

30 AUGUST–4 SEPTEMBER 1782

'*She looked just like a painting, dying to speak.*'

Aeschylus, the *Oresteia*, 458 BC

CHAPTER ONE

✳

IN THE WRONG hands a secret is a weapon.

Caroline Corsham was alive to the danger, to the vulnerability of her position – she had thought of little else since last night's disaster. Yet now that the truth was known – her secret guessed, the blade honed sharp – what choice did she have left, except to believe? *A last roll of the dice. Nothing ventured, nothing gained.* These banalities spurred her on. *God grant me courage.*

Taking a ginger comfit from her enamelled pillbox, Caro slipped it into her mouth, her nausea rising. Muslin, lace and brocade hemmed her in on every side; jewelled buttons flashing on embroidered waistcoats; pastel shades of periwig and kid glove; silver buckles glinting in the light of a thousand beeswax candles that filled the domed roof of the Rotunda with their honeyed scent. It was the opening night of Jacobus Agnetti's exhibition of classical scenes, and half of London society had turned out for the wretched man. Distractedly, she greeted people she knew: allies of her husband in the House of Commons; clients of the Craven Bank; rival beauties, solicitous matrons, admiring gentlemen. Their laughter was shrill, pink faces merged in a smear of complacency. *They smile to bare their teeth, before they rip you apart.*

A young baronet was explaining some technical aspect of the paintings to her, though she doubted he'd ever held a brush in his life. Gazing around the Rotunda, the canvases encircled her in one endless, bloody spectacle. Men in helmets killing one another, killing monsters, killing women. The rape of Lucretia. Medea slaughtering her infant children. It's how history remembers the lady, she thought. By our death or our dishonour or our sins.

Her skin was hot as Hades. Her fears clamoured at her like a Greek chorus. She glanced at the clock on the Rotunda wall.

It was time.

*

Outside, the music had picked up tempo as night had fallen. Before Caro stretched a fantasy-land: ten thousand lights adorning the trees and the supper boxes and the Chinese pavilion. The Vauxhall Pleasure Gardens were busy even for a warm August night, ladies and gentlemen perambulating the lime walks under the stars. Drawing the hood of her sable cloak up over her piled hair, Caro headed for one of the gardens' perimeter paths, where her peacock-blue satin and lack of servant would attract less attention.

The air was rich with the smells of Vauxhall: heady perfumes of flowers, hot pies, gunpowder. The fireworks startled like pistol shots, the revellers' faces flashing green and red and gold. A party of young bucks in carnival masks were swaggering around by a statue of Venus. They tried to waylay her with wine, but she hurried on.

The path grew darker as she progressed deeper into the gardens. Couples giggled in the shadows: young gentlemen sweet-talking shop girls into parting with their dubious virtue; clerks and apprentices fallen prey to Vauxhall's whores. Caro herself was not unfamiliar with this part of the gardens. God might see everything, but husbands didn't – especially when they were sojourned in France, neglecting their wife and child.

Nevertheless, her pulse was erratic. Every danger was heightened now, and anyone who saw her down here would presume she was meeting a lover.

Curls of river fog drifted towards her. The fireworks boomed like a salvo of cannon. On either side, the trees pressed in, the path deserted. Caro turned into the Dark Walk that ran alongside the eastern wall of the gardens, nearly colliding with a man coming the other way. She cried out in horror, drawing back. Two bulging eyes loomed at her over a long grotesque beak, a broad-brimmed hat casting the rest of the face into shadow. Caro backed up against the trees, half-paralysed with terror, but the man in the mask brushed past her without a word.

Collecting herself, a little shaken by the incident, she pressed on. Abutting the gardens' wall were the bowers: a dozen or more little chambers carved into the greenery, invisible from the path. Soft laughter drifted on the breeze, and a voice murmured faint endearments. People hung hats or tied handkerchiefs to the lamps outside each bower, and Caro looked for their agreed signal: an ostrich feather. Spotting it tied to a lamp up ahead, she glanced around herself. Danger upon danger – but she'd come too far to turn back now.

Hurrying into the bower, she stopped, drawing up short. A lantern, a stone bench, willows stirring in the breeze. These were the things she expected to see. Not a woman lying on the ground – her body curled like a question mark, the stomacher of her pink gown stained a shocking dark red. One of her gloved hands clawed at a wound in her throat, the other lay limp next to a bloodstained document on the grass. Caro stared, confused, half expecting the woman to rise and laugh at the joke. It was as if she'd stepped into one of Jacobus Agnetti's paintings.

The woman groaned, a raw, inhuman sound, and more details lodged in Caro's mind: blood in the woman's chestnut hair; one slipper on, one slipper off; her bone-white face, at once alien and familiar. *Oh Lord. Oh no. Oh Lucia.*

Still she stared – at Lucia's contorted mouth, at the blood, so much blood. *Don't just stand there. You have to help her. Move.* Dropping to her knees, the soil wet with blood beneath them, she pulled off her cloak. More blood pumped from several deep, dark wounds in Lucia's stomach. Caro tried to staunch the flow, but her cloak was soon heavy and sodden in her hands. 'Who did this to you?' she cried helplessly. 'Who did this?'

Lucia's fingers found her own. She gazed at Caro as if from a distance. Her lips parted, her words a whisper: 'He knows.'

Chapter Two

WALK AWAY AND do it like you mean it.

Peregrine Child rose from the table and crossed the tavern floor. Eyes focused on the sawdust-strewn floorboards, he counted the seconds as he walked. One . . . two . . . three . . .

'Thirteen guineas,' Jenny Wren said.

Better than fifteen, but still too much. Child paused, but didn't turn. 'The watch is only worth twenty. My client might as well buy himself a new one.'

'Seven guineas is a lot of money, Perry.'

Now Child turned, but only so she could see the seriousness of his intent. 'Not to him. If I go to him with thirteen, he'll laugh in my face. There's pride at stake here. He was robbed.'

Jenny scowled, and a beauty spot wobbled on her cheek like a wart on a toad. Her wig was two feet high, powdered a delicate shade of violet; a convenient repository for stolen goods, Child supposed. Two of her matted-haired swains sat beside her, matching Child stare for stare. Anywhere else, they'd have stood out as singular-looking villains, but here at the Red Lion, ~~~~~ all of a piece. The place had been a thieves' tavern for as ~~~~~ remember: a warren of crooked rooms, hidden trapdoors and secret ~~~~~. The ripe stench of the Fleet Ditch pervaded the cracked plaster walls.

'I'll tell you what's robbery,' Jenny said. 'Ten, that's what.'

'Eleven, but it causes me pain, Jenny.'

'By the time I pay the cove what robbed your client, there'll be arse all left for me. A little goodwill, Perry. That's all I ask.'

They both knew there was no cove. Jenny knew the location of the watch because she'd stolen it herself, probably in the course of undressing his client. Still, negotiating with thieves was a damn sight less arduous than arresting them, and the only sure way of getting his client's property back.

Four . . . five . . . six . . . Child reached the tavern stairs and started to descend.

'Twelve,' Jenny called.

'One for each disciple.' Child was already striding back to shake her hand. 'This is *voluntatem dei*, Jenny. The will of God.'

*

Child should have left it there. After he'd paid Jenny, he should have drained his pot, paid his bill, and gone to find his client. Walk away and do it like you mean it. Instead, he chose to celebrate.

Four hours later, he was still celebrating, having collected a little group of admirers, anxious to share in his good fortune.

'It true you used to be a magistrate?' one asked, eyeing Child's old wig of office with a smirk. It was long and full with thick sausage curls. He couldn't bring himself to replace it, though it had seen better times.

'If I'd known you in my Deptford days,' Child told him, 'you'd have been creeping from chapel to church, praying the eye of Peregrine Child didn't fall on you.'

'So what happened?' The villain asking these questions had a single brown eyebrow that ran across the bridge of his nose, and teeth of a similar number and hue.

'Politics,' Child said, trying to keep the bitterness out of his voice. 'The mayor lost his re-election and the new fellow had another man in mind for my job.'

Admittedly, it was a little more complicated than that. The election had turned nasty amid allegations of dirty tricks. Whores and vagrants had kept disrupting the meetings of the mayor's opponent, because somebody had told them they were handing out free gin. The opponent's import business had also received an implausibly high number of customs inspections – that much Child didn't deny. The missing ballot boxes found under a hedge, on the other hand, had nothing to do with him, but hadn't stopped the blame coming his way. The new mayor's first act, on attaining office, had been to dismiss Child as magistrate. His second had been to issue an unwritten decree: no one was to offer Child employment, no one was to take his business; even his favourite taverns had barred their doors to him.

'Magistrates.' The villain spat an oyster of phlegm on the table. 'Thief-taker's a step up in the world in my book.'

Your book and no one else's, Child thought sourly. It was enough to make a man weep. In Deptford, he'd had status and respect, not to mention a steady stream of income, much of it honest. Now he was reduced to grubbing around after stolen property, arresting the odd thief who tried his patience, and spending too much time in dog-hole taverns like the Red Lion.

The tap-boy returned, carrying another jug. As he set it down, Child felt the lad's hand slide inside his shabby blue greatcoat, reaching for his purse. He moved fast for a man of forty-five, especially one who carried a belly like his. Fist connected with skull, knocking the lad into the wall. As he slid down it, people laughed.

Child shook his head sorrowfully. 'I'd choose a different vocation, son, if I were you. Or you'll end up on a hangman's rope.'

The boy rubbed his ear, pride plainly piqued. 'Thought you was cup-shot, didn't I?'

'I might be drunk,' Child said, 'but I've thirty years' practice. Diligence in what you do, lad. That's the key.'

An hour later, moonlight casting a pewter glow onto the slick cobbles of the Fleetside streets, Child strolled out of the Red Lion, obliviously content, straight into the arms of Finn Daley and two of his thick-necked henchmen. Child reached for his flintlock pistol, but one of them punched him in the stomach, knocking the wind out of him. They dragged him to the edge of the Fleet, grabbing his arms and shoving him forward, so that he leaned precariously out over the murky waters.

Daley, a muscular gnome, his face pocked as a cribbage board, edged in close so that Child could smell his tobacco breath. 'Can you swim, Perry?' he asked, in his soft Dublin brogue.

Craning his neck, Child searched the street for help – but this was a thieves' district, and people hurried on by.

'I'm from Deptford,' he said. 'Of course I can bloody swim.'

Daley produced an axe from beneath his coat. 'Not without arms you can't.'

'Wait,' Child cried. 'I'll have your money soon. I'm serious. I will.'

Daley smiled. 'I've heard it all before, Perry. It's getting tiresome.'

Child's lies came thick and fast. 'I'm working a job worth fifty guineas. I only owe you forty. By next week you'll have the lot. Christ, Daley. I swear it.'

'What kind of job?'

'Something special. Just give me a week and the money's yours. The only reason I haven't been to see you is because I've been so busy.'

Indecision worked its way across Daley's face. His axe-hand twitched – but at the end of the day he was a businessman, and head ruled heart.

'Seven days,' he said. 'At a guinea a day. Then there's all the trouble I had to go to, trying to find you.' He reached into Child's coat and plucked his purse from his pocket, emptying the contents into his hand, tucking it back. 'This will cover the latter. Which leaves us forty-seven guineas apart. Don't even think about running. I'll make it my life's work to track you down. I'm starting to take you mighty personal, Perry, and no one wants that.'

Chapter Three

Sir Amos Fox, the Bow Street magistrate, was a long-limbed, cadaverous man with long white hair and irritated pink skin that clashed with his red waistcoat. He kept clasping his hands together and smiling at Caro over the top of them, in a manner he presumably believed to be reassuring.

Caro forestalled his apologies with a tight smile. 'Please, Sir Amos, it is no inconvenience at all. I have hardly been able to think of anything other than poor Lucia.'

The memory of those moments in the bower still haunted her. She had spent her waking hours reliving them, recalling Lucia's moans and the stench of slaughter. The Bow Street constables had questioned her at the scene, but she'd hardly managed to get the words out. Eventually, Lord March had intervened and told them to leave her alone. Even once she was home, the blood beneath her fingernails had taken an hour of scrubbing to dislodge. Two days later, she was still convinced they smelled of it.

They were sitting around the magistrate's mahogany desk. Many portraits adorned the study walls: King George the Third and his queen; the Prince of Wales; prominent politicians, both Whig and Tory, for Sir Amos trimmed his political allegiance to the prevailing wind.

Mordechai had insisted on accompanying her here. He sat perfectly erect, both hands on the pommel of his walking cane, his knuckles white around his gold signet ring. His profile was slowly becoming their father's: the same hooded eyes and long nose protruding from the gunmetal rolls of his periwig, even the same fleshy growth in the middle of his forehead. He glanced at her unsmiling, still furious.

'My sister would like to know if you have apprehended the murderer, Sir Amos?' he said. 'There has been nothing in the newspapers to that effect.'

Sir Amos offered them another of his solicitous smiles. 'Not as yet, Mr Craven, Mrs Corsham. But I am issuing a reward for ten guineas. I hope it will prompt someone to come forward.'

Caro frowned. She had thought the magistrate's household would be a bustle of activity – a lady of consequence had been murdered after all. Yet she had seen only two of Sir Amos's servants, who hadn't seemed exercised at all, and the magistrate's paltry reward perplexed her.

'Ten guineas? You do know that Lucia was a cousin of the King of Naples? Has a letter been dispatched to her family? I must write myself.'

Sir Amos shifted slightly in his chair, regarding her sympathetically. 'I am seeing to all the formalities, madam, do not fret upon that score. Now I'd like to ask you, if I may, a few questions about your acquaintance with the dead woman. I believe you told my constables that you considered her a friend?'

'Not a close friend. Our acquaintance was rather scant.' Caro sighed. 'But I liked her enormously. We first met about two years ago at a supper party. Lucia was visiting England for the first time. Her husband had died a few months earlier, and she was seeking distraction from her grief in travel. We rather hit it off. I am sure we would have seen one another again, but she was forced to return home to Naples unexpectedly.'

Wine, wit and laughter. That gay spring night when she'd

thought she and Lucia were going to become firm friends. The same heady rush as a new *amour*, followed by a crushing sense of abandonment when Lucia had left London without saying farewell.

'Can I ask who made the introduction?'

'My brother, Ambrose. He knew Lucia's family from his Grand Tour, when he visited the ruins at Pompeii. What does any of this have to do with Lucia's murder?'

'Bear with me, please, Mrs Corsham. You met her again recently, I understand?'

'Three days ago – at a masquerade ball at Carlisle House. Lucia apologized for not having written, and I forgave her. We conversed for a time about trifling matters, until I was taken ill by a bad oyster and returned home. I felt better the following day, and attended the exhibition at Vauxhall as I'd planned. I was walking past the bowers, when I heard a woman groaning in distress. You cannot imagine my horror when I realized it was Lucia.'

Caro's throat was dry. She had anticipated these questions, and had prepared her answers accordingly, but she was conscious of the magistrate's beady eye and Mordechai's glare. Yet she wished to tell the truth, in as much as it was possible.

The magistrate paused delicately. 'May I ask why you were in the vicinity in the first place?'

'I felt a little nauseous and went to take the air. It turned out I wasn't quite so recovered from that oyster as I'd first thought.'

Her lie came more smoothly than it had last night. Mordechai had questioned her for hours, peering at her like a bloody witchfinder: *I am not a fool, Caro, and your husband isn't either. Who were you meeting in the bowers?*

Sir Amos grunted, equally sceptical, doubtless jumping to

the same wrong conclusion. At least their suspicions were better than the truth.

'My sister was quite innocent as to the nature of that part of the gardens,' Mordechai said – family closing ranks, his greatest talent. 'I imagine Lucia was too, being Italian.'

'On that latter score,' Sir Amos said, 'I regret not. That is the principal reason I asked you to come down here today. I have no wish to compound your distress further, Mrs Corsham, but I fear I must. The woman you found dying was not an Italian noblewoman. Nor was her name Lucia di Caracciolo. She was no stranger to the bowers at Vauxhall, nor indeed to the London taverns and coffeehouses. You understand my meaning, I am sure.'

They stared at him aghast, Caro's astonishment quite genuine.

'You mean she was a prostitute?' Mordechai spoke each syllable heavily to underscore the depth of his displeasure.

Sir Amos bowed his head. 'I wanted to tell you in person, out of respect for your family, sir. To have you read it first in the newspapers would never do.'

Caro shook her head. 'I think I would know if I'd been conversing with a prostitute, Sir Amos. Lucia spoke knowledgeably about Naples. We talked of politics and art and fashion.'

The magistrate spoke kindly, but firmly: 'You must not blame yourself for having been taken in by this meretrix. Doubtless your brother, Ambrose, was too. These women learn from an early age how to emulate ladies of fashion. Many have been upon the stage. Their tricks are legion.'

'But her gowns were fine,' Caro said, still unwilling to accept it. 'She wore ostrich feathers. Silks. Her gloves were kid.'

'Do you imagine your average doxy is starving in a doorway? Allow me to disillusion you, Mrs Corsham. Satan's harvest reaps rich rewards, I'm sorry to say. A pretty jezebel can earn five, ten guineas a night from her gentleman callers. They dine out on the town, take boxes in the theatre, some even ride there in their own carriages with their own footmen.'

Mordechai glowered. 'These are not matters for my sister's ear, sir.'

'I saw a woman die before my eyes,' Caro said. 'I assure you that was rather more indelicate. Sir Amos, if it is so hard to tell a woman of the town from a lady, then how can you be certain in this instance?'

'After we removed her gloves, we discovered that at some point in the past, she had been branded upon the hand for thievery. She wore no wedding ring, but she had the marks of childbirth upon her body. By then I was fairly certain what we were dealing with. I had my men take a look at the corpse, and sure enough, some of them recognized her. Lucy Loveless was her name – at least the one she was known by in the taverns. Her landlord identified her this morning.'

Caro was silent a moment, taking it all in. It seemed so implausible, and yet it would go some way to explaining a few discrepancies that had troubled her about Lucia: her sudden disappearance last year, her circumspection about where she was staying, her knowledge of certain matters that should lie far outside the experience of an Italian contessa.

'By all accounts,' Sir Amos said, 'Lucy was the toast of the town for a time, though she was nearing thirty and her star had faded somewhat. The landlord says that artist fellow – Agnetti – liked to paint her. Do you know if Mr Ambrose Craven also met her again recently?'

Caro glanced up. 'Our brother has been abroad travelling for almost a year.'

He made a note. 'And you had no other dealings with the dead woman other than those you've described?'

The magistrate's eyes were searching, and a warmth suffused her skin. 'No, Sir Amos. None at all.'

He inclined his head. 'Then I see no reason to trouble you further. The evening newspapers will report the dead woman's true identity. My reward may entice someone to come forward, it may not. The death of a whore' – he made a gesture – 'doesn't prompt much pity.'

Caro was still trying to reconcile the magistrate's revelation with her memories of Lucia. For the past two days, she'd been consumed by grief and guilt. Despite Lucia's deceptions – Lucy, she supposed she must call her now – those emotions couldn't simply be snipped away like a loose thread. She imagined the magistrate's Bow Street Runners lining up to look at the corpse. Coarse rough men, of the bantering sort, jostling, laughing, their relentless gaze.

'How old is the child?' she asked. 'Losing a mother is a terrible tragedy, whatever the circumstances. I'd like to help in some small way if I can.'

'Your compassion does you credit, Mrs Corsham,' the magistrate said. 'Alas, no child was found to be living at Lucy's lodgings, and her landlord says she never mentioned one in his hearing. I imagine it was given away as a foundling or died in infancy. Some prostitutes even starve their own children at nurse, I'm sorry to say.'

'Then they should hang,' Mordechai said, with a shudder of feeling.

Caro glanced at him in irritation, wishing Ambrose was here instead of him. The thought made her eyes smart and she looked away.

'I suppose she was in the bower to meet a client,' Mordechai said. 'Do you think he killed her?'

'Lucy's clients were men of wealth and status,' Sir Amos said. 'Considering the savage nature of the crime, the number of wounds and so forth, I think it highly improbable a gentleman was responsible. I suspect she was awaiting such a client, when she took the fancy of a passing villain. He desired to sample the goods without paying up, and things took a turn for the worse, as you saw.'

'No,' Caro said, looking up. 'I'm sure she knew her killer. Lucy spoke to me, you see. She said: "*He knows.*"'

The magistrate pondered it a moment. '*He knows.* She might have been talking about anyone. God, perhaps. Her sins would have weighed heavily upon her mind at such a time.'

'So would her murderer. Did the constables tell you about the man I saw in the mask?'

The magistrate sifted through his documents and drew one out. 'Long black coat, black hat, average height, perhaps taller. A plague doctor's mask. Unfortunately, there are many stalls selling such masks and costumes operating within the confines of Vauxhall. It might have been an innocent reveller you saw. And if it was the murderer, then he could have been any one of three thousand men enjoying the gardens that night.' He licked his palm and smoothed his hair, trying to cover one of his bald patches with little success.

'Have you talked to Lord March? He heard me scream and came to my assistance. And there was another man too. Short and shabby, with a beard. Lord March ordered him to fetch the garden constables, I think.'

'I have spoken to Lord March. He doesn't remember seeing anything suspicious.' Again Sir Amos consulted his notes. 'The other man you mention is named Ezra Von Siegel. A Jew. He is a lamplighter employed in the gardens. Did Von Siegel give you cause for suspicion at any time?'

'No. He was shocked, but kind.' Caro remembered Von Siegel procuring blankets to cover the body and to keep her warm. She hadn't been able to stop shaking.

'Do you suspect the Jew of involvement?' Mordechai asked.

'There was no blood on Von Siegel's clothes,' Sir Amos said. 'I'm keeping an open mind. He is a foreign subject, a German.'

'What about the letter?' Caro said. 'I wondered if it might have been dropped by the killer.'

'The letter, Mrs Corsham?'

'It was lying next to Lucy in the bower. At least, it looked like a letter. A document, anyway. I saw a wax seal. It was stained with blood.'

Sir Amos glanced out of the window. He'd done his duty by the Cravens, handling a delicate matter with tact and discretion. Now Caro sensed he was tiring of the conversation. 'We found no letter, madam. Perhaps you imagined it? It would be easy to do so in the moment.'

Had she imagined it? She didn't think so.

'Is the murder inquiry to be handled by Guildford?' Mordechai asked.

'Vauxhall, as you say, rightly falls under the jurisdiction of the Surrey magistrates, but given the sensational nature of the crime and the distances involved, I have offered to look after it myself.'

Mordechai reached inside his frock coat. 'My sister's husband, Captain Corsham, is in France at present, serving on Mr Hartley's diplomatic mission to Versailles. Yet I know I speak for him when I ask that you do whatever you can to keep Mrs Corsham's name out of the newspapers.'

Sir Amos bowed his head. 'Rest assured, Mr Craven, I will do everything in my power to prevent a scandal.'

They shook hands, and Caro saw a folded banknote pass between them.

'What will happen to Lucy's body?' she asked. 'If no one claims her?'

'Her landlord attests that she left considerable debts. These women might earn a good living, but they spend their money like water. I've authorized her landlord to dispose of her possessions to settle her account, but I doubt there'll be much left by the time he's done. Which will mean a pauper's grave, I'm afraid to say. A sad story, all told, but one of the victim's own authorship. Let us hope it gives the young women of this kingdom pause.' Rising to his feet, he held out an arm to assist Caro from her chair. 'I do hope you can put this matter behind you.'

Caro summoned a faint smile, thinking of Lucy's final moments. Her fingers entwined in Caro's own. That bone-white, pleading stare. *He knows.*

She blinked to dispel the image. 'I hope so too.'

PAMELA

5 January 1782
Eight months before the murder of Lucy Loveless

Twelfth Night. The bells of St Anne's striking four of the afternoon. Soho under snow, as though an ermine cloak had been laid across it. Icicles clinging to the leaden guttering of the shops and houses, bright as diamonds in the dishwater light.

The girl's arms ached under the weight of her heavy carpet bag. Her stockings were soaked inside her boots. The cold raked through her thin cloak, her flesh stippled like orange peel beneath her cotton dress. She took the scrap of paper from her pocket and studied the direction upon it, glancing up at the number on the black door in front of her.

For many months she had imagined this moment. On the walk across London, she'd hardly dared accept she was finally doing it. Yet now that the moment had arrived, all the misgivings she'd wrestled with over the preceding weeks assailed her in the voice of Rachel, the cook: *It's all lies, you little fool. There's no feather beds or fancy clothes. Just tricks to cozen vain, lazy baggages like you.*

· She could still go back. Nothing was done that couldn't be undone. Then she thought of her thin horsehair mattress, the ice that froze inside the windowpane. The chill of the flagstones when she was kneeling to lay the kitchen fire. Washing dishes with chapped fingers. Trimming cabbages if she was lucky. Emptying chamber pots.

With sudden resolve, she lifted the heavy iron knocker.

*

The owner of the house was named Mrs Maria Havilland. She was about sixty years old, the girl judged, still thin as a marrow spoon. Her movements were languid and considered, as was her speech. She was seated upon a gold-and-lime divan, wearing a demi-train gown of green watered satin and a choker of emeralds – all of which the girl took to be promising signs. Her hair was a towering edifice of lard, pomade and powder, three silver spiders creeping their way up it. Her rings glittered in the lamplight, as did her narrow eyes.

The girl was naked. Her nipples hard as hailstones, despite the warmth of the fire and the curtains of indigo velvet. She hoped her breasts didn't look too small as a result, and resisted the urge to cover them. Instead she focused on the richness of the parlour's furnishings: the harpsichord between the windows, and the number of candles burning brightly in silver sconces. Over the fire hung a portrait of a much younger Mrs Havilland: bold of eye, a budding mouth, and a creamy complexion that the woman on the divan had attempted to recreate with lead paint and rouge. She was assessing the girl the way men did when you passed them on the street: face first, then bubbies, then legs, then face again, then finally they turned to see your arse.

The parquet floor was smooth against the girl's bare feet. Hannah, the first housemaid, hadn't passed inspection when she'd come here a month ago, but then Hannah had a birthmark on her breast and a missing tooth.

'What trade are you in?' Mrs Havilland asked. 'A milliner? A maid?'

'Maid, madam.'

'Here in London?'

'Yes, madam. In Cheapside.'

'Do you have family nearby?'

'I have no family, madam. At least, none I ever knew.'

Mrs Havilland smiled. 'Oh, we like orphans here. How about your employer? Is he the sort who would come looking? Cause us trouble?'

'No, madam. I don't think he'd care.'

Mrs Havilland had been toying with a long silver hook. Now she pushed it into her hair to scratch her scalp. The girl wondered if it was lice or mice that troubled her.

'How old are you, child?'

'Fifteen, madam.'

'You could pass for thirteen, maybe even twelve. Never younger. We want no trouble from Bow Street, you understand?'

'Yes, madam.' Did the question mean she had passed muster? 'The men say I have a bold tongue, madam. I know how to serve a drop of sauce.'

'No.' Mrs Havilland's tone was sharp. 'I don't want sauce. As you were. *Yes, madam. No, madam.*' She took another long, assessing look at the girl's body. 'Do you know what it is we do here?'

'Yes, madam. I think so.'

'Do you think *you* could do that?'

'Yes, madam.'

'Then we will try you out. But your name won't do. Let us see if we can't come up with something better.' Mrs Havilland's eye fell on a book that lay on the marquetry table at her elbow. 'Can you read?'

'Yes, madam. They taught me at the orphanage. I was good at my books.'

Mrs Havilland pointed to the volume with her scratcher. 'Have you read it?'

'No, madam, but I have heard of it. She is a maidservant too? The girl in the book?'

'Pamela Andrews. Her master was a country squire. He wanted her, but she wouldn't let him have her.' Her manicured finger underscored the book's secondary title. '*Virtue Rewarded*. Are you virtuous, child?'

Utterly confused – wasn't a lack of virtue the point? – the girl tripped over her answer: 'Yes, madam. No. I'm not sure, madam.'

Mrs Havilland smiled, as if the girl had said something clever. 'Take this book. Learn your part. Play it to perfection. And you'll answer to no other name but Pamela. Not while you're here.'

Chapter Four

'Ambrose knew,' Mordechai said. 'Back then, when he introduced you to the prostitute. He must have done. Gad, what was he thinking?'

They were seated in his glossy red coach-and-six heading home from the magistrate's house to Mayfair. Mordechai had lit a pipe, and Caro pulled the window down with a bang. Her ginger comfits were doing nothing to settle her stomach. She leaned against the leather seat, fanning herself.

'Of course Ambrose knew,' she said. 'It probably amused him. To introduce one of his harlots as a lady of quality. Watch us fawn over her.'

'It is unconscionable. His own sister.'

The carriage rocked as they rounded a sedan chair. The Strand was busy with traffic, the foot pavement jostling with pedestrians. From the windows of the milliners and glovers, pretty shop girls eyed the passing gentlemen. Now and then, between the shops, loomed a vast survivor of the old brick palaces that had once lined this stretch of the river. Just now they were passing Amberley House, home to Lord March and his parents, the Earl and Countess of Amberley.

'You didn't mention Lord March was there when we talked before,' Mordechai said. 'Was it him? The gentleman you were meeting in the bower?'

'I wasn't meeting anyone. I was taking the air, as I told you.'

'Harry will hear of it. I might keep it out of the newspapers, but word will get around regardless. When they learn the murdered woman was a whore, the comparisons will invite themselves. You're not to visit Vauxhall again until Harry comes home.'

She stared at her brother, outraged. 'I'm not going to shut myself away. I haven't done anything wrong. It's time you believed me.'

He grunted. 'We can only hope they don't think you were meeting that Jewish lamplighter.'

If only you knew, she thought – and by God, you may do yet. Then you'll understand the meaning of a family scandal.

She turned to watch the bustle around Charing Cross. St Martin's striking three, the whores already out in force. They dipped plumed hats at the cavalry officers coming and going from the Royal Mews, flashing their ankles. Caro thought about her encounter with Lucia at Carlisle House, just three days ago. Her small brown eyes, wide and sincere. *'I can help you, dearest Caro. If you'll only let me.'*

Caro had taken that offer in good faith. Somehow, despite their scant acquaintance, she'd trusted Lucia. Except Lucia wasn't Lucia, she was Lucy Loveless, a prostitute – so why had she offered Caro her help at all? Caro could come up with no answer other than human kindness, and somehow that troubled her most of all. If it hadn't been for that act of kindness, then Lucy Loveless would never have set foot in that bower. Try as she might, Caro felt in some part responsible.

'Did anybody ask about Ambrose at the exhibition?' Mordechai asked, breaking in upon her thoughts.

'Of course they asked. Nobody's seen him in over a year. Everyone wants to know where he is.'

'What did you tell them?'

'Switzerland, as we agreed. I implied he was chasing a woman.'

'More gossip,' Mordechai said darkly.

'It is hardly the same. Ambrose is a man. His conduct need not be beyond reproach. More importantly, knowing our brother, people will believe it.' A thought struck her then. 'Sir Amos said Lucy Loveless sat for Jacobus Agnetti. Do you think that's where Ambrose met her – at Agnetti's house?'

'It hardly matters now.'

'Do you think the magistrate has talked to him? To Agnetti?'

'I haven't the faintest idea.'

'I suspect he hasn't. He didn't seem to care at all. If Lucy had really been a contessa, he'd be out there now scouring the streets.'

Mordechai closed his eyes to signal his limited patience for the topic. 'I suppose dead prostitutes are ten a penny.'

'They still deserve justice, do they not?'

He didn't reply and Caro mused fretfully: 'I know I saw a letter in the bower. And Lucy knew her killer, I am sure of it. She was trying to tell me something, but she died before she could.'

'Caroline,' Mordechai said, in his patriarch's voice, another act stolen from their father, 'your little night in the bowers nearly cost your family dear. You risked making a laughing stock of your husband, and something altogether worse of yourself. If you mean to sit here worrying about something, let it be that.'

*

Gabriel hurled himself at her almost as soon as she'd walked in through the door of her Mayfair townhouse. Laughing, despite her mood, she swung him into the air, holding him close.

'Dog, Mama.' He barked. 'Cat, Mama.' He meowed.

'Oh, aren't you *clever*.' Ignoring the hovering servants in the hall, she kissed him once, twice, three times to keep him safe. Not liking the kisses, he wriggled in her arms, squirming to get free, until she set him down. He ran off into the morning room, calling for his nursemaid, Mrs Graves.

Caro removed her cloak and gloves and handed them to her butler. 'Where are the mails, Pomfret?'

'On your escritoire, Mrs Corsham. May Anna bring you a pot of tea?'

'I'll take tea with Gabriel in the nursery in just a moment.'

Walking into the drawing room, she closed the door. Alone for the first time that day, she breathed deeply, battling her nausea. Everything felt turned on its head. Lucia di Caracciolo, Lucy Loveless. All the emotions running amok inside of her – she struggled to make sense of them. You can't afford to think of the murder now, she chided herself. You have problems enough of your own.

Hastening to her escritoire, she picked up the little stack of letters that awaited her attention, identifying missives from friends, bills from tradesmen, invitations. Her despair mounted, as it had done every day for the past two weeks. No letter in her husband's hand, saying he was on his way home. *Why didn't he write?*

It had been five months since Harry had packed his bags for the Continent, saying he'd be gone three months at most. They had parted on cordial terms, and he'd written regularly enough at first. Now there was only silence and she didn't know why.

Could he be ill? It was a possibility to which she kept returning, and yet if that was the case, then why hadn't she been told? She'd made inquiries with Harry's patron in the ministry, Nicholas Cavill-Lawrence, and had the distinct impression that she was being fobbed off. 'The Americans are resting on their laurels.' 'The French are being stubborn.' 'Peace wasn't built in a day, Caro, these things take time.'

Except time was the one thing she didn't have.

She closed her eyes, refusing to give way to her tears, and the murder at Vauxhall edged back into her thoughts. All the troubling details wormed at her: the letter in the bower, the plague doctor's mask, Lucy's last words.

Pressing a hand to her mouth, she suppressed a wrenching sob. 'Harry,' she whispered. 'Please come home.'

CHAPTER FIVE

PEREGRINE CHILD'S LAMB stew was pale and watery, the meat glistening with pearls of fat and gristle. He stirred it around listlessly, before pushing it aside.

'I'm sorry, love,' he said for the tenth time.

'I told you. It's fine.'

Sophie Hardcastle gave him a tight smile. One of her abundant brown curls had sprung free, and she reached into the top of her stays where she kept her pins, stabbing one into her hair with forceful intent. Child reached out a hand to stroke her cheek, but she pulled away. It was definitely not fine.

He'd planned to take her to a chophouse in Covent Garden which had a new French cook, and then on to the playhouse in Drury Lane. Finn Daley had put paid to that, and so they were sitting in a greasy Holborn watering hole, surrounded by drunk soldiers and penny-fuck whores. Child resisted the urge to put his head in his hands. The watch he'd retrieved from Jenny Wren had been hidden in his shoe, and thus had escaped Daley's greedy clutches. He'd returned it to his client yesterday, for a commission of two and a half guineas, but that was dwindling fast, and he had no other jobs in the offing. Then there was the problem of Finn Daley's forty-seven guineas. Two days had already passed. Only five left.

He'd tried manoeuvring his apostles, borrowing from Peter to pay Paul, but he had so many creditors no one else would touch him. It was why he'd been forced to turn to Finn Daley in the first place. He'd ask Sophie for a loan, but she'd turned him down in the past. *'Money is how lovers fall out, Perry. I've been there before.'*

None of it was his fault; that was the worst part. It had all gone so well when he'd first started out in London. He'd taken on a little debt, just to set himself up on his feet, but it was nothing he wouldn't have been able to repay in time. His London connections had sent a few clients his way and, slowly, word had got around that Child was the thief-taker to go to when a gentleman was in a fix. Lost some compromising letters? Had a diamond necklace stolen? Want to trace an eloped daughter? Perry Child was your man. Little wonder his competitors had been so upset. Child was an interloper on their turf, and they'd clubbed together to work against him. Spreading rumours about his drunkenness and his murkier activities in Deptford. Soon his clients dwindled to a trickle and his debts had become a problem he could no longer ignore.

Five days. And then Finn Daley would come looking for him again.

He gave Sophie a wan smile. 'As soon as I'm back in the game, I'll take you to Drury Lane, I promise.'

'No, Perry, that's not going to work.' Sophie tugged her silk shawl tighter around her ample bosom, and he gazed at her, concerned. It wasn't like her to hold a grudge.

'Then tell me what I can do to make it up to you.'

'It's not that.' She sighed. 'I was going to tell you later, but I didn't want to spoil our night. I had word of my Sam's ship yesterday. She's been sighted off Southampton.'

Sophie's husband was First Officer of an Indiaman, gone for years at a time. The money was good, but Sophie got lonely. Hence Peregrine Child.

'How long will he be in London?'

'Six months, perhaps longer.' She pressed her knuckles against his arm. 'Don't look like that. You knew the way it was.'

He couldn't deny that. It might even have been part of the attraction. They sat there a while longer, making stilted attempts at conversation, but the heart had gone out of their evening, and eventually Sophie rose, gathering her cloak.

'I'd better be getting back to the children. You look after yourself, Perry.' She tied her bonnet under her chin, while he mustered a smile. 'And ease off on the wine, hey? The way you drink, you'll be dead before you're fifty.'

Walk away and do it like you mean it. Child watched her go, and then called the tap-man over. Taking Sophie's advice to heart, he swapped to gin. As he drank, he thought of his dead wife, Liz, wondering what she'd make of him if she could see him now. Not much, was his best bet, but then at least he wouldn't be confounding her expectations. Liz had used to tell him to stop drinking too, but it wasn't like he didn't know. Why did women have to carp on so much about the bloody obvious?

Much later, he walked home through the streets of Holborn. Drunken soldiers' songs drifted up to him from the Fetter Lane taverns: *Fuck the Americans! Fuck the French!* Which was all very well, except everyone knew the war was lost, the colonies gone for good, the British broke and humiliated by their enemies. Child decided he was a fitting metaphor for his once-proud nation.

He lived in a little court off Gray's Inn Lane, on the first floor of a tall, narrow timber house with covered balconies sitting uneasily upon rusting brackets. A carriage was idling at the entrance to the court, and the coachman gave Child a contemptuous look as he fumbled for his key. His neighbours – legal clerks and other scriveners – kept respectable hours, and the landlord was too parsimonious to light the lamps in the halls after ten. So Child was forced to grope his way up the implausibly steep staircase, drawing to an abrupt halt when he made the turn on the landing and spotted two shadowy figures outside his door.

In his time as magistrate, Child had sent many men to the gallows. He never knew who might step out of his past seeking a reckoning. His hand dropped to the pistol in the pocket of his greatcoat. 'What do you want?'

'Mr Child?' A woman's voice, one that bespoke breeding and money and everything else Child resented at that moment.

'I'm Child,' he said. 'You have the advantage of me, madam.'

As she came forward, he caught a waft of expensive scent. In the half-light he could see she was very beautiful. She was looking at Child with a faint trace of disappointment. You and all, love, he thought. You and all.

'My name is Caroline Corsham,' she said. 'I believe you know my husband, Captain Henry Corsham. A woman has been murdered, Mr Child, and I need your help.'

Chapter Six

Child watched Mrs Corsham cast a dubious eye around his lodgings: at the threadbare furniture, the empty bottles, the cobwebs on the beams, the dirty plates. He'd opened a window to give the place an airing, but it just meant the odours of old sweat and liquor mingled with the rising stench of the Fleet Ditch. They were sitting at Child's small round dining table, hastily cleared of the remnants of a kidney pudding from three nights ago. Mrs Corsham's strapping ginger footman lurked near the door, incongruous as a beggar at a ball. He didn't take his eye off Child for a moment.

Mrs Corsham had just finished telling him about the prostitute she'd unwittingly befriended, and later found dying at Vauxhall Gardens. Child had read about the murder in the newspapers. The revelation in the evening editions that the victim had been a celebrated harlot had prompted a shift in tone. A carnal motive was implied, people could rest easy in their beds; no respectable woman was at risk.

'My husband says you are good at what you do.' Mrs Corsham sounded as though she was trying to convince herself. 'He said that in his absence, if I needed help with any delicate matter, I should come to you.'

Her cold, blue eyes travelled over his yellowed stockings and stained coat. Child longed for a drink to steady his thinking, but all he had was gin, which he didn't think would convey the right impression. As she took his measure, so he took hers.

Not yet thirty, but not far off. Her mahogany hair implausibly glossy and coiled. A rose silk gown stitched with seed-pearls and yards of golden lace that probably cost more than all Child's debts combined. A narrow waist and a delicate, angular face gave the impression of fragility, belied by about three seconds in her company. Child had a natural distrust of beautiful women. His instinct was to please them, which was what they anticipated – and experience had taught him that they could turn nasty if you did not. They also had a way of looking at a man, reducing him to the sum of his inadequate parts. Yet the Corshams were rich, and whatever this woman's arcane motives for giving a damn about this dead whore, if some of that money was to find its way into Peregrine Child's pocket, then he wasn't one to look a pretty mare in the mouth.

'I was magistrate of Deptford for over ten years,' he said. 'By comparison, your London villains are a stroll around the garden.'

'Does that include murderers?'

Child inclined his head. 'Murder is a more complicated proposition than theft, but I've caught my share of killers.'

'Can you find whomever killed Lucy Loveless? See him hang?'

'I can try. If she knew her killer, as you suspect, it will prove an easier task. I simply need to find out who had sufficient cause.'

'The magistrate says it cannot be one of her clients, because the crime was too savage to be committed by a gentleman. Is that also your view?'

'I think monsters who wear the masks of men are as likely to be found in the clubs of St James's as they are in the slum-rookeries of St Giles. Whether this is the former or the latter, I cannot yet say.'

She nodded, apparently satisfied by his response. 'How would you proceed?'

'I'd visit her home, talk to her friends, her clients, if I can find them. Go to Vauxhall, talk to Bow Street, and anyone who was in the bowers at the time. Yet without the force of the law behind me, I must offer sufficient incentive for people to talk.'

Her reply was as direct as any Turk in a bazaar. 'How much do you want?'

Enough to get Finn Daley off his back for good – plus a little something to console himself in Sophie's absence. 'A hundred guineas for an arrest, twenty up front.'

'Do you take me for a fool, sir? You can have ten up front, and sixty upon conviction.'

Christ, she was as bad as Jenny Wren. Her kid gloves must cost more than ten guineas. Dimly he recalled that her father had founded the Craven Bank. The old man had certainly taught her to wring the value out of a sou.

'Fifteen and eighty,' he countered.

'Then we have no more business to discuss.' She rose from the table, gesturing to her footman. Child was tempted to tell her to sod off and take her imperious tone with her, but there were other thief-takers out there, and none so desperate.

'Twelve and seventy-five,' he said. 'But upon arrest, not conviction. The cost of taking the case through the courts must be yours alone.'

'Very well.' Unsmiling, she took a purse from her panniers and counted out a stack of guineas on the table as if they were pennies.

Five days to find the killer. Five days before Finn Daley came looking for blood. A murder with no witnesses and few promising paths of inquiry, only a glimpse of a man in a plague doctor's mask who might simply have been a passing reveller.

Child reached for his ledger and inkpot to make notes, trying to summon an appearance of confidence.

'Do you remember anyone else in the vicinity of the bowers other than the lamplighter and Lord March?'

'None who waited around for the constables – and *they* seemed more interested in that poor lamplighter than anyone else. He told them he saw nothing suspicious.'

'And Lord March?'

'The same.'

'I should speak to them both. Your brother too – the one who first introduced you to Lucy.'

'No,' Caro said sharply. 'The lamplighter you can talk to all you like. But I cannot have you speaking to gentlemen of my acquaintance – questioning their movements, their motives.'

'If you want the murderer caught, I cannot afford to be so fastidious. These men are witnesses.'

'My brother, Ambrose, witnessed nothing. He is in Switzerland and has been abroad for almost a year.'

'And Lord March? If he was in the bowers for an assignation, it would give him every reason to lie to the magistrate.' Child could imagine how Sir Amos would have questioned a rich, young nobleman. With every deference and courtesy. 'He might even have committed the crime himself, moments before.'

'Impossible. I have known Lord March since I was in ringlets.'

Child wondered if her attitude was coloured by whatever it was she'd been up to in the bowers. The state of Corsham's marriage was no business of his, but it could complicate matters. 'I am not entirely without subtlety, madam. I have questioned gentlemen before. Even assuming he is innocent, Lord March might have information that is important to my investigation.'

'Then *I* will talk to him. Find out what, if anything, he saw.'

Did she think this was to be a collaborative enterprise? 'Madam, that is not the way I work. This is a murder inquiry, not some drawing-room riddle.'

'Lord March is a peer of the realm. Heir to the earldom of Amberley. Do you imagine you could walk in off the street to Amberley House and put him to the question? His footmen would slam the door in your face. Whereas I know him. He will talk to me.'

'Men lie, madam. It is a skill to divine those lies.'

She gave a hollow laugh. 'I assure you it's one I've learned.'

Child muttered beneath his breath: '*Barba non facit philosophum.*'

'A beard doesn't make one a philosopher,' Mrs Corsham said sharply. 'Nor does a little Latin make you Cicero, Mr Child. We will do it my way, or not at all.'

'Fine,' Child said, which reminded him of Sophie Hardcastle, and he experienced a sudden pang of loss. To mitigate it, he rose from the table and went to the dresser where he kept his books and papers. Taking a pamphlet down from the shelf, he flicked through it until he found what he was looking for.

'Here,' he said, handing it to Mrs Corsham. 'Lucy Loveless.'

She studied the page, and then turned the pamphlet to see the cover. 'What is this?'

'*Harris's List.* A guide to London's leading prostitutes.'

Frowning, she read the entry aloud:

<u>*Miss L—e—s, No. 9 Harley Street*</u>
Artful ways beguile the implicit rake

The above line is highly descriptive of Miss L—y L—e—s, who is a fine, brown-haired, lively girl of about twenty-nine. Her beauty is by no means inconsiderable: clear skin, full breasted, and an agreeable rasp to her speech; her eyes, however, are of no great advantage, as they are small and brown and unremarkable. A small mole mars her upper lip, which she does not trouble to disguise, though her smile is fine enough and, we concede, can prove infectious.

She has little education, but much sharpness of wit, which her company will easily discover. She understands a great deal of her business, and rarely fails to please, though her principal defect is a lack of care in hiding her displeasure should it occur. Just as a lady of the town should be conscientious to paint and patch her face, so she should disguise her imperfections of temper, namely boredom and dismay. How such a piece of goods came to our market, we struggle to guess, for she likes to cultivate an enigmatic air. She will partake in all but the Grecian vice. As such, not less than five guineas will content her.

'It's like a review of a play,' Mrs Corsham said, with a grimace. 'Or as if she is a piece of furniture in a cabinetmaker's catalogue.'

'I'll make Harley Street my first port of call,' Child said. 'Followed by Bow Street to talk to my man there.'

'Her child,' Caro said. 'The magistrate said there wasn't one living at her rooms. He said he thought it must have died or been adopted. I'd like to be certain.'

Child studied his client cautiously, as though she was some new and exotic species, trying to fit her into his study of people. Haughty, spoilt, and too clever by half, was his conclusion, and yet there were some discordant notes, not least the question of her motives.

'Is that why you're doing this? Because there is a child involved?'

'Does it matter why?'

'I like to understand my client's purpose. You met her, you liked her. I understand that. But she lied to you.'

For a moment, she didn't respond, staring down at the pamphlet in her hand. 'I won't deny it hurt. For two days I mourned Lucia di Caracciolo, and now I find no such person ever existed. The magistrate, my brother, the newspapers . . . they see only a harlot now and harlots matter not. Yet a woman still died in that bower. I held Lucy's hand as she breathed her last. They'd like me to forget that I ever met her, but I find I cannot.'

Child examined her sceptically, wondering if there was more to it than that. Then he thought of Finn Daley's axe and Mrs Corsham's seventy-five guineas, and decided to let the matter drop.

CHAPTER SEVEN

CHILD BREAKFASTED AT a little after midday, and then walked across the city to shake off his headache. The skies over north London threatened rain, but Harley Street was always busy whatever the weather. Porters and servants on errands mingled with residents taking the air, and clients calling on the barristers, architects and society physicians who made the streets of Marylebone their home. Child surveyed the women he passed, trying to pick the harlots out from the wives. It was no easy task. They bought their silks and satins from the same mantua-makers, their plumed hats from the same milliners, and, of course, they fucked the same men.

Number nine was five storeys high, the bricks shiny and yellow in their newness. Child had to knock several times before he heard a step in the hall. The door was thrown open to reveal a man of middling years, wearing a nightcap and banyan robe that showed off his brawny chest. His chin bristled with white stubble, his face round and red as a pickling cabbage.

Child introduced himself. 'Are you the owner of this property?'

The man whipped a horn trumpet from his pocket and held it to his ear. 'What's that, sir?' he asked in a Cornish accent.

'The owner,' Child repeated more loudly.

'You're looking at him. Boscastle, at your service.'

'I'd like to talk to you about Lucy Loveless.'

Boscastle gave a heavy sigh. 'I'm afraid she's dead, sir. Up there in Saint Peter's bordello. Though her memory will live on in the minds of many a young gentleman.' He ran his eye over Child, sizing him up. 'And many an older one too. I've another girl upstairs who could inspire just as fine memories.'

Child guessed that as well as Lucy's landlord, this man had been her 'bully': doorkeeper, protector and ejector of unwelcome clients – all in exchange for a cut of the profit.

'I don't want a girl. I'm a thief-taker, here about Lucy's murder.' Child gave him his card. 'I'd like to ask you a few questions, if I may?'

'I already told Bow Street everything I know.'

'My client doesn't find Bow Street as conscientious as they could be. I'd also like to take a look inside her rooms.'

Boscastle gave him a pitying smile. 'Perhaps you confuse this establishment with a philanthropic enterprise, sir?'

'Don't you want the man who killed your tenant caught?'

'Aye, sir, I do. But if you're making a profit from this dreadful business, I don't see why some of it shouldn't be mine.'

It was hard to argue with that logic. A silver crown proved enough to satisfy him, and then Boscastle ushered Child into a hall hung with a dusty chandelier, and up a flight of stairs painted with Bacchanalian murals. The landlord unlocked a door on the first-floor landing, and Child followed him into a large bed-sitting room with three arched windows overlooking the street. The place was furnished ostentatiously: a four-poster bed with silk curtains; a chinoiserie screen; a French-style dressing table with a swing looking-glass; two plush armchairs before the fireplace; and a separate dressing room fitted out with painted armoires and drawers. When lit by candles, the ivory silk wallpaper must sparkle, and the heavy yellow curtains would give the room a lustrous glow. A stage set for love, or the facsimile of it.

'How long had Lucy lived here?' he asked.

'About three years,' Boscastle said. 'Though she'd been in London long before that. She came from Norfolk originally. Used to send the boy out for flounder and samphire when it was in season, because it reminded her of home.'

'And she never had a child living here?'

'No dogs, no children. I make that very plain. Lucy never even mentioned a child in my hearing.'

'She had been branded upon the hand for thievery at some point in her life. Do you know anything about that?'

'Aye, she said she got taken up years ago, not long after she came to London. A lot of girls mix whoring and picking pockets before they find their feet. As long as they're prompt with the rent and cause no trouble, I don't judge.'

Lucy had certainly found her feet. The shelves of the presses and armoires held a rainbow of satin bodices, brocaded skirts, lace petticoats, silk stockings, soft woollen cloaks and fur-trimmed capes, each carefully pressed, folded and laid in tissue-paper. The linens were white, the stays were whalebone, and the parasols were painted silk with ivory handles. Hat- and wig-boxes were stacked on top of the armoires, and a japanned chest was packed with fans, indispensables, and feathers.

'She loved her clothes, Lucy did,' Boscastle said. 'She was selling off her things to pay the bills, but I think these would have been the last to go. They'll have to go now. I'm owed three months' rent, and there's a lot of unhappy tradesmen need paying.'

'Wasn't she making good money? *Harris's List* says she charged five guineas a night.'

'Aye, but that was before all the trouble.'

Child looked up. 'What trouble?'

'First, someone gave her a hiding – beat her all shades of blue. Next, she got the boot from that artist fellow she sat for, Jacobus Agnetti. Then she fell foul of the Whores' Club – they threw her out. She'd already lost half her clients by then, because someone had put it about town that she had the pox. This was another nail in the coffin – if you'll pardon the phrase. She lived off her savings until they ran out, then she was forced to sell her things.'

'When was she attacked?'

'Back in March. Poor girl was laid up for two weeks. She wouldn't tell me who done it. It's my job to protect my tenants, and I pressed her. All she would say was that it wasn't one of her clients. It was personal, not business.'

'If not a client, then who? A lover?'

'Maybe, but I don't think so. Lucy didn't seem interested in men that way. She didn't want a keeper, nor a husband. That's how she got her name: Lucy Loveless. "Men like to tell you what to do, Boscastle, and I cannot be told." She just wanted to get rich and retire.'

'Do you think it was the same person? The one who beat her and the one spreading these rumours?'

'Don't ask me. I only know the rent was late.'

Child closed the final drawer in the dressing room, and walked back into the bedroom. He spent the next ten minutes poking about while they talked. A washstand held a porcelain jug and bowl, sponges, ointments, soap, and a chamber pot. The drawers of the dressing table held a curling iron; jars of lard, powder, red pomatum, whitening paint, and rouge; a patch-box; perfume; and cosmetic water. To Child, who found washing a chore best avoided, being a celebrated harlot looked like hard work.

'Can you give me a list of her clients' names?'

'Are you mad, sir? This is a confidential house. I won't have you pestering my customers, not without some evidence of wrongdoing.'

'How can I get evidence, if I don't know who they are?'

'That's your job, sir, not mine. In any event, I think you're whistling at the wrong dog. I told you the man who beat her wasn't one of her clients. Well, I think he came back for a second go.'

'What makes you say that?'

'Only a few days before she was killed, my other tenant saw her arguing with a soldier in the street. Not a man she recognized from this house. Not a client.'

'Can I talk to her?'

'As long as you make it worth her while, you can do what you like.'

Here and there, during his search, Child caught glimpses of the woman behind the cosmetics and the stage set. A watercolour painting of the Norfolk Broads – her home, Boscastle had said. A memento mori locket containing a lock of soft brown hair. Child wondered if that was proof that Lucy's child was indeed dead.

In one of the bedside cupboards he found a box of almonds in caramel and several rolled pig intestines with ribbon ties, to guard against pregnancy and disease. Also a small glass bottle. Child uncorked it and took a sniff. A waft of old cheese greeted him, instantly recognizable: valerian, a sleeping draught.

'Did Lucy have other visitors? Friends? Family?'

'These girls don't see their families, sir. Not unless they're paying the bills. I got the impression Lucy broke with hers long ago.'

'Friends, then?'

'Her dearest was a girl called Kitty Carefree, a lovely red-head from the Whores' Club. Thick as thieves, she and Lucy were, but there must have been a falling out, because she stopped coming a few months back.'

'Do you think their quarrel was related to her other troubles?'

'Maybe. You should ask them at the Whores' Club.'

'Did she have any other friends that you remember?'

'The wife of the artist, Mrs Agnetti, used to call sometimes on her husband's business. Her and Lucy – sometimes Kitty too – they'd talk, and I often heard them laughing. But you know the story about the Agnettis, I'm sure. It wasn't long after Mrs Agnetti left town that Lucy and Kitty had their falling out. I think Lucy was lonely, truth be told. She took up with an old friend – not the sort you'd find in the Whores' Club, that's for sure.'

'Go on.'

'I never caught the woman's name, but she called several times in the last few months – until I had words. She conveyed the wrong impression for a house like this. My tenants' clients expect the best, not to encounter some rookery moll on the stairs.'

'Can you describe her?'

'Not quite a penny bunter, but she wasn't far off it. Dark curly hair, wild as a gypsy. Scrawny, her cheeks all pox-scarred, yellow teeth. She'd been branded upon the hand too, which made me wonder if she was a friend from Lucy's thieving days. Walked with a limp – no wonder Bow Street caught up with her. After I had words, she stopped coming. I presume they met elsewhere. Lucy was out until all hours in the weeks before she was killed. Sometimes she was dropped off in a hired carriage. Still spending, despite her debts. I had words about that too.'

A shelf next to the bed held writing implements and books: Richardson, Smollet, a few romances, some pornographic pamphlets, and – somewhat to Child's surprise – a volume of the plays of Aeschylus in translation. A walnut writing box was empty, save for a folded map of the environs of London.

'Didn't she have any papers? Letters? That sort of thing?'

'Bow Street took all those. Her drawings too.'

'Drawings?'

'By Jacobus Agnetti.'

Child leafed through the books to see if any papers were concealed between the pages. He found only a few pressed flowers and a card advertising the services of the Magdalen Hospital for Penitent Prostitutes. He showed it to Boscastle.

'Was Lucy thinking about turning her back on this business? Given all her trouble?'

'Lucy? Not on your life. She said: "They mean to stop me, Boscastle, but I'll make them pay."'

'They?'

'That's what she said. I assumed she meant whoever had been trying to ruin her life. I believed her too – that she'd make them pay, I mean. Lucy knew how to hold a grudge.'

On the reverse of the Magdalen card was a jotting in an elegant ladylike script: *50–60 pineapples, 2s 1d.*

Child frowned. It couldn't be a receipt. Pineapples cost a small fortune, eighty or ninety pounds apiece, not two shillings, one pence. Nor, given their expense and rarity, did fifty to sixty seem a plausible number. Child didn't think he had seen more than half a dozen pineapples in his entire life.

'Does this look like Lucy's hand?'

Boscastle squinted, then nodded.

'Can I keep this?'

'If you've a shilling you can.'

Sighing, Child reached into his pocket. He took a final look around that room where Lucy's clients had enjoyed her favours, wishing the walls could talk. Then Boscastle showed him up a second flight of stairs to see his other tenant.

The girl was named Emma and she looked as if they'd just roused her out of bed. Young, with big white teeth, her fashionably brown hair was showing yellow at the roots. For four shillings she agreed to tell Child what she'd seen.

'I was coming home from shopping one afternoon, a week or so ago. Lucy came out of the house, about to get into a hired carriage, when someone called out to her. A redcoat soldier – he had a woman with him, I presumed another whore. He and Lucy exchanged words and then he pushed her.'

'Did you hear what they were arguing about?'

'No, I called over to her, asked if I should fetch Boscastle, and the redcoat and his harlot walked off.'

'Can you remember what he looked like? It could be important.'

'Tall. Short fair hair. Side whiskers. It was an officer's redcoat, with gold epaulettes. He came close to me when he walked past. Gave me a real look of hate. I saw he had a scar just here.' The girl touched her temple. 'Looked like a duelling cut to me.'

'How about the girl?'

'I don't remember. I was looking at Lucy and the soldier.'

'Had you ever seen him before? With Lucy or elsewhere?'

'Not with Lucy, but I think I'd seen him around Covent Garden. He's handsome, see, the sort who draws a lady's eye. If it was the same gentleman, he's one of those who likes to drink too much with his friends and cause trouble for the taverners.'

'There you are, sir,' Boscastle said. 'Not a client.'

Child questioned her a little more, but she and Lucy had

had only a passing acquaintance. He thanked her, and Boscastle walked him down the stairs to the street.

Mrs Corsham's theory that Lucy's murder wasn't the product of a chance encounter in the bowers was gaining credence in Child's eyes. The man who'd assaulted her. The person who'd set out to destroy her livelihood. The soldier who'd accosted her in the street. Her killer. Were they one and the same person, or had Lucy possessed a gift for making enemies? At least Child now had several lines of inquiry. He walked with purpose in the direction of Covent Garden.

PAMELA

10 January 1782

The drums rolled like thunder, interrupting the dance of the dryads. The girls froze, hands cupped to their ears in a variety of poses, amidst a glade of wooden trees with paper leaves. Artfully positioned silk garlands adorned the otherwise naked nymphs, their hair crowned with artificial flowers.

Pamela watched from the wings, heart beating, a little breathless. It was her sixth night in Mrs Havilland's establishment, and already she knew the acts by heart. The brightly lit stage occupied one end of the ballroom. Beyond it, in the darkness, Pamela could see the glow of the gentlemen's pipes, the flash of their pocket watches. Smell their scent.

From between the trees, a girl in a goatskin strolled, holding a bow, a quiver of arrows on her back. Cecily was a little older than Pamela, from a village to the east of London called Dagenham. Her hair was yellow as quince, her limbs long, dusted with gold. The nymphs ran to flank her, crouching on either side.

Next to Pamela in the wings stood George, a former town crier. 'Behold the goddess Artemis,' he bellowed.

Cecily made a show of bending to pluck a silk flower, giving the men a view that set them cheering. She aimed her bow at several members of the audience in turn, and they cried ribald compliments.

When the cheering died, Mrs Havilland walked onto the stage. Regally tall in rich purple silk, with petticoats of yellow crêpe trimmed with fine black lace, her piled hair was adorned tonight with a golden chain of enamelled flowers.

'Gentlemen, I ask that you pay homage to Artemis, huntress of the forest.' She waited again until the applause had quietened. 'Many have attempted to storm Fortress Artemis, yet she stands before you inviolate, untouched by man. In three weeks' time, we shall discover whether there is a stag among you worthy of this skittish fawn.'

Cecily ducked into a defensive crouch, her expression startled, bow ready. An appreciative chuckle arose from the audience.

George gave Pamela a nudge. 'Ready?'

Oh, she was ready. Not that her costume had required much preparation. Her face scrubbed so her skin shone, cheeks pinched to a healthy glow. Her dress thin, made of brown cotton, not unlike the one she'd worn on her arrival. Bare feet. Her ebony hair unwashed and tangled.

On the first night, she'd thought she'd be a laughing stock. She looked like a drudge. Why couldn't she be the goddess Artemis? She'd complained to Mrs Havilland and received a sharp response. Yet at the end of her performance, much to her astonishment, the ballroom had resounded to the gentlemen's cheers.

Even Mrs Havilland had softened: 'You made a good start, child, but there is room for improvement. Put in the work required, and by the end of next month, they'll be queuing all the way to Ealing Common.'

Since then, she had only got better. Pamela stood back as Cecily hurried past her, off to the audience room, a swift pat for luck. The curtain had come down, and the orchestra played a rousing refrain. On stage, Mrs Havilland's footmen were hastily rearranging the tableaux. A stove, an oaken table, a chopping board, a chair. The floor sprinkled with flour and vegetable peelings. In need of a maid.

The curtain rose and the room filled with an expectant hush.

'Behold,' George bellowed, 'the maidservant, Pamela Andrews. Her beauty matched only by her virtue.'

She stepped out onto the stage, and applause swelled like a choir. Taking up her broom, she swept the floor, while the fiddler played a jaunty tune and the men clapped along. The oddness of it all still tickled her. To leave the house in Cheapside to perform a facsimile of her chores here for a paying crowd? Yet she'd never been appreciated at the house in Cheapside like this.

George gave a signal in the wings, and she walked to the table. The music took on an ominous note.

'Behold, the rakish squire, Mr B.'

The ballroom echoed with hoots and hisses. Peter Jakes would be creeping towards her from behind, wearing an oversized periwig and a suit of maroon velvet, a pillow strung under his coat to plump him out. Pamela chopped a carrot as the hoots increased in volume.

He was directly behind her now. Pamela could smell onion and porter on his breath. She tensed as he seized hold of her, pressing his lips against hers, sliding his tongue into her mouth, though she'd told him not to. Her arms flailed, and she pricked him with the knife, a little harder than she was supposed to. He released her with a shout, and she staggered to the front of the stage.

For a moment her mind went blank, though she'd sat up late learning her lines. Relief washed over her as it all flooded back.

'Sir, you are Lucifer himself in the shape of my master, or you could not use me thus.'

Jakes gripped her by the arm, digging in his fingers so it would bruise. 'Since you take me for the Devil, how can you expect any good from me?'

She hung her head. 'I will bear anything you can inflict on me with patience even to the laying down of my life. But I cannot be patient, I cannot be passive, when my virtue is at stake!'

Applause, the loudest she'd had yet. Jakes grimaced and seized hold of her dress with both hands. The bodice had a false seam secured with pins, and the garment rent in artful tatters, exposing her bubbies.

A collective intake of breath. A cymbal crashed. Then she pulled her dress together, so they'd have no more than that one tantalizing glimpse. Gazing out at the gentlemen from beneath her eyelashes, summoning a tear, she made her appeal: 'I am truly sorry for my boldness, but indeed he doesn't use me like a gentleman. I trust that God will deliver me from this Philistine.'

Stamping their feet, the room vibrated to the sound of their acclaim. She basked in their desire, holding the gaze of the gentlemen who looked the richest, as Cecily had taught her. Then she caught sight of another man, and though he had few outward signs of wealth, found she could not look away.

His scarlet redcoat marked him out as a soldier. She knew about them, but this one couldn't be more different to the coarse infantrymen on leave she'd encountered around Cheapside. Sleek. Well groomed. An officer. A gentleman.

He grinned at her, a flash of white teeth. His blond hair cropped short, in the new style she rather liked. A long lean body and a long lean face to match. What looked like a duelling scar cut through the outer edge of one of his eyebrows. *A handsome devil, and he knows it*. It was a favourite phrase of Rachel the cook's. She said it like it was a bad thing, and yet somehow him knowing, and Pamela knowing that he knew, only made her pulse beat a little faster.

Mrs Havilland walked on stage to list her virtues, and Pamela's task was to stand mutely, gazing at the floor. But she couldn't resist another glance at the soldier, and this time when he grinned, she smiled back. As she walked meekly off the stage, to another round of heady applause, she sent up a prayer to Artemis, goddess of virgins: *Let it be him.*

CHAPTER EIGHT

RAIN BLURRED THE vibrant colours of Vauxhall Gardens. Fat drops pitted the paths, washing away the puddles of wine and vomit, flowing in waterfalls off the waxed-cloth roofs of the supper boxes. By daylight the place had lost its magic. Without the lights and the music, it had a squalid, tawdry air.

'Officious little guardsman, isn't he?' Caro murmured to her footman, Miles, nodding at the back of the gatehouse porter who strode in front of them.

She had come here intending to go directly to the bowers, to look for the document she was certain she'd seen next to Lucy's body. Yet the gardens were closed until that evening, and the porter hadn't wanted to let them in. Spotting Jacobus Agnetti's distinctive yellow phaeton tied up in the carriage-park, she'd claimed an appointment. Even then, the porter had insisted on accompanying them to the Rotunda.

'I heard the Prince of Wales is due to visit Vauxhall soon,' Miles said, angling the oilskin umbrella over her head. 'I suppose they have to be careful.'

His broad, freckled face was unusually sullen, his Welsh lilt absent all levity. Caro guessed he still blamed her for giving him the slip here the other night. Mordechai must have torn him off a strip.

He probably also resented her for making him stand so long last night in Mr Child's dingy rooms with their foul odours.

Had it been a mistake to hire the thief-taker? She wasn't sure. Mr Child was an unprepossessing creature in his ill-fitting coat and ridiculous wig, his nose bulging with so many veins it resembled a damson. Yet he had spoken with confidence about the case, and his beady black eyes were sharp. She kept reminding herself that Harry had valued his talents.

The Rotunda's roof resonated to the low drum of rain. The place seemed deserted, and yet someone had clearly been at work. A trestle table stood beneath the dome, with several paintings laid out on it, not all of them framed. Sketchbooks, folders, knives, pencils and other clutter lay between them. More paintings and empty frames leaned against the table.

'I'll wait for Mr Agnetti to return,' Caro said.

The porter squinted at her suspiciously. 'Then I'll wait too.'

Caro paced the Rotunda, footsteps echoing on the tiles. She had never been an admirer of Agnetti's work, though there was no denying his talent, nor his eye for a commercial opportunity. Ever since the controversy over his *Rape of Europa*, everyone wanted an Agnetti for their drawing room – murder and defilement sitting tolerably well with a glass of brandy. The painting before her seemed a case in point.

It depicted a verdant landscape scattered with broken pillars. In the foreground stood an altar of carved stone. A dark-haired girl, little more than a child, lay struggling upon this altar, held down by an older man, a soldier. The girl's robe had slipped to expose one milk-white breast, against which the tip of the man's sword rested, drawing blood. Her face was twisted in terror, imploring eyes gazing into death's abyss. *The Sacrifice of Iphigenia*. It made Caro think of the scene in the bower. Swiftly she moved on to the next canvas.

She was still staring at it a minute later, when Jacobus Agnetti walked into the Rotunda. He stopped when he saw

Caro, black eyebrows drawn together over his hawkish nose. 'Mrs Corsham, good day to you, madam.'

He spoke with a rich Italian inflexion, which was known to drive the society matrons wild. A large, dishevelled bear of a man, his greying black hair was swept back from his forehead in suitably dramatic fashion, his cravat unknotted, worn loose around his neck. In the cathedral light of the Rotunda, his frayed plum-velvet frock coat put Caro in mind of a cardinal's cape: a moth-eaten Medici, which seemed an appropriate analogy, for scandal attached itself to Mr Agnetti like burrs.

He bowed. 'I trust you are well. And your brother Ambrose? It has been some time since I last saw him out on the town.'

Caro murmured her usual story about Switzerland and the hunting season, waiting for Agnetti to smile, as if he could well imagine the manner of feathered game Ambrose Craven was chasing. But Agnetti only said – a little impatiently, she felt: 'What can I do for you, madam?'

'This lady said she had an appointment with you, sir,' the porter said.

'Not an appointment precisely. I should like to talk to you about a private matter.'

Agnetti turned to the porter. 'You heard the lady, sir.'

Muttering beneath his breath, the porter left the Rotunda. Miles retreated to the door.

'A private matter,' Agnetti said. 'I am intrigued.'

Caro turned back to the painting. 'That's her, isn't it? The woman who was murdered? Lucy Loveless.'

The scene depicted another murder: a woman standing over a naked, dying man, axe in hand. He had crawled from a stone bath, his lifeblood streaked across the mosaic floor. The woman's chestnut hair was unpinned, her robes dishevelled, her flesh pliant. She had a high, arched forehead, blazing eyes, and a small mole on her upper lip. Caro imagined her dark hair coiled beneath a black lace headdress adorned with ostrich feathers, her face flushed with the heat of the crowd, enlivened by a puckish smile: Lucia di Caracciolo, dazzling at Carlisle House. She imagined the skin drained of all colour, the lips grey, desperate to speak: Lucy Loveless, dying in the bowers at Vauxhall Gardens.

'Yes, that is Lucy,' Agnetti said softly. 'I heard the sad news from one of my other sitters only this morning. It grieves me greatly. Lucy was an inspiring muse.'

'It was I who found her,' Caro said. 'Whilst taking the air near the bowers.'

His eyes widened. 'How very shocking. I didn't know. I am sorry you had to go through such an ordeal.'

'It was nothing compared to Lucy's.' Caro drew a breath. 'Had you known her long?'

'Since first I came to London – about three years. Here you see her as Clytemnestra murdering her husband, Agamemnon. Lucy loved this painting. I gave her a volume of Aeschylus so that she could read the story behind it. Perhaps I should take it down, under the circumstances.'

'If she loved it, then it should stay,' Caro said. 'I confess I cannot get her out of my head. Will you tell me about her? The manner of woman she was?'

Agnetti considered the question, still facing the painting. 'We talked often when she sat for me. Usually about my work. She enjoyed the myths and history that inspire my paintings, and would ask me questions, sometimes to the point of distraction. About my hometown of Naples too – she said she'd like to visit one day. To walk where the Romans had – to see the sights. Like many of my sitters, she had an earthy wit, but there was a sadness there too. Her life had not always been easy, I suspect.'

'I imagine not, given her trade.'

Agnetti gave Caro a considered glance. 'Do not pity overly much. Lucy's trade gave her the freedom she desired.'

'Do not pity? She died in enormous pain.'

'I was speaking of her life, not her death.' He studied Caro's expression, the colour heightening on her cheeks. 'I too used to pity my sitters, but later I came to admire them. They wear their sins openly. Polite society condemns them, but they hold their heads high. That takes a certain courage, don't you think?'

Agnetti's admiration for his sitters was a well-worn topic in London society. The newspapers liked to dwell at length upon the comings and goings at his gloomy old house in Leicester Fields: the parade of prostitutes through his parlour and the implication that they did more than sit for their supper. Artists had some licence when it came to disreputable conduct, but Mrs Agnetti had plainly had her fill of humiliation. Not that her husband seemed to care, given his behaviour since she'd walked out on him.

'Lucy had no wish to be a maidservant or a milliner,' he continued, 'or any other penniless alternative to a life on the town. She may even have enjoyed her work. Some of my sitters do. She certainly enjoyed spending the money she earned.'

'I cannot imagine any amount of money is worth the risks these women face.'

'Until one has known poverty, how can one judge?'

'Does one need to have known poverty to deplore the degradation of women?'

'Is it not degrading to clean other people's houses for a pittance? That was Lucy's view on the matter. Her options were narrow, and she made her choices as she saw fit.'

Caro's anger, kindling inside her ever since her visit to the magistrate's house, suddenly blazed. 'She was a commodity to her clients, bought and sold like a loaf of sugar. You may choose to believe that she wasn't ground down by those exertions. I do not.'

Agnetti bowed his head. 'Forgive my bluntness, madam. You are upset – and little wonder.'

She drew a breath, fighting to control her emotions. There was little sense in taking it out on Mr Agnetti. 'Can I ask when it was that you last saw Lucy?'

'Some months ago now. I regret to say that I was forced to dismiss her from my employ.'

'Why was that?'

He sighed. 'She stole some drawings from me, and she also stole from another gentleman of my acquaintance. I couldn't have her in the house after that. Of all my sitters, she was the last I'd suspected would betray my trust.'

'The magistrate said she left considerable debts. I suppose she was desperate.'

'You surprise me. Lucy's best years on the town were behind her, but it is only after forty when such women enter perilous times. Her plan was to buy a plot of land in Hampstead, on which to build houses to sell at a profit to fund her retirement. I have no doubt she would have done so, whatever her present difficulties. She was resourceful and determined.'

'The magistrate mentioned that she had borne a child. I thought I might do something for him or her. Did you ever hear her speak of a son or daughter?'

Agnetti smiled sadly. 'Regrettably, I don't think you need worry upon that score. Lucy never spoke of her child. It is my guess that it must have died many years ago.'

'But you knew she'd had one?' The moment she'd spoken, she looked around at the paintings. 'Oh, I see.' He'd seen her naked.

Agnetti made no effort to fill the awkward silence that followed, simply turning back to the painting, lost in private contemplation.

'The magistrate believes she was murdered by a passing stranger,' Caro said, 'but I think she knew her killer. She spoke to me before she died. She was trying to tell me something.'

He turned. 'What did she say?'

'She said: "*He knows.*" I wondered if one of her clients might have killed her.'

As she spoke, it occurred to her that Agnetti might have enjoyed Lucy's favours himself. He had just admitted that he and Lucy had parted on bad terms. Could he have killed her? The possibility chilled her, and she was grateful for Miles's looming presence.

'It is certainly possible,' Agnetti said. 'Many times my sitters come to see me with blackened eyes or other bruises. They see it as a hazard of their trade. Someone attacked Lucy not long before I dismissed her. I presumed it was a client, though she did not say.'

Caro's voice faltered. 'My brother Ambrose knew her. I wondered if he could have met Lucy at your house? He commissioned a painting from you, did he not?'

Mordechai would have a seizure if he knew she was talking openly about Lucy and Ambrose. Agnetti too looked surprised. '*The Castration of Uranus.* It was two summers ago, as I recall. Mr Craven paid several visits to my home to discuss his commission, and Lucy was often around the place. They could easily have talked.'

Which would have been around the same time Ambrose had introduced her to Lucia at the supper party. Little wonder Lucy had discoursed so knowledgably about Naples after her conversations with Agnetti. Had she and Ambrose laughed at

Caro together, amused by her credulity? She tried to summon anger, but felt only despondent.

The sound of approaching footsteps made Agnetti turn. A young woman walked into the Rotunda and Caro was startled to see a knife in her hand. She was very tall, thin and pale, about nineteen years old, her hair so fair it was almost white, cropped shockingly short. With her white muslin gown and the knife, she might have stepped out of one of Agnetti's paintings. The assistant, Caro presumed; the one who had given rise to so much scandal.

The girl gave Caro a cool, assessing glance, and then addressed Agnetti: 'Mr Tyers is asking for you, sir.'

'I apologize, Mrs Corsham,' Agnetti said. 'There is a small problem with the ticketing for tonight and I must attend to it. I trust that I will see you at Carlisle House before too long. I hope by then you will have fully recovered from your ordeal.'

He bent to kiss her hand, and then he and the girl left the Rotunda together. Caro waited a moment, and then walked over to the table. She picked up one of Agnetti's sketchbooks, and leafed through it, looking for Lucy.

Many of the subjects she recognized: gentlemen and ladies of her acquaintance. Others she did not – mostly women, mostly young, mostly beautiful. In the second sketchbook, she found her: Lucy rendered in charcoal, a coil of dark hair resting against her cheek. Her eyes weighed the artist, bold and inscrutable.

A drawing of Lucy would be a useful thing for Mr Child to have, she decided. Agnetti wouldn't miss it. The girl had left her knife on the table, and ignoring Miles's inquisitive gaze, she used it to cut the drawing from the book. Rolling it into a scroll, she concealed it beneath her cloak, and stepped out into the rain-washed gardens.

CHAPTER NINE

'I DIDN'T DO it,' the woman screamed. 'Shitten fucksters.'

The men pulling her along the street carried the distinctive red tipstaffs of the Bow Street Runners. A thin scholarly-looking man in a shabby coat hurried along in their wake, and Child guessed the woman was a whore caught robbing her client.

They dragged her into the Brown Bear tavern, which stood opposite Sir Amos Fox's house on Bow Street. The Runners had used the Brown Bear as their headquarters for years, even turning the bedrooms upstairs into makeshift cells. Child pushed his way through the throng outside, into the crowded taproom.

Several bored-looking Runners sat at tables, writing in ledgers. The queues in front of them stretched out onto the street: mothers holding crying children, people shouting about stolen property, affidavit men come to swear false testimony for money. The woman was dragged up the stairs to the cells, still kicking and spitting. Towards the rear of the taproom, Bow Street Runners between shifts sat around at long tables, drinking and playing cribbage for pennies. Child picked out his friend, Orin Black, another Deptfordian exiled to London.

Orin waved him over, rising to shake his hand. Child liked that he could look him square in the eye, even if Orin could fit through a crack in a door sideways. The other Runners called him 'the jockey' and Child would have punched them in the mouth, but Orin seemed to take it all in his stride. His face was round and dimpled, with the faint ridge of a harelip, and he wore his own hair in a stubby queue, tied back with a yellow ribbon to match his waistcoat.

'I was just going out on my rounds,' he said. 'Take a walk with me?'

They strolled along Bow Street in the direction of the market. 'Lucy Loveless,' Child said. 'What can you tell me about her murder?'

Since he'd turned his hand to thief-taking, he and Orin had established a mutually beneficial arrangement in the trade of information. Orin would pass him the names of victims of theft unimpressed by Bow Street's efforts to recover their property, and in turn Child would pass him the location of any villain with a price on his head who he felt deserved to hang.

Orin raised an eyebrow, one thumb hooked into the pocket of his waistcoat, swinging his tipstaff. 'I didn't attend the scene myself, but the murder's been the talk of the Brown Bear. Who's your client?'

'Between you and me? The lady who found her in the bower. She's decided she cares.'

Orin grunted. 'Only one who does. No one's claimed the body. I'm surprised the Whores' Club haven't. They usually look after their own.'

'I heard they threw her out. I'm going there next.'

Orin grinned. 'Good luck with that.'

Covent Garden was awash with the scents of kindling pleasure: woodsmoke to heat the water in the bathhouses, baking pies, mulling wine, and a hundred varieties of cheap perfume trailing the piazza's working women. Ragged flower girls mingling with wizened penny bunters; buxom bagnio girls

peering from the windows of the brothels and bathhouses; theatre spells strolling arm in arm with coffeehouse molls and
jelly-house tarts; and painted courtesans peeping from the windows of their keepers' carriages. Orin and Child walked between
the fruit and vegetable stalls, the market-men casting anxious
glances towards the ominous skies. Child bought himself an
apple, while Orin eyed the vagabonds and urchins, looking for
trouble.

'Did you know Lucy?' Child asked.

'Not to speak to. I knew who she was. Everybody did. A few
years back you'd have seen her name in the newspapers –
appearances at the theatre on the arm of a duke, or a duel
fought over her favours – that sort of thing. I used to see her
going in and out of the Bedford Coffeehouse. But then she got
older, like they all do, and there's always younger girls for the
newspapers to write about. Next step down from the Bedford
is the Whores' Club. She'd have had another ten years or so at
that level. Then it would have been retirement, if she was lucky,
or more likely she'd have turned bawd, or wound up like that.'
He gestured with his thumb at an ancient penny bunter with a
stick, hobbling across the piazza, offering herself to disgusted
tradesmen for a farthing.

'My client says Sir Amos is convinced it was a random
encounter in the bowers. Wrong place, wrong time.'

'He's probably right. You wouldn't plan a killing like that.
Too many people around. Too much risk of being disturbed –
our killer got lucky. Lucy was stabbed more than a dozen times,
mostly in the lower abdomen. That's a real frenzy, Perry. Either
he couldn't control himself, or he enjoyed it. Mad or bad, that
was the verdict of our lads on the scene.'

'Or someone who had cause to hate her,' Child said. 'She
had an enemy, her landlord says. Perhaps more than one. She'd

been beaten badly a few months back, and someone was trying to ruin her life. My client saw a man in a plague doctor's mask just before she found the body. That would be one way to mitigate some of the risk.'

Orin mused on this a moment. 'If it was planned, why do it there? Why not some place quiet?'

'Because his blood was up?' Child was thinking it through as he spoke. 'Maybe it wasn't planned, maybe he'd just found something out about Lucy he didn't like? Her final words were: "*He knows.*" My client thinks she was talking about the killer.'

'A crime of passion, you mean?'

'A spurned lover. A jealous client. She must have been meeting *someone*.'

'Or a thieves' dispute?' Orin fingered the faint scar of his harelip.

'So you concede it's possible she knew him?'

'I suppose so. There's no witnesses, no suspects, only some Jewish lamplighter who looks as though he couldn't harm a fly. No motive, beyond the obvious, except the sawbones doesn't think she was raped.'

'How about a weapon?'

'Didn't find one. Killer must have taken it with him.'

'Bit of a risk taking a bloody knife out through the gate with all those guards.'

'He takes risks. That's the one thing we do know about him.'

Child pursed his lips. 'How hard did they look? I ask because my client is convinced she saw a document next to the body, only Sir Amos told her he didn't have it. Makes me question how diligent they were at the scene. Can you talk to the Runners who were there and see if anyone saw it?'

'I might leave out the part about their diligence.'

Child grinned. 'They were diligent enough at her rooms.

Took some papers and drawings away with them, I'm told. Can you find out what they were? Get me a look?'

'They'll want paying.'

'Naturally.'

They paused while Orin gave the eye to a pack of urchins idling near one of the fruit stalls, waiting for the stallholder to turn his back. The boys spotted him and ran off in search of easier pickings.

'I had a murder like this last year,' Orin said. 'A whore found beaten to death. The killer's mother turned him in after he came home covered in blood. All he'd say was that he didn't know what had come over him. Maybe Sir Amos's reward will provoke a similar prick of conscience. We've little enough else to go on, I'll be honest.'

'Why did Sir Amos take the case off Guildford's hands?' Child asked. 'Given what you've just said. Doesn't sound like him.'

'Politics, would be my best guess. Perhaps he owes Guildford a favour, or he wants them to owe him one. He's got his eye on a seat in Parliament; perhaps he fancies Surrey? Whatever it is, I'll tell you one thing for certain, it will be to the benefit of Sir Amos Fox.'

Outside the Bedford Coffeehouse, a man was playing a whistle, trying to get his dog to dance for money. It kept sniffing after old food, and a party of young gentlemen sitting at one of the outside tables jeered.

'How about this Lord March?' Child said, eyeing the men with dislike. 'Could it have been him?'

'There was no blood on his clothes. You'd expect there to be if he'd done it.'

'My client says the plague doctor was wearing a long black

coat. Lord March could have discarded it and then returned to assist Mrs Corsham when he heard her scream?'

'You know he's the Earl of Amberley's heir? Mentor to the Prince of Wales? I'd be careful what you say and who you say it to. Look, we had no cause to suspect him. He was helpful and courteous, our lads said. Not often they get to question a peer of the realm.'

Child grunted. 'One of Lucy's neighbours saw her arguing with a redcoat officer only a few days before she died. Said she'd thought she'd seen him around Covent Garden causing trouble.' He described the man, his duelling scar.

'I'll look out for him,' Orin said. 'We get a lot of gentlemen like that down here. They think it great sport to get drunk and break up a tavern, then pay off the taverner. Or start a brawl in a bawdy house. A few years back, a group of them rolled an old lady down a hill for fun. Broke both her arms. Arrest them and they only buy their way out, or their fathers intervene. Half of them have debts that'd make your eyes water, but it don't stop them spending.' Orin gave him a sidelong glance. 'Talking of which, they say Finn Daley's looking for you.'

'He found me. I'm still here.'

'Just watch yourself, Perry. I don't want to be hauling you out of the Thames.'

'If I find this murderer, you won't have to. You'll talk to the Runners at the scene and the ones who took Lucy's papers?'

'Deptford till we die, right?' Orin punched him lightly on the shoulder. 'Come back tomorrow. I'll see you right.'

Chapter Ten

CARO'S BREATHING QUICKENED as she turned into the Dark Walk. Memories assailed her. The constables and the blood and Lucy and Lord March. The man in the plague doctor's mask. The ground outside the bower was a churn of mud from the rain and all the comings and goings. Steeling herself, she walked inside.

The willows slouched under the downpour, the stone bench slick and black. All trace of Lucy had been removed, save for a darkened patch of grass. The mineral stench of blood clogged Caro's nostrils, but memory had seeped into reality. Lucy's fingers clutching her own. *He knows.*

'What are we looking for, Mrs Corsham?' Miles said.

'A document of some kind, perhaps a letter.'

Together they scanned the grass. Caro wondered if it had been kicked into the undergrowth in all the confusion. She crouched down, muddying her petticoats, ignoring Miles's protests. Edging deeper into the trees, her sleeves catching on branches, she felt around on the mossy ground. After a little while spent crawling around, her fingers brushed something small and hard in the grass. A gentleman's signet ring, encrusted with earth. Gold, with a waxy red stone. It looked very old.

'Whatever are you doing down there in the dirt?'

She looked up sharply at the sound of his voice. Lord March stood at the entrance to the bower, an exotic bird amidst the foliage, in a sky-blue coat of moiré silk embroidered with silver thread. She scrambled to her feet, her fingers forming a fist around the ring. 'Miles, wait by the carriage.'

The footman started to object, but she silenced him with a look. He handed her the umbrella and left the bower.

'What are you doing here?' she addressed Lord March.

His face in the dappled half-light resembled an older man's: lined with fatigue, his complexion pale, his cheeks hollow. Too much fast living with Neddy Dodd-Bellingham, she supposed. He'd recently cropped his dark hair fashionably short – Dodd-Bellingham's influence again – tousled on top, with side whiskers over the ears. A waft of civet scent as he moved closer, his dark, intense gaze raking over her.

'I dropped by to see Agnetti,' he said. 'I saw your carriage in the courtyard and came to find you. So what were you doing? Picking mushrooms? Burying treasure?'

'Looking for a document, a letter. It was on the ground by the dead woman. Sir Amos doesn't have it. He thinks I must have imagined it, but you saw it, didn't you?'

'No, I only glanced into the bower. We were on the path outside, remember?'

Caro looked around herself again, distressed by her failure to find it. 'It was here. I know it was.'

'Why does it matter? Haven't you read the newspapers? She wasn't the lady you thought she was – she was a whore.'

Her face and hair were damp, her skirts and slippers muddied, and she was suddenly conscious of how she must appear. 'The letter might be connected to the murder. It could have been dropped by the killer.'

'Surely that is the magistrate's concern.'

'You would think so, wouldn't you?' Caro forced herself to stop looking for it, to look at him. For two weeks, she had sought the opportunity to be alone with him, but now she was doing it all wrong, distracted by Lucy Loveless and her murder. 'How have you been? I didn't get a chance to ask you the other night.'

'Well enough. And yourself? Recovered, I trust? Caroline Corsham is made of Toledo steel, isn't that right?'

'Not always, I'm not. Octavius, I've been concerned. You haven't answered any of my letters.'

'Forgive me. I've been busy.'

'With Catullus? My rival?' She forced a smile. 'Now that we are here, there is something I need to tell you.'

'And I you. That's why I came to find you.' He was looking at her oddly, and a feeling of foreboding rolled over her. 'Clemency Howard is to wear my mother's diamonds to the opera tonight. I didn't want you hearing it second-hand.'

Clemency Howard? She stared at him; all the words she'd practised dried on her tongue.

'I'm past thirty,' he went on. 'Thought it was probably time. My bit for the ancestors. Father's settled my debts, restored my allowance. Mother's delighted. So no more letters, if you don't mind – I know you'll understand. And it had better be Lord March from now on.'

She heard him distantly, the ring cutting into her palm. He smiled to soften the blow, and her eyes grew hot. She said the words very fast, so she couldn't take them back: 'Octavius, I am with child.'

He stared at her for a very long time. 'Why do you tell me this?'

'Because it isn't Harry's. It cannot be. And soon it will be too late to pass it off as his.'

'Are you saying it's mine?'

Her head shot up, and he arched an eyebrow. 'You can't

blame a fellow for wondering. I haven't even asked what you were up to in the bowers the other night.'

'Not that. I swear it.' She gazed at him helplessly. 'I fear Harry will divorce me when he finds out.'

'You really think it will come to that?' His expression softened and he held out his arms. 'Poor girl, what must you have been going through?'

She buried her face in his coat, his silver buttons with the Amberley crest digging into her cheek. If marriages could be broken, she told herself, then so could engagements. If he stood by her, the son of an earl, she could survive divorce. But already he was pulling away from their embrace.

'You'll talk Harry round,' he said gently, holding her by the shoulders. 'Nobody's going to divorce Caro. Especially not a man of sense, like him. He can pack you off to Germany: a quiet place to take the waters, a good family wanting a baby. I hear that's how it's done.'

'But what if I can't? Talk him round, I mean.' Her voice cracked. 'I'll have to leave London, live as an outcast. Lose Gabriel.'

'We won't speak of it,' he said firmly. 'Because it's not going to happen.' He frowned. 'Here, you haven't mentioned this to anyone, have you? Because Father mustn't find out. Things between us aren't yet back on a firm enough footing. And Clemency – Gad, this would break her heart.'

'No,' she said, faintly. 'I haven't told anyone.'

'Let's keep it that way,' he said. 'And try not to worry. Things will work themselves out. They always do.'

CHAPTER ELEVEN

THE COVENT GARDEN market stalls were packing up, the coffeehouses, taverns, bagnios and bordellos busy with a constant stream of customers going in and out. As Child pressed through the crowd, a thin, wan girl selling flowers caught his sleeve. 'Buy me dinner for a half-guinea, sir? Your love would make me very happy.'

If it did, Child thought, thinking of his wife and Sophie Hardcastle and every other woman who'd ever crossed his path, *you would be the exception to the rule.*

The door to the Shakespeare's Head was kept clear of rabble by two stout men in greatcoats. They gave Child a long look-over, but let him pass. In the polished mahogany taproom, well-dressed gentlemen sat around, drinking, laughing, smoking and talking, many with harlots on their laps or hanging off their arms. This was where *Harris's List* was compiled and distributed, and copies were on sale behind the bar. It was also where the Whores' Club met in an upstairs room.

A giant with a ragged ear and a smear of a nose guarded the stairs. 'I'll let you up for half a crown,' he informed Child. 'But if they throw you out, that's your affair.'

Child ascended the stairs, the sound of raucous women's laughter growing steadily louder. The landing spilled with stragglers: harlots fanning themselves, drinking ratafia punch. Child murmured his apologies as he pushed between them, prompting indignant comments and ribald remarks.

The room was a press of women. Blondes, brunettes, redheads, some pleasingly plump, others tiny as children, others again as tall as Amazon queens. A few more exotic faces stood out: a pair of pretty Indian girls, an ebony beauty, and a white-faced girl who looked like she came from the Japans. Child's eyes swam with ribbons, ruffles and lace; soft skin; pert breasts; rouged cheeks; reddened lips. Christ, he thought. A whole damned tribe of them.

A woman on a velvet throne rang a silver bell, and the room fell silent. She had the black tresses and ivory skin of an Italian Madonna, and the gimlet eye of a Smithfield horse broker. On the table by her side sat a squirrel in a golden collar, eating sugared almonds from a china dish. She took a long draw on her pipe, and hashish smoke curled around her face. 'I am Amy Infamy, Chairwoman of the Whores' Club. This meeting is in session. What do you want?'

'I'm a thief-taker,' Child said, 'looking into the murder of Lucy Loveless.'

A murmur broke out amongst the harlots, and the chairwoman rang her bell again, startling her squirrel. 'Lucy Loveless was not a member of this club.'

'She used to be,' Child said. 'Before you threw her out.'

The chairwoman's eyes flashed. 'That's what happens when you break the rules.'

'What rules did she break?'

The chairwoman turned to the only other male in the room: a lad of about sixteen, seated at a secretary desk. 'Hector, proceed to the next item.' She pointed her pipe at Child. 'Time to go.'

'Item six,' Hector read from his leather book in pert, petulant tones. 'Dispersal of the whores' hardship fund.' The lad had the look of a link-boy, with his angelic face and head of tousled yellow hair. Many of the wealthier harlots employed pretty boys like him to light their paths at night, offering a degree of protection in exchange for pennies and the opportunity to meet wealthy pederasts.

'Listen,' Child spoke over him, addressing the assembled women. 'Lucy was stabbed over a dozen times. She died choking on her own blood. There is a monster out there, and it could be any one of you next. Don't you want him caught?'

Another low murmur. Again, the chairwoman rang her bell.

'Lucy knew the risks,' she said. 'Go selling yourself at Vauxhall like a tuppenny jade, what do you expect?'

Hector gave him a slanted grin. 'You never know before you know, Mr Thief-taker, sir, and the moment when you do, it is too late.'

'If Lucy was selling herself in dangerous circumstances,' Child said, 'it was because she'd lost all her clients. You had a part to play in that. A fine way to treat one of your members – that's what people are saying out there on the street – asking why the Whores' Club won't even pay for a funeral. I'm surprised the newspapers haven't learned about your role in this yet. Be a pity if someone were to tell them.'

Child supposed Orin Black counted as a person on the street, even if he was overstating the case a little. The Whores' Club cared about their reputation, but if he hoped his threat would change their minds, he was wrong.

The chairwoman scowled. 'This club was in the right of the matter. Lucy had served time in Bridewell. Not for picking pockets. She'd played the Ring Game.'

Hector made a circle with his finger and thumb, and slid it on and off the index on his other hand. 'You know the Ring

Game, Mr Thief-taker? A sad story in a darkened tavern, a gold ring for sale . . .'

'Switched at the last moment for one of pinchbeck or brass? Aye, I know it. In Deptford they call it the Grieving Widow.'

'Here in London, we call it fraud,' the chairwoman said. 'And any crime greater than picking pockets is against our rules of membership. Our good relations with Bow Street depend on it.'

'How did you learn about her crime?'

'An anonymous letter from a concerned party. We confronted Lucy and she admitted it. A vote was held, and the verdict was unanimous.'

'Aye,' someone called out, 'she'd had enough chances already.'

Child whirled round to find the woman who'd spoken, one of the pretty Indian girls. 'Why do you say that?'

She only grinned.

The chairwoman stroked her squirrel, pointing at him again with her pipe. 'So tell the newspapers what you like. All we did was protect the public from a lying, scheming doxy. Somebody call for Crispin. He needs to go.'

'Just one moment more.' Child made a placatory gesture with his hands. 'I'd like to talk to a girl named Kitty, if she's here? She was a friend of Lucy's once. Whatever their differences, I'm sure she'd like to help find her killer.' He scanned the ranks of whores, eyes fastening on a flame-haired harlot with freckled skin. 'Are you Kitty?'

She batted a silk fan in front of her face. 'Call me any name you like for five guineas.'

He was getting nowhere, and the whores were enjoying that fact. 'Out,' some of them started to chant. 'Out. Out. Out.'

Child raised his voice, his cheeks reddening. 'How about a soldier with a redcoat and a scar? Did anyone ever see him with

Lucy? He accosted her in the street. Might have attacked her before.'

The room seemed to bristle as one. Pursed lips, sullen stares. They knew the man. He was sure of it. The chanting grew louder: 'Out. Out. Out.' Someone threw an apricot and it struck him in the chest. He ducked to avoid a handful of sugared almonds. He appealed to the redhead again: 'Are you Kitty?'

She only laughed. The chairwoman rang her bell more vigorously, and the squirrel leapt from the table, knocking over her glass of punch. The gold chain attached to its collar was secured to a bracelet on the chairwoman's arm. She hadn't noticed the creature's plight and it hung there choking. Hector jumped up to assist, colliding with Child as he did so, just as the giant with the ragged ear strode through the door.

'Crispin, I have asked this gadfly to leave.'

Child appealed to the women one last time. 'This soldier might have killed Lucy. She was one of your own once. I don't understand why you won't help me.'

As he gazed at their hostile faces, the giant seized hold of his collar, steering him roughly through the chanting crowd. He propelled Child down the stairs, and out the tavern door, where he offered a few words of kindly advice: 'You know how they make wine? They crush the grapes with their feet. Come back any time soon and I'll turn your face to claret.'

Chapter Twelve

A BOWL OF warm water sat on the polished marquetry desktop of Caro's escritoire. She was cleaning the dirt from the ring she'd found at Vauxhall with a paintbrush. Miles had drawn the curtains against the darkening Mayfair streets, but a draught was blowing in from somewhere, and the candle flames danced. Gabriel was playing at her feet, building unsteady towers out of painted blocks on the Turkey carpet.

The ring's stone was red and oval – a garnet, she decided – carved with the face of a woman in profile. The stone moved under the brush, as though it was coming loose, but as Caro examined it more closely, she realized that the stone was designed to pivot on a golden pin. Turning it all the way around, she saw that the reverse of the stone was carved with the head of a goat. It was extraordinary. She'd never seen anything like it.

The candles flickered again, and the leaping shadows caught Gabriel's eye. 'Monster, Mama, Monster!'

The ring looked centuries old, heavy and exotic, cold in her palm. Yet one of the assaying marks stamped into the band, a seated figure of Britannia, indicated that the ring had been made on British shores. The remaining assaying marks – those that signified the jeweller and the date of manufacture – were a mystery to Caro, and she decided to take the ring to her own jeweller in the morning.

The candles blurred before her eyes. Lord March was to

marry Clemency Howard. Her grief was not for him, but for herself and her situation. What a fool she'd been to think that he'd stand by her. He'd been more worried about his damn father than about her or the child. Humiliation battled with anger, but neither would serve her now. She forced herself to confront the unpalatable facts.

That evening's mail had brought no letter from Harry. Soon she would have few enough options left. Wait it out, throw herself upon his mercy when he returned from France – or act.

I can help you, dearest Caro, if you'll only let me.

Lucy's words. Or Lucia – as she had been four nights ago at the Carlisle House masquerade. Caro recalled the strains of the orchestra, the swell of conversation, the rattle of dice. Then, as now, all she could think about was Harry and Lord March. Her husband's mysterious absence, her lover's refusal to answer her letters. It had dampened any desire to dance or game, and she was distracted in conversation, watching corpulent Cupids twirl ageing milkmaids across the ballroom floor. Harlequins and dominoes, sultans and vestal virgins – and, walking among them, a lady in a black-and-gold half-mask, drawing the eye of every gentleman in the room. Mysterious, darkly exotic, wearing a black lace headdress with matching feathers, and petticoats of golden crêpe under more black lace. Curious as to her identity, Caro had followed her progress around the ballroom, until the woman lowered her mask for a moment – as if searching for someone in the crowd – and she recognized Lucia. Indignation warred with delight, and she almost sent a footman over. But remembering how she'd felt when Lucia had returned to Naples without saying farewell, she'd only called for another glass of punch.

A short time later, however, when someone tapped her upon

the shoulder and she turned to see Lucia smiling broadly – she'd been unable to resist a smile herself.

'Dearest Caro,' Lucia had said, in that throaty Italian accent, which Caro now knew to be a fraud, 'can you ever forgive me for deserting you? Oh, how I've *missed* you.'

Which had rather settled the matter. They had conversed for an hour over wine: about events in Naples, Harry's trip to France, and Lucia's plans for her time in England. 'This noise, this heat,' Lucia had said, at last. 'Shall we go somewhere quieter? The garden, perhaps?'

Caro, feeling faint herself, had readily agreed. Yet as they walked from the ballroom, the balance of her nausea had suddenly tipped. Clutching a hand to her mouth, she ran into a corridor, reaching the water closet only just in time. Lucia walked in after her, seeing her in all her discomfort. Despite Caro's embarrassed protests, she had taken charge of the situation: loosening her corsets, stroking her back, stroking her hair. Afterwards, she had steered Caro to a cloakroom with a chair, disappeared, and returned with water and a sponge. Somewhat shaken by the incident, overwhelmed by Lucia's kindness and her own despair, Caro had burst into tears.

'There,' Lucia said, holding her as she sobbed. 'Whatever is the matter? You can tell me anything, sweet Caro.'

Which only made her sob all the harder.

'Is it possible that you anticipate a happy event?' Lucia said. 'My sister is always the same. In floods every time, but the clouds will part. Sad in the womb, happy in the world, that's what I say.'

Caro had pulled away, staring in horror. How had Lucia guessed? She was not very far along – just one missed course, nothing to show yet, save a little bloating. Some women might not even recognize the signs in themselves. And yet Caro knew, just as surely as she'd known with Gabriel.

'It is merely a bad oyster. Please, say nothing of this.'

'My mistake.' But a little later, as Caro was straightening her gown, Lucia gave her a long, shrewd look. 'It must be lonely, your husband being abroad these past few months. Perhaps that has contributed in some small part to your distress?' Another look, this one rich in unspoken meaning. 'Maybe you'd like it all to go away? Your sickness, your anxiety? Say the word, and I will forever hold my tongue. But I can help you, dearest Caro. If you'll only let me.'

Looking into her small, brown eyes, Caro had been struck by their trustworthiness – which was ironic, given everything she now knew. Perhaps it was the wine, or Lucia's kindness, or simple desperation, but a single word fell from her lips: 'How?'

'I know an apothecary who makes a particular tincture. It is not without risk – some women react very differently to the herb than others – but it works more often than it does not. I could bring it to you tomorrow night? Where will you be?'

Caro breathed deeply – what Lucia proposed was a very different matter to hot baths and gin. 'I still have time, I think. I expect Harry home any day now.'

'A contingency, then,' Lucia said. 'In case of disaster.'

Disaster was what she feared, every minute of every day. And yet here was Lucia, offering a glimmer of hope. 'I'll be at Vauxhall Gardens,' Caro said hurriedly. 'I could meet you in the Rotunda at ten o'clock?'

'Not the Rotunda,' Lucia said. 'Meet me in the bowers. It will be more private there. We can share our troubles.'

She had argued a little, but Lucia had been insistent, and fearing to annoy her, Caro had agreed. Now she wondered why Lucy Loveless, a prostitute, had taken the trouble to help her at all? An act of kindness – one woman to another facing ruin – which had taken Lucy to the bower where she'd lost her life.

She remembered the dying woman's bone-white face, their mutual desperation. *He knows.* For a brief time, on the night of the murder, Caro had been gripped by a terrible fear that those words had referred to her own secret. Yet in day's rational light, recalling the scene so very vividly, she had discounted this theory. Lucy's words, she felt certain, hadn't been uttered in a spirit of warning, but as a last desperate struggle to convey information about her killer. Caro's secret was safe – for the moment, at least – but every tick of the clock brought her closer to despair.

Lord knows, Harry had few illusions left about their marriage, but whatever unspoken conventions governed their troubled union, this was surely in breach of them? Even thinking about the consequences of divorce made her throat close up and her stomach lurch. Losing her home. The money from her trust in Mordechai's hands. Her brother wouldn't let her starve, but he'd want her gone, banished from London. Locked up in the country for the rest of her days, her name unspoken in society, erased from existence.

Taking a ring of keys from her panniers, she unlocked one of the escritoire's upper drawers. Sliding it all the way out, she placed it upon the desktop. Reaching inside the drawer's cavity, she found the oak fillet tucked flush with the side. She pulled it out, and, with it, came a second, secret drawer. In this latter compartment lay a tiny glass bottle. Caro had found it in Lucy's panniers, snatched it from her dying body – even in the midst of her horror, even as she'd used her cloak to staunch Lucy's lifeblood.

Her salvation or her executioner? There was no way to be certain. Lucy had spoken baldly of the risks: jaundice, tremors – both could last a lifetime; other liver troubles; haemorrhage; death. Potentially an act of suicide, as well as murder.

Then there was the moral question. The Church claimed it was the gravest sin. But then the church said a lot of things, not all of them clever. It was a question of survival, she told herself. A necessity, not a choice. A woman had to be ruthless in defence of herself.

Yet Harry might still return in time. Babies came early and often survived. The timing might raise eyebrows, but if it was possible, it was deniable.

One week, she decided. No longer. Dropping the bottle into the compartment, she pushed it shut, and replaced the outer drawer. Gabriel was chewing on one of his bricks, and she crouched down to prise it from his mouth. 'Mama,' he said, 'when I am dead, will my eyes be shutted?'

His face was brown as a plum stone. He had her husband's colouring and the Corsham smile. Harry won't want to take you from me, she thought, but he won't ever let you go. The thought of losing her son on top of everything else was too much to bear. She clutched him to her breast, her cheek pressed into his soft black hair.

Chapter Thirteen

Child spent the rest of that night visiting the Covent Garden taverns, coffeehouses and jelly-shops. He asked around about Lucy Loveless, and many people were eager to claim an acquaintance with the sensationally murdered whore. Child bought and drunk many toasts to her memory, but nobody could tell him anything useful. The gentlemen were of the opinion that it was a crying shame that a beautiful doxy had gone to waste. The girls either wept or seemed pleased to have less competition. Child recognized several of the harlots from the Whores' Club, but when he approached them they turned away, refusing to talk to him.

He also asked around about the soldier with the scar, and here he had more luck. The owner of a supper house on Chandos Street started nodding even before Child had finished his description. 'Lieutenant Edward Dodd-Bellingham. Neddy to his friends, beshittened arsehole to those of us who have to clean up his mess. He and his friends come here to dine, drowning their sorrows after they've lost at hazard over at the Golden Pear Tree. They like to break things, sometimes tables, sometimes heads. My serving maids are often reduced to tears by their advances. They think every working woman's for sale, and they won't take no for an answer. Bow Street comes when I call for them, but they never lock them up. Friends in the right places, I suppose. I forbid them entry from time to time, but they only stand outside abusing my customers.'

'Did you ever see the lieutenant in the company of a prostitute named Lucy Loveless?' Child described her.

'I knew Lucy. Don't think I ever saw them together, but Dodd-Bellingham's always got women in tow. Don't ask me how he affords them. I hear he's up to his eyes in debt. But then the rules never seem to apply to men like him.'

The doormen wouldn't let Child into the Bedford Coffee-house, where the girls were actresses and courtesans, their keepers earls and dukes. A small crowd of onlookers and journalists stood around outside, hoping to learn a salacious story or to catch a glimpse of a celebrated beauty. Child wound up in the Lamb and Flag, where he watched a puppet show as he drank: George Washington buggering King George, while the Queen looked on.

He made short work of his wine, and signalled to the tap-man to bring another jug. Reaching into his pocket for his purse, he discovered a piece of card, about three inches by four. Black with a gold border, it resembled an announcement card or an invitation, except there was no writing – only the gold silhouette of a man with the horns of a goat. Child had no memory of ever having seen it before.

Had he picked it up whilst drunk one night? He didn't think so. Or had someone slipped it into his pocket? Child remembered his collision with Hector in the Whores' Club. But why would he have put it there?

A satyr, Child thought. Half-man, half-goat. He struggled to remember his rudimentary classical education. Companions of Bacchus, infamous for drunken revels – and the ravishment of women, both willing and unwilling.

PAMELA

10 January 1782

After the performance, came the private audiences.

It cost the gentlemen a guinea to examine Pamela at close quarters – for signs of disease or bad skin or anything else that didn't take their fancy. Clothes on. Three minutes by Mrs Havilland's watch. Keep them wanting more.

As set out in the contract she'd signed that first day in Mrs Havilland's parlour, Pamela received half. She'd already bought herself a new dress of pink silk, the bodice embroidered with leaves and silver flowers. She was permitted to shop, as long as one of Mrs Havilland's footmen went with her – the watchers, the other girls called them; there not to protect her, but to keep an eye on Mrs Havilland's investment. Left to their own devices, young girls might fall in love, or sell themselves cheap.

Here nothing was cheap. Not even time.

Pamela barely had a moment to catch her breath off-stage, before one of the footmen whisked her off to the audience room. So far the gentlemen had proved a disappointment. Brandy-nosed or corpulent or grey or cadaverous, barely a man under forty, some with false teeth, reeking of port and snuff and old man's sweat. It's just a job, she told herself, as their eyes roamed her body. Like emptying a chamber pot. Except this chamber pot will stand you in good stead for life.

She walked through the curtain into the little cell of red velvet. One of the other girls had told her it was supposed to make the men think of virginal blood, and Pamela had laughed uneasily, unsure whether she was joking. The lamps made it glow like the inside of a jewel box. Mrs Havilland waited inside, foot tapping. Two gentlemen tonight, the first not more than twenty-five, but bespectacled and plump. The other a little older . . . Her breath caught, and her stomach turned over.

It was the soldier. Her smiling Adonis.

Some men looked worse in the lamplight, but not him. He had a square jaw and a dimpled chin. Thick blond hair, only lightly powdered. A cool blue gaze, and that scar through his eyebrow, like a buccaneer. And if he smelled a little of port beneath his civet scent, she found she didn't much care.

Mrs Havilland was looking at her, stony-eyed, and Pamela realized she'd missed her prompt. Stepping forward, peeping at them between the strands of her hair, she spread her hands as if to make an offer of herself. 'Good evening, sirs,' she said softly. 'I am glad to know you.'

'And I you,' the Adonis in the redcoat said. His voice was deep, the vowels rich. She could have listened to it all day.

'Well,' Mrs Havilland said. 'Do you like what you see?'

His eyes swept over her. 'I like it very much.'

The plump gentleman sitting next to him shifted on his velvet stool. He had a round, freckled face beneath a yellowed periwig, and pale eyes that blinked at her behind his horn-rimmed spectacles.

'She's too young, Neddy,' he said. 'Just look at her.'

Fat ninny, she thought. Glass eyes. She wasn't supposed to say anything more, but she didn't want her soldier to walk away. Unbidden, her hip jutted out. 'Old enough to know my own mind, sir. Old enough to please.'

The soldier laughed richly. 'So you are. Don't listen to my brother.'

The pair were brothers? She must have looked astonished, for he laughed again.

Mrs Havilland poked her sharply in the back with her silver scratcher, and Pamela cast her eyes down demurely. The soldier asked her a few questions, like the other gentlemen who had viewed her. About her parents. About her life as a maid in the house in Cheapside. Whether she'd ever had a sweetheart, or kissed a boy. She'd rehearsed the answers to all these questions with Mrs Havilland.

When the three minutes were up, Mrs Havilland held up her watch. 'Her auction will be held at the end of next month. Bids will start at a hundred guineas. Will I see you there?'

The soldier gave Pamela that look again, the one that made her skin burn. 'Certainly you will. She's a rare treasure.'

They rose from their stools, and the soldier kissed Mrs Havilland's hand. Then he lifted the curtain, giving Pamela a grin as he went. His fat frog of a brother barely looked at her. The curtain fell back and Mrs Havilland gave her another poke. Pamela realized she was still smiling.

'I told you no sauce.'

'Who is he?'

'Lieutenant Edward Dodd-Bellingham. Don't go getting any ideas, child. He might be handsome as sin, but he's also poor as Job. The Dodd-Bellinghams have had more Jews through their parlour than the Great Synagogue. If he has a hundred guineas to spare, then I'm the Duchess of Devonshire.'

Mrs Havilland might be a nasty old bigot, Pamela thought, but that didn't make her wrong about the lieutenant's debts. Yet that night, as she lay in her feather bed, his smile was her constant companion.

She is a rare treasure. She played the scene many times in her mind. The Pamela in the book would have had strong views about that. What were her words? *Don't let people's telling you you are pretty, puff you up.*

Sound advice. But then the maid in the book had never met a man like Lieutenant Dodd-Bellingham. The girl reminded herself that she was not Pamela. Not really.

Chapter Fourteen

The air around the Bevis Marks Synagogue was thick with the smells of the Jewish Quarter: baking bread, exotic spices, thick black coffee. Caro walked along the street, Miles at her side, a babel of languages swelling and dipping in their wake: Russian, Dutch, Portuguese, Spanish, and the more mysterious tongues of the German and Iberian Jews. Many of the men sported neat, clipped beards.

They turned off Bevis Marks into a crooked row of shops that had been colonized by men of the jewellery trade: goldsmiths, silversmiths, watchmakers, amber-cutters, diamond-polishers and other dealers in gemstones. Halfway along it, she found the shop she was looking for: Solomon Loredo's Emporium of Heirloom Jewellery and Modern Pieces. According to her own jeweller, whom she had visited a little earlier that morning, the maker's mark on the ring she had found in the bower was Loredo's. The shop's interior resembled a box of confectionary: pale green and gold, fitted out with shelves, cases and compartments displaying the jeweller's wares. Necklaces and bracelets; dress-swords and snuffboxes; cravat, hat and hair pins; rings, charms and combs. The jeweller came out from behind his counter to give Caro a sweeping bow. 'Good day to you, madam. Solomon Loredo at your service. What is it that you are looking for this day?'

He was a big, thickset man in a red-and-yellow-striped suit;

his large hands glittered with gold rings. His skull was bald and brown, shiny as a hen's egg, resting upon a thick neck that seemed to flow from his ears. His English was lightly accented, his black eyes lively.

'I have a sapphire choker that would set off your eyes perfectly, madam. Or perhaps something more discreet? A cameo?'

'As it happens, I have a piece to show you, Mr Loredo.'

'You wish to make a sale, madam?'

'Not exactly. I found this signet ring yesterday and I wish to reunite it with its owner. My own jeweller tells me that it was made in this shop. As it is such a distinctive piece, I am hoping you will remember the person who bought it.'

Loredo held the ring up to the light. 'How could I forget? It was made to order, a copy of a much older piece.'

'I've never seen anything like it before.'

'The original is extremely rare and extremely valuable. It is Roman in origin, found in Italy by an antiquarian of my acquaintance, Mr Simon Dodd-Bellingham.'

'I know Mr Dodd-Bellingham.' Caro remembered seeing Simon and his brother, Neddy, at Vauxhall on the night of the murder.

'He sold the ring to a private collector, who wished to have three copies made, each identical to the original piece. Mr Dodd-Bellingham was kind enough to recommend my services.'

'Why did his client want four identical rings?'

'You would have to ask him that, madam. I only fulfilled the commission.'

'May I ask his name, sir? I am sure he would like his ring back.'

'Alas, I make it a rule never to discuss my customers' private business. If you would entrust me to return the ring, I will happily do so. Otherwise, you could speak to Mr Dodd-Bellingham?'

Caro would certainly do so, if necessary, but she wasn't giving up on Loredo yet. 'I confess it is a matter of some delicacy, sir. I recovered this ring at the scene of a murder. The prostitute killed at Vauxhall Gardens – perhaps you read about it?'

Loredo frowned. 'Yes, I did. That poor girl. A shocking thing.'

'By rights, I suppose, I should take this ring to the magistrate. It is possible your client witnessed something that could aid the investigation. But it occurs to me that he might not want people knowing he had visited the bowers. Especially Bow Street – who, regrettably, aren't always as discreet as one might like. I would hate to damage a gentleman's reputation unnecessarily.'

Loredo nodded thoughtfully. 'I do see your dilemma.'

'Which is why I thought we could handle this matter between ourselves. I could return the ring to your client, and at the same time ask him if he saw anything pertinent to the murder. If he did, then I could pass this along to the magistrate without revealing his name.'

Loredo passed a hand across his chin, clearly anxious about his client's reaction.

'But if you feel honour-bound to refuse,' Caro said, 'I will simply take it to the magistrate. I imagine he will then come to see you and compel you to reveal the name. I am sure your client will understand that you had little choice.'

Loredo eyed the ring a moment longer. 'Under the circumstances, I believe your way is best, madam. The name of my client is Mr Jonathan Stone.'

'The moneylender?'

'The same. He lives some way north of London, near the village of Muswell Hill.'

Often to be glimpsed hovering in the background at balls and assemblies, Jonathan Stone had originally made his fortune in India, Caro recalled. Subsequently, he had grown much richer, lending money to young gentlemen against their expectations. Hence he was invited everywhere, mingling with the beau monde, but not truly one of them – standing aloof, usually smiling as if at some private joke. A great sponsor of the arts, he was one of Jacobus Agnetti's patrons. Caro recalled him giving a speech in the Rotunda on the night of the murder.

She thanked Loredo, returning the ring to her panniers. 'I will be sure to explain to Mr Stone that you only had his interests at heart when you provided me with his name.'

Loredo inclined his head, but he still looked nervous. Caro wondered if it had anything to do with the rumours that swirled around Stone. He was said to have mysterious antecedents on whom no one could shed light, though many had tried. Some claimed he was a secret Jew, others that he'd killed a man and had changed his name. He was a notorious libertine, Mordechai said, with a string of country houses, each containing a mistress and by-blow children. But then Mordechai disapproved of anyone and everything.

Yet the fact remained, if you were to pick a gentleman of London society as a potential suspect in a salacious murder, Jonathan Stone would be at the top of everyone's list.

Chapter Fifteen

Felix qui potuit rerum cognoscere causas. Happy is he who can ascertain the causes of things.

For reasons that were unfathomable to him, Child knew that women liked to discuss their troubles with their friends. Lucy had many misfortunes to share: the assault on her person six months earlier; losing her job as a sitter with the artist Agnetti; the anonymous note and rumours that had destroyed her livelihood; her consequent debts. Understanding this chain of disaster, Child felt, was key to finding the man who killed her. He therefore made tracking down Lucy's friends his next priority.

Boscastle, Lucy's landlord, had identified three of them: Kitty, the redhead from the Whores' Club; Mrs Agnetti, the artist's wife; and the pox-scarred prostitute with the limp and the brand on her hand. Neither Kitty nor Mrs Agnetti had called in several months, but the unnamed prostitute had been a much more recent visitor. The landlord had presumed she was a friend of Lucy's from her thieving days, an assumption Child shared. After a midday breakfast of blood sausage at a Holborn chophouse, he walked the short distance to the Bridewell House of Correction, where, according to the Whores' Club, Lucy had served her sentence for fraud.

A vast gloomy brick building on the banks of the Fleet, the prison buildings formed two adjacent squares, each with a courtyard at the centre. One half of the prison housed vagrants and homeless children; the other petty criminals, including a great many prostitutes. Child passed them on his way in: lines of women beating hemp in the courtyard, while an overseer barked orders. In another portion of the yard, a half-naked prostitute was being whipped while spectators watched from a wooden gallery.

Child often had business here, sometimes to speak to inmates who could help with his inquiries, sometimes to give evidence before meetings of the Court of Governors. Oswald Babbage, the Court's secretary, was a sprawling, ungainly man with several chins and small red lips like the mouth of a purse. Upon payment of a modest bribe, he was happy to give Child the run of the Record Office.

'If she came in through these doors, she'll be in there,' Babbage said, gesturing to the banks of wooden cabinets. 'Just be aware that they like to change their names – sometimes many times over the course of a life on the street.'

There was a Register of Inmates for each calendar year. Lucy had told her landlord that she'd been branded on the hand shortly after she came to London. And according to both him and Orin Black, Lucy had been living in the city for many years. Child therefore started in 1775, and worked backwards.

He found no Lucy Loveless in the registers, and he thought it likely, as Babbage had suggested, she'd used a different name in her dealings with the justice system. Child therefore moved on to the more arduous task of consulting the Minutes of the Court of Governors, which passed judgement on the miscreants that came before them. Again, Child started in 1775 and worked backwards, looking for details that would correlate with the little he'd learned from his visit to the Whores' Club.

It took three hours before he found her, in one of the minute books for the year 1767, when Lucy would have been just four-teen years old.

> *Lucy Redfern, 14, and Annie Yearley, 18, on the oath of Mr Jonah Warren, a gentleman of Red Lion Square, for defrauding of ten pounds for a counterfeit ring in the Sun Tavern on Milk Street, and for being common night walkers, wandering abroad at an unreasonable time and picking up men.*
>
> *For Lucy Redfern: Cont. to branding upon the hand and 6 months to be served.*
>
> *For Annie Yearley: Cont. to branding upon the hand, a whipping, and discharge.*

Child took the record through to Babbage's office. 'Do you remember this inmate at all: Lucy Redfern?'

Babbage read the entry, then shook his head. 'Annie Yearley I know. She calls herself Nelly Diver now. Been in and out of Bridewell for years.'

'If Lucy Redfern had brought a child into Bridewell, would it be listed here?'

'Yes, a note should have been made.'

Child wondered if that meant Lucy's child had been born after she'd been in Bridewell, or whether it was already dead by then, or whether the child had been cared for by someone else while she'd served her sentence.

'This Nelly Diver,' he said, 'does she have curly dark hair? A pox-scarred face? Walk with a limp?'

'Got the scars back in '75 in the epidemic we had here. She told the Court one of her pimps was responsible for the limp.'

Sometimes, Child thought, you just got lucky.

CHAPTER SIXTEEN

CHILD'S LUCK DIDN'T last. The Bridewell Register contained no address for Nelly Diver, though she'd served time there only last year. Babbage had told him most whores who came before the Court claimed to have no fixed abode, because they didn't want the authorities keeping track of them. It was frustrating, but at least Child now had a name.

He had several informants amongst the lower sort of whore, especially those who dabbled in thievery on the side. But they'd still be in bed, sleeping off the excesses of last night's business, and wouldn't appreciate a visit until later. He was also due to meet Orin Black that evening, and it was possible he'd come across Nelly Diver in his time. Child therefore decided to defer this particular line of inquiry until then, and in the meantime look into the redhead, Kitty Carefree. He took himself off to a nearby tavern and perused *Harris's List* over a bottle of claret. Kitty Carefree didn't prove hard to find.

> <u>*Miss Ca—ee, No.31 Golden Square*</u>
> *Her eyes enflam'd and sparkling too;*
> *Her cheek, the rose and lily's hue;*
> *Her nose is straight, and just its height,*
> *Her lips than coral far more bright;*
> *Her breasts two little hills of snow,*
> *In which two vivid rubies glow.*

This decent, well-bred young lady, K—ty Ca—ee, is about twenty-eight, and was brought up in Hampshire, her late father being a merchant, whose ambition was the cause of her ruin. The whole of the father's effects went to pay his debts, so that being totally out of subsistence, she applied to one of those handy old women who oblige gentlemen with the newest ware. After losing her maidenhead for a goodly sum, she was taken into keeping by a certain peer of the realm, until they parted by mutual consent. Since then she has had recourse to a more general commerce, and has for some time past obtained a decent livelihood.

Miss C—ee possesses a good deal of vivacity, though on occasion can prove a little fretful. She has a very pleasing nose, dimpled cheeks, and excellent teeth. A Titian Venus would envy her glorious mane of fire, and she has plenty of the same-colour hair upon the enchanting spot of love. Frequently to be noticed in the green boxes of the theatres, and in the season at Ranelagh and Vauxhall, she keeps a chariot and a boy servant. Her education has been liberal; her conversation is easy and unaffected; her taste for literature would not disgrace the greatest genius of the age. The harpsichord and watercolours round out her list of accomplishments. If we could pass over in silence her present mode of life, she has every qualification to render her an ornament to the female world. In her business there are very few who are her superiors. She has a wonderful art in raising up those of her male friends who are inclined to droop while in her enchanting company. It is no exaggeration to say she is one of the finest women upon the town. Her price is from eight to twelve guineas.

Forty minutes later, having walked across the city, Child knocked on the door of thirty-one Golden Square. Soho was as much devoted to pleasure as Covent Garden, and in many of the windows that overlooked the square, women were sitting in their paint and finery, displaying themselves to passers-by. A strapping African footman in blue-and-gold livery opened the door and looked Child up and down. 'You sure you're in the right place? There's a half-guinea bagnio on Carnaby Street might suit you better.'

'I'm looking for Kitty Carefree,' Child said.

'You and everyone else. She moved out back in May. If you've got five guineas to spend, there's other girls here.'

'Did Kitty leave a forwarding address?'

'Afraid not. Think she found herself a keeper. That's usually what happens when they leave suddenly like that. Guess she didn't want her former customers looking her up.'

Then the unhelpful redhead he'd spoken to at the Whores' Club was unlikely to be her. 'She had a boy servant, isn't that right?'

'Hector. She paid the lad off.'

The boy from the Whores' Club, the one Child was convinced had slipped the satyr card into his pocket.

The footman glanced at Child, as if reappraising his interest. 'You with that other lot? They asked about Hector too.'

'What other lot?'

'Couple of coves came yesterday, asking questions just like you.'

'What kind of coves?'

He shrugged. 'Gentlemen. Official sorts. Talked to my mistress about Kitty. Made me wonder if she'd gotten herself in trouble. You're not with them, then?'

'Can you remember what they looked like?' Child held up half a crown. 'I'm paying.'

The footman regarded him coldly. 'I don't take bribes. Be on your way.'

'Can I talk to your mistress?'

'No, you can't.'

'You're not even going to ask?'

The footman bent down to give him a hard stare. 'She don't like shabby little pipsqueaks cluttering up her halls. Now move along before I give you a helping hand.'

Seeing that he'd offended the last honest servant in London, Child walked on. He wondered if the visit of these 'official sorts' had any bearing upon Lucy Loveless's murder. Yet 'gentlemen' didn't sound like Bow Street, and Kitty had moved away several months before Lucy had been killed. It could just as easily be an unrelated matter.

Child knew he'd have little luck with Lucy's third friend, Mrs Agnetti. Like everyone else in London, he'd read about the Agnetti marriage in the newspapers. How Mrs Agnetti had left her husband, the celebrated artist, which was no more than he'd deserved, all things considered. No one knew where she had gone, and it had been suggested she'd left the country. Child decided there were better uses of his time than trying to solve that particular puzzle, especially given Mrs Agnetti's disappearance predated Lucy's troubles by many months.

Glancing at his pocket watch, he saw he still had an hour before he was due to meet Orin Black at Bow Street. So he walked down to the Golden Pear Tree on Compton Street. Like everything else in the capital, gambling clubs came in many different guises to suit different pockets. The Golden Pear Tree was the kind of place where the gaming counters were made of ivory, and a thousand acres of cornfield swapped hands on a throw of the hazard dice. Child talked to the doorman standing guard outside.

'Lieutenant Dodd-Bellingham been in today?'

'Not yet. He owe you money?'

'Something like that.'

He grinned. 'Better get in line.'

'He ever cause trouble here? I've heard he does elsewhere.'

'Good as gold, or we'd stop him playing. Wait and you're bound to see him. He's late today.'

'Did he ever come here with a prostitute named Lucy Loveless?'

'Her who got herself murdered? She came here sometimes. Don't ever remember seeing her with the lieutenant, but it's possible. He usually has a whore or two in tow. Sometimes more, if he's with his friends.'

'What friends are they?'

'Sometimes his brother, sometimes his fellow officers. A few times he brought Lord March, the Earl of Amberley's heir.'

Child noted this with interest. Lieutenant Dodd-Bellingham, the soldier who'd accosted Lucy in the street, was friends with Lord March, who'd been in the bowers on the night she'd been murdered.

The doorman nudged him with his elbow. 'You're in luck. Here he comes now.'

Two gentlemen in army redcoats were walking along the street towards them. Child recognized Dodd-Bellingham by the scar.

He stepped back as the pair drew close, not wanting to draw attention to himself. Gentlemen could be slippery customers, and you only had one opportunity to take them by surprise. He wanted to find out more about Dodd-Bellingham and his acquaintance with Lucy Loveless before putting him to the question.

Taking a long look at his quarry, Child knew instantly that he was a fuckster of the first order. It wasn't just that he was tall and handsome, both qualities Child resented in a man. It was his supercilious gaze, his braying laugh, the way he walked as if he owned the street. The pair swept past them into the Golden Pear Tree, without tipping the doorman. Child wondered if that was why he'd been so forthcoming with his information.

'I thought you wanted to talk to him?' the doorman said.

'Not just now,' Child said. 'He'll keep.'

Chapter Seventeen

The road wound north of London, through a patchwork of green and yellow fields and prosperous villages. Caro's carriage slowed as the horses felt the strain of the incline. She gazed absently at gibbet-like scarecrows, white sailboats on the Fleet River, and a murmuration of starlings shrieking and swelling against the cold-ash sky. This will be my world, she thought, when I am banished to the country – if Harry doesn't come home in time, if I am too scared to take the tincture. There will be nothing but silence and trees and bracing walks and every day will be as purgatory.

Beyond Highgate, the road grew steeper, the houses grander and more intermittent. The village of Muswell Hill, on the edge of the Hornsey woods, was a place of rural retreat for city merchants and stockjobbers. It was here that Jonathan Stone, owner of the ring she'd found at Vauxhall, had built his estate. Caro's coachman, Sam, eased the horses to a walk as they approached the gates. A porter emerged from the gatehouse, and she told him in her most imperious tones that she was an acquaintance of Mr Stone's and wished to see him. The man insisted on taking a message to his master, and she was forced to sit waiting in the carriage for nearly half an hour. From time to time, a gamekeeper with a fowling piece over his shoulder peered at them through the gates. Stone was evidently conscious of his security.

At last the porter reappeared and unlocked the gates. The estate sat on a plateau of a gently undulating hillside, and as they trundled down the drive, Caro admired the views of the city to the south: a dove-grey streak of human endeavour beneath a corona of yellow fog, a hundred steeples melting into the sky above. Stone had pulled down the old red-brick house that had once stood here, but he'd kept the majestic oaks that flanked the drive, as well as an ancient woodland to the north. Between the house and the wood curled a serpentine lake and on the far bank stood a new white building that resembled a classical temple. Evidently an enthusiast for the natural style of landscaping, Stone had planted many copses of trees around the lake, joined by winding paths. They passed more groundsmen and gardeners busy cultivating these miniature Edens – and many more armed keepers patrolling the grounds.

The house was large, white and Palladian, topped with a glazed dome, flanked by smaller pavilions. A butler and several footmen awaited their arrival on the gravel outside. The carriage rattled to a stop, and Miles fitted the steps for her to descend. The butler spoke a few words of welcome, and then escorted Caro into a magnificent hall.

Two curved staircases soared to the *piano nobile* above, light cascading down from the glazed dome. Plasterwork nymphs and youths with lyres danced across the duck-egg blue walls, interspersed with painted panels of Arcadian paradise. In the oval space between the staircases stood an enormous stone sarcophagus. As they ascended the stairs, Caro could gaze right down into its interior. On the galleried landing above, the butler knocked at a pair of ornate double doors. Receiving a command to enter, they walked into a long room with lofty windows overlooking one of the copses of artful wilderness outside. Jonathan Stone and Simon Dodd-Bellingham were conferring over a large urn on a table by one of the windows. A third gentleman she didn't recognize hovered nearby. The master of the house broke off his conversation, walked towards her and bowed. 'Mrs Corsham, what an unexpected pleasure.'

His accent held no hint to his class or his place of origin. Mr Stone was said to enjoy the mystery he inspired and played up to it. About forty, he was trim in the waist, with no physical signs of his rumoured debauchery. His small, elfin face seemed to glow with pleasure at her company. He wore a suit of brushed moleskin – which fitted him like a smooth grey pelt – a silver periwig and silk stockings in silver-buckled shoes. On his right hand he wore a blood-red ring just like the one she'd found in the bower.

'My collection,' he said, with a sweep of his arm, encompassing several life-size sculptures on marble plinths: an athlete poised to throw a discus, a rearing horse, a bearded man reclining in a chair, another holding a bunch of grapes, and a woman in robes so delicately carved they flowed like water. Between the sculptures, glass cases displayed smaller exhibits: pottery fragments, coins and figurines. The walls were hung with classical scenes, much of it Agnetti's work.

Simon Dodd-Bellingham had also walked over to join them. He bowed to kiss her hand. 'Mrs Corsham.'

'Do I take it this magnificent assembly is your work, Mr Dodd-Bellingham?'

'My greatest privilege,' he said, 'though it is a joint endeavour. Mr Stone has a true passion for classical antiquity. His collection is the finest in the country. Perhaps the world.'

An unprepossessing creature, plump, pallid and bespectacled, Simon had a smattering of freckles across his snub nose, matched by a smattering of snuff across the paunch of his striped waistcoat. His yellowing periwig was the same shade as his darned stockings and awkward teeth. The sort of man who edged into rooms, rather than strode.

The third gentleman hung back with servile deference, his lumpen white face and broken nose an incongruous fit with his gentlemanly dress and brown tie-periwig. He had large white hands spattered with ink and sharp, pale eyes.

Stone introduced him. 'My man of business, Erasmus Knox.'

Knox bowed, and then retreated discreetly to the table, where he attended to some papers while they talked.

'Your brothers are well, I trust?' Stone inquired.

Caro inclined her head. 'Mordechai attends to the bank, while Ambrose enjoys Switzerland this summer. Hunting game.'

Stone grinned. 'Bagging many a vixen, I don't doubt.'

Caro took the ring from her panniers. 'I come here on a quest concerning lost property, Mr Stone. Yours, not mine. I found this ring, and I'm told it belongs to you.'

Stone held it up between forefinger and thumb. 'Goodness, what a sleuth-hound you are. Yes, the ring is mine – at least, I paid for its commission. How good of you to take the time to return it.'

'I tracked you down through the jeweller, Mr Loredo. He tells me it is a copy of a much older piece.'

'Here you see the original,' Stone said, holding out his hand. 'Mr Dodd-Bellingham dug it out of the ground at Pompeii. It had lain there in the ash for nearly two thousand years. I consider it one of the finest pieces in my collection.'

'I was digging up a skeleton in the ruins of a bathhouse at the time,' Simon said. 'The ring was on the poor man's finger. Nobody had laid eyes on it since he was killed in the volcanic eruption.'

'A fortuitous find,' Caro said. 'Rather like mine.'

'The ring has an interesting provenance,' Stone said. 'Mr Dodd-Bellingham speculates that the bathhouse was also a brothel, and that the ring signified membership of that establishment. The woman carved on the garnet is probably the wife of the ring's owner. The goat on the stone's reverse signifies Pan, god of fornication. When the owner visited the brothel, he'd simply turn the garnet around.'

It was a habit of Stone's, Caro recalled, to push the boundaries of conversational propriety – in order to discomfort others and amuse himself. His candour didn't offend her, though his motive did.

'Mr Stone, you are speaking to a lady,' Simon said, an ugly pink flush creeping down the side of his neck.

Stone raised his eyebrows. 'Mrs Corsham is not one of your vases, to be swaddled in cotton lest she smash. Society would be a good deal more entertaining, I always think, if we allowed women the freedom to discourse upon the same topics as men. What say you, Mrs Corsham?'

'I accord to the general principle, yes, Mr Stone. As to your Roman and his ring, I am afraid the hypocrisy of your sex is only too often the subject of our discourse.'

Stone laughed. 'There now, Simon. Mrs Corsham is not so easily shockable as you suppose.'

'I confess the circumstances that led to my finding this ring shocked me to my core,' Caro continued sombrely. 'It was lying in the bower at Vauxhall Gardens where the woman was murdered the other night. It was I who found the body, whilst taking the air. I lost a glove in all the confusion, and yesterday returned to look for it. There in the undergrowth, I found this ring.'

Erasmus Knox had looked up from his documents. Simon's face was a picture of consternation. Stone only arched an eyebrow. 'I had heard it was you who found the poor doxy dying.

That must have been distressing. And then you found this ring. Well, I never.'

As Mordechai had predicted, the story had plainly got around. 'I hope you will not blame poor Mr Loredo for giving me your name. It was either that or I took the ring to the magistrate. All told, we thought discretion was the wisest course.'

'You thought to spare my blushes? How kind. Yet you need not have scrupled overly. My reputation is bad as a blight, I'm sorry to say.'

'Did you lose the ring on the night of the exhibition?'

'Are you asking if I killed the woman in the bower?' Stone sounded greatly entertained by the thought.

'Not at all,' Caro replied, though it had certainly crossed her mind. 'I thought you might have seen something that could aid the magistrate's investigation.'

'Alas, had I been in the bowers that night, I would willingly own it. I live my life in the open – sinner that I am.'

'Then you lost it on a different night?'

'I didn't lose it at all.' Again, Stone held up his hand. 'I had three copies of the ring made, and the original here is mine. The others I gave away to friends. Mr Dodd-Bellingham has one himself, though I see he isn't wearing it. Did you drop yours in the bower, you naughty boy?'

A pink flush suffused Simon's throat again. 'No, it is at home. I didn't wear it today, as I was intending to clean the statue of Mercury in your fountain.'

Caro examined them sceptically. 'The dead woman's name is Lucy Loveless,' she said to Stone. 'Did you know her?'

'Possibly, I've met many women of the town.'

'I ask because there she is on your wall.'

Caro had noticed the painting when she'd walked in. It was hard to miss, being about ten feet by fifteen. To the fore of the canvas, Lucy lay sprawled naked on the ground, her face ravaged with pain, blood pooling beneath her. On a bed behind her, a naked man also lay dying. Moonlight glinted on the helmet of the man who had slain them, gilding his anguished face.

'My Clytemnestra,' Stone said. 'Agnetti had six whores line up, and I picked the one I liked best. The poor girl. What a waste of all that beauty.'

It seemed an unlikely coincidence. 'Can I ask to whom you gave the other rings?'

Stone cocked his head. 'No doubt you are also curious as to why I would have three copies made in the first place. If you will walk with me a moment, I shall endeavour to explain.'

Erasmus Knox watched their progress across the gallery. He hadn't taken his eyes off her since the revelation about the ring. Simon followed in their wake, their footsteps echoing across the marble floor. Stone halted in front of another canvas: Agnetti's work again, but a modern scene.

Four gentlemen sat around a table covered with a baize cloth on which lay a book, open at a drawing of an Ionic pillar. At the head of the table sat Stone himself, his hand raised in a curious gesture, his thumb and forefinger pressed neatly together. Next to him sat Simon Dodd-Bellingham, gazing through his spectacles at an oval jewel he held up to the light. To his right sat his brother, Lieutenant Edward Dodd-Bellingham, his redcoat a match in shade to the garnets that glowed richly on each man's hand. The final gentleman, she saw with astonishment, was Lord March.

'The Priapus Club,' Stone said. 'A society for gentlemen with a shared interest in classical civilization. Here you see a painting of the four founders. We are larger in number now, but only the founders have rings. Is it true, as I have heard, that Lord March found you in the bowers after you discovered the dead woman? I imagine he must have lost the ring then.'

The extent of Stone's knowledge made her wonder if he'd spoken to Lord March. The revelation that they were friends surprised her. He had never mentioned Stone as anything other than a loose acquaintance. Nor had he mentioned this club. Nor Agnetti's painting. Yet until recently he'd had debts – said to total over twenty thousand pounds – and it was how Stone was rumoured to work: mingling business with pleasure.

'Lord March found me on the path outside. He barely set foot in the bower. Whereas I discovered the ring buried deep in the undergrowth, near to where the body had been lying.'

Caro had never asked him what he'd been doing in the bowers that night, presuming that he'd followed her from the Rotunda. Now she wondered. He had courted Clemency Howard behind her back – but had there been other women too? Prostitutes? Women known to Stone? Lucy Loveless? Might he have returned to the bower yesterday to look for the ring, having lost it on the night of the murder? Might he have killed Lucy?

He had been her lover, intermittently, for almost a year, and in that time she had rarely heard him utter a harsh word, much less raise a hand. He did have a tendency to a certain roughness in unspent passion, but it had never been the cause of her displeasure – rather the reverse. Beyond the drinking and the insouciance, he was scholarly and clever. She found it hard to imagine him responsible for that blood-soaked scene. Yet how well could a woman ever really know a man? Marriage had taught her about their lies, their hidden selves.

Simon spoke up with a slight stammer: 'My brother couldn't have lost the ring – not on that night at least. I was by his side the entire time, and we left early to have supper in town. We didn't even hear about the murder until the following day.'

His cheeks were damp with sweat. Something wasn't right. Simon's nerves. Mr Knox's watchful gaze. Above all, that Mr Stone had known Lucy Loveless.

'Lord March, I know, has a passion for the classical poets.' She addressed Simon. 'I never had your brother marked down as an enthusiast for historical inquiry.'

Simon's eyes flitted to his client. 'Mr Stone convinced him of its merits.'

'Then he must be a great persuader.' Caro turned back to the painting. 'What does that gesture mean? That shape you are making with your hand?'

Stone wagged a chiding finger. 'You cannot expect me to reveal *all* my secrets, Mrs Corsham.'

'I thought you lived your life in the open?'

'Everyone has secrets. Just ask your brother Ambrose.'

He smiled broadly, as if it were just another of his outré remarks, but to Caro's ears it sounded remarkably like a threat.

'I shall call on Lord March and the lieutenant.' Caro held out her hand for the ring. 'This mystery will resolve itself, I am sure. Thank you for your assistance, Mr Stone. I am sorry to have trespassed upon your time.'

Stone seemed reluctant to let go of the ring, but he handed it over with a distant smile. 'It was no trespass, Mrs Corsham. Do give my warmest regards to your brothers.'

'I shall,' Caro replied. 'To Mordechai, at least. Ambrose is in Switzerland.'

This time there was no mistaking the knowing quality of Stone's smile. 'So you said.'

Chapter Eighteen

THE MOMENT CHILD walked through the door of the Brown Bear tavern, Orin jumped up and grabbed him by the arm. He practically dragged Child out the door, into the narrow alley off Bow Street that ran alongside the tavern.

'What the devil have you got me into, Perry?'

'What are you talking about?' Child said. 'What's the matter?'

'I did as you asked. Tried to get a look at those papers and drawings they found in the dead girl's room. The lads who'd searched the place didn't have them. They'd given them to Sir Amos Fox as per their orders.'

'Why did Fox want them?'

'How the hell should I know? I also asked around about that damn document your client thought she'd seen in the bower. Next thing I know, I'm dragged across the street and given the Inquisition. Sir Amos held my arse to the fire. They wanted to know everything. What I knew about the murder. What I knew about this document. What I knew about Lucy Loveless – who her friends were. I told them I knew arse all. I was just doing a friend a favour. Then they wanted to know all about you.'

'They?'

'He had another gentleman with him. Fat, fifty, white eyebrows like an owl. Someone important. Sir Amos was dancing to his tune, not the other way around.'

'Did you give them my name?'

'Of course I bloody did. They threatened my job. Eyebrows wanted to know if you'd mentioned finding any papers that belonged to Lucy. He also asked about your client. I didn't give them her name – said you wouldn't tell me – but I damn well should have done.'

Official sorts, Child was thinking, remembering the description of the men who'd been looking for Kitty Carefree. The only people from whom Sir Amos was likely to take orders worked down the road in Whitehall. But why would the ministry have an interest in Lucy Loveless? It seemed to have a connection to her papers. Had Sir Amos sent his Runners to Lucy's rooms looking for something in particular? From their questions to Orin, it didn't sound as if they'd found it. Private letters, perhaps? The sort that might compromise an important gentleman's reputation?

'I didn't know this would happen,' Child said. 'I'm sorry.'

Orin threw up his hands, breathing heavily.

'Did you find out anything else?' Child asked. 'About the murder. Or that redcoat soldier? His name's Lieutenant Edward Dodd-Bellingham, I've learned.'

'Weren't you listening? I don't want anything to do with your damn murder.' He turned on his heel and stormed off down the alley.

'What happened to Deptford till we die?' Child called after him.

Orin didn't turn back. 'We're in London now.'

*

Child felt bad that he'd got Orin into trouble, but he didn't see how it was really his fault. It wasn't as though Whitehall normally concerned themselves with murdered prostitutes. The development troubled him. If there was one thing he disliked more than tall, handsome gentlemen and beautiful women, it was politics. Yet, despite these misgivings, he wasn't prepared to walk away. All that stood between him and Finn Daley's axe was Mrs Corsham's commission.

He spent the rest of that night looking for Jenny Wren, tracking her down eventually at an alehouse named the Ape and Apple, deep in the bowels of the slum rookery of St Giles. The place was so fogged with pipe smoke, it was hard to breathe. A man in a patchwork coat was playing an Irish jig on a fiddle, while a warty woman banged time on a bodhrán. Child asked at the bar for Jenny, and was directed to one of the back rooms, where he found her two matted-haired swains guarding the door. One had a brickbat in his hand, cradling it lovingly like a child. The other looked as if he tortured pets for fun.

'Are you going to let me in?'

'No business tonight. Go fuck your grandmother's horse.'

Child smiled placidly. He didn't know why they didn't like him, and he didn't much care. 'She'll want mine.'

'Didn't you hear him? No business. Not from men with broken noses.'

Child tilted his face to the light, though he could guess what was coming next. 'Mine's not broken.'

The fellow with the brickbat grinned, stepping forward, but Child's pistol was suddenly digging into his belly, and all the fun drained out of the man's unshaven face.

'I don't want any trouble, friend. I just want to see her.'

The men exchanged a glance, and brickbat shrugged, evidently deciding Child was more trouble than he was worth. They stepped aside and Child walked through the door. Jenny and her friends – assorted whores and cutpurses – were sitting around a table scattered with playing cards and tin cups of gin.

In the middle was the pot: a pile of ill-begotten coins, snuff-boxes, rings, handkerchiefs, wigs, pocketbooks and buttons. The whores smiled at Child and the villains scowled. Jenny grinned. 'Perry Child, you old soaker. Missing me already? Lock up your bottles, lads, or we'll have to roll him home.'

'I'm told you're not open for business?'

'Always open, Perry. Step into my study.'

Her study was a table in an alcove in the main taproom, a spluttering stub of greasy candle between them.

'I'm looking for a prostitute named Nelly Diver. Do you know her?'

'That poxy salt-bitch whore? More's the pity.'

'Do you know where I can find her?'

'Haven't seen her around in a while. Maybe she's dead.' Jenny grinned happily.

'Can you find out where she is? Do it fast?'

Jenny leaned back in her chair, giving him a lazy smile of appraisal. 'It's time we had that chat about the disciples again, Perry. What was all that you was saying about the will of God?'

Child rolled his eyes, though time rather than money was his pressing issue that night. 'How much do you want?'

PAMELA

12 January 1782

The audience room again. Only one gentleman present. Pamela watching Mrs Havilland. Mrs Havilland watching the gentleman. The gentleman watching her.

He was rather old. Even worse, he looked well-worn. Paunchy, shabby in dress, his own hair thick but run through with grey. A nose like a carrion crow, and bloodshot eyes that bored into her.

'Would you mind turning around, please?' he asked, his accent thick and foreign. Pamela had heard Hannah, the first housemaid, talk at length about Italians and their perversions. Repressing a shudder, she turned all the way around, assuming he wanted to see her arse.

'No, I'd like to look at your face in profile.'

She didn't know what that meant, and just stood there stupidly, until Mrs Havilland, losing patience, took her roughly by the shoulders, positioning her side-on. 'Well? Will she serve?' she asked.

He looked at her for a long time. 'I think I could scour the country for a hundred years and not find a face so fitting.'

'I told you so,' Mrs Havilland said with satisfaction.

'The same price as before. Have her brought to my house tomorrow at ten o'clock.'

Pamela's head jerked up. Was it decided? Was it to be him? Her auction wasn't supposed to be until the end of next month.

Mrs Havilland's face betrayed nothing. Pamela studied the gentleman again. 'Are you to be my first, sir?' she asked, with a sinking heart.

He grimaced as if she'd offended him, screwing up his tired eyes against the light. 'Please, nothing like that. I will not touch you, and neither will anyone else in my house. I wish only to paint you.'

*

It was a great honour, Cecily explained later that night, as they knelt on Pamela's bed in their nightgowns. From the window they were watching the gentlemen leaving Mrs Havilland's – picking out the ones they hoped would win their maidenheads at auction. Earlier, on stage, Pamela had looked for her soldier, but he hadn't come tonight.

'Mr Agnetti is a famous artist,' Cecily said, 'perhaps one day as great as Mr Reynolds himself. Your likeness will hang on the wall of a grand person's house. Generations of people will see it, long after the worms have picked you dry.'

Cecily often said things like this. The daughter of a penniless man of letters, she had literary aspirations herself. She'd told her father she was in the country, staying with a dying cousin on her mother's side. The proceeds of the auction would be passed off as an inheritance.

'He believes you?' Pamela had asked.

Cecily had given a hard little laugh. 'Maybe he's convinced himself he does, but he knows exactly where I am. If we say it out loud, then he'd have to stop me. So we say this.'

'Are you nervous?'

'It will be over soon enough.'

Now she nudged Pamela in the ribs. 'Look, there.'

Opposite the tableaux house was a gambling club called the Golden Pear Tree. A party had just emerged from the doors, and were walking through the snow towards a carriage. Two gentlemen and two ladies. The men had fine clothes, but not much else to commend them. Receding hair and receding chins – Pamela was getting used to gentlemen like that.

The women were a different prospect. The taller had glossy brown ringlets, pinned so that they framed her laughing face. She wore a bright canary-yellow gown, and a broad-brimmed hat sewn with yellow roses. The other had piled red hair, and wore a white silk dress, ruffled in delicate layers, like a billowing cloud. She was trying to catch a snowflake in her mouth, but kept laughing too hard.

'That's Kitty Carefree, the most beautiful woman in the Whores' Club,' Cecily told her. 'A baronet and a Member of Parliament once fought a duel over her favour. The other's Lucy Loveless. They say one of her lovers tried to kill himself because she wouldn't be kept by him. She finds love tiresome, which only makes them love her more.'

The women were hanging on to one another now, laughing uncontrollably. One of the gentlemen called out to them from the carriage to hurry up. Kitty spun around, making a pattern in the snow. Then she ran to the carriage, and was pulled into it by the men. Lucy followed, a little slower, and happened to glance up at the window. Seeing the girls' faces pressed against it, she raised a gloved hand. Then she too was pulled into the carriage, and the door slammed.

Chapter Nineteen

She wouldn't let them put Lucy in a pauper's grave. Caro had decided it last night, after she'd returned from Jonathan Stone's. That morning she'd gone to see Sir Amos and had proposed to pay for a funeral. She'd spent the rest of the day making the necessary arrangements, and afterwards had taken Gabriel to the park.

These tasks gave her respite from her fears. Even in the park, as she'd watched Gabriel run up and down with his hoop, she'd thought about Lucy Loveless and Jonathan Stone, rather than the child growing inside her like a canker. She couldn't shake off the feeling that she had been lied to by Stone, and that Simon Dodd-Bellingham and Stone's man of business, Erasmus Knox, had somehow been party to that lie.

Yet when she returned to the house, to the absence of a letter from Harry, her troubles crowded in. She thought of the disgrace awaiting her, and the little bottle in her escritoire.

A knock at the front door dragged her out of these dismal thoughts. Thinking it might be the penny-post boy, she hurried to the drawing-room door and was surprised to see her brother Mordechai in the hall together with Harry's patron in the ministry, Nicholas Cavill-Lawrence.

She received them in the drawing room. Tea was poured, but not drunk, it quickly becoming apparent that this was not a social call.

'I don't believe in sparing feelings,' Cavill-Lawrence began. 'We've known one another long enough to be able to all speak candidly. Yesterday you paid a call on Jonathan Stone. I'd like to know the purpose of that visit.'

Caro bridled at his tone – and the feeling of being spied upon. 'How do you know that?'

'Never mind how I know. Just answer the question.'

Cavill-Lawrence's voice held an uncharacteristic note of strain. Caro studied him curiously. His coat, breeches and waist-coat were a match in 'true' Tory blue, signifying staunchness to King George, Church and country. Yet in matters of policy he was a pragmatist, hence his survival during the latest round of bloodletting in the government, from which he'd emerged strengthened at the newly created Home Office. Hands upon his substantial paunch, his startling white eyebrows drew together, two albino spiders conferring over their prey. One eye was misted with cataract, the other a watery blue, but sharp. Morde-chai said Cavill-Lawrence now oversaw the kingdom's Secret Office. His motives were often opaque, his methods unsparing.

'If Stone has compromised you in any way, Caro, we must be told,' Mordechai said.

'Compromised me? How? What do you mean?'

'Stone was at Vauxhall for Agnetti's exhibition. We all know his reputation when it comes to the weaker sex. You must have been meeting someone in that bower.'

'You think I –?' Caro started to laugh. 'Jonathan Stone!'

'This isn't a laughing matter.' Cavill-Lawrence frowned. 'If you have struck up a friendship with Jonathan Stone, then I want to know why. Caroline Corsham does nothing except by design.'

'There is no friendship,' Caro said. 'I found a lost signet ring. I took it to my jeweller. He identified the jeweller who made it by the assaying mark. That jeweller in turn told me he'd made it for Jonathan Stone. I simply returned it.'

'A lot of trouble to go to over a lost ring,' Cavill-Lawrence said dryly.

The men's faces were sceptical. She needed them to believe her. The last thing she wanted was them prying more closely into her personal affairs.

'It was in the bower, the same one where the woman was killed. I went back the other day to look for the document I thought I'd seen there. I didn't find it, but I did find that ring.'

Mordechai breathed deeply. 'Why would you do that?'

She glared at him. 'A woman died. It seemed the right thing to do.'

'Why didn't you take the ring to the magistrate?' Cavill-Lawrence asked. 'Why call on Stone yourself?'

'Because Sir Amos doesn't give a damn. To him she's just a prostitute.'

Cavill-Lawrence exchanged a glance with Mordechai. 'Stone didn't ask you any questions? About Harry's work? Nothing political? Or about the bank?'

'No, why would he?'

'You will have nothing more to do with Stone,' Mordechai said. 'Attend to your household duties. Attend to your son.'

Caro was tempted to speak her mind, but this was an opportunity to press Cavill-Lawrence for information. Instead, she adopted a pose and tone of contrition. 'It is hard for a woman when she lacks her husband's counsel. So many weeks have passed now since I last had word from Harry. Please tell me when is he likely to return.'

Cavill-Lawrence's expression was devoid of sympathy. 'I regret to say you must be patient a while longer.' He dabbed a silk handkerchief to his bad eye, regarding her intently with the other. 'What I am about to tell you is highly confidential. I do so in the hope that you understand the precarious nature of our position. The slightest thing could upset that balance.'

'Any hint of scandal,' Mordechai clarified sourly.

'Harry isn't in France,' Cavill-Lawrence said. 'He is in Philadelphia – and may be for some months more.'

Caro stared at him. America! Six, seven weeks' voyage away at best. Hope was stripped from her like a layer of skin.

'Everyone is tired of the war,' Cavill-Lawrence said. 'The French have little money left, the Americans have won their independence in everything but name, and the less said about our own position the better. But these Paris talks have been a French performance from the first. Everything decided upon their terms, Vergennes holding court – only now they find they've overplayed their hand. Even the Americans, their partners in war, are unhappy with their demands. And the more forward-thinking members of our delegation spied an opportunity.'

Caro's head was spinning with the shock of it all, but she was still capable of following his train of thought. 'You mean to offer the Americans better terms than the French?'

'You should put her on the board of the bank,' Cavill-Lawrence said to Mordechai, who didn't smile. 'Cut out France and Spain. Give America all the land south of Canada they want. We get the return of loyalist property, and we get all those eager American customers for our manufactured goods. Embrace a peaceful future as trading partners. It makes perfect sense, when you think about it.'

To those who'd set such great store by English patriotism; to those who'd lost friends, brothers, sons, fighting the rebels for the last seven years; to those who saw every stride by the fledgling American nation upon the world stage as a humiliation – Caro imagined it would make very little sense at all.

'What of the King?' she said. 'He'll never stand for it.'

'His Majesty has shown enormous wisdom in coming to terms with our position. Not everyone will – certainly not in the Commons, certainly not in the country. All that patriotism stirred up in the war – wish it was easy to put it back in the bottle, but it ain't. We'll have our work cut out to bring them round and we like Harry for the task. A war hero who sees the peace. You follow the logic, I'm sure.'

'What he's trying to say,' Mordechai continued, 'is that there must be no more visits to the Vauxhall bowers. No more question marks over your reputation. Much more than your husband's honour is at stake.'

Mordechai knew, Caro thought. He knew about America and he didn't tell me. She supposed he and Cavill-Lawrence must have an arrangement, much like the one Cavill-Lawrence had had with their father: you look after my interests, I'll look after yours. A deal on good terms with America would certainly offer its share of opportunities for the Craven Bank.

Cavill-Lawrence eyed her darkly. 'And no more concerning yourself with matters that lie far outside your province. Like this murdered prostitute.'

Caro heard him only distantly, still coming to terms with the news. Harry wasn't coming home in time. That left only one course.

Cavill-Lawrence rose from the sofa and bowed. Mordechai and he shook hands. *Jonathan Stone is a problem to them*, Caro thought absently. *I wonder why*.

She waited until the front door had closed. 'Jonathan Stone said something odd. He said, "Everyone has secrets. Just ask your brother Ambrose." Were they friends?'

Mordechai gave her a weary look. 'I never kept account of

123

Ambrose's friends. Stone and he are men of shared tastes. It wouldn't surprise me.'

'Do you think it possible that Stone knows – about Ambrose, I mean?'

'They may have discussed it – how can we know?'

'The way he said it,' Caro said thoughtfully, 'it sounded like a threat. Because I'd asked him about Lucy Loveless and the ring. Yet if there was nothing to it, then why did he feel the need to threaten me?'

'Isn't it just another reason to leave all of this alone? I'm at a loss to know what's got into you, Caro.'

CHAPTER TWENTY

WINCHESTER PALACE LAY off the Borough high street, next to the river. Long abandoned by the Bishops of Winchester, much ravaged by time and weather and vandals, most of its buildings had been converted into dilapidated lodgings. As Child walked through the crumbling gatehouse, the bell of St George the Martyr was tolling nine o'clock. Earlier that evening, he'd met Jenny Wren again at the Red Lion. As promised, she'd spent the day making inquiries after Nelly Diver, the pox-scarred prostitute, and had discovered that Nelly presently plied her trade at the Tabard, a tavern on Borough High Street. Child had just come from there. He hadn't seen any woman matching Nelly's description in the crowded taproom, but he'd played dice with some of the regulars, and learned that she lodged here at the old palace.

The medieval hall with its rose window loomed over the palace grounds, surrounded by decaying kitchens, stables, and workshops. A tangled wilderness of a garden encroached upon the buildings. The paths between them were blacker than a Benedictine's cowl, and Child kept his hand on his pistol, watching the shadows. Somewhere a couple were squabbling, their baby crying, another woman keening with what sounded like drunken despair. A dog barked incessantly off in the distance.

A thin-faced girl with tangled hair poked her head out of a window, inviting Child to come inside, murmuring filthy endearments. Winchester Geese, they called the whores down here. In the old days, the bishops had licensed prostitution, reasoning that if you couldn't beat vice, you might as well profit from it. Child had applied much the same logic during his stint as magistrate of Deptford. He asked the girl for Nelly Diver, and she scowled until he mollified her with twopence. She told him to look out for a brick building with a green door next to the bear pit.

Child walked in the direction she pointed, through an overgrown walled garden, into a courtyard full of low buildings that looked like workshops. A heavy stench of yeast suggested that someone had turned their use to brewing. A doorway in the courtyard wall led on to a cobblestone yard, with a sunken bear pit at its centre. Next to it was a brick building, the size of a small barn, with double doors facing the bear pit, and a smaller door dappled with flaking green paint on the other side.

As Child drew closer, he saw that the door stood open a few inches, the wood around the lock splintered, as if someone had put a boot to it. His pulse quickening, he drew his pistol, softly calling Nelly's name. When she didn't answer, he gave the door a gentle kick, and peered inside. A low fire smouldered in a hearth, casting a dim light upon a single, high-ceilinged room. Against the wall with the double doors was a large rusting cage. The barn must once have housed the bear-keeper and his animals. Child didn't like to guess why Nelly had kept the cage.

He collided with something in the dark and swore. Squinting, he made out an overturned table. Casting around for further obstacles, his eyes getting used to the dark, he picked out a horsehair mattress, ripped open, and a splintered chest, the contents strewn across the floor. And a woman, lying on the ground next to the chest.

Child hastened to her side. She was still breathing, but badly beaten; her face covered in blood. Beneath the blood, he could see her skin was heavily pox-scarred. He shook her gently, and her eyes flickered open.

'My name is Child,' he said. 'Please don't be afraid, Nelly. I'm here to help you.'

Her eyes widened in panic. Child sought more words of reassurance, before it dawned on him too late that she was looking beyond him. He rose, starting to turn, just as a cord was whipped across his throat from behind. His head was wrenched back against the body of his unseen assailant, and the breath went out of him. He clawed helplessly at the cord with his free hand, but it dug deep into his neck. His pistol was in the other hand, but he couldn't see his assailant to get off a shot.

His eyes bulged and his vision blurred. Nelly's eyes had closed again. 'Come on,' his assailant said, a gruff voice with an Ulster edge. 'Give it up.'

He was trying to force Child onto his knees, but Child was heavier and wouldn't go down. For a moment, they staggered together, until Child stopped pulling away from the cord, and propelled himself backwards, into his assailant. The man's weight had been braced the other way, and it took him by surprise. They moved fast, coming up hard against the bars of the cage. Child drove his assailant into it, using his weight to heave himself forward and back. The man grunted with pain, but Child's strength was ebbing fast. Summoning the last of it, he slammed his assailant into the cage again. One of the rusting bars gave way, and they fell through the gap.

They landed heavily, Child on top of his assailant. The cord around his throat slackened, and Child rolled off him, drawing a lungful of air. The man's hand went to his belt, a flash of steel in the darkness. Child brought his pistol up and fired.

A white flash and a crack that echoed around the barn. The

ball struck his assailant square in the face, taking half his head with it. Child closed his eyes.

He lay there a long time, letting the fear and the emotion wash out of him. Christ, but it hurt to breathe; his throat felt like a gravel pit. When he opened his eyes again, Nelly was standing over him. She held a candlestick in her hand, and Child could see that she was trembling. She spat on the man's corpse. 'Bastardly gullion.'

His body aching from the struggle, Child sat up. Nelly held the candle up to his face, peering at him through bruised eyes. 'What quarter of heaven did you spring from, then?'

Child knew from the Bridewell record that Nelly was thirty-three, but she looked much older. Her back was bent, her cheeks scarred, her dark hair wild and untamed, crawling with lice. Her dress might once have been yellow, but was much stained with blood and the seed of her customers.

'My name's Peregrine Child. I'm a thief-taker looking into the murder of Lucy Loveless. I wanted to ask you some questions about your dealings with her.'

She gave a mirthless laugh. 'Are you going to start beating me and all?'

Child turned to the corpse, the enormity of what had just happened only now hitting him. It wasn't the first time he'd killed a man, but it was the first time he'd done so without the protection of the law. 'This man was asking you questions about Lucy Loveless?'

Nelly's face was sullen. 'Wanted to know everything she'd told me. What she'd given me to look after. Didn't believe anything I said. Just kept hitting me.'

'Do you know who he is?'

In the candlelight, Child could see that he'd been a heavyset man of about his own age. The clothes of a gentleman, good cloth, sober in cut.

'Never seen him before in my life,' Nelly said. 'I didn't like the look of him, so I tried to close the door, but he forced his way in.'

She crouched down by the corpse and started going through the dead man's pockets, pulling out a purse, a tobacco pouch, a bundle of papers. She seemed to be looking for something, muttering to herself. Child picked up one of the papers she discarded. A letter of commission, stating that the bearer, one Richmond Baird, was an agent of the Home Office. Child closed his eyes again. 'Fuck.'

Nelly had found the thing she was looking for: a folded piece of paper. She gave the corpse a smile of satisfaction as she examined it.

'What's that?' Child said.

'It's mine. He took it from me. Fuckster wanted anything Lucy had given me. I handed it over to stop him hitting me, but it weren't what he wanted.'

It was a drawing of a young girl, the paper stained by grease and fingerprints. She looked about thirteen years old, her hair dark and curly, her eyes dark and expressive with long lashes. In the corner was the artist's signature: Agnetti.

'Who is she?' Child's voice was a dry rasp.

Nelly gave him a look of contempt. 'You're looking into Lucy's murder, and you don't even know that? Her name is Pamela. Lucy knew her. I never did.'

Child shook his head, bewildered. 'What does she have to do with Lucy's murder?'

Nelly gave a soft sigh, pressing a hand to the side of her face. 'This girl, Pamela, she was the cause of all Lucy's trouble.'

Chapter Twenty-One

Before her, Craven House bathed in moonlight. Seventy feet of sandstone frontage on the south side of Grosvenor Square, purchased at auction by Caro's father, along with furnishings, library and paintings, from the estate of a bankrupt marquis who'd put a duelling pistol in his mouth. It was the house in which she'd been born, her haven from her marriage in the early years. Then Papa had died, and Mordechai and Louisa had moved in. Gradually, Craven House had ceased to be hers.

Even then, she'd still had Ambrose. For a year after Papa's passing, she'd called often at the bank, or at Ambrose's rooms in the Adelphi, whenever she'd needed to laugh or cry or be a Craven again. Now there was nowhere left to hide, to forget her marriage for a moment, not even Lord March's rented set of rooms on Duke Street.

The maids had been polishing, and the house smelled of linseed oil. She braced herself in the hall for the onslaught of children, Mordechai, dog, but only old Kendrick hobbled out to greet her. 'Mr Mordechai is working late at the bank, Mrs Corsham. And Mrs Craven is taking supper with the Henekers.'

'And Ambrose?'

Kendrick's watery grey eyes flicked to one of the footmen. 'He's been quiet today, Mrs Corsham. But you'd still be advised to keep a servant close.'

The imperial staircase hall was the heart of Craven House, rising like a tower to a painted dome. Caro followed the footman upstairs, to a door on the second floor, and waited while he unlocked it. Despite his protests, she told him to wait outside.

It had been Ambrose's bedroom as a boy. They'd had his things brought here from the Adelphi when Mordechai had broken up his household three months earlier. Ambrose was sitting in his favourite porter's chair, angled away from the door.

Her mouth was dry, a head of teazle in her throat. 'Ambrose,' she said, 'it's me. Caro.'

He turned at the sound of her voice, and her nails dug into her palms. Ambrose blinked in the lamplight as if it pained him. The doctors said he was nearly blind now. Gaunt, crabbed, his dressing gown hanging off him like a scarecrow, his shrunken yellow hands bandaged, riven with sores. The silver nose he wore shielded her from the worst sight of all: the absence of flesh and blood beneath, eaten away by the unstoppable march of the lesions that covered his body. She found it almost unbearable to look, but he was still her Ambrose, and so she forced herself to come, twice a week, to sit with him, to read to him, looking for any small sign that he still loved her.

The doctors said his mind had been eaten by the syphilis too. Sometimes he suffered delusions and fits of violent rage. He would thrash and groan, until restrained by the footmen. Then he'd weep. She wondered how much of him was still in there, convinced his silence was voluntary – because all the words had become too unbearable to speak. She crouched down by his side, and took his hand.

'I need to talk to you about Lucy Loveless. You introduced her to me as Lucia. That wasn't kind, Ambrose – but let's not dwell on that now. She was one of your women, wasn't she? I can see how you would have liked her. She's dead, Ambrose. She was murdered. She died in my arms.'

Caro waited for a reaction, but he only stared. It was a virulent case, the doctors said, the rot spreading fast. A year ago the sores had become too deep to conceal with cosmetics, and he'd confessed his diagnosis to her, his voice rich with false assurance. Soon he'd been forced to withdraw from society altogether, under the pretence that he was abroad, seeking new clients. He'd refused to step down from the bank at first, conducting business from his rooms via trusted clerks – and he still received a few old friends in private. She wondered now if Jonathan Stone had been one of them.

'Did you meet Lucy at Agnetti's house? He was painting her for Jonathan Stone. I went to Stone's house at Muswell Rise. I'm worried he knows about you – about your condition. Were you friends?'

His Agnetti hung over the fire. *The Castration of Uranus.* Mordechai had thought it in poor taste, painted so soon after Papa had died and Ambrose had taken over at the bank. Caro wondered if that was why Ambrose had commissioned it – to needle Mordechai. But Mordechai had had the last laugh – forcing Ambrose out of the bank, citing his failing wits and some nonsense about unauthorized loans. *How could you take that from him too?* she'd demanded. *Humiliate him before the board like that? How much would it have cost you to wait a little longer?* Mordechai had shaken his head, treated her like a child. *You haven't the first idea what you're talking about.*

Ambrose's grip on her hand tightened, face twitching, as if he was trying to speak. He opened his empty purse of a mouth, his teeth claimed by the mercury cure that hadn't cured. Only a string of drool came out.

'Did you ever hear of something called the Priapus Club?

Jonathan Stone founded it, together with Lord March and the Dodd-Bellingham brothers. They claim to study classical civilization, but I wonder if there's more to it than that. The only Greek known to Neddy Dodd-Bellingham is his vintner.'

Ambrose's days of carousing with men like Stone were long over. He hadn't been able to walk unaided in many months and, Lord knows, no woman would look at him now. But he might still have heard something about the club – through those old friends he used to receive. Stories of all the things he could no longer do, no longer feel.

'One of them dropped a ring in the bower where Lucy was murdered. Can you tell me anything that might help me find the man who killed her?'

More twitching. More drool. She should have known this was a hopeless errand. Overwhelmed by weariness, she blinked back tears. Yet somewhere in there was her brother. She searched his ravaged face for a glimpse, needing his counsel now more than ever.

'I am with child,' she whispered. 'It isn't Harry's. You once told me, if this ever happened, to hop back into bed with him, but he's in America and not coming home in time.'

His silence transported her to another day, another conversation about another lover in another lifetime. Ambrose's rooms in the Adelphi. She'd called and they'd played cards in the thin, grey light of a November afternoon.

'Are you in love with him?' Ambrose had asked. 'Your young architect who looks at you with those calf eyes?'

She'd pretended not to know what he was talking about, until he'd silenced her with a look – brother to sister, their own private language.

'Sometimes,' she'd said. 'In the moment.'

But the moment always passed.

She'd arched an eyebrow. 'Does anyone ever ask if you are in love with any of your women?'

He'd laughed richly at the suggestion, and she'd laughed too. But as their laughter died, and she studied his florid, amiable face, her smile faded. 'Sometimes I think we are not capable of it. Love. The Cravens. Even Mordechai seems to feel marriage to be more duty than delight.'

'You loved *him*,' Ambrose said. 'Harry. You shone like the moon in his orbit, and every gentleman in the room wanted a woman who would look at him like that. What did he do to you, old girl? To make it all go wrong? Come on, you can tell me.'

But she wouldn't speak of it, not to anyone – not even to him.

'Is that why you do it?' he said, after waiting in vain for a response. 'Your pretty gentlemen? To get back at Harry?'

'Perhaps I simply enjoy it. Have you ever considered that?'

'Oh, I don't doubt it. You are a Craven, after all. But one truth does not have to negate the other.'

She had simply let the silence draw out between them, studying her cards. Now, crouched by her brother's side, she gave him an answer: 'My husband loves somebody else, and always has.'

Saying the words aloud gave them a new potency, a new ability to wound. Broken hearts mend – people often said that. But people told a lot of lies – just like husbands. Now she stood to lose Harry altogether, she felt the pain of those old fractures anew. Foolish woman, she told herself. You'd weep for him?

But weep she did, her brother's bandaged hand pressed against her face. Ambrose would have gone to bat for her with Harry – and if that hadn't worked, with Mordechai. How dare a Corsham divorce his sister? Who were the Corshams anyway?

Just jumped-up Wiltshire gentry. If necessary, he'd have bought her a new husband. Scandals could be ridden out, if a family stood by its errant member. But now Mordechai held the purse strings – and he'd see only dishonour.

'I tell you all this so you understand that I have no choice. Lucy gave me a tincture, you see, and I think I have to take it. It is very dangerous and I cannot predict what the outcome will be. So if I don't come to see you any more, it isn't because I don't love you. We'll be together again very soon, I promise.'

If Ambrose was capable of thought on the matter, he gave no sign of it. Her head sunk into his lap – a living morality play or a Hogarth print against the excesses of London life. By the time her sobs subsided, she felt no closer to finding the courage she sought. Only filled with a terrible aching loneliness.

*

Later, at home, Caro stole up to the nursery to kiss her sleeping son. Downstairs she wrote him a letter: pleas for forgiveness, a mother's love. She sealed it and wrote his name. Pray God he won't read it.

A slice of lemon floated in the porcelain bowl of hot water. Caro lifted it out with the aid of a quill knife and laid it on her escritoire next to the little glass bottle. Dipping a finger into the water, judging it to be at drinking temperature, she unstoppered the bottle and added the contents to the bowl. It was almost odourless, a very faint trace of mint. Hard to reconcile with Lucy's dire warnings.

She thought of Harry and Gabriel, then the child in her belly. Was God watching what she did? Many women lost babies a few weeks along – was it really so wrong to give nature a helping hand? And if she had a duty as a mother, wasn't it to Gabriel, her living, breathing child? How would he fare, wrested from her? Without a mother's guiding love? It was unconscionable.

Her skin damp with fear, she murmured a swift prayer. Then she lifted the bowl to her lips and drank it down.

CHAPTER TWENTY-TWO

CHILD DRAGGED THE body outside to the bear pit. Rolling it over the edge, he jumped down after it. The pit was full of leaves and stagnant water. Set into the wall was a rusting gate and Child hauled the body over to it. He opened the gate with a kick, and peered into a long dark tunnel. Nelly had told him it led to a set of disused water stairs on the river. Presumably they used to bring the bears in that way.

He needed both hands to drag the body along, so he was forced to work in the dark. Rats scuttled over his boots, and he kept inhaling cobwebs. After about five minutes of this grim labour, the tunnel grew lighter up ahead. Gradually, the black gave way to the dark blue ink of the river, washed with the reflections of lights on the northern bank. At the tunnel's mouth, Child paused for breath, one hand on the edge of the brickwork, his throat scratched and raw from the dead man's garrotte.

A wherry sailed past, the boatman hunched in the prow, and Child drew back into the shadows. Only when the white sail had been consumed by the darkness did he move. Manoeuvring the body to the top of the stairs, he rolled it down them, into the water. They'd weighted the dead man's pockets with stones, yet he still took an age to sink. Finally, what was left of the man's face disappeared into the murky depths. Farewell Richmond Baird, agent of the Home Office.

*

'People will come looking for him,' Child said, when they were sitting by Nelly's fire. 'Is there somewhere you could go? Out of London? For a while, at least?'

His motives were not purely altruistic. He could end up on a hangman's rope for the part he'd played in Baird's death. That he'd been acting in self-defence would mean nothing to the Home Office. They'd be out for blood.

Nelly had washed her face, but a couple of nasty cuts kept bleeding and she dabbed at them with a cloth. Her nose was swollen, and Child suspected it was broken. As if Nelly needed more bad luck in her life.

'Fuckster had ten guineas in his purse,' she said. 'I've got friends in Shropshire who'll take me in, if I pay my way.'

'Go tomorrow at first light.' Child took a sip of the foul spirit Nelly had served them in tin cups. 'Baird said nothing more about the thing he was looking for?'

'Just that he wanted everything Lucy had given me to look after. I gave him the drawing, but he said he wanted the rest. I said there was no rest but he kept hitting me.'

Baird was probably looking for the same papers that Sir Amos Fox's men had been searching for at Lucy's rooms – presumably also at the behest of the Home Office. Child wondered if they had any connection to the letter that Mrs Corsham thought she'd seen lying next to the body.

'Will you tell me about Lucy?' he asked. 'Anything that can help me find her killer?'

Nelly sighed. 'I can still hardly believe she's dead.' She worked something in her mouth with her tongue and spat a tooth into the fire. Then she started telling him about the early days, when she'd first met Lucy Loveless living in Whitechapel.

'It were a real plague-pit rookery. A penny a night, fifteen to a room. Irish, thieves, you know the sort of place. One night there was an argument on the stairs and I came down to see what all the fuss was about. Saw this girl screaming at a man, a baby in her arms. The man was shouting, the baby was crying, people were screaming at them to be quiet. Lucy was barely fourteen, selling her quim, like we all were. Her customer wanted to put the baby out on the stairs while he did his business, and she wouldn't let him. Eventually, he slapped her in the face, which was when I pulled a knife. Fuckster left, she kept his money, and that was it, friends for life.' Nelly shrugged. 'Almost a year anyway, which is next best thing to life down there.

'Lucy was green as Dutch glass – needed someone to show her the ropes. Didn't know how to spot the cruel ones, or the ones who'd beat you and take your money. Her biggest problem was her daughter, Olivia. With Lucy's face, she could be earning a fortune up west. But they won't take you in a fancy brothel with a baby.'

'Who was the baby's father?' Child asked.

'Some rich city merchant. Lucy's mother had brought her to London when she was twelve. She thought she was being apprenticed to a milliner, but the old woman was one of those who trades in virgin goods. Lucy had a brother, see, and her mother wanted him apprenticed as an attorney. She needed money to do it, which was where Lucy came in. This merchant set her up in rooms in St James's, and it worked all right for a time. Then she got pregnant and he threw her out.

'There were options, I told her – the Foundling Hospital would take Olivia – but she wouldn't hear of it. So we muddled along for a few months and wound up playing the Ring Game.' She grinned, then winced as if it hurt her. 'Lucy was a bloody natural from the first. We pretended we was three orphan sisters of good family – her, me and the baby. Her stories of our woes had people weeping. We had a forty-guinea gold ring what I'd napped off a client, and we looked for a certain sort of gentleman: the tricky sort who'd take advantage of a trusting lady. Lucy made out she didn't know the ring's true value – offered it for sale at ten guineas. She did all the talking, I made the switch. Gentleman takes his ring home to celebrate his cunning, only to find he's paid ten guineas for pinchbeck and polish.' She cackled. 'Must have sold that ring thirty times.

'It was a good enough living, until someone peached on us, and we got taken up by Bow Street. I got off lightly, Lucy didn't – talked back to the Bridewell governors, silly cow. She didn't want to take Olivia into Bridewell, so I found her a wet-nurse. But the old bitch kept the milk-money, and the baby died.' Nelly scowled. 'It weren't my fault. And it was better for Lucy in the end. That baby was holding her back. Anyone could see it.'

'Is that the way Lucy saw it?'

Nelly turned, a shadow passing across her face. 'She was broken, bereft. When she came out of Bridewell, she hired some mountebank parson to say some words in a churchyard. The baby had gone in a pauper's pit, weeks before. Lucy just stared. No tears, just that look on her face. White as parchment, as if every word was a torture. At the end of it all, I took her off to get her drunk on brandy and all she would say was "I am Lucy." She meant the world could go fuck his wife, and anyone else, but not her. She'd survive – just as she'd survived all the rest.' Nelly sniffed. 'I didn't see much of her after that. I heard about her though. She was on the stage for a time. Then off to them fancy brothels in St James's. I got people to read me stories about her in the newspapers. Once I saw her riding past in a carriage, like some duchess, a proper lady. She was doing well. I was happy for her. She deserved it.'

'When did you meet again?'

'About four months ago. She walked through that door, bold

as brass, saying she needed my help. Said I owed her one. I told her I didn't have no blunt to spare. She could look around the place, if she didn't believe me. But she didn't want money.' Nelly pointed to the drawing of the young girl with dark hair. 'Lucy wanted me to look for *her* – for Pamela.'

Child leaned forward. Now they were coming to the meat of the story. 'Who is she? What was she to Lucy?'

'What we call a game pullet: not yet a whore, but soon to be. She was a former servant, Lucy said, selling her maidenhead for a tidy sum. Lucy had met her at that artist's house. He painted Pamela too. She's fifteen years old, but she looks younger. Five feet four, not much meat on her. Lucy said she is sharper than she looks. They're often the worst ones, see. The ones who think they know everything. They're the ones who walk right into danger.'

'She and Lucy were friends?'

'Not as you'd call it. Pamela had only been sitting for the artist a few weeks. Then she disappeared, and Lucy had been scouring London trying to find her.'

'Why did she go to so much trouble if they barely knew one another?'

Nelly gave him a pitying look. 'Don't take much to guess, do it? Pamela was about the same age Olivia would have been if she'd lived. You could see it gnawed at Lucy. She couldn't let it go. Wanted me to talk to the rookery whores, in case Pamela had fallen in with bad company. Visit the Bankside stewpots, talk to the park-walkers. That sort of thing.'

Child was frowning, trying to make sense of it all. 'Did you ever see Lucy with any other drawings by this artist?'

Nelly nodded. 'Four of them. Pictures of different gentlemen. Lucy said they was members of some sort of club.'

'Was one of them fine-looking? Short hair? A scar just here?'

Nelly nodded again. 'Lucy said he knew Pamela too. They all did. I tried to find out more, but she wouldn't tell me much. Said it was too dangerous. Anyway, I looked all over London, but I found no trace of the girl. When I told Lucy, I expected her to be annoyed, but she weren't. She acted unsurprised and I wanted to know why. That's when she told me.'

A very bad feeling began to creep over Child. 'Told you what?'

'That she never thought I'd find Pamela, because Pamela weren't nowhere to be found. Lucy thought she'd been killed – by one of them four gentlemen in her drawings.'

BOOK TWO

✳

5–9 SEPTEMBER 1782

'At home there tarries like a lurking snake,
Biding its time, a wrath unreconciled,
A wily watcher, passionate to slake,
In blood, resentment for a murdered child.'

Aeschylus, the *Oresteia*, 458 BC

CHAPTER TWENTY-THREE

THE CRAMPS BEGAN half an hour later. They came in waves at first, striking Caro without warning. A chill sweat broke over her each time. They grew progressively worse, and Emelie, her ladies' maid, must have heard her moans, for she rapped upon the bedroom door, concerned, until Caro snapped at her to go away.

With the cramps came nausea – intense, visceral, rising from her belly to her throat. She battled it, drawing deep breaths, but the cramps came on again, leaving her gasping. Her stomach swilled like soup, bile flooded her mouth, and then she was leaning from the bed, vomiting into the chamber pot.

She stared down at the contents in dismay. That faint minty odour again. Lucy's words uppermost in her mind: 'If you vomit within an hour of taking the tincture, there is every likelihood that it will not work.'

Racked by another ferocious bout of cramps, she fell back onto the bed, unable to think of anything but the pain inside her. All night, she lay there shuddering, knees bent, back curled, slipping in and out of a hot, feverish sleep. She dreamed of Agnetti's Medea, scorned by her lover, Jason, murdering her infant children by way of revenge. Medea fled aboard a golden chariot sent by the gods who had taken pity, but here there was no chariot and no salvation.

The pain subsided a little before dawn. Dazed and weak, she

pulled back the bedclothes to examine the sheet. Only a few spots of blood. Nothing like Lucy had described. She pressed a knuckle to her mouth, as fear and desperation overcame her.

*

The old brick workhouse cast a long shadow over the graveyard. Caro shivered, pulling her cloak around her. The chattering of rooks in the plane trees mingled with chanting from the poor boys' school. The gravediggers lowered Lucy's coffin into the earth.

It had been two days since she'd taken the tincture. This morning she felt a little stronger, though her stomach still griped. Her skin bore no signs of jaundice, no numbness, no trembling. Her breasts were heavy and sore, a metallic taste in her mouth like she'd been sucking on pennies. She'd had that taste with Gabriel too, all through those hot, angry months she'd carried him. She knew with a mother's certainty that her child lived.

It had scared her, that night she'd taken the tincture. Her nearness to death in all its guises. Slipping from one world to the next. She didn't know where to procure more. She didn't want to procure more. She didn't want to die.

Which meant facing the reality of her situation. There may still be a chance, she thought. Harry's pity might win out. He might let me go abroad, as Lord March had suggested, have the child in secret, give it away. His political prospects, her money, Gabriel: all would weigh heavily against divorce. He claimed to love her – perhaps some part of him truly did? They could put things in train together. Maybe Mr Child would help? Swaying slightly, chilled with cold sweat, she hoped against hope that he would see reason.

The vicar, a lean man with a hooked nose and deep-set eyes,

read the prayers tersely, underscoring his displeasure. He had refused to let her hold the funeral in her parish church of St George's, and looked offended that she had even asked. Only the Cravens' large and regular donations to the parish funds had secured his participation at all. Despite the notice she had placed in the newspapers, only one mourner was in attendance other than herself and Miles: Jacobus Agnetti, standing a little distance off from the grave. He bowed in Caro's direction, but didn't approach.

The vicar finished his prayers at a gallop, closing his book with a snap. Caro thanked him and he departed, pausing briefly at the gate to allow a short, shambolic figure into the churchyard.

'I called at your house yesterday,' Peregrine Child said, as he approached. 'They told me you were ill.'

'I was.' She slipped a ginger comfit into her mouth. The graveyard resounded with dull thuds as the gravediggers shovelled earth onto the coffin. Agnetti made another bow in her direction and headed for the gate.

'Who's that?' Child asked.

'The artist Lucy sat for, Jacobus Agnetti.'

Mr Child gave her a glance of concern. Not that he could be said to look much better. A bruise mottled his cheek and he smelled powerfully of gin.

'I'd like to talk to Agnetti, given what I've found out.'

'I already have. He told me he dismissed Lucy for stealing some drawings a few months ago.'

'I found one.' Child took a dirty square of paper from his pocket and unfolded it. 'This girl, her name is Pamela – she has a connection to all this, I think.'

Caro listened as he told her about his visit to Lucy's rooms, and how he had tracked down the prostitute Nelly Diver. Lucy and Nelly in the old days; the death of Lucy's daughter, Olivia; Lucy's reappearance in Nelly's life, and her quest to find out what had happened to Pamela.

'I've seen this girl before,' Caro said. 'Agnetti painted her. She was his Iphigenia.'

'Nelly said Lucy met Pamela at his house. I spent yesterday asking around about her, but had no more luck than Nelly. None of the pimps and whores I spoke to had ever heard of her.'

'Then you're right. We should talk to Agnetti again.'

Child hesitated. 'This business is more dangerous than we first thought.' Caro listened, astonished, as he told her about the 'official sorts' who'd gone looking for Kitty Carefree; the important gentleman who'd interrogated Orin Black at the magistrate's house; and the attempt on his life by an agent of the Home Office.

'What happened to him, this agent?'

'You don't want to know.'

She frowned. 'The gentleman with the eyebrows – the one who was with the magistrate – he sounds like Nicholas Cavill-Lawrence, Under-Secretary of State at the Home Office. He came to see me the other day to warn me off. Because I went to Jonathan Stone's house in connection with this matter.'

'Stone? The moneylender?'

Caro told him about the ring she'd found in the bower and how it had led her to Stone's estate. 'Cavill-Lawrence wanted to know if Stone had asked me anything political. He *matters* to them in some way, I think.'

Child shook his head. 'You should have left all that to me. This is a serious business, madam.'

'What was he looking for, this Home Office agent?'

'Papers of some kind. He thought Lucy might have left them with Nelly, but she didn't have them. I think that's why

Sir Amos sent men to Lucy's rooms – to look for them. I suspect it's also why he volunteered to take the case from Guildford – only he's acting on the Home Office's account, not his own. For all we know, they're talking to all Lucy's friends and acquaintances. Because they think she entrusted these papers to someone.'

Caro remembered Sir Amos's searching eyes, during that one moment of their meeting when he'd seemed curious. *And you had no other dealings with the dead woman other than those you've described?*

Liars, all of them liars. She'd thought their crime to be indifference, but for some reason they seemed to be protecting Lucy's murderer.

'There's that letter I saw in the bower, but Sir Amos wasn't interested in that. Why not – if it's documents he's looking for?'

'Probably because he already has it. One of his constables could easily have picked it up. This must be something different. Maybe connected.'

Caro shook her head, trying to take it all in. Two documents? Two murders? Both prostitutes – or close enough. Both sitting for Jacobus Agnetti.

'Lucy believed Pamela was murdered by one of four gentlemen,' Child said. 'She told Nelly they were all members of some sort of club. One is named Lieutenant Dodd-Bellingham. I don't know the names of the others. Dodd-Bellingham accosted Lucy outside her lodgings just before she was killed. Lucy had drawings of these four men – probably the ones she stole from Agnetti – but Bow Street took them.'

'The Priapus Club,' Caro said. 'I know their names: Jonathan Stone, Lord March, the lieutenant, and his brother, Simon.' She told him about Stone's painting, and the four rings.

'Stone was wearing the original. We need to find out which of the others dropped his copy in the bower.'

Child gave her a sidelong glance. 'Then you no longer believe Lord March to be as pure as holy water?'

She flushed. 'I am keeping an open mind.'

Child's grin swiftly faded. 'This is more than we ever anticipated. Baird's attempt on my life. The Home Office involvement.'

'Having misgivings, Mr Child?'

'I'd be mad not to. But I'm here, aren't I? Unlike you, I need the money.'

Caro watched the clods fall from the diggers' shovels. *Lucy might have been murdered at any time*, she thought. *If this girl Pamela is the cause of it. The killer simply took his opportunity in the bower. It wasn't my fault.*

A long line of gentlemen's faces spiralled before her eyes: the four members of the Priapus Club, Sir Amos and Cavill-Lawrence. Faceless gentlemen too: the men who'd bought and sold Lucy, the man who'd killed her and who'd killed this child, Pamela.

'Lucy didn't walk away,' she said. 'How could she? Pamela was her atonement for Olivia. To fail her a second time would have been unthinkable. I suppose that's why he killed her – because nothing else he'd done to stop her had worked.' She turned away from the grave to face Mr Child. 'And now he thinks he has won. He thinks nobody cares about his crimes. But he is wrong in that belief, and soon he will know it.'

PAMELA

13–20 January, 1782

In Mr Agnetti's house there was much to love and much to hate.

Pamela hated lying for hours on the wooden altar, her neck stiffening, her limbs turning slowly to ice. The studio was octagonal, on the first floor of Mr Agnetti's house in Leicester Fields, and he often opened the four long windows to disperse the smells of turpentine and paint. The altar was painted to look like stone, and Pamela wore a white robe. To her mind, it was not so very different from the stage in Mrs Havilland's tableaux house, except that the eyes watching her here belonged to goddesses and monsters in gilt frames. Agnetti didn't seem to feel the chill, but then he wasn't the one lying half-naked with his bubbies out.

She hated it when she had to pose with Peter Jakes, dressed in a helmet and loincloth, puffing out his onion breath, flicking her nipple with his wooden sword when Agnetti's back was turned. Still, the artist paid a guinea an hour, half for Mrs Havilland, half for her.

She hated her walks to the house with her watcher, his terse comments and vigilant eyes, trudging through the grimy snow day after day. Agnetti had said it would take three months at least to paint her likeness and many more weeks to paint the drapery and landscape. He'd intimated that in the future he might use her again, and she hoped next time he would paint her as a goddess.

She loved learning about his pictures, listening to Mr Agnetti's voice as he explained, rich as chocolate. Soon he would start on the painting, though he said he would continue to sketch her as it progressed. Chalk and charcoal first. Then black, ultramarine and white. Then yellow ochre, rose madder lake, and vermillion. Even the names of the paints sounded romantic.

She loved the idea of adorning the wall of a nobleman's mansion. The Pamela in the book said that virtue was the only true beauty. But a duke didn't hang you on his wall because you said your prayers at night.

Most of all, she loved spending time with Lucy Loveless and Kitty Carefree . . .

*

They'd first met on the third occasion Pamela had sat for Mr Agnetti. He'd stopped to rest two hours in, as he often did, but this time he'd told her to get dressed.

'My wife wishes to meet you. She invites you to take tea with her and her friends.'

Pamela followed him downstairs, rather nervously. The rippling notes of a harpsichord reached them, and as the player struck the final chords, applause.

Agnetti's morning room was even grander than Mrs Havilland's parlour. Arched windows, rich with drapery, overlooked a small snow-shrouded garden. Yellow silk wallpaper filled the room with a honeyed light. And warmth! A large fire piled high with coals. Pamela felt life flowing back into her frozen limbs. Two ladies sat at a tea table, a silver chocolate pot and porcelain teacups between them. A third woman with tumbling red curls sat at the harpsichord.

'My wife,' Agnetti said, indicating one of the women at the tea table. 'My dear, this is Pamela. My new sitter.'

Mrs Agnetti rose and they studied one another. Much younger than her husband – thirty at most – she was a similar height to Pamela, but all skin and bone. She wore a gown of ruched primrose satin and an extraordinary turban of ivory silk, pinned with a ruby brooch, that wouldn't look out of place in the Sultan's Seraglio scene at the tableaux house. Her face beneath the turban was small and white and hollow: sunken green eyes, a petulant mouth, and tiny teeth.

'You must call me, Theresa, child. Come, take a seat.'

Welcoming words, but her voice was distant, lacking warmth. Agnetti indicated the other women. 'Here are two more of my sitters: Lucy Loveless and Kitty Carefree.'

The celebrated harlots whom she and Cecily had watched that night from their bedroom window. Pamela examined them with mounting excitement, and not a little curiosity. How odd that Mrs Agnetti consorted so freely with whores. Wasn't she afraid for her own reputation?

Lucy gave her a broad smile, wafting herself with a silk fan. Pamela admired her indigo satin and her piled chestnut hair, a long, loose ringlet resting upon one plump breast. Kitty blew her a kiss from the harpsichord. She had ivory skin with barely a freckle, a delicate nose and soft, coral lips. 'Just look at her, Boleyn. Remember what it was like to be young and beautiful?'

Lucy, to whom this remark was apparently addressed, rolled her eyes. 'I wouldn't swap what I know now, not for twenty-five guineas a night.'

'I would.'

Mrs Agnetti poured Pamela a bowl of chocolate with her own hands. Agnetti looked on fondly, and when his wife retook her seat, he went to kiss her. She turned away, so that his lips only brushed her cheek.

His smile faded. 'I shall leave you.'

Kitty played an arpeggio. 'You said if I played Haydn you'd tell us about India, remember.'

Mrs Agnetti glanced at the door through which her husband had departed. 'If you fetch the Madeira, I will.'

Lucy glanced at Kitty. 'It's not yet twelve.'

'Your choice,' Mrs Agnetti said. 'Madeira and India. Or chocolate and London.'

'Oh, Boleyn, don't be a dullard.' Kitty crossed to a decanter on a console table and poured. She handed around the glasses, and then draped herself on a sofa. Pamela sipped tentatively. She preferred the taste of chocolate, but it gave her a thrill to be drinking fine wine, in this fine room, in the company of these fine women on equal terms.

'I grew up in India,' Mrs Agnetti addressed Pamela. 'My father sat on the Council of Bengal. Lucy and Kitty like to hear stories about my time there.'

'I should like to hear them too, Mrs Agnetti.'

'I told you to call me Theresa.' Her tone was sharp.

'Forgive me, Theresa.'

Mrs Agnetti closed her eyes. Lucy and Kitty exchanged another glance. 'India,' Lucy said, with forced gaiety.

The words rattled out of Mrs Agnetti like dice from a box. 'It is strange to think of India now, here in London under snow. In Bengal it is always hot, even in winter, even in muslin, with a punkah-wallah to turn the fan. Our house was a palace of white marble on a hill, and Papa had a stable of elephants with jewelled saddles. And you never saw such gardens! Pomegranates and pineapples, flowers like the heads of dragons. I used to sit under a banyan tree and play with a tiger cub Papa gave me.'

She spoke like this for some time, Lucy and Kitty occasionally piping up to ask questions. Monkeys and Mohammedan servants, hookah pipes and Arabian horses, spiced rice and Hindu gods. Mrs Agnetti refilled her glass twice as she talked.

Feeling that she ought to offer a contribution, Pamela waited for a pause: 'Why did you leave, Theresa? I would have stayed forever.'

'My father was appointed consul to the kingdom of Naples.'

'That's where Theresa met Mr Agnetti,' Kitty said. 'He came to her father's house to paint her portrait and they fell in love.'

'You can see the portrait in the hall, if you have a mind.' Mrs Agnetti glanced at a watch attached to her chatelaine belt.

'I went to Paris with my duke once,' Kitty said, 'before the war. We visited the cathedral and danced in the Palais-Royal. Have you ever been abroad, Pamela?'

'No, I grew up in an orphanage and then was a maidservant in the City.' She was painfully aware how unworldly that sounded.

'There's no shame in that,' Lucy said. 'I've only ever been as far as Ireland myself. Took up with an actor, who convinced me to follow him there. It rained for two months, and it was harder to find a decent jug of wine than the philosopher's stone.'

'Did you know your parents?' Kitty asked, with a sympathetic smile.

'No, I was left at the orphanage as a newborn.'

Mrs Agnetti stared into her Madeira. 'It is very wicked to abandon a child. I can hardly bear to think of it.'

'My mother wasn't wicked,' she said hotly. 'My father hadn't stood by her. She said so in her note. She was only doing what she thought was for the best.'

'Of course she was,' Lucy said gently.

Mrs Agnetti filled her glass a third time, and took up her watch again. What was she waiting for? Agnetti's return?

They passed another fifteen minutes in stilted conversation, until a knock at the front door seemed to answer the question. Mrs Agnetti drained her glass and set it down, smoothing her skirts. They heard the tread of the manservant in the hall. A few moments later, Lieutenant Dodd-Bellingham entered the room. Pamela sat up straight, returning his smile.

He bowed to them each in turn, in his hand a black box tied with a pink ribbon. Could it be for her? Pamela hardly dared hope, yet when he presented it to Kitty, her disappointment was crushing.

'There's one for you too, if you'd like,' he addressed Lucy.

'That's ground we've covered before, lieutenant.'

'So it is.' He turned to their hostess. 'I'm here on Stone's business, but first could I avail myself of an inkpot and pen? A rather urgent letter I need to write.'

Mrs Agnetti inclined her head with a faint smile. 'Of course, lieutenant. Let me show you to my desk in the drawing room.'

She rose and he followed her from the room. No look back this time. No grin to make her skin burn. Pamela glanced uneasily at the box in Kitty's hands. *But he offered one to Lucy too, and he'd hardly have done that if Kitty meant something to him.*

With Mrs Agnetti gone, the mood lightened. Kitty opened the box and took out a card which she laid on the table. It was black with a gold silhouette of a man with the head of a goat.

Inside the box were rows of rose-petal macarons in twists of golden paper.

'Don't mind Theresa if she's sharp,' Lucy said. 'She takes a while to warm up, but she will.'

Pamela smiled, unconvinced. She didn't like people who could turn on a sixpence. Like Mad Miriam at the orphanage, who could lurch from smiles to spite in a heartbeat.

Kitty offered the box around, asking if they'd seen *The Belle's Stratagem* at the Haymarket Theatre.

Lucy and Kitty chattered away for a time – about the stage and the fashions and the town – while Pamela chewed on a rose-petal macaron, wondering when he'd return. So many names she didn't know and places she'd never been. *One day I'll have stories of my own*, she vowed. '*I sailed to Spain with my lieutenant once.*

'Aragon,' Lucy said, at last, 'the poor girl can't follow a word you're saying.'

Kitty beamed at her. 'Forgive me, I do run on. It's all a haze when you're first on the town. I was the same. Such a simple goose. Lucy will tell you.'

Lucy's eye fell on the decanter. 'Put that away, will you?' She rubbed her hip and grimaced. 'I think I pulled something last night. Pamela, be a dove. Ask Agnes to bring a pot of coffee.'

Pamela rose and went into the hall. She called for the maid-servant a little nervously, but when she asked for coffee, the girl responded politely, with a bobbed curtsey. Marvelling at the odd hierarchy in that house, she was about to return to the morning room, when a door opened a little further down the hall.

Mrs Agnetti emerged, followed by the lieutenant. He murmured something which Pamela didn't catch, and Mrs Agnetti gazed up at him and smiled. He brushed the side of her face with his knuckles, his hand moving slowly south to graze her breast.

Pamela stared, her stomach knotting. Kitty called out to her to hurry up, and she turned swiftly, not wanting to be caught spying. She went back in to the morning room and sat down, taking a large gulp of Madeira to quench the flames that burned inside her.

In that house there was much to love and much to hate.

CHAPTER TWENTY-FOUR

LIKE THE COSMETICS of an ageing dowager, the white paint of the townhouses of Bloomsbury Square couldn't quite hide the cracks and blemishes underneath. A century earlier, this part of town had been a fashionable neighbourhood, but the beau monde had long since decamped west to Mayfair, and only a few of the old families remained. The Dodd-Bellinghams were one, Mrs Corsham had told Child on their journey from the churchyard. Blue in blood, short on cash – one of those ancestral lines which had filled the benches of the House of Commons and the ranks of prestigious regiments for generations.

'The late colonel served with distinction in the Austrian Wars and in India,' Mrs Corsham said, as they alighted from her carriage. 'On his return, he squandered his sons' inheritance on women and hazard, and the lieutenant shares his father's reputation.'

'*Young* women?'

'Perhaps. People say he is indiscriminate in his tastes. Every woman a conquest. He was sent to America because the colonel grew tired of buying him out of trouble, but to everyone's surprise he had a good war. They say the King may award him the Order of the Bath.'

'And his brother, Simon?'

'Half-brother. His mother was one of the colonel's mistresses.

He married her after his first wife died and Simon took his name. It caused quite a scandal at the time.'

'How did the lieutenant like that?'

'Better than one would expect. Again, it was a surprise.'

The house had rusting railings and the brassware was in need of a polish. Their knock was eventually answered by a decrepit manservant in blue livery that looked almost as old as he did.

Mrs Corsham asked for the lieutenant, and they were shown into a gloomy hall, the plasterwork riven with cracks. It had that chill peculiar to large, old houses. Masculine voices drifted from one of the rooms. Child glanced at his client, a little concerned by her pallor and the way she held herself.

The manservant returned to invite them into a dining room, the burgundy wallpaper a patchwork of darker squares where paintings had once been displayed. A yellowed chandelier hung over an old mahogany dining table and a moth-eaten tiger's head peered at them from over the fire. Lieutenant Dodd-Bellingham and another gentleman were seated at the table, a dish of herring between them. A musk of sweat and brandy mingled with the fishy odour, and Child got the impression they were not long out of bed.

'Mrs Corsham.' The lieutenant rose, flashing white teeth. 'You are a vision before some very weary eyes.' He kissed her hand.

'Lieutenant. Lord March,' she said, turning to the other gentleman.

Child studied him with interest. Like the lieutenant, Lord March was about thirty, with a long, thin face and elegant features. Thick, dark hair, cropped short like the lieutenant's. Dark, pretty eyes and a thin smile. Child glanced at his hand, but like the lieutenant he wore no rings.

'Allow me to name Mr Child,' Mrs Corsham said. 'He is a thief-taker I have hired, to look into the murder of Lucy Loveless.'

Lord March frowned. The lieutenant raised his eyebrows. 'Odd thing to do.'

'I'm sure you've heard by now that it was I who found the body, lieutenant. Perhaps you also heard that I found a ring when I returned to the bower. Jonathan Stone tells me there are four of them, and that neither he, nor your brother, are missing theirs. Our next port of call was to be Lord March. How fortuitous, then, that he is here.'

The lieutenant inclined his head. 'As it happens, I was intending to call on you later today. The ring is mine. It was stolen from me several weeks ago. We've been keeping it from Stone, or my brother would have told you the other day. The ring was a gift from him, you see, and I knew he'd be annoyed that I'd been so careless. You're my Galahad, Mrs Corsham. I'm much obliged.'

They studied him with scepticism. 'Stolen?' Child said.

'Yes, by your dead doxy, Lucy Loveless. I'll happily tell you the story, though perhaps Mrs Corsham would prefer to wait next door. It's a trifle indelicate, I'm afraid to say.'

'I am a married woman, lieutenant. I'm sure I will endure.'

'Don't say you weren't warned.' He gestured to the empty chairs. 'Won't you sit down? Herring? No? Don't blame you. I'd offer you a bowl of coffee, but the Mohammedan Gruel that Grimmond sees fit to serve is execrable.'

Mrs Corsham placed the ring upon the table. The lieutenant slid it onto his index finger, and Child could see it fitted him perfectly.

'I knew Lucy from Agnetti's house,' the lieutenant said. 'I

am often there on Stone's business, and she was one of his sitters.'

'What business is that?' Mrs Corsham asked.

'Carrying sketches back and forth from his estate at Muswell Rise. Stone prefers not to come into town unless he can help it. When I'm not at his vintner or his bookbinder, I'm at Agnetti's.'

'I never picked you for an errand boy, lieutenant.'

He shrugged, unabashed. 'We don't all have wealthy fathers to settle our debts like March here. Mr Stone lets me work off the interest this way. It suits us both – for the moment at least. I hope my affairs will stand in better shape before too long.'

'Lucy Loveless,' Child said, returning to the point.

'She and I struck up an acquaintance at Agnetti's, and one night she asked me to take her to supper. I engaged a private room at the Prince of Wales, and a very pleasant time was had by both parties. Until I awoke a few hours later, to find the girl gone. My head was spinning, and I believe she slipped a draught into my wine. It was only later, when I got home, that I realized my ring was missing.' He admired it now, turning his hand to catch the light. 'I'm surprised she hadn't sold it. Maybe that's what she was doing in the bower – meeting a villain to do the deal, who then killed her? My brother says Stone paid seventy guineas apiece for these rings. Hell, right now, I'd kill for that.'

'Did you report the ring stolen?' Child asked.

'Of course not. I have my reputation to think of. My superior officers understand that a gentleman has needs, but an official record of his peccadilloes is a different matter. I expect she counted upon it. Scheming jade.'

'You were angry?'

'Wouldn't you be? She denied it, but I knew it was her.'

'I ask because you were seen exchanging words with Lucy

outside her lodgings a few days before she was killed. Can I ask what about?'

'I was passing and saw her on the street. I confronted her again about the ring, but she still refused to admit it.'

'I heard you pushed her?'

'I may have got carried away in the heat of the moment. It was nothing she didn't deserve.'

'Did you also have words with her at Vauxhall?'

'No, I didn't know she was there.'

'You didn't go to the bowers at any point?'

He made fists on the table. 'Does someone say I did? I'm not sure I like the path you are treading, sir.'

Lord March laid a hand upon his arm. 'He's only doing his job, Neddy. Let him ask his questions. It's not as if you have anything to hide.'

The lieutenant eyed Child sullenly. 'If Lucy's dealings with others were similar to her dealings with me, then frankly I'm not surprised that she was murdered. But if you're asking if I killed her, the answer's no. I left Vauxhall early to have dinner with my brother at the Prince of Wales.'

'Lucy's landlord says someone was trying to destroy her livelihood by spreading rumours she had the pox. An anonymous letter was sent to the Whores' Club and they threw her out. Did you have anything to do with that?'

He grinned. 'I might have done. Teach her to steal from me.'

'How did you find out that she had served time in Bridewell?'

'I forget. Someone told me.'

'She was also badly beaten about six months ago.'

'Not by me. I don't hit women.'

'Only push them.' Child met his unapologetic gaze. 'Any inkling who might have hit her?'

'When I saw her bruises, I presumed it was Agnetti. They'd had some sort of falling out.'

'Do you know what their argument was about?'

'Something to do with his wife, I think. She and Lucy were friends.'

'It sounds implausible, does it not?' Lord March put in. 'A prostitute and a diplomat's daughter? But I assure you it's true. I observed the women talking and laughing together myself.'

'You met Lucy too, then, sir?' Child said.

'Yes, I did. Jonathan Stone commissioned a portrait of a club of which I'm a member. I sat for Agnetti a few times during the course of its painting and we became friends. There were often girls around the place. Lucy was one of them.'

Beside him, Mrs Corsham stirred. She had steadily avoided looking at Lord March since they'd sat down, but now she turned.

'Whatever she did to Neddy,' Lord March went on, 'she didn't deserve to die like that. I wish you every luck in your endeavours to find the killer.'

Bluebloods, Child theorized, fell into two camps: arrogant fucksters like the lieutenant, and those who hid their arrogance behind a veneer of condescending charm. At least the fucksters didn't expect you to be grateful.

'Can I ask what *you* were doing that night in the bowers, sir?'

'Just taking a stroll. I explained it all to the magistrate. Regrettably, I saw nothing that could help him. I've racked my memory.'

'Did you tell Sir Amos that you knew the dead woman?'

'No. I didn't know then who she was.'

'You didn't recognize her?'

'I barely glanced into the bower. Mrs Corsham will testify to that.'

She gazed at him coolly. 'Yes, that much is true.'

Her tone intrigued Child, as did her *volte face* regarding his innocence. There is something between them, he thought. Or at one time there was. He wondered if they'd been meeting one another in the bowers.

'A lot of coincidences,' Child said. 'You both knowing Lucy. Both present at Vauxhall. You in the bowers. The lieutenant's ring.'

'Everyone attended Vauxhall that night. And the lieutenant's already explained about the ring.'

'Ask Agnetti, if you don't believe me,' the lieutenant said. 'I talked to him about the theft at the time.'

'Then there's Lucy's interest in the Priapus Club.'

Lord March held his gaze. 'Her interest?'

'She had drawings of the four of you – the founders – pictures she'd stolen from Agnetti.'

'What of it?' the lieutenant said. 'I told you she was a thief.'

'I'm curious about her motive for that crime.'

Lord March spread his hands. 'We are as much in the dark as you, sir.'

'Will you tell me about your club? What you get up to?'

'Very well, though I'm struggling to see the relevance. We have a shared interest in Greece and Rome, and we meet once a month to discuss it. Simon Dodd-Bellingham usually gives a talk on historical or philosophical matters. Often Mr Stone will show off a new acquisition for his collection. Sometimes I give a recitation. I'm working on a translation of Catullus, and I also write a little poetry in the classical vein myself.'

'How many members does the club have?'

'It must be over a dozen now.'

'Can you give me a list of the names?'

'Why would you want to know? Did Lucy Loveless have pictures of the others too?'

'Just curious.'

'Then I'm afraid the answer's no. Not without good reason. No gentleman would thank me for dragging his name into a murder inquiry.'

Child thought about pressing him harder, but doubted he'd get very far. 'Is poetry your metier too, lieutenant?'

'Bores me to tears, if you must know. No offence, March. But I find the club's philosophy enlightening.'

'And what is that?'

He waved a hand vaguely. 'That the Church doesn't have all the answers. The ancients have lessons for us too.'

'What manner of lessons?'

Lord March smiled uneasily. 'Neddy puts it a little bluntly. There is nothing heretical in our thinking, I assure you. The club simply seeks to understand man in his natural condition, as God conceived him to be. We draw upon Rousseau and others, but also on our own studies of the classical world. Mr Stone is particularly interested in the light cast upon Roman society by the excavations at Pompeii. You should talk to the lieutenant's brother, if you want to know more. He's the authority on it all.'

'Is Simon at home?' Mrs Corsham asked.

'In Hampshire on Stone's business,' the lieutenant replied. 'Fitting a statue at one of his houses. He has six, you know, and a mistress in each. Has my brother scurrying up and down the country fitting them out with his precious antiquities. In this house, we're all supplicants at the throne of Stone.'

Child took the card with the satyr from his pocket. 'Does this mean anything to you at all?'

Lord March frowned and shook his head. The lieutenant barely glanced at it. 'No,' he said, in a bored tone. 'Should it?'

'Looks like a satyr to me. Reminds me of the goat on your rings. Clever trick that – the stone that turns around. *Alitur vitium, vivitque tengendo.* Vice thrives by concealment. That's Catullus, right?'

'Virgil,' Lord March said, unsmiling. He took out his watch. Gold, studded with rubies. About two hundred guineas to Child's trained eye. 'Will this take much longer, Mr Child? We're due at the Golden Pear Tree at five.'

'Just one thing more.' Child unfolded Nelly's drawing. 'This girl, her name is Pamela. She was another of Agnetti's sitters. Do you know her?'

The lieutenant glanced at it, then met Child's gaze combatively. 'I know most of Agnetti's girls. Haven't seen this one in quite a while. What does she have to do with anything?'

'She disappeared six months ago. Lucy was trying to find out what had happened to her.'

'Oh, these girls are always falling in love and following their hearts. Or slinking back home to face the music. Or moving in with a keeper. Or getting locked up in Bridewell for a spell.'

'Or getting murdered. That's what Lucy thought had happened here. The four founders of the Priapus Club seem to have been the object of her suspicion. Did she ever speak to you about her?'

The lieutenant brought his fist down on the table, making the cutlery jump. 'I've called men out for less. If you were a gentleman, I'd do so now. Impudent wretch.'

Lord March was still staring at the drawing of Pamela. 'Do you know her, My Lord?'

He was forced to repeat the question, before March looked up. All his charm seemed to have leeched out of him, along with his colour. 'This time I share the lieutenant's misgivings. These questions are at best insulting, at worst they're slander. Repeat them in public and you'll be hearing from my lawyer. I am surprised at you, Mrs Corsham. This lapse of judgement is in poor taste. I suggest you leave before your man does you further discredit.'

*

'Did you see his face?' Child said, when they were outside on the street. 'Lord March went white as winter when I showed him that picture.'

Mrs Corsham didn't look much better herself. She swayed slightly and put a hand to the side of the carriage to steady herself.

'Yes, I did. That girl means something to them, certainly.'

'You are unwell, madam,' he said. 'Why don't I escort you home?'

She glared at him. 'What do you intend to do next?'

'Keep asking around Soho and Covent Garden. See if I can find out where Pamela was lodging. I'll keep looking for Lucy's friend, Kitty, too – and Hector, the lad from the Whores' Club. He was Kitty's former servant, and I'm convinced it was him who slipped that card with the satyr into my pocket. I'll head down to Vauxhall Gardens tomorrow and talk to Ezra Von Siegel, the lamplighter. And that jeweller who made the rings, Solomon Loredo. I have dealings with a lot of jewellers in the City, and Loredo's a canny fellow. If he's done business with Simon Dodd-Bellingham before, then he'll have asked around about him first. I might buy him dinner.'

'Did you believe the lieutenant's story about the ring?'

'I'm not sure. Lucy did have a bottle of valerian in her rooms. It might be the draught she slipped into the lieutenant's wine.'

'He said Agnetti knew about the stolen ring some weeks

ago. If that's true, it seems unlikely the lieutenant invented the story. I will call on him this evening and ask him.'

'Is that wise, madam? Agnetti's name is coming up a lot. He knew Lucy and Pamela. He was also there at Vauxhall on the night of the murder.'

'That's precisely why I should call on him, don't you think?'

'The lieutenant says he thinks Agnetti hurt Lucy before. We don't know for certain that this connects to the Priapus Club at all. Agnetti could have killed her.'

'It would seem a great coincidence, given Lucy's suspicions and all that was going on in her life, if Pamela and those four gentlemen had nothing to do with it.'

Child had to concede the point. 'Didn't you say Jonathan Stone was Agnetti's patron? Even assuming he's innocent, he might not give you honest answers.'

'Then I won't be honest about my purpose. I'll say I want him to paint my portrait. He charges eighty guineas a commission. That should get him talking.'

Child grunted. The woman was stubborn as Noah. 'Just be careful.'

Chapter Twenty-Five

THE GRAND SQUARE of Leicester Fields had a large quadrant of grass at its centre, and a statue of the first King George riding a horse. As Caro's carriage circled the perimeter, she glimpsed several artists at work on the grass, sketching the likenesses of passers-by for pennies. The neighbourhood had long been renowned for its artistic connections. She remembered coming here as a girl, when her father had sat for the great Mr Reynolds. His arch rival, Mr Hogarth, had lived just across the square, their fellow artists forced, quite literally, to pick a side.

The carriage halted outside Agnetti's house, on a corner of the square, the red bricks and octagonal tower giving it the look of a castle in a children's tale. Street-sellers crowded around them: 'Penny pies all hot.' 'Buy a trap, a rat trap, buy my trap.' 'Diddle diddle diddle dumplings, ho!' Miles pushed them all aside, ushering her to the door.

A manservant showed them into a large hall, hung with several of Agnetti's vast canvases. One of the largest was of his wife: a younger, happier Theresa Agnetti. Before she became stick-thin, her hair long and black and glossy, not hidden away beneath those odd turbans she later wore. She gazed at the artist adoringly, and Caro wondered when she'd realized her mistake. Her own happiness hadn't lasted until the altar. Or perhaps Mrs Agnetti had never looked at her husband this way, and the painting was as much a product of Agnetti's fantasy as his classical scenes.

Her use of the word 'commission' elicited the desired effect. The manservant hurried upstairs to speak to his master, then hurried back down again to show her up, explaining that Signor Agnetti preferred his clients' servants to wait downstairs. As they reached the galleried landing, a door opened and a woman hurried out. She gave Caro a bold smile and disappeared into a room further down the hall. One of Agnetti's infamous muses, she presumed.

The studio was large and octagonal, with long windows overlooking the square below. Four easels displayed half-finished works, with another much larger canvas-in-progress propped against a wall, surrounded by a scaffold. A bureau was covered in drawings, and several side tables held the usual artists' tools: bladders of paint, pestles and mortars, canvas knives, turpentine, rags, brushes, palettes, jars of mastic and linseed oil. Agnetti came forward to greet her and they exchanged pleasantries.

'I have long admired the scene you painted for my brother Ambrose,' she said. 'I was fortunate to view more of your work at Muswell Rise the other day. An Agnetti of my own is now my earnest desire. A portrait, I was thinking – a surprise for my husband upon his return from France.'

'A wise decision, madam,' Agnetti murmured. 'Allow me to talk you through some of the different possibilities.'

He showed her around the studio, pointing out paintings. Portraits of ladies and gentlemen. More of his classical scenes: the self-murder of Dido; the rape of Persephone; Ariadne lying naked, Theseus stealing away while she slept. Caro looked for the young girl, Pamela, but didn't see her. Nelly Diver had said that Lucy had only known Pamela a short time. Perhaps *Iphigenia* was the only painting for which she'd sat.

'Some of my clients choose a conventional portrait,' Agnetti said. 'But most prefer to be incorporated into one of my classical scenes. For the younger lady, I suggest a goddess or a nymph.'

'A goddess, I think. One might as well aim high.'

Smiling politely, Agnetti drew her attention to a painting of three naked women in a glade. A young man held out a golden apple, the women eyeing it covetously.

'*The Judgement of Paris*,' he said. 'I would paint you robed, of course, but most ladies prefer to be styled as one of the three principles: Hera, the queen of the gods. Aphrodite, goddess of beauty. Or Athena, goddess of wisdom, the one with the spear.'

Agnetti's Aphrodite had curled red hair. Her tresses artfully encircled one breast, then curled around her hip, one hand resting lightly upon her pudendum. Caro wondered if this was Lucy's friend, Kitty Carefree.

'I choose Aphrodite,' she said.

Agnetti studied her with interest. 'You surprise me.'

'Why is that?'

'Most of my clients choose a subject to address their own deficiencies. A plain woman chooses Aphrodite, but your looks are fine enough. Nor, from our conversation in the Rotunda, are you in any doubt as to your own wisdom. Yet your family money is new. Hence, I would have guessed Hera.'

Caro stared at him outraged. *Your looks are fine enough.* And the presumption! His father might be a count, but in Italy they gave titles to their horses.

'My reasoning is quite different,' she said crisply. 'Aphrodite got the apple.'

Agnetti seemed oblivious to her displeasure. Perhaps he thought being an artist gave him licence to dress impertinence up as honesty. 'It was good of you to pay for Lucy's funeral,' he said. 'I presume that was you.'

She had been wondering how to raise the topic. 'It seemed the right thing to do.'

'I was saddened her friends did not attend.'

'*You* were there.'

'I can hardly call myself a friend. Not given the way things ended between us.' He sighed. 'In truth, my motives were rather more selfish. I thought it possible my wife might have seen the notice in the newspapers and decided to attend. I hoped to persuade her to return home.'

'I heard she and Lucy were friends.'

He studied her face. 'Does that surprise you?'

'I confess it does.'

'People say she objected to my sitters – the newspapers intimate that was the reason she left. It couldn't be further from the truth. Theresa understood their value to my work. And she liked Lucy very much, as well as a girl named Kitty. It would not be a lie to say they were her closest companions.'

It was a bit rich for him to play the abandoned husband, Caro thought, given how swiftly he'd moved his new assistant into the house. Miss Cassandra Willoughby was her name, reportedly of good family, but disgraced. Caro remembered the girl's entrance at the Rotunda, knife in hand. She'd wondered if she might see Miss Willoughby here today, but there was no sign of her.

'I happened to see Lieutenant Dodd-Bellingham this afternoon,' Caro said. 'He tells me he also knew Lucy Loveless, that she stole from him. I confess that saddened me. Was he the gentleman you mentioned when we met in the Rotunda?'

'Yes, he came to see me some weeks ago and told me that Lucy had stolen a ring from him. He was concerned that I had unwittingly invited a thief into my house. That's when I confronted Lucy about the missing drawings. She admitted it readily.'

So the Lieutenant had told the truth. Caro owned her disappointment. Why then had Lucy taken his ring? Her financial difficulties had come later – *because* of the theft and the lieutenant's revenge – and despite those troubles, she hadn't sold it. Given the ring's connection to the Priapus Club, there was surely more to it.

'Did Lucy say why she'd taken the drawings?'

'She had some story ready for me, but I didn't pay it much heed. I was distracted by other matters. Her death still troubles you?'

'It angers me, Mr Agnetti. Nobody cares a fig for that poor girl's life.'

'You speak of Sir Amos Fox, I presume?'

'Among others.'

He nodded. 'Lucy used to call him a walking streak of hypocrisy. She'd say that Sir Amos condemns prostitution in public, but secretly allows it to flourish, because he would upset too many important gentlemen who enjoy the taverns if he did not. She was right, of course. He does just about enough to prevent an outcry from the moralists in Parliament, and no more.'

Caro looked round at the paintings. 'Where do you find your sitters? Do you visit the taverns yourself?'

'Sometimes. There is a club of prostitutes who meet in Covent Garden. I leave advertisements there. If I need an older subject, then I wander the piazza until I find the right woman. They are usually glad of the money. I like to think it helps.'

'And the younger ones? Like your Iphigenia.'

'There are places that trade in young girls. I wish they did not, but they do.'

'Do you never have qualms? About painting them naked, I mean?'

'My scenes may be inspired by myth, but my sitters I paint as they are, not how they should be. For Utopia, go to those daubers across the piazza.'

She sensed she had offended him, and was not entirely sorry after his earlier remarks. Yet she reminded herself that she was not there to pick a squabble. 'Do you still paint her? Your Iphigenia?'

'Pamela is her name, or at least the one she was using then. She left my employ rather abruptly some months ago. I was told by another of my sitters that she'd found a wealthy keeper. It is an occupational trial. My sitters are forever disappearing. They come back when their keepers throw them over, walk in through that door like they'd never been away. I daresay Pamela will do so too one day.' He gestured to another canvas. 'Here you see Aphrodite rising from the sea in a scallop shell. If you wish I could paint you like that – robed, naturally. There are other legends too. Or if you'd prefer, a simpler composition: standing, with one hand on a pillar.'

'The latter, I think.'

Agnetti nodded approvingly. 'Let the subject speak for herself.'

'I saw a simple scene you painted at Jonathan Stone's house,' Caro said. '*The Priapus Club.* I confess it intrigued me.'

'It is execrable,' he said, shuddering. 'I abhor a conversation piece, but Mr Stone is a valued client and he insisted.'

'Are you a member of his club? Mr Stone said it was for gentlemen with an interest in classical civilization.'

'He was kind enough to invite me to join. I attended once, but have not returned.'

'Oh, why is that?'

He paused. 'I am not a clubbable sort of fellow. What did you make of Mr Stone's collection?'

'It is quite the assembly. One cannot fault his passion.'

'Simon Dodd-Bellingham has found him the finest pieces from all over the world. He must have spent tens of thousands of pounds. It is Stone's belief – one I share – that civilization reached its apex during the classical period. That is why we place Greek and Roman forms above all others – in our architecture, our furniture and our art.' He glanced at a longcase clock next to the bureau. 'Forgive me, Mrs Corsham, but I do have an evening appointment. Perhaps we could discuss the terms of business?'

Agnetti would not move from his usual price of eighty guineas. They agreed that the portrait would be painted over several months, the first appointment scheduled in a few days' time.

'I will have my lawyer draw up a contract and my assistant will bring it to your house for you to sign. That is, unless you'd rather I send a servant?'

'No, why would I?'

'Miss Willoughby's reputation precedes her. Some of my clients object to any association with scandal, though not enough to prevent them desiring an Agnetti.' His lip curled. 'I am glad to hear that you are not one of them. Miss Willoughby understands the legal terms and can answer any further questions you might think of later about the painting.'

Disappointed not to have winnowed more out of him, Caro allowed Agnetti to guide her to the door. She paused by the largest canvas, the one surrounded by a scaffold. It depicted a naked man bent in anguish. Around him three winged women hovered, their breasts bared, their demonic faces contorted into howls. In the unpainted upper left corner, a fourth woman was sketched in chalk and charcoal, seemingly emerging from a cloud: Lucy, her eyes burning, her hand raised in condemnation to point at the man.

'*The Torment of Orestes*,' Agnetti said. 'It is the final painting in Stone's quartet, the last for which Lucy sat. Here she appears as the ghost of Clytemnestra, murdered by her own son, Orestes, in revenge for the killing of his father. She appeals to the Erinyes, the Furies.' He pointed to the three leering faces. 'Do you know the legend? The Furies are the daughters of Nyx, the Goddess of Night. Some call them demons, but Cicero described them as goddesses, the detectors and avengers of unpunished crimes and wickedness. They pursued Orestes for the crime of matricide and drove him mad.'

Caro sighed. 'But the gods engineered a trial, and Orestes was found not guilty. I never judged it a satisfying tale. If Clytemnestra deserved to die, then so did he.'

'The outcome may be unjust, but the painting is all the more timeless for it. Lucy herself said as much.' Agnetti smiled sadly. 'She told me that if the Furies flew over London looking for injustices to set right, barely a man in this city would sleep easy in his bed.'

CHAPTER TWENTY-SIX

A ROAR OF uninhibited conversation and masculine laughter filled the dining room. Child dipped his spoon into his mock-turtle soup. The Prince of Wales supper house lay in the vicinity of Drury Lane and the yellow-and-blue velvet booths were packed with patrons enjoying a meal before the playhouse. Each booth sported a portrait of young Prince George, and every now and then someone would stagger drunkenly to his feet to propose a toast to 'Prinny'. No women were present – this being a respectable house – but there was a staircase round the back, and in the upstairs rooms, a gentleman could entertain a lady discreetly. Rumour had it that the Prince himself sometimes met actresses here over oyster suppers, assignations arranged by older friends like Lord March. Child gazed at the patrons' powdered faces, too many chins or too few, framed by lace cravats and scented hair – and concluded that the Prince of Wales would be much improved by a house fire.

'So go on, then,' Solomon Loredo said. 'To what do I owe this generosity? It is, I have to say, uncharacteristic.'

Child had called on Loredo earlier and had invited him to dine on Mrs Corsham's coin. Each man filled his side of the booth more than amply, Loredo's bald brown pate moist from the steam of his soup.

'Simon Dodd-Bellingham,' Child said. 'I've heard you have dealings with him. What can you tell me?'

Loredo looked surprised by the question. 'He is an antiquarian, a classicist. Gentlemen employ him to make them a collection of Roman artefacts, or to assist them in assembling a library. If an older piece comes into the shop – coins, medallions, seals, that sort of thing – then I call Dodd-Bellingham in to take a look. As I said, he knows the collectors, and usually gets a good price. He's worth his commission.'

'Do you know much about his background? I heard he is a by-blow.'

'The fortunate kind. His father did right by the boy, paid for a good education, and when his wife died, he married the mother and adopted the son. Sadly for Dodd-Bellingham, the father had debts as well as a generous heart. I hear the boy is in hock himself. Lives with his half-brother in the family home, neither man able to buy the other out.'

'Is he trustworthy?'

'As much as anyone in this trade. I made the usual inquiries and heard nothing untoward. I certainly haven't had cause to regret our association.'

'Did you ever hear any stories about his dealings with women?'

'No, but I was talking to his clients and the goldsmith's guild, not his bawd.' Loredo frowned. 'What's Dodd-Bellingham supposed to have done?'

'He's a suspect in a murder. The doxy killed at Vauxhall.'

Loredo raised his eyebrows. 'A lady came into my shop the other day, speaking of that murder. She'd found one of my rings at the scene. It had a connection to Dodd-Bellingham.'

'My new client.' Child explained about Stone and the Priapus Club. 'The prostitute killed at Vauxhall believed one of them had murdered another girl. She was fifteen years old, a maidservant turned harlot.'

The eyes of Loredo, who had three daughters, misted over. 'Ah, that is too bad. I see those poor girls out on the street and my heart aches. Even good Jewish girls are tempted – and is it any wonder? They can earn five pounds a year in service or five pounds a night on their backs. My wife struggles to keep a maidservant past six months.' He shook his head. 'But Dodd-Bellingham? He is a scholar, a thinker. And have you seen him? Not a man built for violence.'

'I've rarely met a man who couldn't kill a woman with his bare hands. And whoever killed the whore at Vauxhall had a knife. Could you ask around for me? Any rumours about women or violence that have reached the City?'

'Buy me tickets to the Mascarenhas fight, and I'll ask around all you like. But I think you're up a blind alley with this one, I'll be honest.'

They shook hands, and Child winced at Loredo's grip. The jeweller had himself been a pugilist in his youth, when the newspapers had called him 'The Hefty Hebrew'.

Catching sight of a man who looked like the proprietor, Child waved him over. Bewigged and a little harassed, he was got up like his customers in a smart blue coat with gold frogging. Child slipped him a silver crown. 'You know a gentleman named Lieutenant Dodd-Bellingham?'

'He comes in when he can afford it.'

'Was he here a week ago today? Around ten?'

The man thought for a moment. 'I don't think so. No, I'd remember.'

'What makes you so sure?'

'When he comes in, I keep an eye on him. He's a trouble-maker.'

'You ever see him with his brother?'

'Yes, that one's all right. Tries to calm the lieutenant down when he fancies a brawl.'

'Could the brother have been here that night?'

'I don't remember him, but that's not to say he wasn't here. We were busy like tonight, and he's not the sort to stand out in a crowd.'

Child thanked him, and he hurried off to attend to another table.

Loredo pushed back his bowl. 'A brawling soldier sounds a better candidate for murder than an antiquarian.'

'It never pays to overlook the unlikely ones. People can harbour odd resentments. Being a dirty secret for all those years cannot have left Simon unmarked.' Child scraped up the remains of his soup. It was a specialty of the house, but calves' brains weren't a patch on genuine turtle. 'What can you tell me about Jonathan Stone? Is it true what people say? That he's a secret Jew?'

Loredo laughed a little bitterly. 'All moneylenders are secret Jews according to the newspapers. If an English gentleman is financially embarrassed, it cannot be because of his own ineptitude, but because he has been tricked by a conniving Israelite.'

'Then it isn't true?'

'I don't believe so – and I knew Stone in the old days. He lent money in the City, before he went to India. I borrowed from him myself once – and cursed the day I did so. I almost didn't take Dodd-Bellingham's job because of it, but I salved my conscience by overcharging Stone forty guineas.'

'Is his business legal?'

'Men don't make fortunes like that by lending at five per cent. A few months back some City aldermen tried to have him investigated by the Home Office for dealing in illegal loans, but it all came to nothing. Stone has friends in high places, I suppose.'

Like Eyebrows? Child wondered. Nicholas Cavill-Lawrence?

'Back in the old days,' Loredo went on, 'Stone's rate of interest was twelve: the legal five on the contract, the remaining seven governed by a gentleman's agreement. I daresay that hasn't changed.'

It was just how Finn Daley liked to do business. Child was painfully aware that his own arrangement with Daley had a matter of hours to run.

'Gentlemen's agreements are easily broken,' he said. 'So are legs, which is one way of doing business. But that wouldn't work on gentlemen like this.' Child encompassed the supper house with a sweep of his arm. 'Stone would end up on a hangman's rope.'

'Stone never used violence. Even in the old days. It was beneath him, he liked to say, which is ironic because little else is.'

'Then how did he enforce his debts? If they weren't legal?'

'I shall tell you about my own experience,' Loredo said. 'But you must first swear to me that you will never tell a soul.'

'On my son's grave.'

Loredo placed his hand on Child's arm to acknowledge his sincerity. 'It happened not long after my life as a pugilist came to an end. I was new to the jewellery business, lately married, and I made some bad decisions. I borrowed money from Stone – a small amount at first, but he encouraged me to borrow more, and my debts grew. I could not easily repay at twelve per cent, and so I proposed dropping that rate to the legal five – just until I was in an easier place. Soon after that, his man, Erasmus Knox, paid me a call.' He sighed. 'One of my bad decisions was named Eliza. I thought I had been discreet, but somehow Knox had found out about us. My indiscretion would have destroyed my wife's happiness, and so I came close to bankruptcy trying to put everything right. It was the worst time of my life, Child, I don't mind telling you that.'

'I'm sorry.'

'Stone still uses the same methods and Knox is still his man. A client is slow to pay, or talks about adhering to the legal rate alone, and Knox comes knocking at his door with one of his dossiers. Illegitimate children, forged cheques, ill-treated women, and so on. Unless a gentleman wants to see his peccadilloes in the newspapers, he pays up.'

'Stone has lent money to the Dodd-Bellingham brothers. I wonder if he has anything on them?'

'Not a crime to have secrets, as my own case demonstrates.'

'That depends on the secret.'

They fell silent as the waiter cleared the empty bowls and brought Child a goose pie and Loredo a plate of Turkish mutton with buttered cardoons. 'Your client is a beautiful woman,' Loredo said, when he had gone. 'You can bring her to the Mascarenhas fight, if you like.'

'She's married to a friend of mine.'

'The best kind of friend.' Loredo wiped his mouth, and his smile faded. 'This inquiry of yours – will it bring you up against Jonathan Stone?'

'I think so.'

'We have a saying in the Jewry that comes to mind right now: "The stone fell on the pitcher? Woe to the pitcher. The pitcher fell on the stone? Woe to the pitcher."'

'I take it I'm supposed to be the pitcher?'

Loredo gave him a serious look. 'Stay away from Jonathan Stone. That's my advice.'

CHAPTER TWENTY-SEVEN

THE LETTER CAME that evening. Caro didn't recognize the neat copperplate hand that had inscribed her address, and there was no imprint on the yellow wax seal. Breaking it open, she discovered that the heavy linen paper simply served as an envelope, with no writing on the reverse. Something smaller was inside and she shook it out onto the desk.

A puzzle purse. She stared at it in surprise. Caro and her friends had used to make them for one another as girls: artfully constructed squares of folded paper with poems inside proclaiming undying friendship. This one was painted with an elaborate border and a large pink heart, a message penned around the edge: *My dear, this heart that you behold, will break when you these leaves unfold.* Could it be from Lord March? Could he have had a change of heart?

Prising apart the interlocking triangles of paper, she opened the puzzle purse to the second layer, so that it now resembled a star with four points. She stared at it, appalled. Ordinarily the star would be decorated with images of courtly love or devout friendship, but the painted figures depicted so delicately here were of a different nature entirely. In the first painting a couple were kissing. The woman had brown hair like her own, wearing the same peacock-blue gown she had worn to Vauxhall Gardens. In the second, the pair were engaged in lewd coupling, the man taking the woman from behind like animals on the grass. In the third, the woman wore an expression of fear, looming over her a man in a plague doctor's mask. The final painting had a border of leaves, surely supposed to depict the bower. The dark-haired woman was standing over a lady in a pink dress, bleeding from many wounds to her stomach.

Hardly able to bring herself to touch it, she unfolded the puzzle purse fully, in order to read the hidden message at its heart.

> ### STOP WHAT YOU'RE DOING
> ### OR YOU'LL BE SORRY

*

Later, after she'd put Gabriel to bed, Caro examined the puzzle purse again. The artist was not without talent. Could Agnetti have painted it? It seemed ridiculous to think of the great master turning his hand to this childish task, but then there was nothing childish about the lewd and violent depictions. Nor the threat inside.

Yet Agnetti had talked about Lucy with regret, and he had attended her funeral, which was more than anyone else had troubled to do. And why – if he'd played any part in these events – would he send a threatening message that pointed to an artist? More likely, one of their four suspects was trying to divert suspicion away from himself – and trying to scare her. She resented herself for his success. Closing her eyes, seeking distraction from her fears, she found herself thinking about that strange, unhappy woman, Theresa Agnetti.

When the Agnettis had first moved to London, three years ago, Caro had made an effort to welcome Theresa into London society. She had always enjoyed the company of educated women, and Theresa was said to be learned, fluent in Greek. But in conversation she had proved distant and disinterested, and Caro had judged her a cold, ungrateful creature. This opinion was shared by others in her circle. Only Louisa, Mordechai's wife, had persisted with her acquaintance, saying she thought Theresa's aloof bearing concealed a shyness underneath.

Yet on occasion, when in drink, Theresa's sullenness would desert her entirely, and she could be lively, flirtatious even. Laughing with other women's husbands, probably trying to make her own husband jealous – Lottie Heneker had even overheard her complimenting one of her footmen! It was apparent to anyone that the marriage was unhappy. When the first stories had appeared in the newspapers about Agnetti's sitters, Louisa had been despatched by the wives on a sympathy mission. 'Much good it did me,' she had reported back. 'Consider my head bitten off. She just said it was lies.'

After that, nobody much troubled with Theresa Agnetti. The invitations dried up, and she was rarely seen out in society alone. Then came the scandal when she left her husband – simply walked out of the house one evening, and never returned. Some said she'd fled back to Naples or India. Others that she'd run off with a lover. Mordechai, who was always suspicious of educated, flirtatious women, said Theresa was a drunk, who'd probably thrown herself off a bridge. Agnetti was said to be distraught, but given his reputation for philandering, nobody accorded him very much sympathy. Any residual compassion evaporated just three months later, when he had moved his new assistant into the house. This fresh scandal had eclipsed the first, and now Theresa Agnetti's name was rarely mentioned except in this context.

Caro sipped her wine slowly, her sickness starting to abate

at last. Her breasts were still heavy and sore, her head swimming whenever she rose. *Don't think about the baby*, she told herself. *You will only drive yourself mad. Don't think about Harry.* Yet it was easier said than done. She forced her eye to the puzzle purse again. *Think on this.*

CHAPTER TWENTY-EIGHT

AFTER CHILD LEFT Solomon Loredo, he returned to the Covent Garden fleshpots. No one had heard of Pamela, but everyone knew Hector.

'Little Gannymede gets around,' one coffeehouse moll told him.

'You know where I might find him?'

'Like I said, he gets around. That your thing, is it? Boys?'

'Not on your life.'

She grinned. 'Take me outside for a guinea. I'll show you things a virgin never could.'

'I'm old enough to be your father.'

'Wouldn't ask if it mattered. I don't mind a man with a bit of fat.'

Which was the kindest thing anyone said to Child all night.

In a posture house on Southampton Street, where young girls danced and contorted on silver platters, Pamela's picture was again met with blank faces.

'If I was virgin and looked like her,' one girl said, peering between her legs to study the drawing, 'I'd have sold myself at auction. You get more that way. Try the Horseshoe. People put cards up there.'

'You ever see a card like this before?' Child showed her the satyr.

Her eyes widened. 'You didn't say you was rich. Take me there, will you?'

'Where?'

'Some big house in the country. They have private masquerades there. A girl needs one of those to get in the door.'

'What goes on there?'

'Everything you'd expect. At least, that's what I've heard. I've not been invited.'

'Who does the inviting?'

She shrugged. 'I only know the money's good.'

Child thanked her and walked over to Drury Lane, thinking about the notorious libertine, Jonathan Stone, and his country house at Muswell Rise. Had Lucy or Pamela gone to one of these parties? Was that why Hector had slipped the card into his pocket? He wondered if these masquerades had a connection to the Priapus Club. Was that why Lucy had been so convinced that one of their four suspects had killed Pamela?

At the Horseshoe tavern, Child studied the advertisements pinned to the wall. One card caught his eye, and he took it down to examine it:

> *A Delightful BEAUTY of FOURTEEN years,*
> *NEW to town, appears nightly at MRS*
> *HAVILLAND'S establishment at 16 COMPTON*
> *STREET, as the VIRGIN princess TAPOA of the*
> *SOUTH SEA ISLANDS. On the 17th day of*
> *SEPTEMBER she will be offering her*
> *COMPANY for sale to any GENTLEMAN*
> *willing to RELIEVE her of her present*
> *CONDITION.*

Compton Street, home of the Golden Pear Tree, favoured haunt of Lord March and Lieutenant Dodd-Bellingham.

It being after three, the place would be closed by now. Child trudged slowly home, looking over his shoulder for Finn Daley. His seven days were up.

When that poxy Irishman comes for me, he thought, fingering his pistol, I'll take him down with me. A man should leave a legacy. Let this be mine. Yet, somewhat to his surprise, he reached his front door without incident.

His peace of mind lasted all of twenty seconds, the time it took him to climb the stairs and unlock the door. Moonlight picked out the disarray of his rooms. Drawers pulled out, their contents strewn on the floor, furniture overturned, like the scene in Nelly's rooms.

Drawing his pistol, then lighting a lamp, he checked the bedroom for intruders – but found only the same scene of domestic chaos. They'd opened every cupboard and drawer, swept the contents from every shelf, torn the pages from his books, and slashed open his old feather mattress. Child picked up the remnants of a Toby beer jug that Sophie Hardcastle had given him at Christmas. The handle and spout had broken off, and his distress at its destruction surprised him.

Finn Daley wouldn't take this much trouble: he'd simply torture Child to learn where he kept his money. Any lingering doubt that the Irishman was responsible was dispelled when he lifted the floorboard where he'd secreted three of Mrs Corsham's guineas in a leather pouch. The guineas were no longer in their pouch. They were balanced neatly on top of it. The men who'd searched his rooms weren't moneylenders or thieves. They were Home Office and they wanted Child to know it.

PAMELA

21 January 1782

New gloves weren't a cure for heartache, but they might help.

On the way home from Mr Agnetti's house after one of her sittings, Pamela made her watcher take her to Newport Alley, where Lucy had told her she could find Parisian fashions for a fraction of the prices offered on the Strand. The crooked lane had been entirely colonized by Frenchmen: ormolu workers and clockmakers, jewellers and peruke-makers, milliners, mantua-makers and hosiers, as well as *Maison Bertin*, a haberdashery, where a lady might purchase an entire wardrobe of clothes if she had the funds.

Gazing at the curved shop windows, with money in her purse, Pamela felt like a grand lady in her new pink dress and a wide-brimmed hat trimmed with pale-blue silk. But occasionally, the scene in Agnetti's hallway would nudge into her thoughts, spoiling her pleasure. The lieutenant and Mrs Agnetti's whispered exchange, his hand grazing her breast.

Reaching the door of *Maison Bertin*, Pamela told her watcher to wait while she went inside. She wandered the aisles, fingering swathes of calico, velvet and brocade. The owner was busy with a gentleman on the other side of the shop, but a young Frenchwoman, who might have been his daughter, showed Pamela samples of leather at the glove counter. A rainbow of colours. She touched a pale-blue piece of softest kidskin longingly. Soon, she promised herself.

It was a way of discerning a real gentleman from the imposters, Kitty had told her. Kid gloves or leather. Brass buckles or gold. Watch out for hands too – give them a stroke early on to see if they're soft. A girl didn't want to waste her good years tumbling clerks who'd saved up for the season. She might miss out on a keeper. Even a husband.

Feeling the need to practise the art of looking, Pamela stole a glance at the gentleman across the shop. A shabby brown coat. A yellowed wig. Scuffed shoes with brass buckles. She didn't need to stroke his hands to know to walk on by. Yet as she gazed at the gentleman's profile, familiarity washed over her. It took her a moment to work out where she'd seen him before. Struck by recognition, she stared.

Simon Dodd-Bellingham, the lieutenant's frog-like brother. He looked different without his glasses, in the daylight.

He glanced up and caught her looking. 'Madam.' He bowed.

She approached him, smiling. 'You don't remember me, do you?'

His brow wrinkled in confusion. He'd only ever seen her dressed as a maid. Even after her performance, in the audience room, she'd still been wearing that old brown dress. She liked not being recognized, mistaken for a lady. Already leaving her old life behind her.

'Of course,' he said. 'You're the girl from Mrs Havilland's.' He looked a little dismayed – perhaps by his own myopia.

'I've just come from Mr Agnetti's. I am sitting for one of his paintings. Perhaps your brother spoke of it?'

'No, he did not.'

A little hurt that he hadn't mentioned her, Pamela fingered

one of the ribbons laid out for Simon's perusal. Striped French silk. Expensive.

The owner returned, another two reels of ribbon in his hand. 'I also have the blue-and-gold and the pink-and-gold, monsieur.'

'I'd like it to match the gold of the ring exactly,' Simon said.

He had a little red box in his hand, and Pamela studied the ring he showed the man. Ruby and diamond twin hearts, two smaller diamonds either side. She knew a good stone when she saw one, and these looked very good indeed. Perhaps fifty guineas.

'This one,' she said, pointing to the green-and-gold stripe.

Simon smiled at her, and then nodded at the owner: 'I'll go with the lady's opinion.'

'Very good, monsieur.' The Frenchman held up a list in his hand. 'The lady's clothes are to be sent to the same address as before?'

'Yes please. The ribbon I'll take now.'

The owner returned to his back room to cut it, and Simon put the box in his pocket.

Pamela tried to arch an eyebrow, the way she'd seen Lucy do it, but only managed a squint. 'A lucky lady.'

Simon frowned. 'Here, you won't mention this to Mr Agnetti, will you?'

'The ring? Why not?'

He hesitated. 'I have lately come into a little money – a legacy from an aunt on my mother's side. But I am in debt to a moneylender and, strictly speaking, I should have given my legacy to him. He is a patron of Mr Agnetti's and I wouldn't want this expenditure getting back to him.'

She considered this information. 'Who is the ring for?'

'A cousin who wasn't remembered in the will. I thought it might cheer her up.'

A flush had crept over his skin while he'd been talking. Liar, she thought. She wondered if Simon was keeping a woman. More Dodd-Bellingham secrets, these ones much more palatable.

He gazed at her anxiously. 'So you won't mention our meeting? To anyone at all?'

She smiled. 'It will be our secret.'

Chapter Twenty-Nine

Child looked again for Finn Daley, as he walked out of his front door that morning, but the courtyard and the street beyond were deserted. He breakfasted on bread, cheese and claret at his local tavern, expecting at any moment to spot one of Daley's thick-necked enforcers among the usual mix of drunk soldiers and sleepy whores. All the way down to the river, his hand never strayed far from his pistol. Only when he was ensconced in a wherry, a waterman rowing him down the Thames, did he relax. The trouble with looking over your shoulder the whole time was that it made your neck sore. He rolled his head around, enjoying the feel of the sun on his face. Past the Houses of Parliament, past Lambeth Palace, past the Pimlico marshes, to Vauxhall Stairs.

A small bribe got him through the gate of the Vauxhall Gardens. Child strolled over to the Orchestra, white and ornate as Chantilly lace, blue-jacketed musicians on the balconies rehearsing Handel's *Water Music*. He hadn't been to Vauxhall in years, but he'd brought Liz here once – in the early days, before Arthur was born. They'd watched an automaton play chess, dined on spatchcock chicken, and drunk wine sitting on a bench overlooking the cascade. The memory was like walking on a hobnail – the good ones were the worst. Fuck your feelings, he told himself. Let's get this done.

The garden was a flurry of activity: labourers fixing awnings, replacing lantern wicks, mowing the grass. Stallholders preparing for the night's business. The Prince of Wales's supper box, with its finial of feathers, was crawling with carpenters and painters. He asked a passing man with a barrowful of flowers for Ezra Von Siegel.

'Try down there,' the man said, pointing. 'He's the one with the beard.'

Three triumphal wooden arches framed the Grand South Walk, a painted panel at the end depicting the ruins of Palmyra. Child glimpsed a Chinese Pagoda and statues between the trees. He had progressed about a hundred yards, when he spotted a bearded man up a ladder, tending to one of the lamps.

'Mr Von Siegel?'

The lamplighter wore a red cloth cap, his face gaunt and walnut-brown above his black beard. He was draining oil from the lamp, presumably so he could replace the wick.

Child introduced himself. 'I am looking into the murder of Lucy Loveless. Can we talk?'

Von Siegel climbed down, looking wary. He was even shorter than Child and probably weighed even less than Orin Black. 'You are constable of Bow Street? You think I kill the poor dead lady?'

'I'm a thief-taker.' Child held out two shillings. 'I only want to hear about what you saw.'

Von Siegel glared at the coins. 'I want no money. I have daughter.'

Child smiled. 'Can you tell me what happened?'

'You find the *mörder*? Say to constables of Bow Street to leave me alone?'

'I'll do my best.'

Von Siegel gestured to him to follow, and they walked down one of the paths until they came to another lamp on the borders of the gardens. 'I was here, up ladder. I cut the wick. I see the lady. After she pass, she scream. I go see.'

They continued on to the Dark Walk, Von Siegel counting each bower they passed, until he stopped at the sixth. 'The lady here scream, in arms of gentleman. After they say he is Lord March. I see dead lady in pink dress. Much blood.'

'Did you see a document on the ground? Looked like a letter?'

He pointed. '*Ja, hier.*'

It lent weight to Child's theory that one of the constables had taken it and passed it on to the magistrate, Sir Amos Fox. He stepped into the bower himself, and spent a few minutes poking around in the undergrowth, finding nothing.

'How did Lord March seem to you? Were his clothes disordered? Was he upset?'

'*Nein* so. He try . . .' Von Siegel made calming gestures with his hand. 'Lady upset. He say her name.'

'Mrs Corsham?'

'*Vorname.* He say *Caro.*'

Child took a moment to congratulate himself on his instincts. Perhaps Lord March had arranged to meet Mrs Corsham in the bowers, and encountered Lucy there by chance? Knowing she was a threat to him – because he had also murdered Pamela – he had seized his chance and killed her. It was a good theory, but not the only one he had.

'Mrs Corsham said that as she approached the bower, she nearly collided with a man in a plague doctor's mask. He must have walked past you too, when you were up the ladder?'

He shook his head. 'I not see him. I say to constables.'

'Did you see anyone else acting suspiciously either before or after the murder?'

The lamplighter thought for a moment. 'Small time before

I see Frau Corsham, I see gentleman and lady. They go to bowers. Small time after, come back the lady. She look upset.' He shrugged. 'It is not so very uncommon.'

'Did the gentleman follow her?'

'*Nein*, I not see him again.'

Then this gentleman would have been in the bowers alone around the time of the murder. 'Can you remember what he looked like?'

'Tall, *jung*, red coat like soldier. But with gold here.' He pointed to his shoulders 'And short hair, cut like gentleman.'

'Did he have a scar like this?' Child traced a line through his temple.

He shrugged. 'No lamp. Very dark.'

'What colour hair?'

'Fair, like girl. Her hair short also. Very pretty. Very tall.' He held a hand above his head.

The man could well be Lieutenant Dodd-Bellingham. 'You said the girl looked upset when you saw her the second time?'

'She cry. She go fast.'

Child asked him a few more questions, but achieved nothing more than frightening the poor man further. He allowed Von Siegel to return to his duties and walked back along the path to the place where Mrs Corsham had encountered the plague doctor. Gazing towards the Rotunda, he identified the spot where Ezra Von Siegel had been up his ladder. If the plague doctor hadn't passed him, then where had he gone?

He walked on, peering into the undergrowth on both sides. Spotting a patch of trodden-down grass, he paused. The shrubbery was thick, but not so thick that a man couldn't pass through it. Shielding his face from the branches, Child walked into the undergrowth himself. He soon reached the high boundary wall, topped with broken glass. The killer wouldn't have been able to scale it unaided. He kept moving, the wall to his right, looking into the greenery around him, disturbing a jay that flew out of the bushes in a great bother. An overgrown privet bush blocked his path, and he was about to retrace his steps, when he caught sight of something wedged in a knot of roots at the base of the bush. Pulling on one of his gloves, he crouched down and retrieved it gingerly.

A knife, about eight inches long, the handle tied with red string, the blade thickly coated with dried blood.

The killer walked in here to get rid of it, Child thought. Didn't want to risk taking it out of the gate. Probably changed out of his costume at the same time, but he took that with him. Ezra Von Siegel ran to help when he heard Mrs Corsham scream, so he wouldn't have seen the murderer when he came back out.

Returning to the path, he followed the reverse of the route Mrs Corsham would have taken. Ahead, he could see the Rotunda, rising above the supper boxes and fountains, the shape of one of those little French custard cakes. The door stood ajar and Child walked inside, the shade a relief after the heat of the garden. Circling the walls, he studied the paintings. Pamela, laid out on a stone slab, a soldier readying his sword to plunge it into her. Lucy Loveless as Clytemnestra, butchering her husband and his concubine.

Both women had sat for Agnetti. The Priapus Club sat for him too. The artist seemed to be the lynchpin that connected the different strands of his inquiry.

A trestle table was piled with sketchbooks, unframed canvases and tools. Child picked up one of the canvas knives. It was identical to the one in his pocket, right down to the red string. Which meant it wasn't a chance slaying. The killer had known that Lucy would be in the bower. He took one of Agnetti's knives and went to find her. But why there? Why then? Why take such a risk?

Hearing raised voices and approaching footsteps, he put the knife down and stood back from the table. Jacobus Agnetti strode into the Rotunda, followed by a young, very tall girl with close-cropped fair hair – much like the one Ezra Von Siegel had just described. Child wondered if she was Agnetti's assistant, the one he'd read about in the newspapers. The pair seemed to be mid-argument, Agnetti's expression as dark as January, the girl on the verge of tears.

He stopped when he saw Child. 'What do you want?'

'I was just having a look at the paintings.'

'During the day, this room is private. Come back tonight, if you wish to see the exhibition.'

Feeling the weight of the knife in his pocket, taking a last look around at the bloody scenes on the walls, Child nodded. 'I'll do that,' he said.

Chapter Thirty

CARO PAIRED HER oyster satin with peacock feathers and her mother's sapphires. She applied white lead paint, a little carmine rouge, her eyebrows blackened with burnt cork. Finally, a few dabs of Attar of Roses.

All day she'd been unable to keep anything down. Between the bouts of vomiting, she'd slept, and Gabriel had cried because she couldn't face joining him and Mrs Graves on their trip to the park. Feeling a little better by the evening, she'd forced herself out to Carlisle House because she knew her suspects would be there.

The ballroom was a moving tapestry of damask and brocade; the orchestra playing a *contredance*, the dancers weaving in and out on invisible threads. Lieutenant Dodd-Bellingham cut quite a swathe as he strutted a duet at the head of the line, his partner a rather leaden-footed girl, heiress to a fortune in whale oil and ambergris. His brother, Simon, evidently returned from the country, was surrounded by a party of scholarly-looking men, who'd struggle to cut a swathe in a field of grass. Jonathan Stone prowled the peripheries, before guiding a worried-looking gentleman into an alcove, doubtless to discuss the parlous state of his affairs. And Lord March sported Clemency Howard on his arm, a smiling, dew-faced girl from a long line of Norman barons and minor Plantagenets. He was drinking too much and sometimes Caro felt his hot, angry gaze slide over her.

Other eyes were on her too, faces turning in the crowd. The attention puzzled her. Surely word of her misadventure at Vauxhall couldn't have spread so far, so soon? Not liking their scrutiny, in need of cooler air, she sought the privacy of the water closets off the cloakroom.

When she emerged into the corridor, she found Lord March waiting outside. Grabbing her by the wrist, he pulled her into a deserted billiard room.

'What the devil was all that about yesterday? Inciting that thief-taker of yours to question us like that?'

'I found Neddy's ring in the bower where Lucy Loveless was killed. You don't think that merited further inquiry?'

'Not like that, I don't. The Dodd-Bellinghams are one of us. You can't walk into our houses and question us like criminals.'

One of us, the old families. Even within the beau monde there were ranks within ranks, and those at the top of the tree never let you forget it.

'I ask again what all this is about? Some sort of strange Craven revenge for Miss Howard?'

'You believe highly in yourself, Lord March, if you think I'd use a woman's murder to get back at you.'

She had never seen him like this before. He looked like he wanted to hit her.

'What were you doing that night in the bowers?' she said. 'We both know you weren't taking a stroll.'

'You know what I was doing.'

'Do I? You never mentioned that you knew Lucy Loveless when we spoke the other day.'

'Barely. She was sometimes at Agnetti's house. What? You think I killed her and then waited around for you?'

'Then what *were* you doing?'

'I saw you leave the Rotunda and I followed you. I wanted

to tell you about Miss Howard. Now I wish I hadn't taken the trouble.' He took a folded sheet of newspaper from his coat pocket. 'Have you seen *The London Hermes*? Perhaps this will give you pause.'

A bead of sweat crawled down her spine. The popular scandal sheet was much-read in London society, the identity of those unfortunate enough to grace its pages thinly veiled by pseudonyms. Part of the game was to guess the identities, and it was never especially hard. This was a blood sport after all.

Those in attendance at Vauxhall on the night of the sensational murder of Lucy Loveless, may have descried the disappearance of Mrs Wiltshire from amongst their number. We have learned that this stalwart lady embarked to take the air, and thereby stumbled upon the grisly scene in the bowers. Where, one wonders, was Captain Wiltshire during his wife's hour of distress? In France, comes the answer, Mrs Wiltshire's Arcadian expeditions no less intrepid than they are solitary. How fortunate, then, that a certain gentleman was on hand to restore Mrs Wiltshire to serenity with his tender care. We hear this gentleman, like the lady, is fond of taking a turn in the bowers – such exertions between the pair of them, we wonder there is any air left to breathe!

Caro stared at the scandal sheet, appalled. This would explain why people had been looking at her in the ballroom: gossiping, speculating, casting judgement. Mordechai would be incandescent when he heard of it. And it would hardly make things easier with Harry.

'You need to stop all this, Caro. Think of your present situation. Why would you seek to draw attention to yourself at such a time?'

Scenting danger, her eyes narrowed. 'Breathe one word of my present situation, and I'll tell your father the child is yours. I shall name it after you, a little Fitzmarch. Harry will bring a suit against you for criminal conversation and I will give evidence in court on his behalf. What will Clemency Howard and her parents make of that?'

He held up his hands. 'Steady on, Caro. I won't tell a soul. Why would I?'

Because you don't like my inquiry into Lucy's murder. Because you played some part in all of this – I just don't yet know what. But he'd say nothing. Not when he stood to lose Clemency Howard, and with her his father's favour. Not when his inheritance was at stake.

'But my point still stands,' he said, moderating his tone. 'Why would you seek to make enemies of everyone who matters in London?'

'You and your friends are not everyone, Lord March. And if I make enemies by hiring a man to look into a brutal murder, then I have to ask myself why that is.'

'"Why" is the damn question. I don't understand why you're doing this. Nobody does.'

There wasn't one answer she could give him. Not one that he'd understand. *Because if she hadn't tried to help me, Lucy would never have been in that bower. Because when we thought she was* one of us *she mattered – and then she did not. Because a dead child casts a long shadow. Because where there is guilt, there is rage. Because even those at the top of the tree don't have impunity from murder, and their fall, when it comes, is the furthest of all.*

'That girl we asked you about: Pamela. Don't deny that you knew her.'

'The one in the drawing? I met her once or twice at Agnetti's house. I didn't recall it before, but Neddy reminded me.'

It sounded like lines he'd rehearsed for a play. 'No, I saw your face. You know what happened to her, don't you? You all do.'

He spoke coldly. 'I will submit to no further interrogations from you, madam. Your inquiry is ill-advised, your speculations fanciful. I intend to speak to Sir Amos Fox, to your brother too. Perhaps they can talk some sense into you, where I cannot.'

*

She had barely set foot back in the ballroom when he appeared by her side. Jonathan Stone, wearing his private smile and a sleek moleskin suit.

'I hear you reunited the ring with its owner. And hired a man to look into the Vauxhall murder. I trust your inquiry proceeds apace?'

'It has led us to a girl named Pamela – as I am sure you've also been informed.'

'My Iphigenia. Lucy developed a strange obsession with her. I counsel you not to do the same.'

'Lucy thought she'd been murdered. She suspected you, among others.'

'People often look for the worst in me. It is a cross I have to bear.'

'One you do not seem to find especially burdensome.'

Stone watched the dancers, unblinking. 'Appearances can be deceptive. Oh, don't mistake my meaning. I have no fear of the hangman's rope, but no man likes to stand accused of a crime he did not commit. Did you talk to him, as I asked? Brother Ambrose?'

'How could I? Ambrose is in Switzerland.'

He glanced at her askance, and his smile broadened. 'Talk

to him. Ask him about Jonathan Stone. I guarantee you'll see things differently once you do.'

She gazed at him, uncertain, not wanting to admit that she couldn't ask Ambrose anything; not liking his allusions, not knowing what they meant. 'I'm quite capable of forming my own opinion about you, sir.'

'Everybody does.' He swept an arm across the ballroom to encompass the beau monde. 'They call me a man of appetite, as if I should be ashamed of it. As if they themselves had never tasted forbidden fruit. It doesn't stop them taking my money, they leave their sanctimony at the door. Some even attend my parties – ask Brother Ambrose. A woman of appetite is, I regret to say, a different proposition. Her indiscretions are not just a scandal. They are a moral outrage. She is not just to be condemned, she must be cast out.'

His tone gave Caro pause. 'A story regarding my discovery in the bowers has somehow found its way into the pages of *The London Hermes*.'

'Then you'll understand,' he cried, delighted, 'how unpleasant it is to have people casting aspersions about your good name. Like me, you must be hoping this is the end of it.'

She held his gaze, eyes equally serious in their intent. 'Do you mean to threaten me, Mr Stone?'

'Sorry, was I too opaque? It was ever a failing of mine.' He gestured again to the chattering beau monde. 'This snake pit is not to my pleasure. I abhor their hypocrisy, but beneath this idealist lurks a shameful pragmatist. Know that I will use whatever tools I have to hand.'

Chapter Thirty-One

Child bought his dinner from a pie-man on Dean Street. The man jabbed his thumb through the crust and poured meat liquor into the hole, while Child kept a nervous eye out for Finn Daley. That he hadn't paid Child a visit yet disturbed him. The Irishman's laxity was so uncharacteristic as to be implausible.

He ate the pie as he walked down to Compton Street. The Golden Pear Tree was busy with gentlemen going in and out, many of those leaving heading for the tableaux house opposite. Child followed them, handing over a half-guinea to the doorman with a grimace.

The room was dark and cavernous. Perhaps two-score gentlemen sat at tables in front of a stage. A fiddler was playing pizzicato, an oriental tune, and several dark-haired girls onstage danced rhythmically. Seashells covered their breasts and their straw skirts swayed. 'Behold the maidens of the South Sea,' someone bellowed off-stage.

A lady of about sixty sat at a table to the rear, the only woman over twenty-five in the place. Surrounded by yellow-haired girls – presumably those who hadn't made the cut for the South Sea scene – the footmen jumped to her orders and the patrons treated her with respect. Mrs Havilland, Child presumed.

He edged his way through to her table, and the girls assessed him with bored eyes. Mrs Havilland's hair was artfully piled, adorned with silver shells and a golden starfish. Her unimpressed gaze travelled over Child's coat, belying her thin red smile.

'Beauty is bought by the judgement of the eye, sir.' She swept the air with a silver scratcher to point at the girls. 'But in this house, not by judgement alone.'

'I'm not looking to buy, but I am looking for a girl.' Child took out the drawing. 'Her name is Pamela. She was selling her maidenhead about six months ago. Did she do so here?'

The smile vanished, replaced by a flinty stare. 'All my girls are here of their own free will. They don't appreciate men asking questions. Neither do I.'

'I'm not here to cause trouble. Will you look at the picture, please? This girl has disappeared, I suspect unwillingly.' He held the drawing up so all the whores around the table could see it.

Mrs Havilland raised her scratcher to point at him. Seconds later, two pairs of big hands gripped him, and he was dragged from the room, bundled back down the corridor, out onto the street. One of the footmen put a boot to Child's arse, and he landed hard on the cobbles.

'Can I have my half-guinea back?' he called after them.

The door slammed. He wasn't getting back in there tonight. Child decided to return tomorrow, when he'd try to bribe one of the girls, or one of the servants. Cursing Mrs Havilland's name, he limped in the direction of Covent Garden, intending to resume his search for the link-boy, Hector. As he waited to cross the road at the junction with Greek Street, he felt a light touch on his arm. His hand leapt to his pistol, drawing it as he turned. His assailant let out a cry of alarm, stumbling back. Not Finn Daley, but one of the yellow-haired girls from the tableaux house. Heart pounding, Child returned his pistol to his pocket and held up his hands. 'Forgive me. I didn't mean to frighten you.'

She stared at him indignantly. 'Well, you did.' Glancing around, she lowered her voice. 'My name is Cecily. Pamela was my friend. Buy me a coffee and I'll talk to you – but I need to be quick.'

*

The coffeehouse was quiet, just a few whores sitting around the polished wooden interior, nursing cups of milky capuchin coffee, so-called because the colour of the coffee resembled the brown cowls of the monks. Drinking one was a signal to customers that a girl was for sale.

Cecily sipped hers daintily, occasionally smiling at Child so that onlookers would think he was a client. Broad-shouldered, with overly plucked eyebrows that gave her a startled look, she was well-spoken, with a slight edge of Essex.

'Pamela and I were up for sale at the same time. We shared a room. After I was auctioned, I didn't see her for a while. But I had some trouble at home, and I came back to Mrs Havilland's just before she left for good.'

'When was Pamela auctioned? Can you remember?'

'The end of February. But the gentleman who bought her didn't want her right away, so she stayed on at the tableaux house for another week. Then one night he came and collected her in a carriage. Pamela promised to come back and see me, but she never did.'

'Can you recall the date?'

'The first of March. She said it was the start of her new life.'

'Do you know who he was? The gentleman who bought her?'

'A redcoat officer named Dodd-Bellingham. I'd seen him in the tableaux house from time to time. Pamela talked about him a lot. She was sitting for the artist, Mr Agnetti, and she'd met him again there.'

'Was the lieutenant alone when he came to collect her?'

'He was with another gentleman – somebody said they were brothers. They came in a hired carriage full of girls from the Whores' Club. Pamela said they were heading to a private masquerade in the country.'

'Did you recognize any of the girls?'

She smiled shyly. 'I know all the members of the Whores' Club. I hope one day they'll let me join.' She counted four names on her manicured fingers. 'Rosy Sims, Ceylon Sally, Kitty Carefree, and Becky Greengrass. Pamela knew Kitty. They'd become friends at Agnetti's house.'

'This woman wasn't one of them?' Child showed her the second drawing.

'That's Lucy Loveless. She wasn't there that night. But she came later, like you, asking questions.'

'When was this?'

'In April. Mrs Havilland sent her away, but I followed her, just like I did with you. Told her the same things I'm telling you now.' She stirred her capuchin, looking at him intently. 'I read about Lucy's murder in the newspapers. Do you think it had something to do with this? With Pamela?'

'Yes, I do.'

'I knew it. That Pamela was dead, I mean. Even before Lucy came. Mrs Havilland said she had found a keeper, but I knew it couldn't be true.'

'Why not?'

'Because she never came back for her money. Mrs Havilland said she did, but she was lying. That's why she won't help you – she kept it for herself. A hundred and twenty-five guineas minus expenses. Nobody walks away from that.'

Child was inclined to agree, but he asked his next questions anyway. 'Is there any possibility that Pamela could be with her family? Or returned to service because she didn't take to this life?'

'Pamela never knew her parents. She grew up in an orphanage. And she hated being in service. That's why she was doing all this, for a chance at a better life. Something bad happened to her, Mr Child. I know it did.'

Child showed her the card with the satyr. 'Did you ever see Pamela with one of these?'

'She had one with her that night she left. It was an invitation to the masquerade. I asked her about the satyr and she said it was the symbol of their club.'

'The Priapus Club?'

'Yes,' she said, nodding, 'that was it. Pamela was nervous to be going, but excited too. She was sweet on the soldier, you see. Had a nosegay he gave her, which she kept until it fell to pieces. He wasn't rich, but that didn't stop her moping around.'

The lieutenant, who'd pretended not to recognize the invitation at his house only yesterday. 'How did he buy her at auction if he wasn't rich?'

'Perhaps he wasn't as poor as she thought? He couldn't have been, could he? Her maidenhead went for two hundred and fifty guineas. She looked young, see, which always gets a girl more.'

'Did she say anything else about him that you remember?'

Cecily thought for a moment. 'She said she had a rival. Another woman. She didn't say who.'

Child wondered if that rival was Agnetti's assistant, Cassandra Willoughby – he strongly suspected that she and Dodd-Bellingham were the couple that Von Siegel, the lamplighter, had seen heading for the bowers.

'I've heard the club has over a dozen members. You didn't see any other carriages? Other girls?'

'There weren't any others. Just five girls for five men. Pamela told me this night was special. Only the very best girls invited. But when I said that to Lucy, she shook her head.'

Child frowned. 'Who told you there were five men?'

'Lucy. She asked me if I knew who the others were. I told her I only saw the lieutenant and his brother.'

A fifth suspect. Nelly had thought Lucy only had four in mind, but that had been because of the four drawings. Perhaps this fifth man had never sat for a painting? Or perhaps he had been the one wielding the brush?

'Did Pamela ever talk about Agnetti?' Child was thinking of the knife he'd found that afternoon, and the scene he'd subsequently witnessed in the Rotunda.

'She said he was kind. I think she liked him – but not like that. He was old.'

'Did he ever try anything with her?'

'I don't think so. She would have said.'

'How about the lieutenant's brother, Simon? Did she ever talk about him? Or a gentleman named Jonathan Stone? Or a friend of the lieutenant's named Lord March?'

Cecily nodded. 'The last one, Lord March. Pamela liked to tell us about all the fine people she was meeting at Agnetti's house. We'd roll our eyes, but she didn't care. Proud as a peacock.'

'Did she ever mention an argument with any of these men? Or anything that made her feel uncomfortable?'

'She said Lord March had a fancy for her, and we teased her about wanting to be the next Countess of Amberley. To hear her talk, there wasn't a man on God's earth who didn't show an interest in her, but it didn't make her uncomfortable, she enjoyed it, played up to it.'

And maybe one of them hadn't liked that. Maybe he'd wanted to be the one in control. Some men did.

Child needed to find Hector. He needed to find Kitty Carefree and the other girls in that carriage. *But I'm getting there, Lucy*, he thought. *I'm on your trail.*

Chapter Thirty-Two

Lord March was talking to Lieutenant Dodd-Bellingham. Caro watched them across the ballroom, guessing from their tense faces that it wasn't their usual easy banter. Clemency Howard was watching them too. By her side, Jacobus Agnetti was talking to Lord March's mother, the Countess of Amberley, doubtless angling for a commission. Caro looked around for Simon Dodd-Bellingham, but she couldn't see him. She wished Jonathan Stone's threat had unsettled her less than it had.

Nicholas Cavill-Lawrence was laughing with the Earl of Amberley, but every time she moved, she felt his cold fish-eye upon her. She thought of the missing document in the bower, Cavill-Lawrence's interest in Jonathan Stone, the Home Office agents looking for Lucy's friends. *What's your part in all of this?* she wondered.

Lord March and the lieutenant walked across the ballroom, weaving between the dancers. Caro followed at a distance, through the courtyard garden, into the Star Room. The pair passed between the gaming tables, disappearing through a doorway that led to the kitchens.

Caro waited for a little while, but they didn't come out. Eventually, she walked over to the doorway herself, stepping back to avoid a striding waiter bearing a tray of griddled kidneys. There was no sign of her quarries. She couldn't imagine they had business in the kitchens. But halfway down the corridor was another door that looked as if it led outside.

Walking swiftly, she tried the door, and found that it opened onto a small dark courtyard. There was nothing much to see: a midden of kitchen waste, a few old pallets, a line of drying dishcloths and a rusting bucket. Over the strains of the orchestra, she could hear a murmur of male voices close at hand.

An alley led off the courtyard, and Caro edged around the wall to peer into it. Lord March and the lieutenant stood some yards away. She couldn't hear what they were saying, but from their movements it didn't look convivial.

The lieutenant held a fist before his face and, for a moment, Caro thought he might strike Lord March. Moonlight flashed on something clutched in his gloved hand. Lord March snatched it from him, and flung it away. The lieutenant said something else, and Lord March pushed past him, heading back towards the courtyard with a face like thunder. Caro drew back into the shadows, praying he wouldn't spot her in the dark. But he seemed intent only upon his own unsteady progress, stumbling into Carlisle House.

Turning back, she watched the lieutenant, who was gazing at the ground, walking up and down, presumably looking for the thing Lord March had thrown. He wandered around for a while like this, and then unbuttoned his breeches, urinating long and loud. Once he had finished, he emitted a soft belch and gazed around the alley again. Muttering beneath his breath, apparently giving up on his search, he walked back towards Carlisle House. Again Caro drew into the shadows.

At the door, the lieutenant paused, and took a long look around him. Then he ran a hand through his golden hair, brushed something from his redcoat, and walked inside. The door closed behind him, and Caro allowed herself to breathe again.

She walked down the alley to the spot where she'd seen them talking. It stank of cat and urine and rotting food. At the end of the alley, in the distance, she could see carriages trundling past on Soho Square. What had they been arguing about? The thing in the lieutenant's hand? She looked around her, trying to work out how far Lord March might have thrown it.

She walked back and forth across the alley, poking mounds of unpleasantness with her slipper. After about ten minutes of careful searching like this, she caught sight of a metallic glint in a pile of vegetable peelings and rags. Wincing, the stench of urine sharp in her nostrils, she retrieved it with her handkerchief. A silver necklace with a charm on the chain: a tiny hand with a turquoise bead on either side. It had an exotic look, not English in design. She wondered if it was old, like the jewellery she'd seen in Stone's collection.

The music stopped, and she heard applause and approaching footsteps. Slipping the necklace into her panniers, she turned. A man was striding towards her from the Carlisle House end of the alley. He wore a wide-brimmed hat, and she made out the long beak of the plague doctor's mask. Fear curdled in her stomach. She turned and ran.

She could hear him behind her, the rasp of his breath, the fall of his feet. Her own feet skidded on the cobbles, and her muscles burned. Up ahead, she could see lights and passers-by. She tried to call out to them, but couldn't find the air. Then he was on her, dragging her back, an arm across her throat. She fought him, clawing for the mask. At any moment, she feared a knife would slide between her ribs, but he only forced one arm behind her, marching her on towards the lights.

Hope flared. What was he doing? Why was he taking her

towards safety? Carriages rattled past, their lamps dazzling. She was still fighting him, but he was too strong, forcing her on into the square. Caro could see her own carriage and footmen, drawn up with many others outside Carlisle House. She took a breath to call out to them, but the man released her without warning, throwing her away from himself with tremendous force.

She landed hard on the cobbles, the air expelled from her lungs. Her ears filled with a tremendous clatter, and twisting, she saw a carriage bearing down on her. Foam on the horses' nostrils, the sharp iron of their hooves. A stench of horse sweat hit her hard. She rolled.

Her face struck the cobbles and she tasted blood. She cried out as one of the coach wheels grazed her leg. Then as the carriage rattled on, she drew a sobbing breath, and all she could hear was Miles calling her name.

PAMELA

23 January 1782

Pamela stared at the canvas. The lines of chalk and charcoal. Light and shadow. She could discern arms, legs, a nose: her and Peter Jakes. The line of his sword. A bulge of muscle in his arm as he held her down.

'Who is she, Mr Agnetti? The girl I'm supposed to be?'

'Her name was Iphigenia, the daughter of a Grecian king named Agamemnon. The Greeks were going to war with the kingdom of Troy, and on the eve of their embarkation, one of his soldiers accidentally killed a deer belonging to the goddess Artemis.'

He was growing on her, the Italian, despite his grizzled jowls and his paunch and his salt-and-pepper hair. He liked her to ask questions, and thought about the answers he gave. This one she knew.

'Artemis is the goddess of virgins.'

'Strictly speaking, that is Hestia. But Artemis was renowned for her virginity too, as well as her capacity for vengeance. Alarmed, the Greeks consulted a seer who said that in order to appease Artemis, Agamemnon must sacrifice Iphigenia.'

'His own daughter?'

'He told her she was going to be married. That's what she thought the altar was for.'

'The poxy gullion.' She clapped her hands to her mouth. 'I'm sorry.'

He smiled. 'No, it is probably a fair description. What would be going through her mind, do you think? Fear, hope, confusion? Something more?'

'Anger,' Pamela said. 'Her da is the person supposed to keep her safe.'

'Anger wouldn't make her father change his mind. Pity might. Tears and so on. Wouldn't that be a woman's calculation?'

'You can't calculate for feelings. Not the ones that bubble out of you. Anger's the worst for doing that.'

'So it is.' Agnetti considered a moment. 'But I think fear is what people will expect. I might make a few more sketches. Can you think of something frightening while we work?'

Returning to the altar, she thought of the cupboard in the two-room orphanage, the darkness, the smell of must, the spiders. Mrs Rosell had used to lock her inside it when she refused to say her prayers. She tried to recall terror, but remembered only rage: at her parents for abandoning her; at the other orphans for their compliance; at Mrs Rosell for her grating voice and old patched shoes.

Fake it, she thought. Like the Pamela on stage at the tableaux house when Squire B tears her dress. Eyes full of submission, the way they like it.

*

Two hours later, the door opened and Mrs Agnetti entered the studio. She was wearing another of her ridiculous turbans, this one a vibrant scarlet in hue.

'Jacobus,' she said, 'Greyling says you told him I wasn't to take the carriage out today.'

'Dr Latimer says it isn't wise for you to go out. I thought we could take supper together. Vermicelli, to remind us of Naples.'

'But we agreed that I would go. I accepted the invitation.' She turned to Pamela, who was suddenly conscious of her bared breast. 'Leave us. I want to talk to my husband alone.'

Agnetti frowned. 'Speak to her kindly, Theresa.'

'I will speak to her any way I choose in my own home.'

Bitch. Pamela smiled sweetly. 'I don't mind.'

Agnetti put down his brush. 'Go and join Lucy and Kitty. I will send for you shortly.'

Downstairs in the morning room, she found Kitty at the tea table, playing solitaire. The lieutenant's box of rose-petal macarons was by her arm. Lucy was lying with her feet up on the sofa.

'They're arguing,' Pamela said. 'Mr and Mrs Agnetti.'

'Last time *he* wanted to go out,' Kitty said, 'and *she* didn't want to go. Whatever he wants to do, she wants the opposite.' Her eyes flicked to the decanter. 'He's right. She shouldn't go. Theresa needs to take better care of herself now.'

'If she drinks,' Lucy said, 'it's because she's unhappy. He bears a responsibility for that, don't you think?'

'He is kind to her,' Kitty said. 'Tries to make her smile. Could have any harlot in town he wants and chooses not to. Would that I were so unhappy.'

'A prisoner in your own home? Him your gaoler?'

'Since when was it a crime for a man to care for his wife?'

'There are no crimes between husbands and wives. Short of him cutting your throat. That's the trouble with marriage.'

Lucy and Kitty seemed to have slipped away from the Agnettis, into some wider argument they'd had before.

'Not all marriages are unhappy,' Kitty said. 'Some are full of love.'

'And some of hate.'

'Will Lieutenant Dodd-Bellingham be there?' Pamela said. 'Wherever she wants to go to supper?'

Lucy frowned. 'She said it was just ladies. Why do you ask?'

'No reason.' She poured herself a bowl of chocolate, wondering if Agnetti suspected what his wife was up to. 'Does Mr Agnetti really never tumble his sitters?' The newspapers suggested otherwise.

'Never, though many have tried. He only has eyes for his wife.'

'When he's not ignoring her for days,' Lucy said. 'Closeted away up there painting.'

Kitty sighed. 'One day you'll meet the right man, Boleyn. Handsome, rich, kind, and he'll *adore* you, just like Mr Agnetti adores his wife. And you'll turn your back on happiness because you're stubborn.'

'And will he ride into town on a unicorn, this man?'

'Why do you call one another that? Aragon? Boleyn?'

'We first met at a brothel in St James's called Hampton Court Palace,' Kitty said. 'Six girls, each named for one of King Henry's wives. Nobody ever wanted poor Ann of Cleves, so they changed the name.' She popped a macaron into her mouth. 'Here, there's only two left. Do you want one?'

'What was that card the lieutenant gave you?' It had been nagging at Pamela for days. 'The one with the man-goat.'

'An invitation to a masquerade out in the country.'

'At the lieutenant's house?'

'Lord, no. The Dodd-Bellinghams haven't owned a country house in thirty years.'

'But he'll be there?'

'And plenty of better gentlemen. It's the sort of rout where a girl might find herself a rich husband.'

Lucy snorted. 'Dreaming don't make it so.'

'It happens,' Kitty protested. 'Remember Lavinia Fenton, who became the Duchess of Bolton?'

'When you're a duchess, then you can say "I told you so".'

'When I'm a duchess, I'll find good husbands for you all.'

'You can keep mine,' Lucy said. 'Buy me a country house instead.'

'I'll buy you nothing if you don't stop being such a cynic.' Kitty flounced. 'The money's good anyway. Twenty guineas a night.'

'No constables. No watch. No one to hear you scream.'

Kitty threw the last macaron at Lucy's head. 'Stop scaring the girl. Mr Stone would never let a harlot get hurt.'

A door slammed upstairs.

'She'll be crying,' Lucy said.

Tears . . . a woman's calculation. Except Mrs Agnetti wouldn't even convince at the tableaux house.

'They were happy once,' Kitty said. 'Maybe they can be again. If she's a little kinder. If he tries talking to her properly. Maybe things will change, when . . .' She curved a hand in front of her stomach.

'When a baby isn't being sick, it's screaming,' Lucy said. 'When was that ever a wand to wave over a marriage?'

Pamela frowned. Was Mrs Agnetti with child? And if so, then who was the father?

Chapter Thirty-Three

'You could have been killed,' Mr Child said.

Caro studied his horrified face. 'Well, I wasn't. Just a little bruised.'

She had covered the graze on her cheek with lead paint, and Emilie, her ladies' maid, had bandaged the cut on her leg. The jolting of the carriage along Oxford Street jarred her aching bones, but all told, she'd been lucky. Haltingly, she told Child about the attempt on her life.

'My footman, Miles, picked me up off the street and I sent him after the plague doctor. There was no sign of him in the alley. He must have gone back into Carlisle House. Miles asked around inside, but nobody had seen him. I suppose he had removed his costume by then, just as he did at Vauxhall Gardens.'

'He's bold,' Child said. 'I'll give him that.'

Mordechai had turned up at her door at ten, having heard all about it. He'd whisked her off to Bow Street, where he'd torn strips off the magistrate.

'It is unconscionable,' he'd said. 'I insist that you do more. We're no longer talking about a dead whore. A man who would murder my sister might murder anyone.'

Sir Amos had been much less solicitous today. 'There was a reason he chose you, though, wasn't there, Mrs Corsham? I understand from Lord March that you have engaged a thief-taker to look into the murder at Vauxhall.'

Mordechai stared at her incredulously.

'Yes, I have,' Caro said. 'I want Lucy's killer caught.'

'As do we all,' Sir Amos said. 'But I hope last night demonstrated the folly of your actions. Leave this matter where it belongs, madam, in my hands.'

Remembering the business with the missing documents, and the magistrate's closeness to Nicholas Cavill-Lawrence and the Home Office, Caro was past trusting a word he said. The attack last night had frightened her, but it had angered her too – her rage hardening her resolve.

Mordechai had lectured her all the way home, as much about the scandalous story in *The London Hermes* as about the attempt on her life. She'd barely bothered to argue. How could she expect him to understand? Mordechai, who had never in his life felt the compulsion of desire. The heat of a lover's body. The rush of watching the hazard dice tumble and fall. The need to know who'd killed a woman who'd died in your arms.

'Dismiss this thief-taker from your service,' had been his parting words. 'Do it at once.'

'Did you get any sense of him?' Child asked now. 'Height? Weight?'

'He wasn't a short man, but I had my back to him most of the time. He was strong enough to manhandle me along the street.'

'You have the waist of a wasp, madam. Ninety-nine men out of a hundred could do the same.'

The carriage had halted again, caught up in Oxford Street's endless tide of coaches, chairs, curricles and phaetons. Bewildered country folk, come to London to see the sights, stared at the shop windows with their displays of painted fans and china plates, the pyramids of sugar plums and exotic fruits.

'They were all there,' Caro said. 'Our four suspects. Jonathan

Stone threatened me not long before it happened. And Lord March and Lieutenant Dodd-Bellingham had been in the alley just minutes before.'

'Would they have had time to get changed into the costume?'

'Yes, I think so. Just about.'

'Why throw you in front of the carriage? Why not just knife you in the alley – forgive me, madam – like he did with Lucy?'

'If my death was thought to be a murder, my brother wouldn't have rested until the killer was caught. This way it would have looked like an accident.' She breathed deeply. 'We have him rattled, Mr Child. It suggests to me that we're doing something right.'

'Oh, we're making progress, that's for sure.' She listened as he told her about his visit to the tableaux house and his conversation with Pamela's friend, Cecily. 'I think we can safely presume that the Dodd-Bellingham brothers took the girls to Stone's estate that night, and that Lord March too was a guest at this masquerade. Neither he nor the lieutenant mentioned it, and if they didn't precisely lie, that's a devil of an omission. As far as I'm aware, nobody's seen Pamela since. Cecily shared Lucy's view that something bad happened to her there. I'm inclined to agree.'

'As am I.' Caro frowned. 'And she mentioned a fifth suspect? Why, this inquiry does not narrow, it only expands!'

'My best guess is Agnetti.' Child told her about the knife he'd found at Vauxhall Gardens and the scene he'd witnessed afterwards between the artist and his assistant. 'He knew both Lucy and Pamela, he has a temper, and he isn't shy of losing it with women. He also had the means and the opportunity to kill Lucy. The murder weapon belonged to him.'

'Couldn't someone else have taken the knife from amongst Agnetti's tools? I saw several at the Rotunda the other day.'

'It's possible. Was Agnetti at Carlisle House last night?'

'Yes, he was. And he did say he had once attended the Priapus Club. Perhaps he was talking about that night with Pamela?'

'There's more,' Child said. 'I went to the offices of *The Public Advertiser* this morning, and read up on our friend Agnetti. Want to know something interesting? Theresa Agnetti disappeared on the first of March, the same day Pamela went to the masquerade.'

'You think there is a connection?'

'It seems rather a large coincidence. Two women who likely knew one another, both disappearing on the same day. The newspapers say Mrs Agnetti walked out of her house that evening, taking no money and no clothes. She left no letter, no explanation. She simply vanished.'

'Are you suggesting that Agnetti might have killed her too?'

'He wouldn't be the first husband to dispose of an unwanted wife that way. The newspapers say the marriage was unhappy.'

'I think it was.' Caro thought for a moment. 'Mr Agnetti hired a thief-taker to find his wife, as I recall. My sister-in-law, Louisa, answered his questions. Why would Agnetti do that, if he had killed her?'

'To make it look as if he hadn't. Did your sister-in-law know the wife well?'

'Louisa tried harder with Theresa than anyone. She wasn't always easy company.'

'Could you talk to her? You must concede the timing's odd.'

'Very well. But there are other possibilities for our fifth suspect too. Nicholas Cavill-Lawrence, for one. The Home Office must be taking an interest in Lucy's murder for a reason.'

'Couldn't Lord March be that reason? Pamela told Cecily

that he had a fancy for her. His father, the earl, could surely pull strings with the Home Office?

'Yes, he could.' Caro was long past any instinct to defend him. Courting Clemency Howard behind her back. Whoring with Jonathan Stone. Lusting after a fifteen-year-old virgin.

She showed Child the necklace she'd found in the alley. 'Lord March and the lieutenant seemed to be arguing over it. It made me wonder if it had belonged to Pamela or Lucy.'

Child examined it. 'I'll show this to Cecily. And if she doesn't recognize it, then I'll take it to Lucy's landlord.'

'It's rather exotic: that odd little hand and the beads. I wondered if it was old, like the jewellery in Stone's collection?'

'I could ask Solomon Loredo. He would know.' Child slipped the necklace into his pocket. 'The lieutenant certainly has questions to answer. The owner of the supper house he gave for an alibi says he wasn't there – he doesn't remember seeing Simon either. But the lamplighter, Von Siegel, places a gentleman matching the lieutenant's description in the bowers at the time of the murder.' He told Caro his theory that the woman Von Siegel had seen with the gentleman – the one who'd left the bowers in tears – was Agnetti's assistant, Cassandra Willoughby. 'Cecily told me that Pamela had a fancy for the lieutenant, but that she had a rival for his attention, another woman. I thought it must be Miss Willoughby, but according to the newspapers, she didn't come to London until the spring.'

'That's right,' Caro said, recalling all she'd read and heard about Agnetti's scandals. 'It was an elopement gone awry. Her lover abandoned her. She'd not been in London long when Agnetti took her in.'

'Then Pamela's rival must have been someone else. You did say the lieutenant was something of a rake. Did you talk to Agnetti about the ring?'

'Yes, he confirmed the lieutenant's story that Lucy had stolen it. But then I suppose Agnetti could be lying too – if he is involved, as you suspect. Why would Lucy steal the ring? To what purpose?'

'I can't think of one. Von Siegel remembered seeing a letter in the bower, by the way. I think we can safely presume that it's now in the hands of the Home Office. And my rooms were searched the other night. They must still be looking for this second document, whatever it is.'

They had come to a halt in Broad St Giles's, caught up in a herd of sooty sheep being driven to slaughter. The animals jostled against the carriage, and the feral smell of their fleeces only heightened Caro's nausea. She closed the window, sucking on a ginger comfit.

'I think all four of them know what happened to Pamela,' Child said. 'Stone, the Dodd-Bellingham brothers and Lord March. Perhaps they're all involved. Or the other three are scared of Stone. Loredo said that he likes to learn his debtors' secrets.'

'I hate to think what else they might have been up to. As for Stone, he is cavalier about his reputation, but even he'd struggle to shrug off the murder of a fifteen-year-old prostitute at his estate.'

'He certainly has no shortage of enemies who would like to see him brought low. Loredo told me that some City aldermen recently tried to have him investigated for dealing in illegal loans, but the Home Office wanted no part in it. I wonder if that was Cavill-Lawrence's doing too.'

'Stone put a nasty story about me in the newspapers, and threatened to do more.' Caro sounded more light-hearted about it than she felt. 'I received this in the post too.' She showed him the puzzle purse.

Child unfolded it to examine the paintings and the message inside. 'Could this be Agnetti's work?'

'Whoever painted it has talent, but why would Agnetti have sent it? It only points suspicion his way.'

Child grunted, conceding the point. 'Well, it wasn't an idle threat. I ask you once again, madam, to leave this business to me. Let me talk to Mr Dodd-Bellingham alone.'

'We have been over this, Mr Child. I know these men – the way they think. Besides, the killer already knows that you're working for me.'

'At least promise me you won't put yourself in danger again. I don't want you talking to any of our suspects alone. No more situations like last night.'

'Very well. I'll keep my footman close.'

They turned into Bloomsbury Square and the carriage rattled to a halt outside the Dodd-Bellingham residence. Child opened the door and jumped out, holding up a hand to assist her down.

Caro looked up at the house. 'I can hardly believe they went along with it. The buying and selling of a fifteen-year-old child at auction. I wouldn't have put anything past Stone or the lieutenant, but I thought better of Simon and Lord March.'

From Child's expression, he had no such reservations. 'I wonder which one of them did the deed. Took Pamela's virginity, I mean. The lieutenant? He was the one who bought her.'

Caro's voice was quiet and hard. 'Let us find out.'

Chapter Thirty-Four

Grimmond, the Dodd-Bellinghams' elderly manservant, stood back to allow Child and Mrs Corsham through the scullery door. The mews yard was weed-strewn, with high, lichened walls on either side and a dilapidated coach house. A young man of about twenty-five, whom Child presumed to be Simon Dodd-Bellingham, was standing in front of the open coach-house doors, applying some sort of paste to a marble statue of a naked woman. She was pointing into the distance, her extended arm held in a clamping device.

He straightened when he saw them. 'Mrs Corsham, good heavens. Grimmond, what were you thinking? This is no place to receive a lady.'

'Don't blame poor Grimmond,' Mrs Corsham said. 'I insisted.'

She made the introductions, and Simon eyed Child warily. With his horn-rimmed spectacles and bad teeth, he was a sorry specimen indeed compared to his brother. Child recalled Mrs Corsham saying that his mother had been a celebrated beauty. Not much evidence of it here.

'I am relieved to see you looking so well, madam,' Simon said. 'I heard there was an incident at Carlisle House last night.'

'Thank you for your concern, but I survived unscathed, as you see.' Mrs Corsham studied the statue. 'She's rather fine. Who is she?'

He smiled uneasily. 'Persephone, my older woman – by about two thousand years. One of my agents in Athens dug her out of the ground at Delphi. Mr Stone has a new fountain at a Berkshire estate which will suit her perfectly.'

'The arm was broken?'

'In transit. Greek porters are perfect vandals, but I have secured the arm by knocking in a pin. Once I've filled the gaps and sanded her down, no one will know.'

'We're also looking to fill some gaps,' Mrs Corsham said. 'We'd like to talk to you, if we may, about Lucy Loveless.'

Simon glanced from one to the other, his face slick with sweat. Mrs Corsham hadn't been lying about his nerves.

'My brother told me that you called the other day. I'm afraid I can add little to what he told you. I was in the Rotunda until just after nine, when Neddy and I left to dine at the Prince of Wales supper house in Covent Garden.'

Mrs Corsham gave him a flinty look. 'Lucy Loveless believed a fifteen-year-old girl named Pamela was murdered six months ago. She had several suspects in mind for that murder, and you were one of them. We know you and your brother collected Pamela from a tableaux house in Soho, and took her to a masquerade at Stone's estate on the first of March. Nobody has seen her since. The owner of the Prince of Wales doesn't remember seeing you on the night of Lucy's murder and he is certain that your brother wasn't there. Which means you've already lied to us once. So if you want us to believe you had nothing to do with any of this, I suggest veracity, Mr Dodd-Bellingham – and much of it.'

Child shot her an admiring glance. It was like having Torquemada on your team.

Simon blinked his dismay. 'Then you'd better come inside.'

The coach-house walls were lined with shelves, a chaos of

paint pots, glass bottles, and jars of coloured powders. More clutter filled the room: racks of chisels, brushes and knives; coils of rope and spools of string; a barrel of nails; another of saw-dust; and more clamping devices. Several tables were scattered with bits of broken statue: disembodied arms, feet, heads, as well as fragments of mosaic and broken pots. A desk groaned under the weight of papers and leather-bound volumes. The air smelled of paint, a welcome respite from Mrs Corsham's ginger comfits, which reminded Child, all too painfully, of his dead wife. In the centre of the dusty floor stood a large pottery urn.

'Don't touch it,' Simon exclaimed, as Child wandered over to take a look. 'The paint's not yet dry.'

The urn was decorated with a frieze of glossy black figures. A man poised to penetrate a woman, who was writhing against the buttocks of a second man; he, in turn, poised to enter another man from behind, who was kissing a woman between her open legs.

Child grinned. 'Looks like quite a party.'

'My apologies, Mrs Corsham.' Simon closed his eyes. 'The Athenians could be rather indecorous.'

'Is that piece for Mr Stone?' she asked. 'It looks to his taste.'

'I hope to sell it to him, yes, once it's restored. Such pieces are highly collectable, with prices to match.'

He pulled out a chair for Mrs Corsham – the only one in the room – and she sat, arranging her skirts around her.

'Let's start with Lucy Loveless,' Child said. 'Did you know her?'

Simon's gaze flicked between them. 'My brother says I must have met her at Agnetti's house, though I don't recall doing so. I don't consort with his sitters as a rule. But I certainly met her in May. She came to see me.'

'To ask you about Pamela's disappearance?'

'Yes. I told her I knew nothing untoward, which is the truth.'

'Do you deny that your brother bought Pamela at auction, and that you were with him when he collected her from the tableaux house?'

'No, why should I? We did nothing wrong.'

'A fifteen-year-old girl,' Mrs Corsham said. 'Traded at auction like horsemeat.'

His voice faltered. 'It was her choice to sell herself. The age of consent is twelve.'

'It shouldn't be.'

'Your brother and Lord March said nothing of this when we questioned them the other day,' Child said. 'Why do you think that was, if you did nothing wrong?'

'For the same reason I didn't mention knowing Lucy when I saw Mrs Corsham at Mr Stone's the other day. I had no desire to set hares running again. Lucy, as you say, had constructed certain notions about us. Pointing fingers, crying murder – and no truth to it at all.'

'So where's Pamela now?'

'I haven't the first idea. My brother dropped the girls back in Soho the morning after the masquerade. He says Pamela seemed perfectly content, and was looking forward to getting her money. You can ask him.'

'I'd rather ask the girls.'

'They'll tell you exactly what they told Lucy. Neddy brought her back safely to London. Nothing happened.'

'Who else was there that night at Stone's estate?' Child said. 'Apart from you, your brother and the girls?'

'Just Mr Stone and Lord March.'

'How about the fifth man?'

His Adam's apple bobbed. 'What fifth man?'

'Five girls for five men. That's what Lucy said.'

'She was wrong. There were only four of us. One girl is – forgive me, madam – rarely enough to satisfy Stone.'

The trouble with nervous men was that they looked as guilty when telling the truth as they did when they were lying. Which made them hard to judge. Child watched the sweat roll off him, gathering his thoughts. 'Doesn't the club have over a dozen members? Why so few of you on that night?'

'This meeting was just for the founders. We discussed some administrative matters that would have bored the wider club, and then had dinner with the girls.'

'Had you ever met Pamela before that night?'

'Yes, once at Mrs Havilland's, and then a few times at Agnetti's. She was a bold little piece for her age. Always stopping to talk. I could hardly avoid her.'

'Where did your brother get the money to buy her virginity? Two hundred and fifty guineas, wasn't it? From Stone?'

'I presumed so. Neddy is always bringing him girls. When you owe Stone money you can't repay, he finds a use for you.'

'You bring him antiquities. Your brother brings him girls. What does Lord March bring him?'

'Nothing any more. His father settled his debts upon his engagement. But previously he introduced Mr Stone to many gentlemen of his acquaintance: noblemen like himself, seeking to borrow money against their expectations. Or men who might otherwise advance Stone's business interests. A name like Amberley opens many doors.'

'Do these gentlemen ever come to the Priapus Club?'

'Some of them are members, yes. But I've told you – it was only the four of us who were there that night.'

'So you did. Tell us about your club, if you will. What does it mean, Priapus?'

Looking extremely reluctant, Simon took a box down from

a shelf and rummaged through it. He set a small bronze figurine on the desk. A little man with a beard and an ugly, leering face. In his hands he held his enormous, erect penis.

'Priapus was a fertility god to the ancient Greeks and Romans. A son of Aphrodite, he was cursed by Hera in revenge after his mother won the golden apple. Shunned by normal society, he joined Pan and the satyrs in bacchanalian revels.'

'Satyrs like the one on Stone's invitations? The cards your brother hands out to the girls?'

'That's right.'

'Satyrs are rapists, are they not?'

Simon shook his head. 'There are many different myths, most in conflict with one another. But if you mean to make an inference about our club, then you couldn't be more wrong. All the women who come to our masquerades do so willingly. They are more akin to muses than whores.'

'I heard they are paid well for their time. That sounds like whores to me.'

'Naturally they are paid, but Stone insists the girls are treated with respect. Equality between the sexes is one of the foremost principles of our club.'

'Your brother mentioned the club's philosophy. Can you tell us more about it?'

'We revere the natural condition,' Simon said. 'Man as God intended: tolerant, free, given full liberty to his desires. I have made an extensive study of the cult of Priapus, from artefacts found at the sites of Pompeii and Isernia, and they suggest these beliefs were once commonplace in ancient Rome. As club members, we try to uphold these same principles in our daily existence.'

'By fornicating with harlots?' Child pointed to the urn. 'Something like that?'

Simon took off his glasses and wiped them on the sleeve of his shirt. 'There is a physical expression of the club's beliefs, I don't deny it. We call it the generative principle.'

'I can think of a few other names for it,' Child said.

'Many of the great men of Athens visited the temple prostitutes. The women were said to bring enlightenment through ecstasy. Socrates himself is known to have frequented the brothels.'

'What is that gesture Stone makes with his hand in his painting of the Priapus Club?' Mrs Corsham asked.

Simon bowed his head. 'Please don't make me say it in front of you, madam.'

'I thought you believed in equality between the sexes?'

He screwed up his eyes, looking utterly miserable. 'It is supposed to represent the private parts of a lady. Mr Stone believes that women – in their natural condition, freed from the bondage of marriage – have the same appetites for pleasure as do men. The Church has always feared female desire and shamed women for it.'

'And Mr Stone is to be our liberator?' Mrs Corsham said dryly. 'My sex is fortunate indeed to have such a champion.'

'Pamela certainly had desires,' Child said. 'For your brother – that's what we heard. Was it Neddy who took her virginity that night?'

He sighed. 'I don't know. I wasn't there.'

Child frowned. 'You just said that you were.'

'I was, at first. But when the debauchery began, I went for a walk.' Simon's gaze fell on his statue of Priapus. 'It is an odd thing, desire, is it not? As red-blooded men, we are supposed to want every woman we meet, the younger the better. But I often wonder how much of that performance is a fear of looking foolish in front of one's friends?'

'You don't like women?'

'I like them very much. Virtuous, kind women. Not whores with their wanton humour and bawdy tricks. I rarely touch the girls at the masquerades – and I certainly didn't touch Pamela. If you must know, I also thought she was too young. After I left the masquerade, I wandered around Stone's estate, until I thought they'd all be asleep. Then I returned to the house. The place was in darkness, but I roused a servant and went to bed. When I awoke, Neddy and the girls had already gone.'

'From what you've told us,' Mrs Corsham said, 'the physical side of the club is largely the point. If you dislike it so much, then why not leave?'

'Because I owe Stone money I cannot repay, and I have no desire to end up in the Fleet Prison. As long as I am useful to him, I have value. I fit out his houses with antiquities, I seek out writings to support his philosophy, I attend his club and, to my shame, sometimes I demean myself with his whores. Perhaps in time, I'll get out from under this wretched debt. Until then, I go wherever Mr Stone points.'

'Then you don't believe in it? The club's philosophy?'

'I believe in tolerance and difference. How could I not, given my background? I am interested in the study of the fertility cults and early religion, but that doesn't mean we should adopt their practices ourselves. The Church can be dogmatic, certainly, but marriage, when it is founded upon mutual regard, is the highest expression of God's love.' He gazed at them, a picture of anxious sincerity.

'There was little mutual regard in the Agnetti marriage,' Child said. 'Mrs Agnetti disappeared on the same day as Pamela. Do you know anything about that?'

He looked surprised by the change of subject. 'No, I barely knew Agnetti's wife.'

'Did she know Pamela?'

'I presume so. Pamela was sitting for Agnetti, and he maintains a liberal household. I believe Mrs Agnetti often spent time with his sitters.'

'Did you ever hear any talk about where she might have gone?'

'Only the usual unkind rumours – lovers and so forth. My mother was the subject of gossip all her life, and so I try to pay it little heed.'

Child grunted. 'Your lie about being with your brother at the supper house on the night of the Vauxhall murder: was that to protect you or him?'

'We may have lied, but our intentions were entirely honourable. Neddy was with a lady at Vauxhall that night. He didn't wish to compromise her reputation, but given his history with Lucy, he was worried about not having an alibi.'

'He was right to be worried.'

'Look, Neddy is hot-headed sometimes. He likes women, as our father did. Sometimes he can be an ass when in drink. But he is good-hearted beneath it all, not a killer.'

'Do you know who this lady was? His companion?'

'No, he didn't say, and I didn't ask.'

'So where were you that night, if not with your brother?'

'In the Prince of Wales dining alone. I can't help it if they don't remember me.' He smiled ruefully. 'I have a forgettable face.'

The earnest, blinking scholar. As an act, it did well to convince. But looking at Mrs Corsham, Child judged they'd reached the same conclusion: Simon Dodd-Bellingham was still lying through his teeth.

CHAPTER THIRTY-FIVE

✳

THEIR INQUIRY WAS becoming a many-headed Hydra, writhing and dangerous in its multiplicity. Back home in Mayfair that afternoon, Caro felt a need to impose order on her thoughts. Her nausea had passed, but her back ached like Tartarus, so rather than sit at her escritoire, she took her ledger and inkpot to the wingchair in Harry's bookroom. A small square chamber, fitted out in walnut and painted panels; the smells of leather and beeswax reminded her of her husband.

What would he say if he could see her now? Embroiled in a sensational murder – after she'd reacted with such anger last year, when he'd embarked upon his own murder inquiry in Deptford. His friend, Tad, had been killed, and Harry had refused to stand aside. Call it justice, call it vengeance. Now she understood a little better.

Thinking about her husband and the past, old resentments slid into her mind like needles. Every lie. Every memory of her trusting foolish self.

Ambrose would have told her to forget, if she couldn't forgive. *You're a Craven – we don't give a damn, remember?* Lord knows she'd tried, but her anger had proved impervious to reason. Now she'd need to be a new Caro: humble, contrite. Could Harry ever forget? Could he forgive?

As terror at her situation threatened to creep back into her soul, she forced herself to concentrate upon her inquiry. Picking up the card from the Magdalen Hospital, the one that Mr Child had found in Lucy's rooms, she examined it again. The cryptic jotting on the reverse: *50–60 pineapples, 2s 1d*.

She shared Mr Child's opinion that it could not be a receipt – not at those prices. Could it be a reference from a book? A note of a conversation? Some sort of cipher? Could it have a connection to the Magdalen Hospital – given it was on the reverse of the card? Or did it have nothing to do with their inquiry at all?

Coming up with no good answers, she put it to one side, and picked up the puzzle purse. No ambiguities there. Caro studied the paintings again: the rutting couple, the plague doctor, Lucy's bleeding corpse. She read the threat inside, unable to suppress a shiver.

Opening her ledger, dipping pen in ink, she made a list of all those connected to their inquiry whom she knew could paint. Jacobus Agnetti was the obvious place to start, though she still thought it unlikely that he'd have implicated himself in such a fashion. Then there was Simon Dodd-Bellingham – she recalled the vase with the copulating figures he'd been restoring in his workshop that afternoon. Lord March had dabbled in all the artistic pursuits – as had Kitty Carefree, whose entry in *Harris's List* had praised her accomplishment at watercolours. Caro hadn't the first idea about Jonathan Stone, nor Lieutenant Dodd-Bellingham, though the latter seemed unlikely.

Pomfret knocked and entered the bookroom. 'A Miss Willoughby is here to see you, madam. Something about a contract and a painting? Oh, and Mr Cavill-Lawrence called earlier. He waited for a time, but when you didn't return by two, he had to leave.'

What had Cavill-Lawrence wanted? To chastise her again? To question her about her inquiry? Or had he taken the opportunity of his visit here to have a poke around her things – just as his agents had poked around Mr Child's rooms, looking for this mysterious missing document?

Why were the Home Office protecting a killer of prostitutes? Why did Jonathan Stone have Cavill-Lawrence looking so troubled? Was he the fifth man at Muswell Rise on the night of the masquerade, or was he simply protecting his influential friends?

Mulling over these questions, she walked into the drawing room to find Miles standing over Miss Willoughby. The pair were talking, though they broke off when they noticed her in the doorway. The girl rose, and they shook hands.

'Do sit down, Miss Willoughby. Would you care for tea? No? Miles, be so good as to wait in the hall.'

Cassandra Willoughby cut a boyish figure with her height and flat chest and close-cropped fair hair, blue eyes stark against her porcelain skin like Delft china. A wide canary-yellow sash brightened her muslin gown, yellow slippers peeping beneath the hem. She produced some papers from a calfskin case.

'Mr Agnetti asked me to tell you how much he is looking forward to beginning work on your portrait. All you need to do is sign this document and return it, along with your deposit of forty guineas.'

'I will have my lawyer look at it and, assuming everything is in order, I will bring the deposit to Leicester Fields tomorrow. But if you don't mind, I do have one or two questions first. Mr Agnetti said you were an authority on his work.'

She smiled. 'He flatters me. But I will endeavour to answer any questions that you have.'

'Do you assist him with his painting, as well as with his clients?'

'I prepare his canvases. And sometimes I work on the

drapery and landscapes. Though please be assured that Mr Agnetti does all the figurative work himself.'

'Where did you learn to paint?'

'I had a drawing master. He saw I had ability – as did Mr Agnetti.'

'I am glad of it. A woman should be able to fulfil her talents.' Caro paused. 'Miss Willoughby, I wish to discuss a delicate matter. I am sure you heard about the woman lately murdered at Vauxhall Gardens? It was I who found the body, and consequently I have an interest in seeing the killer caught – as I hope all right-thinking people would. Can I ask if you left the Rotunda at all that night?'

'That is a very strange question, given the context.'

'Strange, but also important. A woman matching your description was seen entering the bowers not long before the murder, together with a gentleman in an officer's redcoat. My thief-taker and I believe that officer to be Lieutenant Edward Dodd-Bellingham. You are acquainted with him, are you not? From Agnetti's house?'

Miss Willoughby flushed. 'I never left the Rotunda.'

Caro spoke gently. 'I would never normally pry into a personal matter, you understand. But there can have been few other women present at Vauxhall that night matching such a striking description. The witness who saw you said that when you left the bower, you looked upset.'

As she did now, her fingers twisting the fabric of her dress.

'Perhaps you are afraid that Mr Agnetti will find out? I give you my word that he will not. I ask you only to trust me. More lives might depend on it.'

Miss Willoughby could be no more than twenty years of age, but sitting there like that, her long limbs constrained by tension, she looked younger. 'You think more people could get hurt?'

'I think it's possible, yes. We believe Lucy was not the killer's only victim.'

She drew a sharp breath.

'Was it you my witness saw?' Caro pressed again. 'And Lieutenant Dodd-Bellingham?'

Miss Willoughby gave a swift nod, staring down at her hands. Her voice, when she spoke, was little more than a whisper. 'I am sure you have heard the stories of how I came to London. How I was duped by a man I thought I loved. Had Mr Agnetti not taken me in and offered me employment, I cannot say to what depths I might have sunk. Through that act of generosity, he gave me a reason to trust again – which led to a mistake almost as grave as the first. The name of that mistake, as you have correctly conceived, is Lieutenant Dodd-Bellingham.'

Caro smiled sympathetically. 'Do I take it that he, too, deceived you in some fashion?'

'Perhaps I also deceived myself.' She bit her lip. 'The lieutenant comes often to Leicester Fields on business for Mr Stone, who is an important patron of my master. Over the past three months, I have had many dealings with him concerning Mr Stone's commissions. I confess that at first I found him charming. Eager to stay and talk once our business was concluded, considerate in conversation, ready to laugh at himself. In short, an intimacy formed. I was not so naïve, given his debts and my own situation, as to think that the lieutenant was in any position to act upon his feelings. Yet I had no doubt that those feelings were sincerely held.

'On the opening night of the exhibition, he came to the back room of the Rotunda, where I had been working, to ask if I would take a walk with him in the gardens. I should have refused, but I have few enough other friends in London, and as I said, I enjoyed his company very much.' She drew another long breath and her words came out in an angry flood. 'We strolled and talked, until I found myself in an unfamiliar part of the gardens. Drawing me into one of the bowers, he tried to kiss me. I slapped him and he grew angry. His attentions became more forceful, but I managed to push him away, and in drink, he stumbled. I ran back to the Rotunda, and I have not seen or spoken to him since.'

Caro shared the girl's anger, and placed a hand on her arm. An attempted rape would explain why the lieutenant had asked his brother to lie about his whereabouts on the night of the murder. Especially when that incident placed him in the bowers – alone, angry, his blood up – at precisely the time Lucy was killed. If he made a habit of such attacks, then it also gave him a motive for Pamela's murder. She might have had a fancy for him, but a woman could change her mind. And even with a willing woman, certain men could turn violent.

'I am sorry,' she said. 'What the lieutenant did to you was unforgiveable. It makes me wonder what else he might be capable of. Did you see anyone acting suspiciously as you ran away? A man in a plague doctor's mask?'

'Not that I remember.'

'Did you ever see the lieutenant with such a costume?'

'No, never.'

'Or recall if he carried a bag that night?'

'I don't. I am sorry.'

'Was Mr Agnetti in the Rotunda when you returned?'

'Yes, I'm sure he was.'

'How about Mr Stone?'

'I don't remember.'

'How did Mr Agnetti seem that night?'

'Preoccupied with the exhibition. Concerned about how his work would be received.' Miss Willoughby smiled through her tears. 'There was no need for him to worry. These paintings are his finest to date.'

'You admire him?' *Enough to lie to protect him?*

'Of course. He is a great artist.'

'The man I have hired to look into the murder heard him speaking to you in anger yesterday at Vauxhall. You were upset on that occasion too.'

'Oh, that.' Her gaze slid to the floor. 'Someone saw the lieutenant and I together as we were walking in the gardens that night and reported it to Mr Agnetti. He was very angry, which distressed me. Normally he addresses me with every courtesy.'

'Mr Agnetti never struck me as a moralizing sort of man. Quite the reverse.'

'That's why I was so upset. I didn't understand his fury. If he found out that we'd gone to the bowers, I think he'd dismiss me.'

'Well, he won't hear it from me. Do you think it possible that Mr Agnetti was jealous?'

'Of the lieutenant? Why would he be?'

Did she need it spelled out? 'Your residence in his house has given rise to speculation.'

Her eyes blazed. 'First you ask if I am the lieutenant's whore, now you ask if I am Mr Agnetti's. You dishonour me, and you dishonour him with these questions. He has offered me only kindness since I met him.'

Caro studied her heated face with a mixture of curiosity and pity at her predicament. Some might call her a gullible fool – to be taken advantage of twice – but some men were adept at preying on sad, lonely women. So much sadness there, she felt. So much anger too – at Caro, at the lieutenant, at all the world save Mr Agnetti.

'I only meant that Mr Agnetti might have feelings that he himself cannot acknowledge. If the question was indelicate, then I apologize. I simply seek the truth about this murder.'

'Then you are talking to the wrong person, for I know nothing that can enlighten you, save that Mr Agnetti is an honourable man, and Lieutenant Dodd-Bellingham is a liar and a brute.'

*

Miles escorted Miss Willoughby to the door. Again, Caro heard them talking in the hall. When the footman returned, she gave him an inquiring look. 'You and Miss Willoughby seemed to have much to discuss.'

He raised his russet eyebrows. 'The other day, while you were upstairs at Agnetti's house, she asked me my opinion on his paintings. She showed me one of her own too. I was just asking her if she'd finished it.'

'Why did she care what you thought about her painting?'

'I have eyes, madam.' He grinned. 'It was just a ruse to get me talking. She wanted to know about you.'

Caro frowned. 'What about me?'

'Whether you might commission any more paintings, and whether you used other artists. She has an eye for Agnetti's business, I suppose.'

'I don't want you talking to her about my private matters.'

'I never would, madam.' He looked offended. 'She asked me about myself too. Now there's a rarity.'

Caro gave him a look. 'Is there something you wish to tell me about yourself, Miles?'

'Not really. My mother's been sick. But it's nice to be asked.'

'Talk to Pomfret, if you need time to visit, or an advance

upon your wages.' She closed her eyes, overwhelmed by weariness, and Miles took the hint.

A little later, when she felt rested, she returned to Harry's bookroom. Looking again at her list, she thought about adding Cassandra Willoughby, but decided against it. The girl hadn't even been in London when Pamela had disappeared, and her connection to Lucy's murder seemed purely peripheral.

> *Jacobus Agnetti*
> *Simon Dodd–Bellingham*
> *Lord March*
> *Kitty Carefree*

She added the names of Jonathan Stone and Lieutenant Dodd-Bellingham to her list, resolving to find out if either man was skilled at painting.

A long list. Too long. Too many people with motives opaque. The truth concealed by lies and obfuscation, like the folds of the puzzle purse.

Chapter Thirty-Six

CEYLON SALLY, ONE of the four girls on the list that Child had been given by Cecily, was the same pretty Indian who'd spoken out against Lucy at the Whores' Club. A hard-eyed, hard-bitten little meretrix, about eighteen years old, her arms jingled with silver bracelets, signalling her irritation with Child's questions. He had already spoken to two of the other whores on the list, Rosy Sims and Becky Greengrass, tracking them down in Soho and Covent Garden respectively with *Harris's List* as his guide. Sally's replies were proving depressingly familiar.

'Pamela?' she said, in soft, accented English. 'I remember her. She came with us to a masquerade. Virgin.' Her finger traced ancient graffiti in the tavern tabletop. Around them young gentlemen diced and drank and sang bawdy songs.

'Did Lucy Loveless come to speak to you about that night?'

'Three times.' She yawned. 'Dull questions on a dull subject.' Her black eyes flashed. 'Must be contagious.'

'Then you'll know that Pamela hasn't been seen since. Do you know what happened to her there?'

'She cracked her pipkin. Sold it for two hundred and fifty guineas. Then she slept with the smile of Venus, as did we all. One of the gentlemen dropped us back in Soho the following morning. Last time I saw Pamela, she was off to collect her money. She's probably in the arms of a handsome swain, sipping the finest Lisbon by the sea.'

'You're sure that's all that happened?'

Another fierce jangle of her bracelets. 'Quite sure.'

'I know that the lieutenant and his brother picked you up in Soho and that the masquerade took place at Mr Stone's estate. Lord March was there too. Which one of them took Pamela's virginity?'

'I don't recall. There was wine, hashish.' She made a vague gesture. 'You pay attention to the man you're with if you want to be invited back.'

'So who were you with?'

She shrugged. 'I don't recall.'

Child sighed. 'Tell me about the fifth man. Could he have been the one with Pamela?'

Her eyes were unreadable, the pupils dilated, perhaps with laudanum. 'What fifth man?'

The other girls had given him much the same story, and Child didn't believe a word of it. They hadn't asked for money to answer his questions – that was the first clue they were lying. And their stories were too similar, often word for word. They'd been paid off, was his best bet. Either that, or they were scared. Perhaps both.

Yet he still wanted to find Kitty Carefree, the fourth woman on the list. Until a few months ago, she had been Lucy's dearest friend. Even if she'd also been paid for her silence, Lucy's murder might be enough to prick her conscience.

Child spent the next few hours touring the Covent Garden fleshpots, buying drinks, talking to whores and their clients. He never stopped watching out for Finn Daley, still baffled that the moneylender hadn't yet paid him a visit. Was it too much to hope that he'd dropped dead?

In the course of his tavern travels, he discovered that Kitty was well known and well liked, the toast of the Bedford

Coffeehouse in her youth, her past a long trail of titled gentlemen and wealthy merchants who'd loved her then discarded her when they'd grown bored. Nobody could tell him who was keeping her now, only that she'd not been seen out on the town since the spring, which was when the footman at the brothel in Soho had said she'd moved out.

'Kitty Carefree?' one young gentleman said, lifting his head from his tankard just long enough to squint at Child. 'Girl has a cunt like a split fig.'

Which sadly wasn't going to help Child find her.

Pamela: missing, presumed dead. Kitty Carefree: missing, presumed alive. Theresa Agnetti: missing, presumed alive, murdered, dead by suicide – depending on who was doing the presuming.

Too many missing women to Child's mind. They'd all known one another, all spent time in Agnetti's house – just like Lucy Loveless. He was convinced that the fates of those four women were connected.

As day slid into dusk, and he was walking past a jelly-house in Maiden Lane, he glimpsed a familiar face through the curved window. Pushing open the door, he squeezed past the counter of blancmanges and jellies, sparkling like jewels in the candlelight.

'Remember me?'

Hector grinned. 'How could I forget?' His pert, knowing voice was all at odds with his downy cheeks, expressive eyes and tousled blond hair. The boy dipped his spoon into his glass – a ribbon jelly set in coloured layers – and sucked on it suggestively.

Child took out the invitation. 'Did you put this in my pocket?'

'Felt sorry for you, didn't I? Blundering around like that. Inspire pity in a Puritan, you would.'

Child sat down at the table, lowering his voice. 'Lucy believed a girl named Pamela had been murdered. She thought Jonathan Stone or one of his friends might have been responsible. Is that why the Whores' Club wouldn't help me? Because the girls risk losing their money from his masquerades?'

'You learned something then.' Hector gave Child a round of mocking applause.

'Do you know anything about Lucy's inquiry? From your time working for Kitty?'

He took another mouthful of jelly. 'I might do.'

'I take it you didn't put this in my pocket out of civic duty?'

'Now you come to mention it, I do like a present, sir. A silver nutmeg, a golden pear.'

'The King of Spain's daughter?'

'I'd rather have the King.'

'I'll give you five shillings – but only if I consider your information worth it.'

'Oh, I'm always worth it. I'll take a golden guinea in lieu of that golden pear.'

'Half a guinea. Take it or leave it. Your choice.'

'You old skinflint.' But he was smiling. 'Meet me by the entrance to the King's Mews in half an hour.'

'Why can't we talk here?'

'Because I have no great desire to have my belly cut open at Vauxhall Gardens. Never know who's watching, do we?' Hector scraped back his chair, raising his voice: 'No, I won't talk to you, you dirty old goat. Stop touching me.'

People looked round. 'Nasty pederast,' someone said.

Flushing, Child turned an indignant face on Hector, but he'd already danced out the door, laughing.

CHAPTER THIRTY-SEVEN

DEFINE PURGATORY. FOR Caro, it was time spent in the company of her sister-in-law, Louisa, and her friends.

It being a remarkably fine evening, their hostess, the Duchess of Shropshire, had announced that badminton would replace cards as the game of choice. Her footmen had set up a net in the half-acre of private garden to the rear of her Piccadilly mansion, and brought chairs, sofas, and tables out onto the grass. Caro, lying on a Chippendale daybed, watched Clemency Howard and another girl bat a shuttlecock back and forth in the golden sunlight.

Around her, the duchess, Louisa, and half a dozen other ladies sipped bergamot punch and nibbled cheese wigs and other pastries. The moment Caro had arrived, she had been besieged with questions, everyone wanting to know about her brush with death outside Carlisle House. The ladies laboured under the misapprehension that the near-miss had been a dreadful accident, and Caro said nothing to disabuse them. Only Louisa, who would have had the real story from Mordechai, raised the occasional eyebrow. Eventually, they tired of the topic, and the conversation moved on to indolent servants and inattentive husbands.

'I'm having my portrait painted by Jacobus Agnetti,' Caro said, during a suitable pause in these discussions.

'Is that wise?' Louisa asked. 'All things considered?'

The women exchanged glances, all doubtless having read *The London Hermes*. 'I meant Agnetti's scandals,' Louisa said hurriedly.

Pregnant again, her sister-in-law sat proud and pink and placid in a pale-blue bergère hat and a sack-back gown let out in front. Caro would have to tread carefully if she didn't want the conversation getting back to Mordechai. Louisa was one of those calm, sensible women who rarely contradicted their husbands, but behind her round blue eyes was a mind ticking away like a Janvier clock.

'Agnetti is a perfect poppet,' the duchess declared from beneath her wide straw hat. 'Oh, he's a little stiff at first, I grant you, but when you sit for him, you'll find him really quite charming. He opens up about himself, and really sees the person one is. He says a good artist has to – see into the mind of his sitter, I mean. He painted me as Aphrodite and we hung the portrait in the red dining room. We're to use him again, to paint the ceilings at Stonelands.'

The duchess had false teeth of mottled jasper that clattered when she talked, an old-fashioned fondness for white French wigs, and a penchant for bees. Occasionally one would drift over from the hives at the bottom of the garden and everyone would pretend not to mind.

'Have you met her yet?' Lottie Heneker asked. 'The assistant?'

Caro had known someone would ask, and she might have guessed it would be Lottie. A silly, dimpled creature, wife of the Solicitor General, you could always count on her to cheat at cards and spread slanderous gossip.

'Miss Willoughby brought my contract over earlier today,' Caro said. 'I'm not sure there's any truth in the rumours.'

Sally Carmichael gave a cynical smile. 'Why would Agnetti

invite scandal if it wasn't in some way to his benefit? A man doesn't take a woman half his age into his house unless he wants one thing.'

A penniless cousin of the duchess, Sally often took her resentment at her situation out on others with a brutal bluntness. *I would too*, Caro thought, *if I was forced to traipse around as a companion, condemned to read novels aloud and collect honey dressed in rural costume.*

'She assists him with his work,' Caro said. 'Even paints the scenery in his portraits.'

'Just because she's deft with a brush, doesn't mean she's devoid of other talents.' Lottie said.

'I am with Caro,' the duchess declared. 'Nor did I ever give any credence to those stories about him and his sitters. Agnetti loved his wife and misses her dreadfully.' She broke off to applaud. 'Oh, good hit, Clemency.'

'Evelina Missingham met someone who knows the Willoughbys,' Sally said. 'They're old Northumberland gentry. Evelina says the mother died, and the father doted upon the girl. Perhaps too much. The foolish child should have waited and got herself married off. Instead she eloped with her father's secretary.'

They had all heard variations upon the tale. 'After they married, the money soon ran out,' Lottie said. 'First the secretary abandoned her. Then it turned out they weren't really married after all. He'd simply got a friend of his to dress up like a parson. I've heard she lived for a time at a boarding house in Paddington, earning money from her painting – if you believe that, which nobody does. Agnetti met her in Leicester Fields and admired her work.'

'He admired something,' Sally observed dryly.

'Perhaps Agnetti was lonely,' Louisa said. 'Without Theresa, without children, in that big house all by himself. He still hopes Theresa will come back to him, I've heard.'

The duchess reddened. 'He should take a horsewhip to her if she does. I never liked her from the first. There was something dark and cold and secretive about that woman.'

'She could be warm enough when she wanted to be,' Sally remarked slyly. 'Remember that time you caught her flirting with His Grace?'

'I've heard, on occasion, she did rather more than flirt.' Lottie smiled, with an arch of an eyebrow.

They turned as one. 'What?' 'Do tell?'

Lottie took her time, enjoying the attention. 'Christopher Whitaker tells a story of a ball at Spencer House last year. He was looking for the cloakroom, and walked into the billiard room by mistake. He found it already occupied – by Theresa and a certain gentleman of our acquaintance. He wasn't teaching her how to pot the balls either.'

'Good heavens.' 'Who?' 'You must say!'

'Lieutenant Edward Dodd-Bellingham,' Lottie pronounced with satisfaction.

Well now, Caro thought, amidst the murmurs. Even for the lieutenant this was swift work. First, he'd seduced Agnetti's wife – then with her out of the picture, he'd moved on to his assistant. She wondered if Agnetti had heard the rumours about the lieutenant and his wife – it might explain why he'd been so angry with Miss Willoughby. And presumably Theresa was the rival whom Pamela had mentioned to her friend, Cecily.

'Now that's a pretty revenge,' Sally said. 'For Agnetti's dalliances with his sitters, I mean.'

'Theresa told me she didn't believe the stories about his sitters.' Louisa sounded distressed. 'And I always thought, beneath the flirting, that she loved her husband very much.'

'Come now, Louisa,' the duchess said sternly. 'You know how you always think the best of everyone.'

Louisa sighed. 'She wanted a child, that much was obvious. I saw the way she looked at mine. And do you remember the time Imogen Chandos-Murray said she was expecting, and Theresa made her cry? I think that was the cause of the unhappiness between her and Mr Agnetti. Perhaps Theresa felt the fault of their barren marriage was not her own? Women in such situations have been known to resort to desperate measures. It's the only explanation I'll entertain.'

'She'd never have got a baby this way . . .' Lottie glanced over at the younger girls playing badminton, and dropped her voice to a whisper. 'Christopher says Theresa was on her knees and she had the lieutenant's member *in her mouth.*'

Sally gasped. Louisa blanched. 'You should not say such things, Lottie.'

'I'm only saying what I heard. Christopher swears it is true.'

'I wonder if we ever really knew Theresa at all.' Louisa sighed.

'Could the lieutenant be keeping her somewhere, do you think?' Caro said.

'Of course not,' Sally said. 'He has no money for a start. He was sniffing around Emily Chandos-Murray for a time, until Imogen told her she couldn't possibly afford him.'

A collective sigh arose as the women ruminated upon the tragedy of penniless men with faces like Lieutenant Dodd-Bellingham's.

'He is certainly his father's son,' the duchess said, and there was a chorus of agreement, every woman present having a story about the time the colonel tried to kiss her in a cupboard.

'Poor Neddy,' Lottie said. 'He returns from the colonies a hero, only to find a rather unattractive cuckoo in the family nest. I wonder, having seen Simon, that the colonel owned him at all. Not a bit of the old man there.'

'What do you make of him?' Caro asked. 'Simon Dodd-Bellingham?'

'Mordechai says he is a fine scholar,' Louisa said. 'He's thinking about getting him in to take a look at our library.'

'I wouldn't, if I were you,' the duchess said.

'Why ever not?'

'I was going to get him in too. Thought he could help Freddie start a collection: engraved gemstones or fossils. He needs something to fill his evenings now he's given up politics. I had our steward make inquiries and he heard a troubling rumour about wandering hands. Not up ladies' skirts like his father, but into his clients' pockets.'

'Good Lord.' Louisa frowned. 'How very shocking.'

Mr Child had said that Stone liked to deal in his clients' secrets, Caro recalled. She wondered if he could be blackmailing Simon? Yet how much of a secret could it be, if the duchess knew it?

'Simon has never struck me as dishonest,' she said. 'Who is he supposed to have stolen from?'

'Ansell Ward, the City alderman. You know how merchants like to try it on with a library of Latin – well, Simon was employed to catalogue his books. And apparently Ward is convinced that he stole from him. There wasn't enough evidence for an arrest, but he was summarily dismissed. Freddy thought we shouldn't run the risk.' She raised her voice to a boom. 'Very well done, Clemency.'

They applauded as the players walked back to join them. Miss Howard's face was flushed and smiling. 'I do like to win. I know I shouldn't.'

Caro moved up to make space for her, and Clemency smiled her thanks. 'Will you play, Mrs Corsham?'

'Not today. I don't much like to run around. Did anyone ever hear a suggestion that Theresa's disappearance was not as voluntary as we all thought?'

Lottie looked up, eyes shining. 'Foul play?'

'Well, why not? It wouldn't be the first unhappy marriage to end that way.'

'An outrageous suggestion,' the duchess said. 'Agnetti hired the best thief-takers in the kingdom to find his wife.'

'Not just here in England,' Louisa said. 'Mordechai says he has an agent in Naples looking for her right now. And he has written to India to engage a man there. Whatever Agnetti's deficiencies as a husband, he can't be faulted in his efforts to find her.'

'What good would it have done him to murder her anyway?' Sally Carmichael asked. 'If he wanted to be rid of her, he could have put her in the country – he's rich enough. Without a funeral, he can't remarry, so what's in it for him?'

'Who is to say it was planned?' Caro said. 'People say he has a temper. Perhaps he found out about Theresa and the lieutenant?'

'I never heard him speak unkindly to her – even when her behaviour warranted it,' the duchess said. 'He was always gentle and kind, and Freddie says he is fierce in her defence at the club.'

'The lieutenant, then?'

'Neddy Dodd-Bellingham would sooner kill for a beefsteak than for love,' Lottie declared. 'I doubt this *amour* with Theresa was a matter of the heart. On his side, at least.'

'What then, suicide?'

'Oh, Caro. Surely not.'

'Then where is she?'

Answer came there none, and signalling her boredom with the topic, the duchess remarked upon Clemency's gown. That sparked a debate upon India cotton versus lawn, with one daring voice speaking up for tamboured muslin.

Was Theresa Agnetti even relevant to their inquiry? Caro could not help but think that she was. Mr Child was right. Her disappearance so close to Pamela's own did raise troubling questions – especially if both women were rivals over Lieutenant Dodd-Bellingham. Did this mean that their inquiry had grown again: three murders, rather than two? Or had Theresa Agnetti played a darker, more active role in this strange story?

CHAPTER THIRTY-EIGHT

CHILD FOUND HECTOR leaning against the gatepost of the King's Mews, watching the cavalry officers riding in and out. Lights wove around Charing Cross: footmen with torches leading sedan chairs; carriage lamps bouncing with the movement of the horses; link-boys escorting whores from job to job. Hector held his own torch in front of him suggestively, reminding Child of Simon's statue of Priapus.

'That wasn't funny back there.'

'A little bit, it was. You follow me and we'll talk. Agreed?'

Child took an uneasy glance around, thinking about Finn Daley again. The boy might be leading him into a trap. 'Where are we going?'

'Got to look the part, sir. Anyone sees us together, I don't want them thinking it's information you're buying.'

Reluctantly, Child followed him down Cockspur Street. 'Lucy thought it was all odd from the start,' Hector said softly, his words drifting back to Child. 'The girls who are usually invited to the Priapus Club are women of the town: young and beautiful, but experienced. This particular night, they wanted a virgin and Lucy wanted to know why. It wasn't usual for them to meet like that either, just a few of them. The masquerades are normally held at full moon, a dozen or more gentlemen, perhaps two dozen whores. This night, Lucy suspected they were up to something they didn't want the rest of the club to see.'

'Something involving Pamela.' Child's face was grim.

Hector nodded. 'Lucy said Stone trusted the others, the Dodd-Bellinghams and Lord March, because they owed him money and he knew their secrets.'

'I heard there was a fifth man. Did you ever hear anything about that?'

'Lucy asked me about him too. She was trying to find out who he was.'

'When was this?'

'A little while after Kitty moved out.'

'What did you tell her?'

'That the girls talked about a fifth man the morning after the masquerade.'

'Go on.'

'The lieutenant dropped the girls off at Kitty's rooms at about nine. It was earlier than I was expecting – I wasn't long in bed. Kitty had twisted her ankle and the others helped her up the stairs. They were acting strange, quiet, like something was up. While I was making them tea, I heard them talking. One of the girls, I think it was Rosy Sims, asked the others about the fifth man – "the one with Pamela". Well, everyone got angry then, and Ceylon Sally said that Rosy should never speak of it again. Then Kitty saw that I was listening, and told me to go and buy more tea, though we didn't need any. When I came back, the girls were gone and she gave me a hug, a little tearful. Told me she'd buy me a present for being so good, but she never did.'

The fifth man, the one with Pamela.

'This girl definitely wasn't with them?' Child showed him Pamela's picture.

Hector shook his head. 'Is that her? Kitty talked about Pamela sometimes, when she'd come home from Mr Agnetti's. She liked her, but then Kitty liked everyone.'

'Did you ever hear any talk about a document? Some papers? Or a letter? From Kitty or Lucy or anyone else?'

Hector turned, his eyes blazing in the light of his torch. 'They asked me about that too. I told them I didn't know anything about it.'

'They?'

'A couple of coves came to see me last week, asking me questions about Kitty. Big. Well dressed. Knew the law.'

Official sorts. Like the men who'd been looking for Kitty at her rooms. Like the late Richmond Baird, agent of the Home Office.

'Were you telling them the truth?'

'Don't you start. Took me an age to convince them. They held a knife to my balls. Most fun I've had in months.' Despite his bravado, Child could tell the episode had rattled him.

They cut through an alley that brought them out on the fringes of St James's Park. Ahead of them stretched the Mall, a wide, gravelled path flanked by lamps, park-walkers and their customers flitted in and out of the shadows like bats. Hector headed away from the lights, towards the Horse Guards parade ground, the night air pierced by a shriek from the waterfowl patrolling the pond.

'Tell me about Lucy and Kitty, their falling out,' Child said. 'Was that because of Pamela?'

'That's obvious, isn't it? Kitty tried to talk Lucy out of doing what she was doing – she said Pamela had left town, she was alive and well. Lucy didn't believe it, not for a moment. Kitty had come into some money lately and Lucy wanted to know where it had come from. Kitty said her duke had given it to her for old times' sake, but Lucy called her a liar and Kitty cried.'

'Were you in the room when they argued?'

'No, but I have ears, and doors have keyholes. They didn't

speak after that. It upset Kitty. She and Lucy had been friends for years. I think that had a lot to do with her moving out. She didn't tell me where she was going. I think she thought I might tell Lucy. Lucy came looking for her, you see, after she left.'

'Could it be true what they say on the street? That she found herself a new keeper?'

'Not one I ever met. She'd only been seeing her regulars.'

'Where else could she be?'

'Sometimes she'd leave town to take the waters, used to say she needed a rest from all the men. Given how she'd been acting lately, that's what I presumed.'

'How had she been acting?'

'Anxious, distracted, upset about Lucy. She'd always been that way – the sort who'd cry after the men went home – but this was worse. She was praying a lot. She'd always done that too. But lately, she'd been doing it more – and going to church, over at St Andrew-by-the-Wardrobe.'

'Had she ever dismissed you before when she went away?'

'No, but usually she only went for a week at a time.'

Four months was a long rest. And Kitty had been anxious, praying. Perhaps guilty about whatever had happened to Pamela.

'Did Kitty ever talk about giving it up? Prostitution?'

'Sometimes. I didn't take it seriously though. What else would she do? Where would she go?'

Throw herself upon the charity of the Magdalen Hospital for Penitent Prostitutes? Child was thinking about the card he'd found in Lucy's rooms. Had Lucy guessed that Kitty had decided to change her life for good, perhaps motivated by remorse? Had she gone looking for Kitty at the Magdalen? That would explain why no one had seen her out on the town.

They had reached the corner of the park, the black hulk of

the abbey looming large over the old houses. Birdcage Walk stretched off to the right, a darkened promenade of trees. Ragged boys of Hector's age stood in little clusters by the shrubbery, talking and smoking pipes. A man sidled up to them, coins were exchanged, and one of the boys led the man into the bushes.

'Oh no, you bloody don't.' Child grabbed Hector's collar, pulling him up short.

He grinned. 'You never know, you might find out you like it down here, sir.'

'A man can hang for what they're doing in those bloody bushes.' Child resented the distraction, still trying to think everything through. 'What did Ceylon Sally mean at the Whores' Club, when she said Lucy had used up all her chances already?'

'They'd tried to blackball her once before. About a month before they threw her out for good.'

'Who did?'

'Sally, Rosy and Becky. Kitty had already left town by then.'

'They targeted her because of Lucy's inquiry?'

'Looks that way, don't it?'

'You don't know?'

'It was before they took me on as secretary.' Hector looked at him askance. 'I could find out, though. Take a peek in the club minutes. For the right price.'

'I'll give you another half-guinea,' Child said, 'but I want you to do some other things for me too. Ask around at the Whores' Club, find out if any of my suspects have a taste for young girls.' He produced a list of names that he'd made earlier in the jelly-house. 'I also want to know if any of them have a reputation for violence. You'll see Agnetti's name on that list too. I want to know what he does with his sitters – what he does with Cassandra Willoughby. Whether he did anything with Pamela or Kitty or Lucy. And anything the girls witnessed between him and his wife. Arguments, flying fists, that sort of thing.'

'Don't want much, do you?' But Hector took the list. 'It'll take me a couple of days. You know St Bennet's, by the river? Meet me there at midnight, the day after tomorrow.'

Child gave him the first half–guinea, and the flash of gold attracted the attention of the boys by the bushes. One made a move towards them, but Child stopped him with a look.

'I liked Lucy,' Hector said, perhaps feeling the need to justify the money. 'I had to take the news to her when the Whores' Club threw her out. She'd lost almost everything by then. Her job sitting for Agnetti. Most of her clients. She said the lieutenant had got Jonathan Stone's man of business to look into her past – that's how they'd found out about Bridewell. I asked how she was going to survive, and she said: "How I always do, H. I am Lucy." Only this time she didn't, did she?'

'She was playing a dangerous game,' Child said, gazing back across the park towards Covent Garden.

'I told her to stop,' Hector said. 'Her inquiry, I mean. I said the Whores' Club might take her back, make an exception. I asked how she expected to beat them, even if she did find out the truth. Those gentlemen were important, powerful, protected. She smiled then, like she knew something that I didn't. "They think they are," she said, "but their greatest strength is their greatest weakness." Don't even ask me what she meant. I've no idea.'

PAMELA

28–30 January 1782

In the days that followed, Pamela discovered many more secrets.
She learned, for instance, that Lieutenant Dodd-Bellingham
had an enemy, and she was responsible for delivering him from
that enemy herself.

She had been walking across Leicester Fields to Agnetti's
house – her watcher, as usual, by her side. Her boots were worn
and patched, her feet damp in the snow. Peddlers selling kindling and chestnuts stamped their own feet for warmth. Their
whistles followed Pamela across the piazza. 'Show us your bubbies, miss. We won't bite.'

She turned to give them a piece of her mind, but the words
dried on her tongue. She'd spotted the lieutenant striding across
the piazza, vivid in his redcoat. As she watched, a man walked
up to him, short, but powerfully built. He had long black hair
and a straggly black beard, his clothes dirty and torn. The lieutenant stopped when he saw the man and Pamela slowed her
own pace. Their words were snatched away on the wind, but
their faces weren't friendly. The lieutenant put his hand on the
man's shoulder, and pushed him away.

Pamela was close enough to see the man bare his blackened
teeth. The lieutenant walked on, but the man ran at him full
pelt, launching himself onto his back. The pair went down in

the snow, and the man rained punches upon the lieutenant. Pamela ran, taking her watcher by surprise. She grabbed the man by the collar, trying to pull him off. The peddlers clapped and whistled. Turning, the man lashed out, striking her on the arm. It gave the lieutenant the opportunity to punch his assailant in the midriff.

Winded, he fell back. 'Bloody bitch.'

Her watcher had caught up with her, and kicked a flurry of snow at the man. 'Be off with you, churl.'

The man looked from him to the lieutenant, evidently deciding the odds were against him. He staggered away and the lieutenant clambered to his feet, brushing snow from his redcoat. His face sported a nasty bruise. 'My champion,' he said, with an elaborate bow that made her blush. 'Next time you ride into battle, you must wear my colours on your sleeve.'

He offered her his arm, and she longed to take it, but her watcher scowled. The three of them walked on to Agnetti's door.

'You're a bastardly gullion, Dodd-Bellingham,' the man with the beard shouted after them. 'I'll fix you, you son of a mutt-bitch whore.'

Pamela glanced up at the lieutenant, concerned, but he only smiled down at her in that way that made his eyes crinkle.

'Who was that?' she asked.

'Just a man I used to know. Put him out of your mind. I already have.'

*

Then there was Lord March, who dropped by to see Agnetti two days later. Pamela was lying on the altar, and from her awkward vantage point she examined the newcomer curiously. Agnetti put down his charcoal and went to shake his hand, addressing him with deference.

'I came with Neddy,' Lord March said. 'He's brought you a letter from Stone. I said I'd bring it up, as I wanted to talk.'

Much of their conversation was a mystery – snatches in a language she presumed to be Latin, odd names, books – but she understood well enough the way Lord March kept glancing at her bared breast well enough. Cecily had told her that the lieutenant was friends with the son of an earl, the heir to a great estate. Lord March wasn't a patch on the lieutenant, but he had a thin, fine-boned face and dark pretty eyes. She smiled at him, trying not to think about what the lieutenant and Mrs Agnetti were up to downstairs.

Lord March dragged his eyes back to Agnetti. 'I wondered if I might borrow that volume of Dracontius we spoke about?'

'Of course,' Agnetti said. 'If you wait here, I'll fetch it. Pamela, you may take a rest until I return.'

She took her time sitting up, slipping her breast into her robe, enjoying the effect she had upon the young nobleman.

'So you're his Iphigenia,' Lord March said, drawing closer. 'Neddy's told me all about you.'

She gave him a bold eye. 'Promise not to sacrifice me to the gods?'

He laughed richly. 'Do you know the rest of the story? Here, I'll show you.'

Pamela joined him in front of another of Agnetti's giant canvases: the one he was working on with Lucy and Peter Jakes, as well as Julietta, a girl from the Whores' Club, and a handsome tenor from the Royal Opera House. The painting was nearly finished. Julietta lay dying on a bed, slain by the tenor – who was as flatulent as a bull-calf, according to Lucy. Peter Jakes was crawling across the floor, his blood streaking the mosaic tiles, Lucy standing over him with an axe.

Lord March touched her arm as he spoke, pointing to the

painting. 'Iphigenia's murder sparked a chain of recrimination and killing that rocked the Hellenic world. Here you see the murder of Agamemnon, Iphigenia's father, who had returned victorious from the conquest of Troy. The dying girl is his Trojan concubine, Cassandra. His wife, Clytemnestra, furious about Iphigenia's murder, enlisted the aid of her lover, Aegistus, to kill them both.'

'He sacrificed his daughter. He deserved it.'

'Their son, Orestes, didn't think so. In the third scene that Mr Agnetti is to paint, he murders his mother and her lover in an act of revenge. In the final painting, Orestes is driven mad by the Furies, winged demons who demand justice for his crimes.'

'He loved his father, even though he'd killed his own sister?'

'I suppose he must have done.'

Pamela mused on this a moment. 'I wouldn't give my da the time of day. Not even if someone was standing over him with an axe.'

Lord March smiled. 'Sometimes I think the same about my own father.'

'I'd kill for love though – like him there in the painting.' She pointed at the tenor, Clytemnestra's lover. 'Murder a rival, or someone who hurt him.' She thought about that man down on the ground in Leicester Fields.

Lord March pointed at Lucy as Clytemnestra. 'Love must have played a part there as well. Love for her husband, I mean. If it was just about her murdered daughter, then why kill Cassandra too?'

'Jealousy can do that to you,' Pamela said. 'Mix you up inside, so you can't see straight.'

His eyes locked on hers, and he spoke softly:

'I hate and I love.
And if you ask me how,
I do not know.
I only feel it,
and I am torn in two.'

'Yes,' she said. 'Hate and love. That's it. Did you write that?'
Cecily had said Lord March was a poet.

'It's Catullus,' he said. 'A Roman who lived two thousand
years ago. His verses, like the feelings he writes about, are eter-
nal.' He paused. 'I could read you more poetry, if you wish. I keep
a set of rooms in Duke Street. You could meet me there tomorrow afternoon?' He ran a hand down her back, grazing her spine.

'I cannot,' she said, her throat dry as dust. 'There is to be an
auction.'

'I know,' he said. 'Neddy told me. I'll do nothing to risk your
money. Nothing you won't enjoy. You have my word as a
gentleman.'

She wondered if it was a test – of her chastity, her virtue.
Maybe the lieutenant had sent his friend to try to seduce her?
How to respond? She didn't want to offend him. A peer of the
realm, a potential keeper. Her heart was with the lieutenant, but
a girl couldn't live off her heart alone. Be open to every option,
Lucy always said.

'I can't get away from my watcher. But you could bid for me
at auction? Or later, after I am sold, you could invite me to your
rooms again?'

He smiled, stepping away. 'Perhaps I will.'

She wondered why he kept a set of rooms in which to meet
women, when he could visit any brothel in town. Perhaps he
had a mistress? A lady of quality, high-born, who needed somewhere discreet to meet him in private. It hadn't stopped him

wanting Pamela. She was a match for any lady in town, and soon the whole of London would know it.

*

When Agnetti returned with the book, he asked her to wait downstairs, as he had a private matter to discuss with Lord March. As she descended the stairs, the door to the drawing room opened, and Lieutenant Dodd-Bellingham emerged. She caught a glimpse behind him of Mrs Agnetti, sitting on the sofa, and her blood curdled. He closed the door and looked up, catching sight of her.

'I hoped I'd see you here,' he said. 'I have something for you.'

Smiling, she walked to meet him. From his pocket he produced a white and purple nosegay tied with a ribbon. 'To thank you for riding to my rescue the other day.'

She smelled it appreciatively. 'Your poor face.' Reaching out a finger, marvelling at her own audacity, she traced the outline of his bruise. He turned his head to brush his lips against her finger.

'Dear God, girl,' he said, stepping away. 'Jonathan Stone would have my heart, liver and lights fried up in a skillet.'

She remembered Lucy and Kitty talking about a Mr Stone, the one who had the masquerades out in the country. 'What does Mr Stone have to do with anything?'

'I owe him money, which means I have to do what he says.'

'Why wouldn't he want you talking to me?'

'Oh, take my word for it.' An uncharacteristic trace of unease seemed to settle on his features.

'Does your brother owe him money too?'

'Owns us both – lock, stock. You don't happen to have a spare three thousand pounds?'

She shook her head, and he grinned. 'Pity. Then I could marry you. You're kinder on the eye than any heiress.'

She stared at him. 'You mean to marry?'

'God willing. When the Order of the Bath is announced. My brother says the heiresses will come flocking and I can get out from under Stone at last.'

The furrow in her forehead deepened as she distilled this information. She committed the name to memory: Jonathan Stone.

Chapter Thirty-Nine

Midday, the Thames shiny as a new sixpence in the sun. Peregrine Child, sweating out last night's liquor, trudged through the dingy streets of Southwark. From everything Hector had told him, he was convinced that finding Lucy's friend Kitty was the key to unlocking this conspiracy of silence. Run her to ground, appeal to her tortured conscience, find out which one of these blueblood fucksters had killed Pamela. Then they'd all start talking, trying to save their own skin – gentlemen always did when they felt the lick of the hangman's rope.

On the edge of St George's Fields, he paused to catch his breath. A great expanse of heath and bog on the southern fringes of the city, Child sometimes came down here to attend a fair or watch a riot. Today the only attraction was a gang of itinerant horse dealers showing off a frisky pony to an eager crowd. *Caveat emptor,* Child thought. He knew all the tricks. Stick a live eel or a wedge of ginger up a horse's fundament, and any broken-down old nag could look lively. He gave them a wide berth, taking a circuitous route across the grass to the gates of the Magdalen Hospital for Penitent Prostitutes.

Not dissimilar to the Bridewell Prison, the Magdalen comprised four brick buildings forming a square, with a quadrangle in the middle. Yet compassion, not condemnation, was the prevailing principle here: the inmates enrolled of their own volition, the high brick walls designed to keep undesirable elements out.

Child spied a few undesirables waiting around outside the gates: pimps and bawds hoping to catch a glimpse of their former charges and entice or bully them back to life on the street.

The heavyset porters on the door examined Child sceptically, probably taking him for a pimp. Judging that they would be impervious to bribery, he presented his card, saying that he was looking into the murder of Lucy Loveless.

'Poor girl,' one of the porters said, with a little more warmth.

'I think she might have come here recently.' Child showed him Agnetti's drawing.

The porter nodded slowly. 'I remember her. What man would forget? She came here about a month ago. I forget the name she used, but it wasn't Lucy Loveless. She looked and sounded every inch the respectable lady. She talked to Mrs Rainwood, our matron.'

'Can I talk to Mrs Rainwood? I'm sure she'd want to see this animal caught.'

The porter gave a decisive nod. 'So would I.'

Child waited in the lobby. When the porter returned, he invited Child to follow him. They walked out into the quadrangle, where several women were taking exercise, strolling arm in arm around a pond. Wearing gowns of sky-blue wool, and small-brimmed hats shielding their faces, their eyes were cast demurely down, and they talked in whispers. Child glimpsed other women at work in the surrounding buildings: sewing or washing laundry, skills to equip them for lives as respectable servants. They walked past a large octagonal chapel, through a door, and up a flight of stairs. The porter knocked at another door on the landing, and received a soft command to enter.

A plump, smiling woman of about thirty rose behind a desk to greet him, extending her gloved hand. 'My name is Hester

Rainwood, matron of the Magdalen. Please, Mr Child, take a seat.'

She had a soft, well-spoken voice, and a round face thickly plastered in white lead paint, with two little circles of rouge painted high on her cheeks. Judging by her sober attire – a high-necked grey gown with a cameo at the throat and a cream house-bonnet – she didn't seem like the sort of woman who would trick herself out for attention's sake. He presumed her skin was scarred by pimples or the pox.

The room was small, but comfortably furnished: lace curtains, a bookcase, and a biblical scene over the mantelpiece: Mary Magdalen washing the feet of Christ. A teapot sat next to a fruitcake on the desk. 'I am afraid you catch me at the guilty hour, sir. Would you care for a slice?'

Child declined, but accepted a cup of tea. While she poured, he repeated the reason for his visit.

'As my porter told you,' she said, studying the drawing he'd placed on the desk, 'this woman did come here about a month ago, but she called herself Mrs Pearson, not Lucy Loveless.' She sighed, lips downturned in distress. 'I read about the murder in the newspapers. Such a terrible thing.'

'Did Lucy come here looking for a prostitute named Kitty Carefree?'

'Yes. That's right. How did you know?'

'I found one of your cards in Lucy's rooms.' He pointed to a small stack of identical cards on Mrs Rainwood's desk. 'Kitty had talked about giving up her trade, and had lately embraced religion. I knew Lucy was looking for her, and I put two and two together.'

'Mrs Pearson claimed to be trying to find her estranged sister. Their father had lately died, she said, and she hoped to reconcile with Kitty. Especially as she'd been told that Kitty had recently turned her back on prostitution. I told her we had no inmate here registered under that name, and none who answered her description. Strictly speaking, I should not have provided Mrs Pearson with any information at all, but she was extremely convincing in her distress.'

'She did not deceive you lightly,' Child said. 'Lucy thought Kitty had information about another murder, the victim a young prostitute, just fifteen years old. Now Lucy too is dead, and I fear that Kitty might be next.'

Mrs Rainwood's eyes widened with concern. 'What makes you say that?'

'People are looking for her, and I'm not at all sure they wish her well. But I'll keep looking too, and I hope to find her first. Can I ask you one other question?'

'Of course.'

'It will sound foolish, but do these words and numbers mean anything to you at all? *50–60 pineapples, 2s 1d*. It was a note written on the back of Lucy's Magdalen card. I wondered if it could be connected to her visit here.'

She looked bemused. 'No, sir. I'm sorry. They do not.'

'Never mind,' Child said, a little dejectedly. He'd truly hoped he'd find Kitty here, but it was another dead end. 'I'm sorry for taking up your time unnecessarily.' He rose, hand outstretched, but she didn't take it.

'Please, sir. Sit down. I have something else to tell you.'

Intrigued, he did so. 'Madam?'

'Do you give me your word that you will do nothing to compound the danger for this young woman, Kitty Carefree?'

'Of course. If I find her, I'll try to help.'

She took another sip of tea, and set it down, rattling the china. 'When I told Mrs Pearson – I still struggle to think of her as Lucy Loveless – that her sister wasn't an inmate here, she asked me if I'd speak to those who were – to see if any of the girls might know Kitty or have an idea where she might be. I was reluctant to do so. We are not supposed to remind our inmates of their former lives, you see. The lure of Mammon and the bottle and the flesh are too near in their minds. We give them counsel, wean them from drink, but the smallest disturbance to their serenity can set them off course. Yet I was moved by Mrs Pearson's compassion and determination.' She regarded him seriously. 'I did not tell you this at first, because I have only been in my post a few months, and I feared my actions could get me in trouble with the governors. But, given what you have told me about the danger this poor girl, Kitty, might face, I cannot in all good conscience remain silent about the little I learned.'

'Anything you tell me will be in the strictest confidence,' Child said. 'I promise you the governors will not hear of it.'

She inclined her head. 'As it transpired, some of the girls here were acquainted with Kitty, though none of them could tell me where she was living now. I wrote and told Mrs Pearson, but I also told her I wouldn't give up. She had left quite an impression, as you can probably tell. I questioned every new inmate as they came in, with little success until last week, when I spoke to a girl who claimed to have seen Kitty very recently. She was riding in a fine carriage upon the Strand, in the company of an older gentleman. According to the girl's account, the pair were kissing.'

Child frowned. 'Then Lucy was wrong? Kitty never reformed at all?'

'She may have tried,' Mrs Rainwood said. 'But change is hard, and poverty grinding, and temptation lies everywhere. My inmate did not get a good look at the gentleman, but she did provide me with a description of the carriage. It was distinctive, she said, lacquered with red, white and blue diamonds, like a harlequin, or a playing card. I thought if Mrs Pearson could find the owner of the carriage, he might be able to provide her with information that would help find her sister. She never replied to my letter, and now I know why. Lucy Loveless would have been dead by the time it arrived.'

Did this mean Kitty was still in London, plying her old trade? If so, it was odd that none of her other friends and acquaintances had seen her. Perhaps, as Mrs Rainwood suggested, she had moved out of Soho with every intention to reform, but had subsequently met a gentleman who'd made her a handsome offer. If her new keeper was a jealous man, the sort who didn't like his mistress frolicking in the taverns, then it might explain why she hadn't been seen out on the town. He decided to ask around Soho and Covent Garden, to see if anyone remembered seeing this carriage. Given the man was a likely whoremonger, he might be a regular visitor to those parts.

'Thank you, Mrs Rainwood,' he said.

'I pray that you find her.' She walked out from behind the desk to shake his hand again. 'If you meet with success, and Kitty hasn't entirely closed her mind to reform, please tell her that I would happily welcome her to the Magdalen. You said she is a religious woman?'

'Her servant said she prayed. And she'd been going to church, over at St Andrew-by-the-Wardrobe.'

'The preacher there is a great evangelist,' Mrs Rainwood said. 'Do you know what they say? That a person can be cleansed of sin. Born again.'

Child gave a crooked smile. 'I wish I believed that.' He paused by the window on his way to the door, gazing down at the women in the yard. A waft of his own brandy-sweat greeted his nostrils. 'How do you do it?' he asked. 'Wean them from drink?'

'It depends on the woman. For some the bottle is a hedonistic pleasure, and giving them fresh occupation is enough. But for others, girls who have suffered – often unspeakable cruelties – or who are consumed with guilt about all the things they've done, the drink serves to deaden the pain of their existence. If they are to fall out of love with liquor, they need first to love themselves.'

Child grimaced. 'You say it as if it was easy.'

'I tell them to imagine their life as if it belonged to another. Were they to hear the tale of their own sins, would they condemn, or would they forgive? So often we are kinder to a stranger than we are to ourselves.'

'And if they heard the sins of that stranger and still felt inclined to condemn? What then?'

Mrs Rainwood smiled at him sadly. 'I wish I knew.'

Chapter Forty

On the good days, Caro's nausea was less pronounced, her tiredness lifting a little, her spirits livelier. Taking advantage of just such a day, she had spent the morning attending to some household matters that could not wait, and had then taken Gabriel to the park. After lunch, she visited her lawyer, and finding that everything was in order with Mr Agnetti's contract, she called in at the Craven Bank to withdraw his forty-guinea deposit. Sam then drove her to Agnetti's house in Leicester Fields. She was hoping to use her visit to Agnetti's as an excuse to talk to him again, but his manservant informed her that both his master and Miss Willoughby were at Vauxhall Gardens.

'Then please tell him that I look forward to our first sitting tomorrow.'

Chafing at the delay, seeking another line of inquiry to pursue, she recalled the allegation against Simon Dodd-Bellingham that she'd heard at the duchess's garden party. Theft was a far cry from murder, but it did speak to character – further suggestion that Simon wasn't the earnest innocent he appeared.

Other possibilities occurred to her too. The duchess had said that Ansell Ward, Simon's alleged victim, hadn't possessed enough evidence to have him charged with any crime. Caro didn't discount the possibility that this was because Simon was innocent. Yet if he *was* guilty of this theft, then perhaps Jonathan Stone had found proof of his culpability – evidence that could see him hanging from a rope? Perhaps Simon had been threatened into silence upon the subject of Pamela's murder, just as Stone had threatened Caro herself the other night. Understanding the ties that bound her suspects together was, to Caro's mind, imperative if they were ever to snip them loose.

Providentially, Alderman Ward was both a client of the Craven Bank and an old friend of her late father. 'Lyme Street,' she told Sam, and as he whipped the horses to a trot, she settled to the jolting tempo of the carriage.

The streets of the City of London swarmed with stockjobbers and clerks, and Company men coming and going from East India House. Caro's grandfather had once sold groceries from a shop in Lyme Street, and her father had established his first counting house not a stone's throw from here. 'City people,' Louisa's mother had said with a sniff, when Mordechai had first paid his addresses to her daughter. Yet she'd given her blessing eventually, as Papa had known she would. In London, increasingly, money held court.

Ansell Ward lived in a large half-timbered, leaded-windowed survivor of the Great Fire. A progression of jettying storeys, each larger than the one below, gave the house the appearance of a giant merchant ship – much like the ones that carried Ward's clocks and pocket watches to China and the Japans. Caro was greeted by a tall bewigged footman with large flared nostrils and an insolent smile. She waited in the hall while he conveyed her request, and then escorted her in to see his master.

Inside, the house was rambling and low-ceilinged, the floors all angles askew, the boards creaking. Caro was shown into Ward's study, which had so many pictures hanging or pasted to the panelling that barely an inch of oak could be glimpsed between them: maps of the world and the American colonies; plans of battlefields clipped from magazines; a pair of oil paintings depicting patriotic scenes – the death of Major Peirson and the repulse of the Spanish at Gibraltar. Ceramic busts of Admiral Keppel and General Clinton flanked an automaton clock on the mantelpiece.

Beaming, Ansell Ward rose to shake her hand. 'I remember when your father brought you to the Mansion House for the Farewell Dinner – when was it? '68? '69? You told us all you were going to sit in Parliament one day.' He chuckled.

Given his passion for *la guerre*, a less martial man than Ward it was hard to imagine. Small, soft and smiling, with a white, pitted face like bread dough, he wore a pastel-blue suit like a little boy dressed up for church. Caro fielded his inquiries about Ambrose with practised dexterity, and when he asked after Mordechai, she seized the opening it offered.

'As it happens, I am here on my brother's account. Mordechai wishes to expand his library and is thinking of engaging Simon Dodd-Bellingham for the task. I believe he worked on your own library?'

Immediately she sensed his unease. The fingers of one hand tapped on the table in double time to the clock, while the other slid back and forth between his chins and his cravat. 'Dodd-Bellingham, yes. I would counsel against it.'

She blinked, as if in surprise. 'Can I ask why?'

'You may, though it's not a pleasing tale. About eighteen months ago, I purchased a large lot of rare books at auction, which needed cataloguing. I hired Dodd-Bellingham for the task, and for three months he fulfilled his duties quite satisfactorily. Then I discovered that a pair of jade figurines had gone missing from my library. It soon became obvious to me who was responsible.'

'Not Mr Dodd-Bellingham? Good heavens.'

'I couldn't prove it, or I'd have involved the law. But I know it was him. He was one of only two people who had the opportunity, the other being a servant who has been with me for years. And it is well known the boy has debts. My wife was convinced of his guilt, and she is an excellent judge of character. He'd been at the sherry decanter too, we think.'

'I must say, you surprise me,' Caro said. 'Simon always struck me as a trustworthy, if rather pitiful, creature. And he is so very passionate about his work.'

'Oh, he puts on a good show, but that's all it is – a wicked masquerade intended to deceive the unwary. I suppose it's hardly surprising. His mother was little better than a common harlot. Thievery and drunkenness must flow through his veins.' He shook his head. 'But I don't mind admitting that it upset me greatly at the time. I admire the name Dodd-Bellingham, you see. That's why I chose Simon in the first place. His father, the late colonel, fought alongside Clive at Plassey. And his brother, Edward, further adorns the family tree. Did you know the King is to award him the Order of the Bath?'

Caro smiled politely. 'The lieutenant saved a starving camp, isn't that right?'

'In the winter of '76 to '77, a few months after the recapture of New York.' He jumped up to point to one of his maps. 'General Howe had established a string of outposts across New Jersey, from the Hudson here to the Delaware there. Dodd-Bellingham was stationed at a godforsaken little hole named Van der Linden's Mill, along with three hundred British regulars. All around was neutral ground and a bitter winter ensued, rebel militia scouring the countryside looking for British foraging parties to pick off. Our troops were receiving the worst of it, and so Howe ordered the northern outposts to fall back to the Hudson River. But Van der Linden's Mill was cut off by the snow, in a dire situation.

'All through January, into February, those brave men held out, harried by enemy militia whenever they ventured forth. Food dwindled and disease was rife, men dying in their beds or at their station. But their commander refused to surrender, which would have meant losing six valuable cannons to the enemy. They would stand their ground or die trying – as English lions. The end seemed all but certain, when Lieutenant Dodd-Bellingham took it upon himself to act. He took six of the strongest, bravest men, and they crept out, under cover of darkness, through enemy lines. They captured a supply train against overwhelming odds, and rode the wagons back disguised as rebel militia. That food kept the company alive until the thaw. They say His Majesty himself likes to recount the story.'

So too, it seemed, did Ansell Ward. Catching himself, he smiled, cheeks dimpling. 'Do forgive me, Mrs Corsham. My wife says I love a battle more than pound cake.' He sighed. 'And now the fruits of that sacrifice are to be bartered and sold at Versailles like so many trade beads. Menorca for Grenada, and so forth. Oh, I don't blame men like your husband. They are merely cleaning up the mess the Cabinet made. Those gentlemen aren't fit to lick the boots of Captain Corsham and Lieutenant Dodd-Bellingham.'

Caro inclined her head, acknowledging the compliment. 'There was one other matter I wanted to ask you about, sir. Jonathan Stone. I heard some City aldermen wanted him investigated for dealing in illegal loans, but the Home Office refused to get involved. Can that be true? I ask because Captain Corsham has had concerns about Stone for some time. I wanted to write and let him know.'

It was the best she could come up with, but fortunately Ansell Ward was an unsuspecting man. 'It is gratifying to know that we have allies in Parliament, though rather too few, I think. It runs too deep.'

'It, sir?'

'Corruption,' he said. 'The ministry complicit, the law not worth a candle, the authorities looking the other way, paid off. It's how Stone really made his money. I've gone to the heart of that little mystery. Another sorry tale.'

'I thought that, like so many others, he made his fortune in India.'

'So he likes people to think. Oh, I don't deny that he returned to England moderately prosperous, but no more than that. Yet very soon he was lending vast sums at interest. Tens of thousands of pounds, a nabob's ransom. What do you make of that, then? Eh?'

Caro made the appropriate noises of bemusement he seemed to anticipate.

'Stone was just a broker,' Ward cried. 'A middling-man. For the banks. That's what he was back then, and little has changed. Now don't look like that. Not every counting house is as respectable as the Craven, and some of your competitors aren't shy about breaking the law. Usury doesn't pay, see, not with the legal rate of interest at five per cent. But that's where Jonathan Stone comes into play. He brokers the loan, the bank lends on paper at five per cent, but the real rate is twelve, the bank and Stone splitting the difference. Stone's part of the endeavour is to ensure that their debtors pay up at the higher rate, which they do with a regularity that should alarm the righteous man. A group of us aldermen, as you say, were determined to put a stop to it. Go into the banks, open the books, identify the guilty parties, hold their feet to the fire. But the Home Office made plain where their interests lie. Too many powerful gentlemen up to their necks in it, I suppose.' He peered at Caro. 'Mrs Corsham, are you quite all right?'

Memories assailed her: the still, tense faces of Mordechai and Cavill-Lawrence, her feeling that Stone mattered to them in some way. Wanting to know if Stone had asked her about politics. Or the bank.

She recalled Stone's coded warnings about Ambrose, which she'd taken to refer to his syphilis, but now she wondered. *Did you talk to him, as I asked? Brother Ambrose?*

Ward's martial mementoes stirred other memories too: those terrible days back in the spring, when her brothers had gone to war over the bank. Ambrose's quiet despair; Mordechai's fury. The refusal of the pair of them to answer her questions about what on earth was going on. And afterwards, when the board had voted and installed Mordechai as chairman, Ambrose had taken to his bed and stopped speaking at all.

Gazing at Ward's concerned face, she murmured a few words about what a disgrace it all was, and how she was sure that Harry would want to see something done. Glowing with pleasure, he took her hand in his soft paw.

'If only every parliamentarian was as staunch as your husband, and every banking house as honest as the Craven. Virtue will prevail, of that I am in no doubt. Until then,' he raised a fist, '*A la bataille!*'

Chapter Forty-One

CHILD SPENT THE next few hours wandering the streets of Covent Garden, stopping to talk to tavern doormen and grooms in stable yards. No one remembered the distinctive carriage with the harlequin pattern, in which Kitty Carefree had been seen riding. Child asked the whores he encountered too, but none of them recalled a client with a carriage like that.

At eight o'clock, fortified by a bowl of cockles and a quart of gin, Child walked up to Soho, to continue his inquiries there. First, he stopped off at Compton Street, where he watched the girls arriving for work at the tableaux house. Spotting Cecily, he hurried across the street to intercept her.

'What do you want?' she said. 'I got into trouble the other night for disappearing.'

'It won't take long. I just need a minute of your time.'

Back in the coffeehouse, Cecily stirred her capuchin, while Child held up the necklace for her to examine.

'It was Pamela's,' she said, after a moment. 'Her father gave it to her mother. It was the only thing she'd ever had from either of them. She'd never have parted with it willingly. Where did you find it?'

'Two gentlemen were arguing about it. One of them threw it away. My client was watching.'

'Was one of them that soldier? The one who picked her up?'

Child nodded.

'A pox on his eyes. Do you think he killed her?'

'Quite possibly.' The necklace span between Child's fingers. He examined the silver hand and the turquoise beads. As Mrs Corsham had said, they looked exotic. 'Did Pamela ever say anything else about her parents?'

'Only that she was left as a baby at an orphanage. Pinned to the blanket was a note from her mother, and that necklace. Her father had abandoned them, the note said, and her mother couldn't afford to keep them both – it's a common story. That didn't stop Pamela making up other stories about them, mind. Most orphans do.'

'What kind of stories?'

'She said that when she was at the orphanage, and the girls used to walk to the park, a gentleman would sit and watch her from his carriage. Silly cow had convinced herself he was her father, when he was probably just tugging at himself over the girls.' Cecily smiled sadly. 'Pamela was always dreaming up tales to make herself seem grander. I told Lucy that, when she asked.'

'She asked you about Pamela's parents too?'

'No, about another piece of silliness on her part. Pamela said she knew a secret that was going to make her rich. That's what I mean, she was always making up stories. She had great plans for the future, said she was going to marry her handsome soldier, be the next Lavinia Fenton. I told her she was already rich. A hundred and twenty-five guineas! But she said that was nothing compared to the value of her secret.'

Child frowned. 'She never said what it was?'

'Of course she didn't. Like I said, it was just another of her stories.'

*

Soho was coming to life, lamps flaring in the windows of the chophouses and brothels, the taverns filling up, laughter rising. Child decided to begin his inquiries after the carriage at the Golden Pear Tree across the street. He also had a few questions for the doorman about the lieutenant and Lord March.

Weaving his way between the revellers on the street, he was forced to step aside as a very large man, probably drunk, veered into his path. He turned to make a sardonic remark, but it died on his lips as the man stepped in front of him again, no longer looking drunk, but very alert. Someone else seized him from behind, and the large man drove a fist into his stomach. Winded, Child doubled over, vomiting onto his assailant's shoes.

'Fuckster,' the large man said, and hit him again.

People stared, but no one intervened as the pair manhandled him towards a waiting carriage. He struggled and shouted, to no avail. The second man reached into his pocket and removed Child's pistol. They opened the door to the carriage and bundled him inside, where the large man sat on him. The door slammed, and the carriage moved off.

Shite, Child thought. Finn Daley.

BOOK THREE

9–12 SEPTEMBER 1782

'*We should know what is true before we break our rage.*'

Aeschylus, the *Oresteia*, 458 BC

Chapter Forty-Two

❋

Ambrose sat in his porter's chair, the hood shielding his eyes from the lamp, a fragment of light glinting at the end of his silver nose. Caro held his bandaged hand.

Footsteps in the hall. The door opened and Mordechai entered, dragged away from a supper party by Caro's note.

'Come down to the study,' he said.

'I want to talk here.' Skewering him with her gaze, she cast about for questions, so many to choose from she didn't know where to start. 'Answer me honestly. When Ambrose was chairman of the bank, did he authorize loans brokered by Jonathan Stone?'

Mordechai gazed up at a painting, Cronos castrating his father with a scythe. 'The bank has always used men like Stone, ever since Father's time. You think he went from grocer to banker by following the rules?'

She closed her eyes. 'Breaking the law.'

'Everyone does it. Everyone with any sense.'

'Do we use Stone now? Is that why you were so troubled when you confronted me with Cavill-Lawrence the other day?'

'Yes, we still use Stone – among others. I'll not apologize for it. The laws on usury are clerical cant. Parliament can't repeal them without upsetting the Church, so we just ignore them and everyone looks the other way.'

'Then why did you force Ambrose out of the bank?'

Mordechai glared at her. 'Every day I take decisions in the best interests of this family. I don't anticipate gratitude, but I do expect to be obeyed. I told you to dismiss your thief-taker. Have you done so?'

'No, and I won't consider it. Not without answers.'

More footsteps were heard in the hall. The door opened to reveal a footman. Behind him, Nicholas Cavill-Lawrence, who stopped when he saw Ambrose. 'Good God. It's as bad as that.'

'What's he doing here?' Caro asked.

'I sent for him when I received your note. This concerns him too. The damage our brother has caused goes far beyond our family, I regret to say.'

Caro waited until the footman had withdrawn and closed the door. 'What damage?' She looked from one to the other. 'Why do the Home Office care about Stone if everyone makes illegal loans? Why does the bank?'

Cavill-Lawrence walked to the window and threw it open, one of those men who couldn't abide disease at close quarters. Taking an enamelled snuffbox from his waistcoat pocket, he took a pinch, then nodded at Mordechai. 'You might as well tell her.'

Her brother frowned. 'Are you sure?'

'What's she going to do? Bring down her own family's bank? It might make her see sense.'

His gaze stony, his voice hard, Mordechai addressed his words not to her, but to Ambrose. 'He was never cut out for the chairmanship. The responsibility. The hours. I knew it. The board knew it. Everyone except you and Father.' He looked up. 'That damn painting.'

'Just the facts, please,' Cavill-Lawrence said. 'Everyone here is aware of the family history.'

Mordechai dragged his eyes to Caro. 'In November last year,

when Ambrose was in his last months as Chairman, he authorized a new loan brokered by Jonathan Stone. Nearly a hundred
thousand pounds, larger than any we'd ever made. When I
found out, I queried the sum, as one would. Who, I wanted to
know, could afford to borrow so much? What guarantees did we
have that the money would be repaid? What Ambrose told me
was even worse than I had imagined.'

'The Priapus Club,' Cavill-Lawrence said. 'That's where they
did their business, your brother and Stone. Did it together, until
a year ago, when Ambrose was forced to withdraw from society.
After that, Stone did the seduction part alone. Enticing young
men of good family into debauchery and debt. Masquerades,
drink, women, God knows what. Stone used Lord March to
make his introductions. He brokered the loans, and Ambrose
came up with the money. Everybody happy – except the
fathers – but fathers die eventually. Ambrose always had an eye
for the future, much like your own father. And these young men
stood to inherit some of the largest estates in the kingdom.
Catch them while they're young, Ambrose used to say, and you
have their business for life. And one day, late last year, Jonathan
Stone walked into his rooms at the Adelphi, and told him that
he'd hooked the biggest fish of all.'

Caro stared at him, realization dawning. 'Good Lord,' she
said. 'You mean Prinny.'

Prince George Frederick Augustus. Nineteen years old, in
fierce pursuit of pleasure, kept on a tight purse string by his
moralist of a father, who'd told the banks not to lend him
money on any account. Caro saw how it would have happened.
All Lord March would have had to do was dangle the prospect:
Stone's money, his club, his women – to Prinny it must have
been as tempting as the apple in the Garden. The future King

of England in the pocket of Jonathan Stone – and the Craven Bank.

Ambrose made a noise, more than a gasp, not quite a moan, and they all stared at the hollowed-out man in the porter's chair. Caro shook her head. 'If the King found out that we had illegally lent money to his son . . .'

'Then Ambrose and I would be facing prison,' Mordechai said. 'Perhaps worse.'

'But it makes no sense. Ambrose was daring, but never reckless.'

'His wits were failing. Presumably Stone took advantage. Ambrose should have stepped down as Chairman long before he did.'

'But his wits weren't failing back then. Physically he was worse, but he was only a little forgetful in the mind. That came later.' She looked from Mordechai to Cavill-Lawrence, wondering if there was something else they were not telling her. 'This document your agents are searching for – does it have something to do with the Prince?'

'A witness account of the Priapus Club,' Cavill-Lawrence said. 'A potted history, if you will. Names, dates, and all manner of detailed depravity. It was in Lucy's possession before she was killed, and now we can't find it.'

'How do you know?'

'Because she took it upon herself to write to the Home Secretary and tell him. The letter was found next to her body after she was killed. A constable passed it to Sir Amos Fox, who acted entirely properly by involving my office. Lucy claimed in her letter to have a dossier of evidence pertaining to the murder of a young prostitute named Pamela. These papers include the witness account I mentioned: a document that could cause enormous embarrassment to many important families, not least the House of Hanover. Lucy demanded a Home Office investigation into this alleged murder, and the arrest of the guilty party. Failing that, her dossier would be sent to the newspapers. The public, she felt certain, would want to see justice done. One has to rather admire her presumption.'

In the wrong hands a secret is a weapon. Oh, Lucy, Caro thought, *you were playing with fire there.*

'Lucy said in her letter that her dossier was in the possession of a friend,' Cavill-Lawrence went on. 'She was afraid for her safety – and when you're blackmailing the Home Secretary, you're right to be. She said that if anything happened to her, then that friend would ensure the newspapers got their dossier. We didn't kill her, we weren't even aware of any of this until we read her letter. But I don't see how this friend is supposed to know that. Every day since Lucy's murder, we have braced ourselves for the dossier's appearance in print. Perhaps this friend was not as reliable as Lucy thought. Perhaps it was merely a bluff and there is no dossier. But if that document exists, then we must find it. I ask you now, as a loyal subject, if you or your thief-taker knows where it is?'

'I'd hardly be here now, asking these questions, if we did.'

Cavill-Lawrence took another pinch of snuff and sneezed his frustration. Mordechai paced the room. Ambrose had tipped back his head, as if to study her, but seemed to gaze through her.

'Lucy had five suspects in mind for Pamela's murder,' she said. 'Jonathan Stone, the Dodd-Bellingham brothers, Lord March, and a fifth man. Was Prinny at Muswell Rise that night?'

Cavill-Lawrence gave her a look, the kind that had cemented his reputation in Whitehall as a man never to be crossed. 'I will pretend you never said that. Prinny was hunting in Northamptonshire throughout March, and for that we can be thankful.'

Except that Northamptonshire was not so very far from Muswell Rise.

'In any event,' Cavill-Lawrence said, 'it makes no odds. The royal heir, nights of depravity, whores and masks and all the rest, a fifteen-year-old virgin. The newspapers won't care who was where when. Any scandal that touches the Priapus Club, touches Prinny.'

'So the murderer is to walk free? Perhaps to kill again?'

'What murderer? We have no evidence that this girl, Pamela, is even dead. Only the ravings of a whore in the grip of an obsession.'

'A woman who is now dead. You certainly have evidence of murder there.'

'Sir Amos Fox tells me he arrested a suspect for Lucy's murder last night. A lamplighter named Ezra Von Siegel.'

Caro stared at him aghast. 'Von Siegel didn't do it.'

'On the contrary, it seems that he confessed.'

'Under what duress?'

Cavill-Lawrence's cold gaze never left her face. 'Less than forty years ago, a bloody battle was fought on British soil for the crown of our kingdom, and across the water, the Stuart Pretenders watch and wait. It is only because of this King's steadiness, his sense of duty, his private morality, that their cause has diminished. Other enemies plot from within: Papists, foreign spies, those who would have us follow the American example. A scandal that rocks the House of Hanover, that threatens the bond between King and heir, would be a gift to those enemies. There's very little I would not do to prevent that happening.'

'Father indulged you,' Mordechai said. 'Ambrose and your

husband too. But I am not prepared to do so any longer. I am stopping your allowance until your husband returns home – I have spoken to the other trustees, it's all in order. If you need any household bills settling, then you may come to Louisa or myself. But don't think we'll be subsidizing thief-takers, or nights trysting at Vauxhall Gardens.'

'If this story about the Prince becomes public knowledge,' Cavill-Lawrence said, 'the fall of the Craven Bank won't be far behind. Let destitution concentrate your mind, if nothing else will.'

Chapter Forty-Three

❋

THEY HADN'T KILLED him, and Child didn't know why.

He was sitting in a small, ornate dining room lit by several lamps. From somewhere, he could hear the swell and dip of conversation and the chink of crockery. He guessed he was in a private dining room in a supper house – judging by the short distance they'd travelled, somewhere in the vicinity of Covent Garden. It might even be the Prince of Wales. When they'd arrived, his assailants had dragged him from the carriage, into a darkened courtyard. Through a door, up a flight of stairs, into a corridor decorated much like the room he was sitting in now. They had pushed him through another door, into this chair, and the big man had held up a finger. 'We'll be right outside. Cause any trouble and I'll hurt you again.'

Child took an inventory of the room. On the wall, a portrait of the King. On the mantelpiece, a clock. On the table, a dish of figs, a bowl of walnuts, a bottle of good claret and three glasses. As a weapon, he'd take the bottle over the glasses. But if they wanted him dead, then why hadn't they killed him already? Child's unease warred with his confusion. This didn't feel like Finn Daley's doing. The Irishman didn't entertain his overdue debtors, he put a knife between their shoulder blades, and dropped them in the river.

Hearing louder voices in the corridor, Child sat up straight, wincing at the effort. The door opened, and a slim gentleman

with an amiable, elfin countenance entered the room. He was
followed by a second man, with a long white face and a broken
nose. Child guessed from their dress and demeanour that the
first man was the one in charge. He was about Child's own age,
though wearing his years a hell of a lot better. On his index
finger was a blood-red ring, just like the one Mrs Corsham had
found in the bower.

'Good evening, Mr Child,' he said. 'My name is Jonathan
Stone. This is my man of business, Erasmus Knox.'

They took the chairs opposite him. 'Wine?' Stone asked.

Child's gaze flicked from one to the other, knowing this
presaged nothing good. 'You're damn right.'

Broken-nose poured, while Stone produced a sheaf of
papers from a leather document case. He slid one across the
table so Child could see it.

'Eighty-three guineas, eight shillings and fourpence,' Stone
said. 'The sum total of your debts, Mr Child. Your creditors were
only too happy to have them taken off their hands. The amount
in its entirety is now due to me. We are here to discuss the terms
of your repayment.'

Child stared at him in horror, not doubting his word. It
would explain why Finn Daley hadn't been to see him. He took
a long pull on his wine, trying to wash the sickness away. 'Let
me guess, you want me to resign from Mrs Corsham's inquiry?'

'As it happens, no, I don't. At least, not for the moment. Mrs
Corsham is a stubborn woman. Were you to leave her service,
she would simply hire someone else, perhaps someone better. I
want you to remain by her side, but report back to me.'

Child's mind was labouring fast. If he refused, Stone could
have him taken to the Fleet Prison. Men died in that dank
hellhole. Yet in such dire circumstances, surely he had friends
who would help? Sophie Hardcastle, if he could get a message

to her discreetly. Orin would do what he could, despite their present disagreement. And there was always Mrs Corsham. Eighty-three guineas was a trifling sum to a woman like her, and if he explained about Jonathan Stone, she might even pay the lot just to spite him.

'No,' he said. 'I won't do it.'

Stone regarded him placidly, tapping his steepled fingers together. 'I rather feared you would say that.' He nodded to his companion. 'Mr Knox.'

Broken-nose had been rolling a walnut across the table from hand to hand. With Child's uneasy eyes upon him, he took a brass seal from his waistcoat pocket, and brought it down on the nut with a bang. He picked a nugget from the splintered shards, chewed and swallowed.

'I have recently had the misfortune to spend a few days down in Deptford,' he said, with a Brummagem twang. 'There I made the acquaintance of a young man named Andrew Drake. The brother of your late wife, Elizabeth.'

Child drained his glass, hoping the pulse beating in his neck wouldn't betray his fear. 'How is the lad? I could tell you some stories about him.'

'And vice versa.' Stone gave a faint smile.

'Andrew was just a little boy when you married his sister,' Knox continued. 'But his older brother, the late Frank Drake, was a close friend of yours.'

'I wouldn't say that,' Child replied carefully. 'He came in a package with Liz. The Drakes are close-knit. Always were.'

'And up to their armpits in all sorts of unsavoury ventures. Counterfeiting being one of them. Frank was the head of the enterprise. One Drake cousin, a woodcarver by trade, made the moulds out of cuttlefish shells, which Frank would bring back from his slaving voyages. Gives a very delicate design, or so I'm told. Another cousin, a blacksmith, clipped the coins, mixed the scraps, and melted them down to make new coins. And then there was young Andrew himself, scarcely old enough to know better, who had the task of mixing those shiny new coins into a barrelful of nails, then riding out on a pony with the barrel tied to the tail. When the coins were sufficiently scratched, they could be passed into circulation. A capital crime, which, as a former magistrate, you would surely know.'

'Like you said, Frank was trouble. That's why we weren't close.'

'Close enough that you'd pay regular visits to that smithy down by the river. Andrew saw it all. The Spanish brandy you'd drink with Frank, the forge blazing away in the background. The money you'd take as magistrate to turn a blind eye. Andrew doesn't seem to like you very much. We won't dwell on the reasons why. But suffice to say, under the right inducement, he is willing to give evidence against you. I hear the new mayor doesn't like you much either. He wouldn't take much convincing to bring a prosecution. The new magistrate is his man, isn't that right?'

And then not even Mrs Corsham could buy him out of trouble. Child stared at his interlocutors, seeking words of bravado that would not come. He had grown to respect Mrs Corsham. He wanted to catch the murdering bastard who had killed Lucy and probably Pamela too. But not at the cost of his own life.

'Well, Mr Child?' Stone said, breaking in upon these dismal thoughts. 'Do we have a deal?'

Hating himself, Child grabbed the bottle and refilled his glass. 'What do you want to know?'

Stone smiled broadly. 'Everything.'

Child's words came slowly at first, then picked up speed,

tumbling from his lips like pieces of silver. He told Stone all their progress to date, leaving out only Cecily and Hector. His conscience had enough to bear, without the responsibility for more deaths.

'There now,' Stone said, when he had finished. 'That wasn't so hard. And it will be easier the next time, it always is.' He cocked his head, considering. 'Tell me, what was Mrs Corsham doing in the bowers on the night she found Lucy's body?'

'How should I know?' Child said. 'That has nothing to do with my inquiry.'

'It does now. You must have wondered who she was meeting. So let's hear your theory.'

Child sighed. 'I wondered if there was something between her and Lord March. He was in the bowers that night. A witness heard him call her by her given name.'

'He swears not.' Stone tapped his fingers together again. 'If Mrs Corsham has taken a new lover, then I want to know who he is. What was it your namesake said about falsehood, Mr Knox?'

Broken-nose regarded Child stonily. 'That man's mind is more susceptible to lies than to the truth.'

'Not mine,' Stone said. 'I have a keen ear for falsehood, but a keener ear still for the truth – and I want to know the truth about Caroline Corsham. Not the face she presents to the world, but the part of herself she hides away. Observe her, Mr Child. Report back to me.'

PAMELA

2–7 February 1782

Other secrets in that house proved harder to penetrate. Three days later, the lieutenant called again. He spoke to Mr Agnetti about Stone's business and then went downstairs to see Mrs Agnetti. As soon as Pamela had finished sitting for Mr Agnetti, she looked for him. But he must have already left, for she found only Lucy and Mrs Agnetti, talking intently in the morning room. From the way they broke off their conversation and glared at her, she knew she'd interrupted a private talk. By now, she was used to Mrs Agnetti's hostile looks, but Lucy's hurt.

Cecily was auctioned that night, her maidenhead sold for a hundred guineas. She and Mrs Havilland were disappointed by the sum, and the fat old lawyer who'd bought her looked pleased with his bargain. The girls commiserated with Cecily, and she and Pamela hugged in the hall – until Mrs Havilland barked at Cecily to hurry up, and she was ushered into the gentleman's waiting carriage.

The next day, when Cecily came to collect her money and her things, she hadn't wanted to talk about it. 'It's easier than some will tell you,' was all she'd say. 'Harder than others. Follow Mrs Havilland's instructions and you'll be all right.'

Pamela watched the hackney carriage drive away, a black fog settling upon her mood. Kitty always made her feel better about the things a girl needed to do to make her way in the world, and she resolved to talk to her at Mr Agnetti's.

But when she walked into Agnetti's morning room later that day, she found Kitty locked in conversation with Lucy. Another discussion swiftly curtailed by her entrance. Kitty was dabbing at her eyes with a scrap of lace.

'What are you talking about?' Pamela asked.

'Running away,' Kitty said. 'A new life.'

'Why would you want to do that? You love your life in London, don't you?'

Kitty only rose from the sofa, closing the door too hard behind her.

'It's not you,' Lucy said. 'Don't take it to heart. Come, sit with me. Tell me about your day.'

Secrets she didn't understand. She didn't like it.

Over the next few days, Pamela maintained a stealthy presence in that house. Listening at doors was a skill: one which, like most servants, she'd perfected as a maid at the house in Cheapside. But her endeavours proved fruitless. Everyone talked in whispers, creeping about.

Only the Agnetti marriage was quite without mystery. To hear Mrs Agnetti wax on about her husband's genius, or how they fell in love, or how dutiful a husband he was when he could be convinced to step away from his work, you'd think she was as innocent as milk-water. But then she'd be scurrying off to meet the lieutenant the moment her husband's back was turned, or greeting Mr Agnetti with cold silences, or picking a quarrel with the maidservant, or giving Pamela one of her hard stares. Never Lucy or Kitty, who seemed quite taken in by her wiles. As was the lieutenant.

He called often at the house, supposedly on Mr Stone's business. But Pamela knew it was largely on Mrs Agnetti's account. The transformation that came over her on these occasions was marked. She'd be nervous when she knew he was coming. But when he walked through the door, she would greet him with the softest smiles, shy and girlish. He lapped it up. It's all a performance, Pamela wanted to tell him. She's calculating, cold, unkind.

She was also an obstacle to Pamela's plan.

Kitty had told her that once she lost her virginity, she should find a keeper as soon as possible. And if she was going to be with one man only, then she wanted it to be him. His debts were another obstacle, but if he married an heiress, then things could be different.

On the morning of the seventh of February, she arrived at the house to be greeted by a loud crash. Alarmed, she put her head into the drawing room. Mrs Agnetti was glowering at her husband. At his feet were shards of china.

'That was one of your favourites,' he said softly. 'These things you do, you only ever hurt yourself.' He walked over to his wife and tried to take her in his arms.

Mrs Agnetti – she was never Theresa except to her face – caught sight of Pamela in the doorway, and her face contorted with rage. 'Get out,' she screamed.

Pamela fled upstairs, and when Agnetti joined her a little later, he spoke to her for the first time about his marriage.

'I am sorry you witnessed that scene. Theresa's spirits have always been turbulent, but since we moved to England, her unhappiness sits on her like a cloud. Sometimes I think that we should never have come here, but I have had success in London I never could have dreamed of in Naples.'

'You don't have to explain,' Pamela said. 'I'm sorry.'

His face was etched with sorrow. 'I think on it like an illness.

One to which there is no cure except patience and love. Only sometimes I am rather lacking in the former.'

'You are a good husband, Mr Agnetti. Don't do yourself down.'

'It will be different when the baby comes. Motherhood will restore her to happiness. It is God's blessing.'

Deluded old fool, Pamela thought. You could see the elation shining out of him when he talked about the child. Apollo if a boy. Juno if a girl. They had picked the names together, he said.

It's not God's blessing, she wanted to say. It's Lieutenant Dodd-Bellingham's. But if she told him, then he might challenge the lieutenant to a duel. The lieutenant would win, of course, but with Mr Agnetti dead, Mrs Agnetti would be rich and free to marry again. No, things were better as they were. Soon the lieutenant would tire of her wanton ways.

How could he not?

CHAPTER FORTY-FOUR

NEMO MALUS FELIX. Peace visits not the guilty man. Not unless he drinks himself to oblivion.

The sun hurt Child's eyes, the streets busy with people talking too loudly, in cheerful morning voices. In lieu of breakfast, he stopped off at a Puss and Mew in Carnaby Market. The shutters of the house were closed, one of them carved with a relief of a cat, holding out a wooden paw. 'Puss,' Child called. 'Puss, are you there?'

A pause, then a shuffle behind the window. 'Mew,' came the answer. 'Mew mew mew.'

The shutter remained closed, a necessary precaution given the gin laws. This way buyer couldn't inform on seller, and everyone went away happy, except the magistrates. Child pushed two pennies through the slot in the cat's open mouth. Then he reached into his pocket for the leather cup he carried for this purpose, and held it under the cat's paw. The gin gurgled as it flowed from the concealed spout.

The spirit tasted foul, in keeping with Child's mood. Illegal distilleries like this adulterated their gin with vitriol and turpentine. A pint of it could kill you. Today the prospect seemed quite tempting.

He had betrayed his client to their mutual enemy. He would be forced to do so again – give Stone information that could hurt Mrs Corsham. Unless he could talk her out of continuing with her inquiry.

But a short time later, when he faced Mrs Corsham in her dining room, she wouldn't hear of it.

'Stop?' she said. 'How can I? The magistrate has arrested poor Mr Von Siegel. For no other crime than for being Jewish, and in the wrong place at the wrong time. Sit down, Mr Child. I have much to tell you.'

Gloomily, he sat listening as she told him about her conversation with her brother and Cavill-Lawrence. Occasionally, her tale was interrupted by her infant son, who sat opposite them at a table that could have sat twenty, making messy work of a bowl of pottage. Mrs Corsham's own plate of food was untouched. Her ginger footman hovered discreetly, looking at Child as though he was about to make off with the silver. Seeing Mrs Corsham here, in this domestic tableau with her son, his guilt returned full-force, so that he was hardly able to take in what she was saying.

The Prince of Wales. Mixed up with Jonathan Stone and his masquerades. Little wonder the Home Office were in such high dudgeon.

His client seemed more troubled by the involvement of her family's bank than that of the heir to the throne. First her lover was embroiled in this, Child thought, then her brothers. But that was the trouble with the beau monde. They were a tight, exclusive circle, because that was the way they liked it. Marrying sisters and cousins. Keeping their money close. But throw a man like Stone into the barrel and the rot spread closely too.

'Mrs Corsham,' he tried again, when she had finished. 'I beg you to see reason. The Prince of Wales could be the fifth man at the masquerade.'

'I dearly hope not. But he could have easily travelled from

Northamptonshire to Muswell Rise. It's two days' ride at most, one at a gallop.'

'What if he killed Pamela?'

'Surely not. He's just a boy.'

'He's nineteen years old. Men far younger than him have committed murder. I don't much fancy taking a stroll up to St James's Palace to arrest the heir to the throne. And even if the Prince is innocent, the Home Office will never allow these crimes to come to trial. Not as long as the House of Hanover risks being drawn into it.'

'We will find a way to make it happen,' Mrs Corsham said, doggedly. 'Lucy did – her letter to the Home Secretary might even have worked, if she hadn't been murdered. And we can keep the Prince and the Craven Bank out of it, I am sure. I'll not let them hang poor Mr Von Siegel for a crime he didn't commit. Nor will I be bullied into silence.'

Child wondered if there was some other route out of this mess. A way to bring down Stone, before he could hurt Mrs Corsham. Whatever had gone on at Muswell Rise that night with Pamela, Stone was plainly up to his neck in it – and quite conceivably guilty of murder himself. If Child could get to the truth and do it fast, perhaps it would give him the means to fight back against Stone? It wasn't much of a plan, but it was the only one he had.

'Lucy said to Hector that the Priapus Club's greatest strength was also their greatest weakness,' he said. 'She must have meant the Prince.'

Mrs Corsham nodded. 'My brother and Cavill-Lawrence weren't telling me everything, I think. There is more to it, but I don't yet know what.'

Her son looked up from his bowl to point at Child. 'Monster, Mama, monster.'

'Hush,' she said, smiling fondly. 'This is Mr Child, a very clever man who catches villains.'

Still thinking about Jonathan Stone and his betrayal, Child decided that the boy had it about right.

'Do you have any children, sir?' Mrs Corsham asked. 'I know so little about you.'

'I had a son once. He died.'

She stared at him aghast. 'I'm sorry. That was a thoughtless question.'

He made a hopeless gesture. 'It was a long time ago.'

To cover their awkwardness, she tacked back to their inquiry. 'I found out something interesting from a friend of my sister-in-law. Before she disappeared, Theresa Agnetti had taken a lover: Lieutenant Dodd-Bellingham.'

Child raised his eyebrows. 'Miss Willoughby, Theresa Agnetti, Pamela. Was there a woman in Agnetti's house whom the lieutenant didn't try to seduce?'

'That's how he is – just like his father. And he's handsome, of course, charming enough when he wants to be – and persistent. For every ten women who say no, like Miss Willoughby, there will be one who says yes, like Mrs Agnetti.'

'Perhaps he doesn't like it when they say no – and when they're poor and friendless, like Miss Willoughby, it makes no odds. Perhaps he tried to rape Pamela and she fought back?'

Mrs Corsham glanced at her son, seemingly anxious about the topic, but he seemed happily absorbed, scraping up the last of his pottage.

'Lucy thought that Stone wanted Pamela at the masquerade for a purpose,' Child went on. 'That he trusted those men because he knew their secrets. If Simon is a thief and his brother is a rapist, then perhaps Stone has evidence of those crimes? Did you ever hear anything untoward about Lord March?'

'No, but I do know he would never have introduced the Prince to Stone willingly. He took great pride in his role as Prinny's mentor – perhaps the only thing he ever took seriously, apart from his poetry.' She shook her head. 'I hate to think of Pamela out there at Muswell Rise in the middle of the night, with no one to help her.'

'Kitty was there.' Child told her about his discoveries since they'd last met. 'I think she felt guilty about whatever had happened to Pamela. It makes me wonder if it is her testimony that the Home Office are searching for. We know Lucy was looking for Kitty – perhaps she found her.'

'Then we must find her too.'

The little boy jumped down from the table. 'Mama, may I hunt the mouse again?'

'He spotted it two days ago upon the nursery stairs,' Mrs Corsham explained. 'It's sparked quite the obsession. You may hunt the mouse, my love, if Mrs Graves says you can. Miles, see him upstairs, will you, please?'

Frowning, she turned back to Child. 'Do you think Kitty is the friend Lucy mentioned? The one who was supposed to give her dossier to the newspapers, but never did?'

'It's possible.' Child thought of Nelly Diver's battered, bleeding face. 'If we're right, then I hope to God that we find Kitty before the Home Office do. Assuming they haven't already.'

'I have my first sitting with Mr Agnetti this afternoon,' Mrs Corsham said. 'I'll ask him about Kitty. And I'll try to find out more about what went on in his house in the weeks before Pamela disappeared. I think you might be right that Theresa Agnetti is connected to all this somehow.'

'You promised me that you wouldn't meet with any of our

suspects alone,' Child objected. 'Mr Agnetti might still be our fifth man.'

'Miles will be downstairs. Agnetti will hardly try anything with him around.'

'Lucy was surrounded by six thousand people. That didn't help her.'

She smiled at his concern. 'You are a stalwart servant, Mr Child.'

Chapter Forty-Five

Mr Agnetti proposed to paint Caro standing in front of a ruined temple in a glade. She would have flowers in her hair and growing at her feet. Orange blossom for her married state; lilies for wealth; cinquefoils for motherhood.

He positioned her on his stage, next to a broken pillar, adjusting her stance several times in a way she felt somewhat impertinent, turning her shoulder, raising her chin, like she was a doll. Morning sunlight poured through the open windows and the cries of the street-hawkers carried from the square below.

'At first I will simply make some sketches,' he said. 'Probably for two or three sittings, after which I will commence painting. I cannot predict a finish date, but most commissions take between three and six months.'

Without her allowance, she wouldn't have enough money to pay the outstanding amount. But Harry would surely be home by then, and Mr Agnetti's bill would be settled one way or another. As would her own account with Harry. She shivered, not wanting to think of her unborn child and all it entailed.

Mr Child's commission was another matter, and she would need money to pay her own way – she was damned if she'd let Mordechai keep her shut up at home like an errant child. Earlier that morning, she'd therefore dispatched Pomfret on a discreet mission to a pawnbroker's in Marylebone with a pearl necklace she'd never liked. He'd returned with thirty pounds. A trifling sum, but for the moment, it would have to do. She could always pawn the Hilliard miniature, if it came to it.

Agnetti sketched upon a secretary desk, rather than his easel, working in both chalk and charcoal, his hand moving rapidly across the paper. Caro's eyes flicked to the giant canvas leaning against the wall. He'd worked on it since her last visit. The faces of the Furies were further defined with highlights and shadow.

'Look at me, if you please, madam,' Agnetti barked, and her eyes slid obediently back to his face. Remembering Mr Child's warnings, she suppressed a shiver. Had those big hands, which brought such vivid life to his canvases, also wielded the instrument of death at Vauxhall Gardens? Had they thrown her under the wheels of that carriage at Carlisle House?

'I have been thinking a little more about Lucy Loveless,' she said. 'And about Pamela, your Iphigenia. Did they know one another?'

'I was wondering whether you were going to raise the topic,' he said. 'Lord March tells me you have employed a thief-taker to look into the murder. Do I take it your sudden admiration for my painting is connected to your inquiry?'

Caught out, she hesitated, before deciding to own the charge. 'It seemed a good opportunity to learn more about Lucy.'

'I see. Something strange happened the other day. I discovered that another drawing, one of Lucy, had gone missing from one of my sketchbooks. That book was in the Rotunda when you called on me there. Was it you who stole it?'

She flushed under his stern gaze. 'Borrowed it, rather.'

Agnetti tossed his charcoal onto his desk. 'You never thought to ask me for the drawing directly? Or put your questions to me honestly?'

Given that Miles was downstairs, within earshot if she

screamed, she spoke boldly: 'I didn't know if I could trust your answers. My thief-taker found the murder weapon hidden in a bush at Vauxhall. It was one of your knives, the handle tied with red string.'

'*Madre di Dio.*' He closed his eyes. 'There were knives, frames, other tools in the storeroom located off the corridor in the Rotunda. It wasn't locked. Miss Willoughby and I needed to go in and out. Anyone could have slipped in there and taken the knife.'

'Were you in the Rotunda between half past nine and ten o'clock?'

'Many people can attest to it.'

'Yet you just said you went often to the storeroom?'

'Yes, but only for a matter of minutes each time.'

A matter of minutes was all you'd need to get from the Rotunda to the bowers and back again. A man would barely be missed. But then the same held true for all of them.

'If I ask my questions honestly now, will you answer them?'

'Of course. Whatever my past disagreements with Lucy, I want her murderer caught. The magistrate's ambivalence angers me too. But I will return your deposit.' He crumpled his sketch into a ball and tossed it over his shoulder. 'The work of Agnetti is not for the walls of false admirers.'

Determined not to be chastened by his censure, Caro began combatively. 'We have heard that your quarrels with Lucy pre-dated the theft of your drawings. That you had an argument with her around the time she was beaten.'

'I wouldn't call it an argument. I was looking for my wife and I thought Lucy might know where she was.'

'Did you lose your temper?'

'I may have done. I was worried for Theresa and my emotions were heightened. Lucy had strong views on marriage and men, and I thought it possible she'd helped Theresa leave, without realizing the full extent of her troubled mind. She insisted not.'

'Were you the one who beat her?'

'Of course not.' He sounded weary. 'She'd hardly have carried on sitting for me, if I had.'

'She might have done. She wanted to steal those drawings.'

He threw up his hands. 'I just wanted to know where Theresa was. But that was six months ago. I didn't kill Lucy.'

'Did you know that Lucy was looking into Pamela's disappearance?'

'Yes, she told me after I confronted her about the stolen drawings.'

'Pamela had attended a masquerade at Stone's estate on the night she disappeared. The four gentlemen in your stolen drawings were present – as well as a fifth man. Was that you?'

'Lucy asked me the same question. I wasn't there.'

'Yet you said you'd been to the Priapus Club before?'

'In January, two months before Pamela disappeared. It was not what I was led to expect. Mr Stone might be a valued client, but as a married man, his club was not to my taste.'

Caro gazed at him sceptically. 'Can you give me the names of the members? Other than the four in your painting?'

'I'm afraid not. Everyone was wearing masks. And once I'd witnessed the true nature of the club, I swiftly left.'

'What did you do after Lucy raised her concerns with you?'

'My mind was on other matters at the time, namely the disappearance of my wife. But I did question Kitty, another of my sitters, regarding Pamela's whereabouts. She assured me that Pamela had simply found herself a wealthy keeper.'

'It didn't occur to you that Kitty could have been lying?'

He sighed. 'You sound like Lucy. There is no evidence to

suggest it. Some of my sitters I wouldn't trust to tell me the grass was green, but Kitty was an uncomplicated girl, with a romantic heart. She is the last person I believe would be complicit in a murder.'

Caro's eyes fastened on his *Judgement of Paris*: his red-headed Aphrodite. 'Is that Kitty?'

'Yes, it is.'

'Do you know where she is now? My thief-taker is trying to find her.'

'They told me at her lodgings that she too had found a keeper. That has always been the pattern of Kitty's life: a year or two as the personal property of a wealthy gentleman, followed by stints in the brothels in Soho and St James's, when they tire of her company.'

'Did you know Pamela never went back to the tableaux house for her money? She walked away from a hundred and twenty-five guineas.'

He frowned. 'No, I did not.'

'I know Pamela met the Dodd-Bellingham brothers and Lord March in this house. Did she meet Mr Stone here too?'

'I don't believe so. Mr Stone rarely visits my studio. That's what he has the lieutenant for.'

'Did she ever talk about him?'

'She asked me some questions about him once or twice. My sitters like nothing more than talking about rich, important gentlemen.'

'Did Pamela ever mention feeling disturbed by any of those gentlemen? An unwanted interest? A forceful advance?'

'If she had raised any concern with me, then I would have acted upon it. Pamela was my sitter, under my protection.'

'You said your wife and Lucy were friends. Was she also a friend of Pamela's?'

The furrow in his brow deepened. 'What has Theresa got to do with this?'

'They disappeared on the same day. Did you never think that odd?'

'I confess I barely noticed Pamela's absence at first. I was too busy looking for Theresa. When I did, as I said, I was told she'd found a keeper. I certainly had no cause to make a connection. But in answer to your question, no, they were not friends. In truth, there was a tension between them.'

'Oh?'

'I never fully learned the cause of it. Perhaps Theresa resented the time I spent on the Iphigenia painting. Sometimes she desired my company at times when I couldn't give it. Often when I could, she did not.'

'Could Theresa have been jealous?'

He gave her an icy glare. 'Forsaking all others. It was not a vow I took lightly, whatever the newspapers might say or people might believe. Besides which, Pamela was a child.'

'Can you think of any other reason for their antipathy?'

'No, but Theresa could be . . . difficult with people sometimes. She was slow to trust and sometimes her manner turned people against her.'

'My thief-taker spoke to a friend of Pamela's who says she had a strong liking for Lieutenant Dodd-Bellingham. Did you ever witness any affection between them?'

'No, and Pamela would never have let anything progress very far. She was auctioning her virginity for a large sum, and whatever her feelings, I don't believe she'd have risked losing it. She is young, but not a fool, and above everything, she wants to improve her lot in life. If I possessed as little as she does, I daresay I would too.' He paused. 'She really left her money at the tableaux house?'

'That's what I've been told.'

His heavy brows drew together again, and she assessed his troubled expression with a critical eye.

'I asked my previous question, Mr Agnetti, because I wonder whether the lieutenant might have played some part in the tension between Pamela and Theresa?'

He turned away, and she could see the question had hurt him. 'The gossip has spread so far?'

'I did hear a rumour. Is it true?'

'I don't wish to speak of it,' he said. 'Theresa has nothing to do with any of this. Of that, I'm certain.'

'But Mr Agnetti—'

'No,' he said fiercely. 'If you have any more questions about Lucy or Pamela, then you may return at any time. But the struggles Theresa and I faced as husband and wife are a private matter.'

Chapter Forty-Six

A SPRAY OF blood flew past Child's eyes. The pugilists circled one another, keeping their distance. Three hundred voices roared as they came at one another again.

Mixed doubles always brought the crowds out, and this bout was a grudge match. Last year the Mascarenhas, a husband-and-wife pairing from Lisbon, had defeated Mr Wheatacre, a stevedore, and his partner in sparring, Mrs Johnson. The blood was hers: her close-fitted jacket and Holland drawers already spattered.

Child had met Solomon Loredo in a tavern on Old Street at two o'clock. All the spectators had gathered there, the streets around the tavern swarming. The organizers had circled the crowd, looking out for informants, the London magistrates particularly zealous when it came to boxing. Then one of them had cried out that the location of the match was to be Black-heath, and they'd all piled into their carriages, a long line of sixty vehicles trundling south.

'I feel bad that you paid for my ticket,' Loredo said, his little black eyes never leaving the fighters in the ring. 'For I have nothing for you. I asked all over the City. Spoke to other dealers in antiquities, other jewellers. Nobody had a bad word to say about Simon Dodd-Bellingham. No rumours about women or violence, no visits to the City brothels. I went to several myself, spoke to the bawds and the girls.'

'That must have been a hardship.'

'I am a diligent man, Child, what can I say?'

'Dodd-Bellingham claims not to like whores. Only respectable women.'

'That fits with what I heard. In that respect, as a bachelor, he is unusual.'

'Maybe his tastes run in a different direction. There are other sorts of brothel. Ones that deal in men or little boys. Or little girls.'

Loredo looked troubled. 'Not Dodd-Bellingham. He has been to my house, met my wife, met my daughters. I never witnessed anything to give me cause for concern.'

'Sometimes the biggest rakes are just talk, and the quiet upright men the ones you ought to watch. I knew a merchant in Deptford who went to church every day, and strangled three whores before we caught him.' Child took Pamela's picture from his pocket. 'This is the one we think was murdered back in March. She was older than she looked, but not by much.'

Loredo dragged his eyes from the fight, and frowned, seemingly troubled by the girl's youth. 'I hope to God you're wrong about Dodd-Bellingham. I still think you are.'

The crowd surged forward as Mascarenhas caught Wheatacre a hefty peg on the chin and he went down. The Portuguese, in the manly and proper way of pugilism, kicked the fallen man in the ribs, a practice known as 'purring', until he managed to roll away, and reclaim his feet. This prompted a flurry of bets upon the Portuguese, a man calling out new odds to entice those supporting the English.

'Did you ever hear a rumour about Dodd-Bellingham stealing from one of his clients? A man named Ansell Ward?'

'Yes, I heard it,' Loredo said.

'You weren't going to mention it?'

'Only because I concluded that there was no truth to the allegation. I looked into it when I first had dealings with Dodd-Bellingham – a man who would steal from his clients wouldn't think twice about deceiving another dealer. Yet aspects of the story didn't sit right with me from the start. Dodd-Bellingham was trying to build his business, make a name for himself with his clients. He had grand ambitions. That's why he got himself into debt in the first place.'

'Debt is a good motive for theft.'

'He was making far more from Ward's commission than he'd get for a pair of jade figurines – that's even without the risk to his reputation. And that part about him drinking on the job?' Loredo pulled a face. 'Does he look like a drinker to you?'

Child had to concede the point. He knew drinkers, looked at one in the mirror every day.

'His other clients couldn't have been happier with his work,' Loredo went on. 'He has a reputation for honesty. That's why the whole tale was so strange.'

'Did you ask him about it?'

'Naturally. He said it was all a misunderstanding. Oh, the theft was real enough. Dodd-Bellingham suspected that one of Ward's footmen was responsible. Initially, it seemed that's where the blame would lodge. But Ward's wife didn't like young Simon, he suspects because of his illegitimacy, and she pointed the finger at him. You know how women can be when they take against a man. Ward is a doting husband, and she talked him round.'

'You took Simon's word for it?'

'Of course not. I made inquiries amongst my acquaintances, thief-takers like yourself. No dealer in stolen goods remembered Dodd-Bellingham trying to sell a pair of jade figurines. None of it added up, Child. The boy is not a thief. I'd bet my house on it.' Loredo cried an oath. 'Watch this. She's got a choke-hold like you wouldn't believe.'

Senhora Mascarenhas had Mrs Johnson down on her knees and was strangling her. Mrs Johnson looked in desperate straits, and the crowd, judging by the betting, assumed that it was all over. But she managed to jab an elbow into her opponent's groin, and wrenched herself free. The men were also bloodied and tiring, Mascarenhas's eye badly gouged.

Child showed him Pamela's necklace. 'Can you tell me anything about this?'

Loredo took it in his big fist, frowning again. 'Is this also connected to these murders?'

'Yes, it belonged to the girl in the drawing.'

Loredo examined it, glancing up occasionally to watch the action. 'You sometimes see Lascar sailors selling necklaces like these down at the docks. The little hand is a token of good luck. Sailors buy them for their sweethearts for a few shillings.'

'It's not old or valuable, then?'

'There's no way to date it for certain. The Calcutta silver-smiths don't use assaying marks. I'd guess it's younger than you or I.' He gave Child a sidelong glance. 'Jonathan Stone was in India. Could he have given it to her?'

'I'm told that her father gave it to her mother. The girl grew up in an orphanage.'

'Hardly uncommon,' Loredo observed. 'A girl gets sweet-talked into bed by a sailor, believes she's going to be married, then gets left high and dry when the next ship sails. She is disgraced, often with child. Most end up turning whore.'

Child grunted, returning the necklace to his pocket. He winced as Mrs Johnson thrust her thumbs into her opponent's eyes, kneeing her several times in the breasts for good measure. The senhora stumbled back, unable to see for all the blood, and

Mrs Johnson delivered an uppercut that knocked her out cold. The crowd cheered as the English pair rounded on Senhor Mascarenhas, buffeting him one between the other.

'*Basta!*' he cried out, but the crowd wanted blood, and seeing that they would not give quarter, Mascarenhas jumped from the ring. Wheatacre and Johnson held their arms aloft, while the crowd sang 'Rule Britannia'.

Loredo, who had a hatred of the Portuguese for their persecution of his Lisbon forefathers, hugged Child. 'There now. You have brought me luck, my friend. Have dinner with me tonight. What do you say?'

CHAPTER FORTY-SEVEN

THE GREEN PARK was hot as hay harvest. Caro sat on a rug on the grass, watching Gabriel and Miles race the boy's wooden wheeled horses up and down the grass. Every now and then, her son would stop to beam at her, and she and Mrs Graves were required to applaud.

Ladies shaded by parasols strolled in the sun, the gentlemen swinging Malacca walking canes. Footmen made little processions carrying hampers and cushions and silver coolers of ice and wine from the grand mansions that lined the park's borders. Sometimes one of the gentlemen would tip their hat to Caro, or one of the ladies stop to talk. But others of her acquaintance hurried on by. Her entire circle would have read *The London Hermes* by now.

'When I am four, I'll have a real horse, won't I, Mama?'

She couldn't even remember making the promise, but for Gabriel it had become etched in stone. *Will I even see your fourth birthday? Will you hate me when you know what I've done? Will another woman take my place, be your mother?*

Last night she'd had a dream: her belly swollen almost to term, the child she'd tried to murder squirming inside her, a vengeful Orestes trying to claw his way out. Lord knows, *The London Hermes* wouldn't help her chances of talking Harry round. She kept rehearsing the conversation in her mind, all her pleas and promises countered by talk of honour and principle, and all the other things men cited when pride made them do foolish things.

'Look,' Miles said, pointing. 'There's Miss Willoughby.'

Agnetti's assistant was walking across the grass towards them, her face shaded by a white hat adorned with pale-pink roses. She smiled at Caro a little nervously, and raised a white-gloved hand.

People turned to stare. This is all I need, Caro thought. The company of a scandalous outcast. But she rose to greet Agnetti's assistant nevertheless.

'I called at your house,' Miss Willoughby said. 'They told me you were here.'

'Please, do sit down,' Caro said, gesturing to the rug. Miles hastily moved the basket and her parasol out of the way, and stood back smiling. Miss Willoughby has made a conquest there, Caro thought.

Gabriel was staring trance-like at an older child running a hoop.

'A handsome boy,' Miss Willoughby said.

Caro smiled. 'He's growing up too fast.'

Miss Willoughby took a folded banknote from her panniers and held it out to Caro. 'Mr Agnetti asked me to return your deposit.'

'You didn't need to come out of your way,' Caro said, secreting the note in her own panniers. 'You could have left it at the house.' Given Mordechai's actions, she was glad of the money. 'I suppose Mr Agnetti told you how I deceived him?'

'Yes.' She frowned. 'That is why I offered to come, rather than send a servant. I wanted to talk to you about your inquiry.'

'Oh?'

'Lucy Loveless left Mr Agnetti's employ some weeks before I came to London. But this afternoon, when we were discussing your visit, Mr Agnetti pointed her out to me in his painting of the Furies. I realized then that I had seen her before.'

The boy with the hoop had wandered off, and Gabriel ran up to Caro. 'Boat, Mama?'

Caro glanced at him distractedly. 'Yes, my love. I will join you there in just a moment. Go with him, Miles.'

Looking extremely reluctant, the footman picked up Gabriel's wooden boat, giving Miss Willoughby a last considered glance. Then he set off across the grass towards the Queen's Basin, followed by Gabriel and his nursemaid, hand in hand.

'Do go on, Miss Willoughby,' Caro said.

'It was only a few days before Lucy's murder. Mr Agnetti had asked me to collect some paints and oils from a shop in Marylebone, and I encountered the lieutenant in Leicester Fields as I was leaving. He offered to escort me there.' She flushed, looking down at her hands. 'This was when I still thought well of him, you understand. As we were walking along Baker Street, a woman came out of one of the houses and when she and the lieutenant noticed one another, they exchanged cross words. I realize now that this woman was Lucy Loveless.'

This must be the same conversation that Lucy's neighbouring tenant had described to Mr Child, Caro realized. 'Did you hear what they said?'

'Lucy accused the lieutenant of ruining her life. He laughed at her, and this seemed to anger her further. Then she said something that wiped the smile from his face: "Maybe now that I have so much time upon my hands, I'll visit Somerset." I thought it an odd thing to say, given the nature of their exchange, and her expression suggested that it was an allusion she thought the lieutenant would understand. And he seemed to – for he pushed her violently. Then he walked off in a fury, leaving me to hurry after him.'

Caro frowned. 'Did the lieutenant ever mention Somerset in passing?'

'Not that I recall. But it clearly meant something to him.' She sighed. 'That incident should have told me everything I needed to know about the man, but he told me some story, casting himself as an innocent victim of theft, and I told myself that he had a right to be angry. We believe the truth we choose to see, do we not?'

Caro wondered if Lucy's threat had a connection to the lieutenant's secret? Another rape? One committed in Somerset?

'Tell me,' she said, 'does the lieutenant like to paint?'

She looked surprised by the question. 'He never said as much, though he was highly complementary about my own work. I presumed afterwards that this interest was feigned, like so much else.'

'And Mr Stone?'

'I believe Mr Agnetti once gave him some private lessons. He says Mr Stone has talent, but then he is a valued client, and I imagine all valued clients are said to have talent.'

Caro returned her trace of a smile. 'Thank you,' she said. 'I will pass your information on to my thief-taker. In return, I have something to tell you. A mystery I believe I have solved, one that might help you understand Mr Agnetti's anger over your stroll with the lieutenant. People say he was the lover of Mrs Agnetti.'

Miss Willoughby's eyes widened and her mouth went slack. 'Now I feel even more of a fool,' she whispered.

'I think Mr Agnetti was only trying to protect you. Under the circumstances, one can understand his anger.'

'Yes, poor Mr Agnetti.' She bit her lip.

'It was not your fault,' Caro said, gazing at her with sympathy. 'Not for trusting the lieutenant. Not for what happened in that bower.'

She blinked away her tears. 'It feels as if it is. Everything does.'

Caro wondered if she was talking about her father's secretary, the man who'd abandoned her. Or something else in her past. *Evelina says the father doted upon the girl. Perhaps too much.*

'It is our tragedy to assume upon our own shoulders responsibility for the misdeeds of men,' she said. 'But we should be kinder, I think. To one another, as well as to ourselves. Do call on me if ever you should need a friend.'

Miss Willoughby gave a wan smile. 'Thank you, Mrs Corsham. But my duties leave me little time for making calls.'

They shook hands, and Caro watched her walk off across the grass, a little put out by the girl's refusal of her offer of friendship. For a few minutes, she sat quietly, watching the children play, thinking about everything Miss Willoughby had told her. She hated the idea of her sweet little boy being drawn one day into that world of twilight pleasure. Buying women, or seducing them, discarding them once they'd succumbed. *And how will I be able to teach him differently, if I am not there?*

Someone shouted her name, and she looked up sharply. Miles was racing across the grass towards her.

Sweat broke out on her skin. 'What is it? Where's Gabriel?'

'He's not with you?' Miles turned, scanning the children. Caro felt a rush, as the world seemed to tilt on its axis.

'Why would he be with me? You were supposed to be watching him.' Her eyes swept the crowds. 'Gabriel!'

'It was busy.' Miles was panting. 'He was running around

after his boat. I can't have taken my eyes off him for more than a moment. Mrs Graves . . .'

But Caro wasn't listening. She was running towards the Queen's Basin. People stared, time moving like treacle. *Is this happening? Yes, this is happening.* Her stomach contracted and a hundred dark thoughts entered her mind. *He's drowned in the pond. A kidnapper has him, for ransom, for unspeakable purposes. No, he's just hiding, this is all a game. No, he's being hurt right now, and you're doing nothing.*

She rounded a bend in the path, almost colliding with a passing couple. 'Have you seen a little boy with black hair in a pink gown?'

They only stared at Caro blankly. *Why weren't people helping?* She ran on, but what if she was running the wrong way? She screamed his name again, hands shaking, her vision a tunnel. She ran past the little wilderness that shaded the Tyburn pool.

'Mrs Corsham,' Miles shouted. 'There he is.'

She turned and saw him, crouched by the pool, pushing his boat. She ran, grabbed him, held him so tight she was afraid his ribs might crack. Her tears flowing, she kissed him again and again.

'Mama,' she heard Gabriel say. 'Lady gave me for give to you.'

'What lady?'

He had something in his hand, and as she took it from him, bile rose in her throat. It was another puzzle purse – this one painted with a pair of masks, one black, one white. With trembling fingers, she prised the folds apart.

Inside were more paintings: a lady, dressed in the same oyster satin she'd worn to Carlisle House; the same lady held by the plague doctor; the lady crushed and bleeding beneath the wheels of a speeding carriage; a little boy crying, perhaps for his mother.

She unfolded the puzzle purse fully to read the message inside:

YOU FIRST. HIM NEXT.

PAMELA

8–14 February 1782

Mrs Agnetti did not bloom during her pregnancy. It was as if she was being devoured by an incubus. Her face pinched and hollow, her eyes sunken and dark-rimmed, her belly distended over her tiny frame like a starving urchin. Sometimes Mr Agnetti would ask Pamela to take tea with his wife, and Mrs Agnetti would sit there glowering, stabbing at her sampler, reminding Pamela more than ever of Mad Miriam at the orphanage.

She didn't know what she'd done to earn the older woman's enmity, but she presumed it must have something to do with Lieutenant Dodd-Bellingham. Perhaps Mrs Agnetti had sensed a dwindling of his affections? Or noticed the attention he paid Pamela whenever he saw her? In front of her husband, Mrs Agnetti would speak with forced politeness, but sometimes her mask would slip, and she'd snap or speak coldly, her hands clenched like rat's claws. Pamela was fed up with Lucy's and Kitty's excuses for her behaviour. *She's anxious about the baby. Don't take it to heart. Theresa doesn't mean to be unkind. It's just her way.*

Mrs Rosell used to say similar things at the orphanage, whenever Mad Miriam shouted or cried or swore. Then one day, Miriam had produced a pigeon from beneath her dress and put out its eyes with a needle, while all the girls screamed.

One afternoon in mid February, Mr Agnetti decided to finish painting early, and invited her downstairs to take Madeira with him and his wife. He talked to Pamela kindly, Mrs Agnetti sitting very still, turning the pages of her book too fast to be actually reading it.

'You pose very well,' Mr Agnetti told her. 'You must sit for me again. You will make a fine goddess when you're a little older.' He rose to tilt her chin, turning it to the fading light. 'What do you think, Theresa? With such beauty and those fine black eyes, she could be my Andromeda.'

Mrs Agnetti looked up from her book, just long enough to skewer Pamela with her gaze. 'I fear she'd struggle to convince as a princess.'

Nasty old witch. Pamela sat up straighter, tilting her chin in a regal manner.

Agnetti smiled. 'There now. Her bearing is perfect.'

'What are you reading, Theresa?' Pamela asked sweetly, enjoying the moment.

'The plays of Euripides.'

'A Greek tragedian,' Agnetti explained. 'One of his plays was about Iphigenia. You should read it – shouldn't she, my love?'

Mrs Agnetti answered woodenly, scarcely bothering to pretend. 'Yes, Jacobus. I am sure Pamela would enjoy Euripides very much.'

*

Know your enemy. It was a favourite saying of the lieutenant's. He liked to tell Pamela about his exploits on the battlefield. And that's what this house had become. Unacknowledged but understood. Mrs Agnetti knew it. So did she.

Lord March called late that afternoon to return Agnetti's

volume of Dracontius. 'I have some thoughts on it, if you'd be interested?'

'Very much,' Agnetti said. 'Pamela, let us finish for today. You may wait for Mrs Havilland's footman in the morning room.'

She slid off the altar, enjoying the heat of Lord March's eyes. So predictable. She smiled at him, tucking her breast away.

Downstairs, she found the morning room empty. The Agnettis had argued earlier. Theresa had wanted to attend a party of supper and cards at a place called Craven House, but Mr Agnetti hadn't wanted her to go. Pamela wondered if that was where she was now, laughing with the lieutenant. So devious. So cold. A woman like that might be hiding other secrets too.

Returning to the hall, she listened out for the servants, hearing only a distant murmur from the kitchen. Taking a candle from the table in the hall, she crept back upstairs. Past the door to the studio, up another flight of stairs, to the second-floor landing. Here she paused.

From the servants' talk, she knew the Agnettis had separate bedrooms. His was at the front of the house, and she presumed this second door must lead to hers. Pressing her ear to the door, she listened, but could hear nothing. Turning the handle very slowly, she opened the door and stepped inside, closing it behind her.

The curtains were open to a charcoal sky, the room in shadow. Pamela made out a canopied bed, an armoire and a dressing table. She lit her candle with a tinder from her pocket, and placed it on the dressing table. Studying the jewellery boxes and the bottles of scent, the silver pots and brushes, she wondered why such a plain woman needed such an extravagant toilette – and then decided that the answer spoke for itself. Opening one of the boxes, she took out a diamond brooch. Good silverwork, the stones cushion-cut. About fifty guineas. She wondered if it had been a gift from Mr Agnetti. Or from him.

'Put it back.'

Startled, she almost dropped it. Turning, she glimpsed a figure sitting on a stool in a darkened recess of the room. Theresa Agnetti. Whatever was she doing there in the dark? Lying in wait?

Her heart racing, grappling for an excuse, she seized upon the first that came to mind. 'Forgive me, Theresa. I was looking for a hairpin. I thought you were out.'

Mrs Agnetti rose and came forward into the candlelight. A pair of scissors flashed in her hand. 'Do you spy for my husband? Or do you do this on your own account?'

Pamela gave a nervous laugh. 'What are you talking about, Theresa?'

'You want him, don't you? Does he ever touch you? When you are alone?'

'Do you mean your husband? I never would.'

Mrs Agnetti's voice rose in pitch. 'You know who I mean.'

It was out there now. No point pretending otherwise. Battle lines drawn.

Pamela drew a breath, and the lies tumbled out unbidden. 'Every chance he gets. We'll be together when he tires of you. Sometimes he laughs at you when we are alone.'

The scissors flashed, cold steel pressed against Pamela's neck. 'Try to take him from me and I will kill you.'

Chapter Forty-Eight

CARO'S ANGER WAS fierce and bright, burning like the fireworks over Vauxhall Gardens. She was hardly aware of the crowds, the bangs, the whiff of gunpowder, reliving the terror of losing Gabriel again and again.

Her son had seemed quite unscathed by the experience. She'd had Gaston grill him a miniature beefsteak, and he'd tucked into it quite happily. When she'd questioned him about what had happened, all he could tell her was that a lady had given him the puzzle purse. What lady? What woman could do such a thing to a mother? Miss Willoughby had been in the park only a short time before Gabriel was taken, and she certainly had the talent to have painted the puzzle purse – but to what end? Could she be in league with the killer? With Mr Agnetti? But why would a pair of artists implicate themselves like this?

More likely the killer had paid a woman to do it. Her heart tightened, as she thought of her innocent boy led into danger, his life threatened. *I will find you*, she promised, *and I will enjoy your hanging day.*

The night was cooler, the end of the season drawing near. It seemed to infect the Vauxhall crowds; the wine tents raucous, the women bolder, the men more forward. Carnival masks leered in the crowd, brittle laughter rising, men shouting bawdy remarks to one another across the lime walks.

Instructing Miles to look out for the Dodd-Bellinghams and Lord March, they made a perambulation of the Grand South Walk, scanning the snaking rows of supper boxes. So many eyes were upon her, people whispering, not troubling to hide it. She nodded at acquaintances, ignoring their sly smiles.

Catching sight of Simon Dodd-Bellingham strolling alone amidst the crowds, she fought to master her anger. *They think that they have won. Because Ezra Von Siegel is under arrest. But I will turn their misplaced confidence to my advantage.*

Spotting her, Simon smiled. 'Mrs Corsham, I trust you've heard the news?'

No stammer tonight. No sweating.

'About Mr Von Siegel?' she said. 'Indeed, I have.'

'The man confessed, so they say. You must be relieved.'

She regarded him evenly. 'As must you.'

'A murderer off the streets? Who wouldn't be?'

Caro gazed around at the crowds. 'I thought you gentlemen hunted as a pack? And yet, here you are, a solitary creature. Are Lord March and your brother not at Vauxhall tonight?'

'Lord March has taken Miss Howard to a levée at the Palace. Neddy is around somewhere. He's with his friends.'

'I am glad to hear it, for I wanted to ask his advice. All this adventure has proved a little much, and I am thinking of taking a trip to visit an aunt down in Somerset. I hear the lieutenant is quite the authority upon that county.'

Immediately, she sensed his caution. He moistened his lips with his pink tongue. 'Somerset? Why do you say that?'

'Did he not visit before the war? I'm certain that's what I heard.'

'I wouldn't know,' he said slowly, as if choosing his words carefully. 'I was living with my mother then, as you recall. But I must say, it sounds unlikely. For one thing, Neddy can't abide the

339

countryside. He suffers dreadfully from the summer sneezes – likes to say the best thing our father ever did was sell up his country estates.' He smiled ruefully, warming to his performance. 'But then Neddy always does like to put a bold face on things.'

'Oh, he certainly does that,' Caro said. 'Perhaps he endured the countryside in order to work on his watercolours?'

'Watercolours? Neddy?' Simon laughed.

His reaction seemed genuine, but 'Somerset' had clearly meant something to him. A reason to be wary. A weakness. A secret. Probably his brother's, rather than his own.

'Well then,' she said. 'I shall have to seek the lieutenant out and ask him. Enjoy your night, Mr Dodd-Bellingham. I am sure our paths will cross again before too long.'

He bowed, and she felt his eyes follow her as she walked away.

Together with Miles, she searched the crowds for the lieutenant, eventually running him to ground at the food stalls near the Rope-Dancing Theatre. He was with a small party of redcoat officers and ladies, part of a much larger crowd gathered around one of the stalls. The object of their interest was an obese man eating a vast tray of pies, another man taking bets on when he might vomit.

Recalling Miss Willoughby's story of the attempted rape, thinking again of Gabriel, her anger burned. Yet tonight she needed to play a subtler hand.

'In the thick of the action, as ever, lieutenant,' she said, joining his side.

He gazed down at her unsmiling. 'If it isn't Mrs Corsham. Where's your fat friend? Licking his wounds? He'd be enjoying a nice reward right now, if he'd spent less time harassing his betters, and more time quizzing that murdering Jew.'

'We can all be grateful for the magistrate's efforts, I am sure. You might also be pleased to know that Mr Child spoke to the girls who attended your masquerade on the first of March. They confirmed everything your brother told us.'

'There you are, then,' he said. 'Simon did try to tell you.'

She sighed. 'I still worry about that girl, Pamela, though. Where she is – why she hasn't been seen around town. I am thinking of engaging Mr Child to find her.'

'Then you're a fool. Throwing good money after bad. I told you, these girls like to go wandering off, following their hearts.'

'Nevertheless, Mr Child has got me thinking. Did you know that Pamela disappeared on the same day as Theresa Agnetti? Mr Child thinks there might be a connection.'

'Theresa?' He frowned. 'That thief-taker of yours is simply after more of your money. Wherever Pamela is, she'd be laughing if she knew she was putting you to so much trouble.'

'I'd like to believe you are correct,' she said. 'Could I ask you a few questions about Theresa? I know the two of you were close. It will help me come to a decision about Mr Child.'

He hesitated, suspicion writ large upon his face. She could almost hear his mind working, debating which course would serve him best.

'After all,' she pressed, 'how could it hurt? If you're so certain that Pamela is alive and well?'

She was counting upon his arrogance, his conviction that he could seduce any woman around to his way of thinking.

The crowd had quietened to a hush. The obese man belched, leaned over and a cascade of vomit spilled from his mouth. People surged around the man taking bets, shouting.

The lieutenant crumpled his ticket. 'Very well, then. But I just lost my last crown, so dinner's on you.'

CHAPTER FORTY-NINE

IN THE CARRIAGE back to London, Child resisted Loredo's entreaties to stay out drinking by agreeing to dine with him in two days' time. The jeweller dropped him at the north end of London Bridge, taking the carriage on to his home at St Mary-le-Bow.

Child found a Thameside tavern, where he sat dwelling upon his predicament, trying and failing to think of another way out. If he didn't do Stone's bidding, then he'd face a trial, the jury bought, which would mean transportation at the very least, more likely a hanging. Do as Stone demanded, and Mrs Corsham would pay the price. Draining his pot of porter, he called for another. While he drank, he wrote a letter to Mrs Corsham cancelling the meeting they'd arranged for tomorrow afternoon. He couldn't face seeing her again so soon.

He thought of all the things Mrs Rainwood at the Magdalen Hospital had said. To love oneself. Easy for her to say – that gentle, kind woman who'd probably never committed any sin greater than a fart in chapel. All those loved by Peregrine Child ended up unhappy and then dead – and if that was the way things were going to go, he'd just as soon do it in the company of the bottle.

A little before midnight, he rose. To go on. That's all he had.

*

Hector was waiting for him in the dark, damp shadow of St Bennet's church, the light of his torch flickering across the lichened bricks and puddles.

'Mr C,' he cried. 'Want to step inside? For six shillings, I'll let you touch the divine.'

Child gave him a weary look. '*Me vexat pede*. It means behave yourself, or I'll drop you in the river.'

They walked along Thames Street, passed by the occasional coal wagon and once by the odorous cart of a night-soil man.

'I took a look at the minutes of the Whores' Club like you wanted,' Hector said. 'It seems that back in June, not long after Kitty moved out, Lucy stole a ring from Lieutenant Dodd-Bellingham.'

'So he told us.' Then the lieutenant had been telling the truth about one thing, at least. 'Go on.'

'Lucy used that ring to trick a whore named Moll Silversleeves into telling her something she shouldn't have done. Lucy made out that the lieutenant had lost the ring at her rooms. She told Moll he was trying to persuade her to give the Priapus Club a try. Moll was young, a little green, the wine was flowing, the ring convinced her – and she opened up.'

'About Pamela?' Child frowned. There had been no 'Moll' on Cecily's list.

'No, Moll wasn't there that night, she didn't know nothing about Pamela. But she'd been to other masquerades at Stone's estate. Lucy asked her if the Priapus Club would be worth her while. Well, Moll laughed at that – the members were rich, powerful men. Most harlots would give their eye-teeth for an invitation. Still, Lucy scoffed, which was when Moll started throwing names around. The girls aren't supposed to know who the gentlemen are, that's why everyone wears masks. But masks fall off, or don't fit well, and the girls make it a sport to guess.'

'Lucy was still looking for the fifth man,' Child said.

'Seems that way, sir.'

They turned into an alley that led downhill to the river, the cobbles a carpet of stinking excrement. The cranes on the roofs of the warehouses resembled a row of gibbets in the moonlight.

'When Moll found out she'd been duped, everyone went mad,' Hector said. 'Rosy, Becky and Sally led the charge. Lucy won the vote against her, but only just – people felt she hadn't behaved in the spirit of the club, that she'd risked their income from the masquerades in pursuit of her strange crusade. Not long after, we had the anonymous note about her time in Bridewell, and that was that.'

Child wondered if the trick with the ring was how Lucy had first found out about the Prince, and come up with her plan for blackmailing the Home Office.

They fell silent as they passed a busy tavern packed with sailors, lightermen and their whores. Hawkers stood in the shadows by the door, hoping to tempt the patrons into private pleasures: a toothless crone selling milk of the poppy; a spotty youth with a bag of lewd prints; a pair of young, muscular stevedores – known down here as water rats – lounging in the warehouse doorway opposite, giving Child the eye.

'Do you know where I can find Moll Silversleeves?' he asked.

Hector sighed. 'I doubt she'd have talked to you before, but she certainly won't now.'

'What do you mean?'

'They found her three nights ago. She'd hung herself in her rooms. It happens from time to time, but this one took the girls by surprise. Moll always seemed such a cheerful girl.'

They locked eyes. It could be a coincidence – but Child didn't think so either. Perhaps the murderer – or one of

Richmond Baird's friends from the Home Office – had paid Moll a visit.

'Did you find out anything interesting about my suspects?'

'A little. The girls say Mr Stone's not a violent man, quite the reverse. Prides himself on his proficiency at the art of love. The girls play up to it. The louder their cries of pleasure, the more he pays. Your lieutenant now is the opposite. All about his own pleasure. Not violent as such, but so clumsy it borders upon it. That's the trouble with the handsome ones. They never had to try.'

'No rumours of rape?'

'He wouldn't need to. The girls would never refuse him. He's the gatekeeper to Mr Stone's masquerades.'

They had reached the wharves, a chaotic jumble of ladders, piers, cranes, masts and timbers. Light spilled across the water from the brothels of Bankside opposite, oyster- and eel-boats drifting with each swell of the tide. Hector led him down a set of crumbling waterstairs, along a stretch of muddy beach, past a lone mudlark searching the flats for treasure. They stopped under one of the piers, sheltered from the wharves above, the kind of place the water rats came to do their business.

'How about Agnetti?' Child said.

'The newspapers have it all wrong. He don't touch the girls. Pines for his wife, they say. The girls I spoke to didn't like her, by the way. Said she was a real stone-cold bitch. I heard a good story about Agnetti, though. Want to hear it?'

'That's what I'm paying you for.'

'His father, the count, was a notorious philanderer. In Italy they called him *L'Ariete Dorato*, the Golden Ram. His mother entered a convent when Agnetti was only five years old, and he was brought up in a house full of his father's whores. Never knew who or what he might walk in on – his father or his friends, girls everywhere you looked. Sounds like fun, don't it?'

'Not really. Where did you hear this?'

'One of the girls who sat for Agnetti. He told her the story himself – said his father's women were more of a mother to him than his own.'

'Did you learn anything more about relations between Agnetti and his wife?'

'No, but I can keep asking.'

'How about the others? Lord March? Simon Dodd-Bellingham?'

Hector skimmed an oyster shell, the splashes punctuating his words. 'Didn't get a chance. Something came up.'

His tone gave Child pause. 'Oh?'

He shrugged. 'Someone was asking after me last night, a gentleman, at Birdcage Walk. I thought it might have been one of the men who threatened me before. So I spent the day down at Moorfields, out of sight.'

'I've changed my mind,' Child said. 'Forget what we agreed. I don't want you putting yourself in danger.'

Hector's voice rose. 'Do I look scared to you? If they catch up with me, then I'll convince them that I don't know nothing, like I did before. Come on, sir. Do a lad a service. I've got my heart set on that little yellow-boy in your pocket.'

Child hesitated, but the lad's information had proved useful so far – and there were few enough others willing to help him out. 'There's a carriage I want you to look for,' he said. 'Kitty was seen riding in it.' He described the harlequin pattern. 'Find it, keep asking around about my suspects, and I'll give you double what I promised. But for Christ's sake, watch your back, do you hear?'

'Didn't know you cared, sir. Consider me touched.'

Child listened to the lad's footsteps splashing and sucking through the mud back up to the wharves. He waited a little longer, skimming a few oyster shells himself, thinking about everything that Hector had told him. The lieutenant a little rough. Mrs Agnetti a stone-cold bitch. *Moll always was such a cheerful girl.*

Chapter Fifty

The lieutenant's party dined in the Grove, a grassy piazza at the heart of Vauxhall Gardens. The rows of supper boxes around the perimeter resembled boxes at the theatre, enclosed on three sides, with a view of the octagonal Orchestra and the dancing. In the silences between the music, the boxes buzzed with conversation, over the chink of silver and crystal. A cork popped, followed by applause.

The lieutenant's friends were named Cartwright and Hennessy, redcoat officers like himself. A trio of ladies accompanied them, introduced to Caro as Hennessy's sisters on a visit from Dorset. Caro could detect little family resemblance between them, and the looks Hennessy gave them were far from fraternal. She wondered if Lucy had ever sat in these boxes, masquerading as some gentleman's sister or niece.

Miles was the only servant present, standing with his back to the wall, which was painted with a scene from *Midsummer Night's Dream*. Liveried waiters poured wine, and brought platters of roast meat, bread and butter, olives and salad. The lieutenant seated himself and Caro at a slight distance from the others, and their intimacy soon drew the attention of passers-by. More grist to the scandalmongers' mill, Caro thought, with an inward sigh.

The lieutenant chewed on a mouthful of chicken, washing it down with a rich yellow wine. 'Theresa used to assist her husband with his clients,' he said, 'much as Miss Willoughby does now. She'd consult me about her husband's sketches, any quibbles over contracts, all of us wanting to keep Mr Stone happy. Sometimes when we'd finished talking business, Theresa would offer me tea, and we'd discuss other things.'

'I heard she offered you rather more than tea.' An image came to Caro of Theresa, down on her knees before the lieutenant in the Spencer House billiard room.

He grinned. 'We shared some private time together, I don't deny it. Theresa was a sweet girl. And she deserved better than Agnetti. Parading his whores in front of her – a gentleman should at least attempt discretion. No wonder she came looking for me, is all I'll say.'

'Mr Agnetti denies ever touching his sitters.'

'Up there on his own all day with half-naked strumpets? Believe that and you'll believe anything. Theresa certainly didn't.' The lieutenant lost his thread for a moment, turning to watch a pair of girls and their chaperone walk past. 'Whatever the truth, Theresa wasn't happy. Agnetti was fifteen years her senior, and there comes a time when a woman stops needing a father, if you know what I mean.'

Caro remembered all those nights at supper parties and balls: Theresa's awkward flirting, her husband's watchful glower. 'People say she was trying to make Agnetti jealous.'

'Perhaps she was, but not with me. This was different.'

They made an unlikely pairing, Caro reflected. Theresa not a plain woman, but not a great beauty either – not the sort of lady she imagined would interest the lieutenant for very long. As for Theresa, with her interest in Greek and art and philosophy, Caro struggled to imagine what she had found to talk about with the lieutenant.

'Truth be told,' he went on, 'I didn't think much of Theresa at all, at first. She was just Agnetti's wife. Stone's business, not my pleasure. But she had that rare ability to really listen to a man. It wasn't long after Father had died, and one day, to my surprise, I found myself telling her all about it. Mother's illness, and that woman he married when Ma was barely cold. About Simon, wanting to hate him, finding that we rubbed along all right, and then feeling dashedly disloyal.'

Caro wondered if this story was one he often told the ladies – a glimpse of the little boy beneath the braggadocio, each woman flattered to think that she was the first to hear it.

'Did she flirt with you?'

'Sometimes – she'd blush, wouldn't meet my eye. I sensed what she wanted, what she needed. One day, when Agnetti was out, I thought: Dash it, I'll chance my arm. Half expected a slap, but she responded like a – well, let's just say that she responded. After that, we'd meet in private: at a ball, or here at Vauxhall, sometimes at her house. Agnetti was so busy with his wretched paintings, he didn't even notice.'

'Did Theresa confide in you about her marriage?'

'A little. Just what I've said. That she was unhappy. Well, that much was apparent to anyone.'

'Was there ever any indication that Agnetti was violent?'

'She didn't say so. I never saw any bruises.'

'Did you ever witness him being unkind?'

He thought for a moment. 'He could be curt with her sometimes, when she was in drink. Towards the end, I think he caught on. Began to suspect that she was in love with someone else.'

'She told you that? That she loved you, I mean?'

'Not in so many words, but one gets to know the signs. She wrote me letters, gave me little presents, painted me a miniature.'

'Theresa painted?'

'She said Agnetti taught her when they were courting. She wasn't half bad.'

Cartwright, Hennessy and the girls had risen to applaud a passing entertainer, who was juggling with live mice and sticks of fire. The lieutenant rose to watch too, and Caro waited impatiently until he sat back down.

'If Theresa was in love with you, then why do you think she left?'

The lieutenant busied himself with his dinner, uncharacteristically coy about answering. 'If you must know, she'd become rather overbearing. Always asking me to call, demanding to meet. Sometimes all smiles, sometimes on the verge of tears when we parted. If I asked her what was wrong, she just said I was her only happiness. It's not the kind of thing a gentleman wants to hear.'

'You'd tired of her?'

'No need to make it sound so callous. I'd never led her to believe it was anything other than a diversion. I'd been thinking about ending it for a while, but she was sweet and willing and always there. Then Agnetti found out about us, and I decided it was time to do the deed.'

'Agnetti knew?' Caro said sharply.

The lieutenant had the grace to look a little abashed. 'I didn't intend to rub his face in it, but there we are. We were at the Amberley Ball, and she slipped away from Agnetti to meet me in the garden. One thing led to another, and afterwards I happened to glance up, and there he was, out there on the terrace, looking down at us.'

'You're certain he saw you?'

'Stared right at me, and he didn't look happy. I thought he

might call me out, but he was too much of a coward. Just went back inside.'

'So you broke it off with her?

'Didn't see that I had any choice. If Agnetti had decided to divorce her, he might have named me in a suit of criminal conversation. I could have ended up rotting in the Fleet, liable for thousands. I certainly didn't want to do anything that would give him further cause.'

'How did Theresa take it?'

He shifted a little in his chair. 'I don't know. I sent Simon with a note. Look, I'm not proud of it, but you can't put it all on me. I've spoken to people who knew the family in Italy, and Theresa had always been a strange, secluded girl. And if she was melancholic, the fault surely lies with her husband?'

'You think she killed herself? Because she couldn't live without you?'

'Don't think me unfeeling about it. I lit a candle for her at Easter.'

Caro frowned. 'It never occurred to you, given what had happened, that Agnetti might have hurt her?'

'He wouldn't have it in him. Besides, Agnetti spent hundreds on thief-takers trying to find her. He even spoke to me about it, demanded to know if I was keeping her. That would have cost him pride, I don't doubt. I told him I could barely afford to keep myself. Things were fraught between us for a time, but then they settled down. Neither one of us wanted to upset Stone.'

It had the ring of an honest account, though Caro reminded herself of all his other lies.

Could Theresa's disappearance have nothing to do with Lucy's murder after all? A tragic death, but no man culpable – unless you counted an imperfect husband and a heartless lover?

'Did you know that Pamela and Theresa disliked one another?'

He waved a hand. 'It was just some petty women's squabble, nothing more. Theresa said she'd caught Pamela nosing around in her bedroom. She wasn't happy about it. And Pamela said that Theresa had sent her a nasty note.'

'Were you the cause of their dispute?'

'Neither of them said as much, but it wouldn't surprise me. You ladies and your claws. I'd sooner face a hundred Hessian mercenaries.'

'You knew Pamela liked you then?'

'She made it pretty plain, but I never touched her. Stone wanted to bid for her virginity. He'd have been furious.'

'Pamela was for him, then? For Stone?'

He shovelled a last forkful of salad into his mouth, pushing back his plate with a belch. 'Who else would she be for? I certainly couldn't afford her.'

'Lucy thought there was a fifth man at the masquerade, and that Pamela was intended for him.'

He seemed ready for the question – ran a hand through his hair and yawned. 'What fifth man?'

Caro longed to confront him with his lies, with his attack on Miss Willoughby, to threaten him with the word 'Somerset', as Lucy had done. But, for the moment, it suited her for him to think that he'd won her round.

'So there you are,' the lieutenant said. 'No more mysteries for your fat thief-taker. No more murders.' He took another long pull on his wine and wiped his mouth. 'Finding Lucy's body was a shock to you. It's taken its toll – that's plain to see. And now that thief-taker has got you chasing after chimeras. You need to find a new diversion. Something to stop you getting bored while Harry's away.' He reached for the bottle again, his fingers brushing against her own. 'I know a little supper house where we could take a private room.'

Cartwright and Hennessy were watching them with sly amusement. On the path, a woman of her acquaintance noticed them, and nudged her companion.

Caro rose, nodding to Miles, who hastened forward with her cloak. 'Do forgive me, lieutenant, but I am feeling a little faint. I rather think it's time that I went home.'

PAMELA

17 February 1782

When Mrs Agnetti wasn't around, and they weren't having one of their secretive conversations, Pamela still delighted in spending time with Kitty and Lucy. At first she'd liked Kitty best, being the more beautiful, the more famous, the more ambitious. Yet Lucy was the more level-headed, less prone to flights of foolish fancy – sometimes Kitty seemed like an innocent for all her experience.

Occasionally Lucy would give her a hug, not just a squeeze, but a proper embrace. Other times, she looked at Pamela with a distant expression. Perhaps mindful that their whispered huddles had made her feel left out, Lucy also went out of her way to include her.

'My baronet called again last night.' Kitty played a little refrain upon the harpsichord. 'But I had Hector look into his affairs, and he only has three hundred a year.' She glanced at Lucy. 'It's all right to say I told you so, you know.'

Lucy only smiled.

'Jonathan Stone,' Pamela said. 'Tell me about his affairs.'

'Oh, Stone's worth thousands,' Kitty said. 'The newspapers call him the Midas of Muswell Rise. That's the name of his country estate.'

'Did he inherit his money?'

'No, he made his fortune in India. That's where he first met Mrs Agnetti. He was a friend of her father.'

'And now he lends money to other gentlemen, to the lieutenant and his brother?'

'That's right.'

Lucy put down her book. 'This play is very strange. One man has just tricked another into eating his sons in a pie. When they're not murdering, they're being murdered, or appearing as ghosts. When I'm dead, I shall haunt you, Kitty. Tell you off for your bad choices.'

'Oh, stop it, Boleyn.'

Lucy glanced at Pamela, who'd been thinking about Mrs Agnetti and the scissors. She hadn't seen her since, had stayed out of her way.

'Pamela needs a name,' Lucy said. 'Another of Henry's wives?'

'The young, pretty one?' Kitty said. 'She was another Catherine, wasn't she?

'Howard. She had her head cut off, you silly goose.'

'Jane Seymour, then, who won the King's heart?'

'I always liked Katherine Parr best myself. She survived the old bastard and kept his money. Well, Pamela? Money or love? Which is it to be?'

It was a stupid question. Both was plainly the answer. But Pamela didn't want to disappoint their eager faces. 'I choose Jane Seymour,' she said, and Kitty shot Lucy a triumphant look.

*

Later that afternoon, when Mr Agnetti wanted to take another rest, instead of returning to the morning room where Lucy and Kitty were talking, Pamela slipped upstairs. Mrs Agnetti was definitely out this time. Pamela had watched her getting into her carriage from the studio window.

She prowled the room, opening drawers and jewellery boxes and Mrs Agnetti's black lacquered paintbox. In a cupboard by the bed, she found a box of sugarplums, but little else of interest. Popping one into her mouth, she gazed around the room, considering.

Where would Mrs Agnetti keep her letters from the lieutenant? Pamela knew they existed – had seen them slipping little notes to one another, sometimes right under Mr Agnetti's nose.

Pamela slid her hands under the mattress, looked beneath the pillows, then paced the floor, testing each board to see if it was loose. Next she peered under the bed. Spotting a round wicker basket, she pulled it out, only to discover that it contained Mrs Agnetti's monthly rags. She considered the pile with distaste. Not a bad place to hide something from the prying eyes of a husband and servants. Pamela didn't believe the old tales that a woman could miscarry, or a man lose his mind, simply from touching monthly blood. But many did. Grimacing, she plunged her hand up to the elbow into the old, stained linens, and felt around inside the basket. Something was under there, something small, cold and hard. Pulling it out, she gazed at a little glass bottle.

It had no label, and she wondered if it was laudanum. But when she uncorked it to take a sniff, she recognized the faint minty odour at once. The girls in the tableaux house sometimes took pennyroyal when they'd missed their courses. And Hannah, the first housemaid in Cheapside, had taken it after a mistimed tumble with David, the second footman.

Yet Mrs Agnetti wanted a child more than anything. She'd wax on about it to Kitty and Lucy, often to the point of tedium.

Surely she wasn't planning to get rid of her own baby? As for Mr Agnetti, he talked of little else except his joy at impending fatherhood. There was no chance that the little bottle had come from him. It came to her in a flash. The lieutenant must think the baby is his. He must have given Mrs Agnetti the pennyroyal, but she was refusing to take it. The knowledge pleased her. She'd been right. He could not love her.

Downstairs she heard Kitty calling her name: 'Seymour?'

Hastily, she put the bottle back, piling the rags on top of it, and slipped out of the room, closing the door behind her.

Chapter Fifty-One

Something was up with Mr Child. Caro had sensed it yesterday. He'd seemed ill at ease during their meeting, which, judging by his odour, she'd put down to gin and lack of sleep. Then just now she'd received a letter from him, cancelling their meeting that day as he wanted to continue looking for Kitty Carefree. Caro didn't dispute his assessment that Kitty was key to their inquiry, but she couldn't shake off the feeling that Mr Child was avoiding her. Perhaps he was simply embarrassed by his lack of result to date? It was an understandable reaction – warranted even – but also frustrating. She had wanted to talk to him about Lucy's mysterious reference to Somerset.

Child's letter included an account of his conversation with Solomon Loredo, which intrigued her. Simon had claimed to Loredo that Ansell Ward's wife had turned her husband against him because of his illegitimacy. Yet Elspeth Ward had a reputation as a sensible, kind, philanthropic woman, not the sort to cast around for fire and brimstone. It didn't ring true that she would dislike a man because of the sins of his father. It made Caro wonder if Simon could be guilty of the theft after all.

She couldn't bring herself to leave Gabriel's side until he went down for his morning nap, but once he was asleep, she called for her carriage. An hour later, back in the bustle of Lyme Street, she knocked on Ward's door once more, and asked the insolent-looking footman if his mistress was at home.

'Mrs Ward is visiting her sister in Cambridge,' he told her, with a flare of his overlarge nostrils. 'She returns next month.'

It was frustrating – and yet, recalling Simon's claim that a footman had been responsible for the theft, a new plan occurred to her.

'Is your master at home?' she asked.

'Yes, madam.'

'Pray ask Mr Ward if he will receive me.'

In the hall, while they awaited the footman's return, Caro held a whispered conversation with Miles that was soon inter-rupted by the sound of running feet and wild laughter. A mo-ment later, a door flew open and a young woman burst into the hall, followed by a boy in hot pursuit. The girl was holding a book above her head, and the boy made repeated grabs for it. Noticing Caro, she lowered her arm, enabling the boy to seize it at last.

'Forgive us,' the girl said, recovering her breath with diffi-culty. 'We did not know that Father had company.'

The family resemblance was marked: both children small in stature, rather plump, with their father's white doughy face and dimples. The girl was perhaps seventeen, the boy a little younger.

Caro smiled. 'My name is Mrs Corsham.'

'Julia Ward,' the girl said, bobbing an ungainly curtsey. 'And this is Sebastian, who promised not to read Mr Fielding until he had minded his Latin verbs.'

'It was less a promise,' Sebastian said, equally breathless, 'and more a declaration of intent. Didn't Phaedrus say that some-times the mind should be diverted, in order that it should return to better thinking?'

'And Ovid said that little things please little minds,' Miss Ward said. 'Don't hold me to account when your wife cries because she married a dullard.'

More footsteps in the hall heralded the arrival of Ansell

Ward, followed by his footman. He smiled at his children, but as he bowed to Caro, his natural amiability dissolved into a more neutral expression. It made her wonder if he'd read *The London Hermes*.

'Mrs Corsham, another unexpected pleasure.'

'I am quite the pest, I know,' she said, 'but another matter has arisen at my brother's table, coincidentally also concerning the Dodd-Bellinghams. I informed my brother that you were the authority upon that family, and he dispatched me to make inquiries on his behalf.'

Caro could not help but notice the marked effect the name of Dodd-Bellingham had upon Ward's children. They stared at one another in apparent dismay. The boy clutched his sister's hand. Her face had reddened.

Ward pulled out his watch and frowned at it. 'Very well, Mrs Corsham, but I cannot be long. I have an appointment at three.'

With a last curious glance at the children, Caro followed him to his study.

'I know I may speak freely to you, sir, in the strictest confidence,' she said, adopting an expression of concern. 'My visit concerns a friend of my brother's – or rather, it concerns his daughter, to whom Lieutenant Dodd-Bellingham has lately been paying his addresses. Her father is not opposed to the match in principle, but he has heard a troubling rumour about Dodd-Bellingham's reputation.'

Ward drummed his fingers on the desk. 'You mean women, I suppose? I have heard such tales myself. Whilst not precisely laudable, is it not perhaps understandable in a military man? Staring death in the face, carpe diem, and all that. Once he is married, I am sure he will apply himself to that happy state with the same dedication he has displayed on the battlefield.'

Caro leaned forward confidingly. 'This particular rumour is

of a more serious nature, sir. An allegation concerning Somerset that has caused my brother's friend grave concern. I wondered, given your knowledge of the family, if you had heard the story?'

Ward gazed at her intently, his brow furrowing. 'Indeed I have, madam, for I've friends in the War Office. They will be dismayed to hear that the slander has spread so far. Pray reassure your brother's friend that the accusation was thoroughly investigated and found to be baseless.'

The War Office? Caro frowned. 'I understood that some doubt remained,' she said vaguely, hoping to draw him out upon the topic.

'Not in the least. It was a vicious lie from start to finish.'

'Perhaps you would be so good as to talk me through the investigation, sir? That way I can set the mind of a concerned father at rest.'

Ward shook his head furiously. 'No, madam, I cannot. These are affairs of state, not drawing-room gossip. And the more people talk, the more others will assume that there is no smoke without fire – when the only thing burning is the reputation of an honourable man. Forgive me if I grow warm. This is a matter upon which I feel deeply.'

All very interesting. If the Somerset allegation had been investigated by the War Office, then it must concern something the lieutenant was said to have done whilst serving in uniform. Yet Caro knew that he had never been stationed in Somerset, having sailed directly to fight in the colonies after enlisting. Her eye fell upon Ward's maps and battlefield plans, and she wondered whether there could be a place called Somerset in America?

'I quite understand,' she said. 'Your certainty comforts me greatly. I will reassure my brother's friend in the most general terms, and persuade him that he should pay no heed to unkind rumours.'

'I am glad to hear it, madam,' Ward said. 'Reputations are a fragile commodity. Once shattered, there is no putting them back together.'

Not a subtle man, he gave her a long hard look. She sensed the story in *The London Hermes* had offended him deeply. Fat, judgemental fool.

Ward escorted her back to the hall, where his footman and Miles were waiting. There was no sign of the children. She and Ward exchanged the appropriate politenesses, and as the front door closed behind them, she turned to Miles. 'Is it done?'

He inclined his head. 'You can count on me, madam.'

She smiled. 'I know I can. Thank you, Miles.'

They walked on, past her carriage, into Lyme Street Square. A little gate between the houses led into a half-acre of public garden, land that had somehow resisted the attentions of the property speculators. Deserted apart from an old lady feeding starlings, they made a perambulation of the paths in the warm September sun. Eventually Miles nodded towards the gate. 'There he is.'

Ward's footman was crossing the grass towards them. He bowed to Caro. 'I hear you'd like to talk to me, madam.'

'Yes, I would. What is your name?'

'Bob Carruthers.'

'I would like to ask you some questions, Mr Carruthers, about a gentleman named Simon Dodd-Bellingham. He worked for a time in your master's house.'

'I remember.' The footman's eyes flicked to Miles. 'He said there would be a reward.'

'Ten shillings, if you answer to my satisfaction.'

He pulled a face. 'T'other one paid me fifteen.'

'Which other one?'

'Fellow who collared me in the Blackbird last year. Had a

broken nose. He wanted to know about Simon Dodd-Bellingham too.'

Erasmus Knox. Caro remembered his sharp, pale gaze and his inky fingers.

'Very well,' she said. 'If you tell me precisely what you told him, I will match his price.'

He nodded, apparently satisfied, and they resumed their stroll. 'Dodd-Bellingham worked in Mr Ward's library,' the footman said. 'I brought him refreshment from time to time. Funny fellow, up to his ears in books and dust, but the Wards doted on him. He dined at table with the family, notwithstanding that he was a by-blow.'

'I heard Mrs Ward didn't like him?'

'Who told you that? He was the family pet. She was forever fussing about his lack of prospects – even suggested to Mr Ward that he teach the children Latin to supplement his income.'

Caro frowned. This was a very different tale to the one that Simon had told Solomon Loredo.

'Did the children like him?' she asked, remembering their curious reaction in the hall.

'I haven't the first idea. But they're the sort who mind their books.'

'Tell me about the theft,' Caro said.

'It was Mrs Ward who discovered it. Two jade figurines – expensive pieces from China – had gone missing from the library. No visitors had called that day, and so Mr Ward had all the servants brought in and questioned. Then Mrs Ward recalled that she'd seen the figurines that morning, *after* the maids had been in to dust. Well, that put me in a bind, for I was the only servant who'd been into the library since, when I'd taken Mr Dodd-Bellingham his afternoon tea. I protested my innocence, and pointed out that no one would have had such a good opportunity to take them as Dodd-Bellingham himself. But Mr Ward refused to think any ill of a gentleman he trusted.

'Just when it all looked bleak for me, Mrs Ward pipes up again: "Ansell, the boy does have debts." Seizing my moment, I said I thought Dodd-Bellingham had been at the sherry too – that part really was me, but I was past caring about anyone other than myself. Mrs Ward, she shook her head, tears in her eyes, and said, "I fear we have been taken advantage of, sir." Well, I knew then that I was safe. Ward usually listens to his wife, and so it proved. They asked me to leave so they could discuss the matter in private, and the next thing I knew, Dodd-Bellingham was dismissed, still protesting his innocence.'

Nothing about the story seemed to sit quite right to Caro. Why had Mrs Ward changed her views about Simon so dramatically?

'Did you take those figurines? I won't involve the law, but I need to know.'

'No, madam, I did not.'

'Do you think Simon took them?'

Carruthers grinned broadly, his nostrils flaring wider. 'Oh no, Dodd-Bellingham was as innocent as I was myself. I know it for a fact.'

'Go on, Mr Carruthers. Don't keep me on tenterhooks.'

'About a month later, after everything had quietened down, Mrs Ward asked me to take a box of old clothes to the charity for distressed gentlewomen on Fenchurch Street. Her and Miss Ward often donate their cast-offs, but they don't always check the pockets, and sometimes I find the odd sixpence, or a ribbon a girl might like. Well, this time, guess what I found?' He grinned again, enjoying the moment. 'In the bottom of that box, wrapped up in an old shawl. Those figurines.'

CHAPTER FIFTY-TWO

EACH BANG RAISED Child fraction by fraction back into the world of his betrayal. His face was in his pillow, dried spittle on his face. *Bang bang bang.* Daylight. He winced, fumbling for his watch. Midday. Christ. *Bang bang bang bang.* It took him a few more moments to work out that someone was beating at the door to his rooms.

Rolling out of bed, he pulled on a pair of breeches, tucked in his nightshirt, then stumbled to the door, trying to rub the spittle from his face. *Bang bang bang.* He pulled back the bolts and opened the door.

'Hey,' Child said, his sheepish grin fading as he took in Orin Black's expression.

'I've been sent to fetch you.'

While Child dressed, Orin paced the sitting room, unsmiling. Then he led the way downstairs to a waiting carriage. He wouldn't answer any of Child's questions, his face set and sullen, clearly still annoyed about the other day. As if Child needed anyone else to make him feel bad.

His stomach swirled uneasily at the jolting of the carriage, the Holborn streets bright with coloured parasols. Gazing from the carriage window, unable to get any answers from Orin, he tried to work out what the devil was going on. He presumed they were heading for Bow Street, but when they reached the turning on the Strand, they drove on, through Charing Cross, towards Westminster. To the Home Office? Could they have found out about Richmond Baird, the agent he'd killed? But nobody could prove that Child had done it, not unless they'd caught up with Nelly Diver and she'd talked.

They drove on, past the Home Office, past the Privy Garden, past Parliament and its spires, crossing the abbey precincts, coming to a halt on Petty France, a quiet street of residential houses on the edge of the Pimlico Marshes. Orin opened the door and they climbed out. Child followed him along an alley running between two of the houses, emerging into St James's Park, about a hundred yards from Birdcage Walk.

Orin turned left, hugging the rear walls of the Petty France gardens, until they came to a larger walled plot, which extended out into the park itself. A Bow Street Runner was stationed by the gate, and he stood back to let them pass. Child's spine tingled with nerves, a sickness on his palate that wasn't only down to last night.

Beyond the gate was a vineyard, the plants standing in ordered rows, wasps darting in and out of the fat bunches of grapes. Spotting more Bow Street Runners standing over something on the ground, Child's ears filled with a high-pitched hum, which he wasn't sure came from the wasps or his own head.

Running forward, he pulled up short, staring down at Hector's body. The boy's shirtfront was stiff with dried blood, the fabric torn where a knife had plunged into him several times. His white face resembled a startled angel's, his blue eyes drained of their knowing glint.

Child's throat swelled, as rage flooded through him – at the world and its hardship and misery, at the men who'd bought and sold Hector, at the killer who'd tempted him here and butchered him, just like he'd butchered Lucy. And at himself. He had foreseen this nightmare, and then pretended he hadn't, because he'd wanted the boy's information. Just another customer seeking to satisfy his needs.

'Your card was in his pocket,' Orin said. 'They thought you should see it.'

They. Child looked up and saw two thickset gentlemen walking towards him. They wore sober black coats too hot for this weather, and grim expressions beneath their brown powdered wigs. *Official sorts*.

'I'm sorry,' Orin said, already moving away. 'I had no choice.'

The men grabbed Child under his armpits and hauled him to a corner of the vineyard. He barely put up a fight. One pushed him up against a wall.

'Do you have it?'

'Do I have what?'

'You know what.'

'Kitty's testimony? No, I don't.' Part of him noted that they didn't dispute it.

'Does she?'

'Does who?'

'Mrs Corsham.'

'No.'

They exchanged a glance. 'We're looking for a friend of ours,' the second man said. 'Name of Richmond Baird. You seen him?'

'No,' Child said.

'You sure?'

He started to deny it again, but the first man, losing patience, drove a fist into his mouth. His head struck the wall, and he slid down it. They worked him over well: face, ribs, stomach. Child almost welcomed it: penance for Hector, for his betrayal of Mrs Corsham, for Liz and their boy and all the rest.

When they eventually released him, he lay there fighting for breath, wincing at the pain each one caused him.

'Tell her you resign. No more Lucy Loveless. No more chasing after missing doxies. No more Priapus Club. Understand?'

How can I resign? Child wanted to say. *Jonathan Stone won't let me.*

Not that they'd have cared. Either they took his silence as affirmation, or the question was rhetorical, for they walked off, leaving him down there in the dirt.

PAMELA

22 February 1782

Pamela stared at the painting. It was like looking at herself in the mirror, her body and the altar just lines in charcoal and chalk, but her face flesh and blood, her eyes alight with fear. She found it incredible that all those tiny brushstrokes could produce this smoothness, like real skin. Vermillion and lead-white for her, a touch of carmine for Peter Jakes's ruddy face.

'Now that I have started painting, I will only need one or two more sessions of sketching,' Agnetti said. 'But I should like to use you again. When you find new lodgings, you must let me know your address.'

She smiled. 'I'd like that, Mr Agnetti.'

'Here, I have a present for you.' He held out a package wrapped in blue-marbled paper, tied with a yellow ribbon. 'To thank you for being so patient a sitter.'

She unwrapped it eagerly. A book.

'It is Euripides,' Agnetti said. 'The play about Iphigenia that my wife was reading the other day.'

Disappointed, she forced a smile. It was kind of him, and the volume was plainly expensive, bound in rich green calfskin, like Mrs Agnetti's own edition. Turning the pages in a show of enthusiasm, a piece of paper fell out and wafted to the floor. She picked it up and gasped.

WHORE

'What is it?' Agnetti said, turning back from the painting.

Hastily, she slipped the note into her pocket. 'Does Theresa know that you gave me this book?'

'Yes,' he said. 'She wrapped it up for you herself.'

Pamela nodded, seeing the escalation for what it was. 'Then I shall be sure to thank her, when I next see her.'

*

Did Mrs Agnetti think Pamela would take it lying down? First the threat to kill, now this nasty note. Such acts of hostility demanded a response.

Lord March called later that afternoon. Usually he came with Lieutenant Dodd-Bellingham, and Pamela presumed he was downstairs with Mrs Agnetti. Normally she would have enjoyed the looks Lord March gave her, but not today.

When Mr Agnetti sent her out, she crept upstairs again. In the bedroom, she pulled out the basket of rags and groped around for the little bottle. Putting it into her pocket, she went downstairs. In the hall, she listened at the drawing-room door. She could hear the lieutenant's heavy breathing. A soft moan escaped the lips of Mrs Agnetti.

WHORE. It was ironic, all things considered.

The morning room was empty, neither Lucy nor Kitty around today. A half-drunk glass of Madeira sat on the tea table. When Mrs Agnetti returned from her tryst with the lieutenant, she would surely drink it.

It is a kindness, she thought. To Mr Agnetti most of all. Surely she cannot expect him to raise another man's child? And if he discovered the deceit and divorced her, then the lieutenant, an honourable man, might marry her out of obligation.

Unstoppering the bottle, she hesitated. One of the girls had said that the herb could make a woman ill. But it surely could not be that bad if so many girls took it? Before she had time to change her mind, she added the tincture to the glass. To win great love, you had to be prepared to kill for it.

CHAPTER FIFTY-THREE

CRISPIN, THE DOORMAN at the Shakespeare's Head, took one glance at Child. 'You looking for more bruises to add to that collection?'

'Hector is dead.' The words hurt Child's mouth. 'He was murdered last night – by the same man who killed Lucy Loveless.'

Crispin's vicious smirk twisted into a thunderous scowl. He jerked his head towards the staircase. 'Go on up. She'll want to know, and I don't want to be the one who has to tell her.'

Hauling his aching body up the stairs, Child was greeted by the familiar haze of perfume and hashish smoke. The Whores' Club was in session and he pushed his way through the girls on the landing, ducking under batted fans and coils of hair.

Amy Infamy, the chairwoman, scowled at him. 'How did you get past Crispin? Someone call him.' Flicking one of her black tresses over her shoulder, she nearly dislodged her squirrel, which was perched there nibbling on an apricot.

Child gestured to the empty chair next to her. 'Hector is dead.'

All around him, beautiful faces crumpled. Child spoke into the stunned silence, telling them about the scene at the vineyard he'd witnessed.

'Then this is your fault,' the chairwoman said, when he had finished.

'In part, but it's also yours. If you had helped me in the first place, then Hector wouldn't have decided to seek me out. He wanted me to find the bastard who killed Lucy. And he paid the price. Now will you help me?'

A murmur rippled through the room. Becky Greengrass, one of the whores who had gone to the Priapus Club with Pamela, raised her skirts to show him her cunny. 'Go boil your piss, you fat old fuckster.'

Ceylon Sally spoke up in agreement: 'Hector shouldn't have got involved. He knew this club's decision, and he went behind our backs.'

'What if Lucy's story was true?' someone said. 'What if those men really did kill that young whore at Muswell Rise?'

'How is that our business?'

'Many of us go to those masquerades. Who is to say the killer won't try again?'

'We were wrong to throw her out,' another girl cried. 'I've always said it. Lucy died thinking that we hated her. And now Hector too.' She started weeping.

'I told you, nothing happened that night,' Rosy Sims said. 'They've arrested some lamplighter for Lucy's murder. And Hector was probably killed by a murdering molly. Didn't you just say he left Birdcage Walk in the company of a gentleman?'

Child had gone down there earlier and had questioned the boys by the bushes, but nobody could give him a description of the man. They were shaken by Hector's murder, and from the look of them, scared stiff. He wondered if the Home Office had paid them a visit.

'Someone had been looking for Hector for a couple of days,' he said. 'I think word got back to the killer that he'd been asking around about the murders. That's why he was killed.'

The chairwoman encompassed the room with a sweep of her

pipe. 'Our members are plainly conflicted. The Whores' Club must stand neuter. We cannot help you.'

'You could take a vote on it,' Child suggested. 'A secret ballot.'

'Who the pox do you think you are?' Rosy Sims demanded. 'I've seen stains on my bedsheets that look better than you.' She looked around at the others. 'You're not seriously listening to this fat jackanapes?'

But they were listening. Child could see it in their frowns and their tears and their clenched fists.

'I say let's vote,' another voice said. 'I was with you on Lucy. But this is different. We can't do nothing.'

Rosy Sims started shouting and others shouted back. The chairwoman rang her bell for silence, and the arguments gradually quietened to whispered insults. She pointed at Child with her pipe. 'This club will discuss the matter. You will wait downstairs.'

Child descended to the taproom, where he nursed a gin that cost a shilling and tasted of turpentine. The voices upstairs grew increasingly rancorous, and half an hour later, Rosy Sims, Becky Greengrass, and Ceylon Sally trooped down the stairs. They turned to glare at him as they passed, walking out of the tavern with an air of outraged dignity. A small, dark girl followed in their wake. She beckoned to Child. 'You can come up.'

The chairwoman gave him a look that said he was there on sufferance. 'This club has voted to help you, if we can. Three of our members chose not to, and that is their prerogative. You may ask your questions, sir.'

Child gazed at their expectant faces, marshalling his thoughts. 'Did any of you ever hear any talk about Pamela's disappearance? Or know anything about a fifth man who was there at Muswell Rise that night?'

His words were greeted by a long silence.

'All we know is that Lucy thought a girl had been killed,' the chairwoman said. 'But Becky and the others swore it wasn't true. They said Lucy was going mad. She often sounded it.'

'How about Lucy's murder? Did anyone ever hear any rumours about that?' He gazed out at a sea of blank faces.

'Only what was in the newspapers.' The chairwoman pursed her lips. 'They shouldn't have talked about her like that. It wasn't right.'

'Does anyone know the whereabouts of Kitty Carefree?'

Several women started talking at once, but it was only the same old stories about a wealthy keeper with no name.

'Kitty was spotted riding in a gentleman's carriage on the Strand about two weeks ago,' Child said. 'If she has found a keeper, then it seems likely that this was him. The carriage was distinctive.' He described the harlequin pattern.

'I've seen that carriage.' The speaker looked about fifteen, with soft skin and piled fair hair. 'I saw it pull up outside the Devil tavern in Fleet Street a couple of weeks ago. Might have been the same day. A gentleman got out. There was a woman inside, but I didn't see her face.'

'Can you describe him?'

'Well dressed, about fifty, maybe a little older. They had a guild dinner that night, in one of the upstairs rooms. A lot of rich merchants coming and going. I called out to him, but he didn't stop, just walked inside.'

This was something to go on, at least. The Devil was only down the road.

'Am I right in thinking that some of you sit for Jacobus Agnetti?'

A few hands shot up.

'Did any of you ever meet Pamela at his house?' Child held up her drawing.

'I did.'

Child swivelled in the direction of the voice. The girl had coiled black hair and a strong-featured face with thick black brows and a Roman nose.

'My name's Julietta. I was Agnetti's Cassandra. I don't mean his assistant,' she clarified. 'The one in his painting.' She wound a finger round one of her ringlets. 'Pamela's painting was part of the same quartet as mine. So we got to talking.'

'How did she feel about Agnetti?'

'She liked sitting for him and she wanted to do it again. He'd talked about painting her as his Andromeda, though I know at least three other girls he was considering.'

'What about Agnetti's wife? How did Pamela feel about her?'

'They didn't get on. I don't know why. Theresa could be mean sometimes. Take against a girl for no reason. It ought to have been a happy time for them – the Agnettis had wanted a baby for so long – but Theresa went around with a terrible scowl, and Pamela seemed to get the worst of it.'

'Theresa was pregnant?' This was news to Child.

'Until she lost the baby and nearly died. The doctors came and went for three days and three nights. Lucy, Kitty and I took it in turns to sit with her. The poor thing all yellow and shrunken, sweat pouring off her, shivering. She was delirious too, saying all sorts of terrible things.'

'Such as?'

'That Pamela had tried to kill her. That she'd murdered her baby.'

'Was she serious?'

'Like I said, she was in a fever, delusional. The next time I saw her, she was a little better, sipping gruel. She cried about her baby, but she never said anything more about Pamela.'

But maybe she still believed it, Child thought. And if so, that was a powerful motive for murder. Not that he believed Mrs Agnetti had killed Pamela with her own hands, but it spoke to his conviction that she had played a part in it somehow.

Child listed the names of their four main suspects. 'Did Pamela ever talk about any of these men?'

'She had a fancy for the lieutenant,' Julietta said. 'He's a fine-looking fellow, I told her, but not worth breaking your heart over. A girl needs to think about what a man will put in her purse, not in her cunny. But her feelings were all mixed up. They often are at that age.' She thought for a moment. 'She mentioned Mr Stone too. Asked me a lot of questions about his money and his background.'

Child addressed the room: 'Have any of you ever had a violent encounter with any of these men? Or heard a rumour to that effect?'

The girls all started talking at once. The chairwoman rang her bell, and once order was restored, she called out each name in turn. Those of Lieutenant Dodd-Bellingham and Jonathan Stone were greeted with silence, and Child reminded himself that many of the girls benefitted from the masquerades, and might not want to stick their necks out.

'Lord March,' the chairwoman announced, and one of the girls put up her hand.

'He tumbled me a few times, when I was working at the Nunnery over in St James's.'

Child had heard of the Nunnery. The sort of place where the girls spoke French and played the harp, and a man didn't get much change from twenty-five guineas. If Lord March was a regular visitor, then no wonder he had debts.

'He was rough with you?'

'Not exactly. He liked brandy, and struggled to hold it. Sometimes he'd drink himself into a stupor, and the next morning he wouldn't remember what he'd said and done. One night, he'd had a skinful, and he could be real trouble to get primed when he was in his cups. I raised him up eventually, but it had taken a real effort. He was pleased and gave me five guineas as a tip. But in the morning, when he awoke and found his purse empty, he claimed he'd been robbed. He grabbed hold of me and searched me, and found my guineas. I thought he was going to hit me, so I screamed for the bullies. They calmed him down, and I told them what had happened, but he wouldn't believe it. Neither did the bullies. They threw me out.' She bristled with indignation at the memory.

'Another time,' she went on, 'he got into a brawl with some friends, and they broke the place up. Smashed a looking-glass, pulled down some curtains. The bullies locked him in a cupboard until he sobered up. In the morning, they showed him the damage and he couldn't even remember doing it. A man like that, who knows what he could do.'

And he'd wanted Pamela, Child reminded himself. Had Lord March been drunk that night too? Out of control? Orin's words came back to him: *Mad or bad. A real frenzy.*

The chairwoman called out the final name: 'Simon Dodd-Bellingham.'

Several of the girls glanced at one another. One pulled a face.

'What is it?' Child said.

He was answered by a girl with a long aristocratic face and silver earrings. 'I've never seen him in the brothels, but we've all met him at the masquerades. He talks about his old pots and statues and bores everyone to tears. The other men, they're there for the girls, but not him. Some of us wonder if he's a molly, but a molly wouldn't look at us the way he does.'

'Go on,' Child said, his interest stirring.

'Like he wants us and hates us all at the same time – and hates himself for wanting us too. One time, he just sat there watching me. Stone noticed and told me to attend to him. I didn't want to, but you don't argue, or you don't get invited back. And afterwards, he treated me so coldly.'

'Contempt isn't a crime,' Child observed, remembering Simon's disgust when he'd talked about whores that day in his workshop.

She shrugged. 'I don't say he murdered anyone, only that we don't like him. But a girl learns early to be careful when they're quiet like that. The hot, angry ones might break your nose, but it's the cold, distant ones who'll kill you. Then afterwards use your hair to wipe your blood off their shoes.'

*

Limping a little, Child walked east to Fleet Street, thinking about Lord March and Simon Dodd-Bellingham. One with a propensity to be hot-headed, violent, and irrational in drink; the other cold, perhaps nursing a hatred of prostitutes. As for Pamela and Mrs Agnetti, their disagreement over Lieutenant Dodd-Bellingham was sounding less like a petty jealousy and more like a full-blown feud. But did that rivalry have any bearing upon whatever had happened that night at Muswell Rise?

The Devil tavern lay just beyond Temple Bar. Child stooped under the old wooden lintel. The place was popular with men of letters, and a number of gentlemen in the taproom were listening to one of their number declaiming poetry. Child ordered an ale, and bought the tap-man one too. They enjoyed a moment in companionable silence, and then Child asked him about the harlequin carriage.

The man shook his head. 'I never saw it, but I wouldn't, not stuck behind here.'

'Apparently, you had a guild dinner on that night. It was about two weeks ago?'

He nodded. 'August the thirtieth, it must have been. The Worshipful Company of Fruiterers booked one of our upstairs rooms.'

Fruiterers. Child stared through him for a moment, searching for the connection his answer inspired. When it came to him, he smiled. 'Pineapples.'

CHAPTER FIFTY-FOUR

❋

THE NEW FRENCH lamps lately installed at the Theatre Royal, Drury Lane, were so bright they bathed not only the stage but also the entire auditorium in light. Not that the audience cared. They were there to watch one another, not the play.

The galleries were full. The Prince of Wales sat in the royal box, surrounded by friends and sycophants, powdered to the point of pastiness, already running to fat. Caro watched him through her opera glass, wondering if he was the fifth man. *The one with Pamela.*

On stage, the actors perspired in the heat, white stage paint sliding off the face of the man playing Sir Oliver Surface. Swivelling her opera glass to observe those seated down in the pit, Caro watched Jacobus Agnetti, his arms crossed, unsmiling. The Dodd-Bellinghams were sitting nearby: Simon laughing, the lieutenant scanning the boxes with his opera glass, looking up at the ladies.

Earlier, at home, she had consulted Harry's atlas, and discovered that there were three Somersets in the American colonies: one in New Jersey, one in Massachusetts, and one in Maryland. She would talk to Mr Child about it tomorrow.

She had also given some thought to the footman's story about Simon. Why had Mrs Ward been so desperate to get Simon out of her house? To the point where she'd manufactured an entire theft to manipulate her husband into dismissing him? Caro had a theory, which she'd talk to Mr Child about too.

Training her opera glass upon the Amberley box, she watched the earl and countess, the latter smiling benevolently upon Lord March and Clemency Howard. The door to their box opened, and a footman in the distinctive livery of Amberley blue handed Lord March a note. He read it, and then looked across the auditorium to meet her gaze. Rising, frowning, her note in his hand, he murmured something to his mother and Miss Howard, and left the box.

He arrived in her own box a minute later. She nodded at Miles, and he left to stand guard outside.

'What is the meaning of this?' Lord March said quietly, taking the seat beside her. He turned the note to face her, the only message she'd been certain would bring him running:

I KNOW WHAT YOU DID

'The plague doctor tried to kill me outside Carlisle House,' she said. 'And somebody took Gabriel from the park. They gave him a note that threatened his life.'

'You think *I* did that. That I'd hurt a child?'

Opera glasses swivelled in their direction. Normally it would not raise eyebrows – a gentleman could visit a lady in her box without judgement being passed. But as that season's scandal *du jour*, Caro's every movement was now scrutinized. Judging him in part responsible for her predicament, her anger surged.

'I'm not sure I know any more what you would and wouldn't do. I never thought that you'd lead Prinny into danger.'

Was that a flicker of relief she saw in his dark eyes? 'That's what this note is about? Prinny?'

What else would it be about? she wanted to ask. Only she

knew the answer: a cold winter's night at a masquerade at Muswell Rise with a girl named Pamela.

Studying his face, she wondered if the lines of weariness and strain were the product of more than a few late nights with Neddy Dodd-Bellingham. Had whatever had happened at the masquerade exacted a toll upon him? Did it gnaw at his poet's heart and his underworked conscience?

'It was the thing you valued most,' she said. 'That the King placed his trust in you. You were supposed to keep Prinny away from men like Stone.'

'You say it as if I had a choice,' he said, wearily. 'After Father cut off my allowance, I couldn't make my repayments to Stone. He bleeds a man dry.'

'Because he knows their secrets. What did he know about you? You might as well tell me. We are the keepers of one another's secrets, are we not?'

He stared at the actors on the stage: Joseph Surface flirting with Lady Teazle. Her husband knocked at the door and, hastily, she concealed herself behind a screen.

'Stone got hold of a book of my verses,' he said. 'Poems about ladies I knew. It was in my private collection, and I think he bribed one of my servants to steal it. He threatened to have it printed up as a pamphlet: *The Libidinous Lord*. Each verse entitled with a ladies' initials – women who'd trusted me, exposed to ridicule. I couldn't let it happen.'

'So chivalrous,' Caro said. 'Tell me, did you armour yourself while you were bedding half of London?'

'Of course I took precautions. And don't look like that. You're married, remember? Hardly in any position to judge.'

They were long past the time for such quarrels. 'Well, at least let's not pretend that you had anybody's interest in mind but your own,' she said. 'Your father had already threatened to cut you off once. I imagine you feared he might go through with it if faced with such a scandal. And so Prinny pays the price for your misadventures.'

He spoke sullenly, from a place of guilt. 'His Highness has merely taken on a little debt.'

'A hundred thousand pounds? You call that little? Prinny – in the clutches of a man like Stone?'

His lips grew white with the intensity of his whisper. 'Given the source of that loan, you'd do as well as I not to speak of it.'

They studied the stage, pretending to watch the actors. 'Was *I* in this book of yours?' Caro said.

He wouldn't meet her eye. 'I'm sorry. I shouldn't have done it.'

'Then Stone knows about us?' The news alarmed her. 'Did he return the book? When your father settled your debts?'

He nodded. 'He won't use me against you. He can't.'

She arched an eyebrow. 'Because you're all in this together?'

'Because Stone keeps his word. His business depends upon it. But he'll have Erasmus Knox looking into your life, and if he finds out about the child . . .'

'He won't find out. Not unless you tell him. And you know what I'll do then.'

He glanced uneasily across at Clemency. 'I told you, I won't say a word.'

Not when his inheritance was at stake.

'Why didn't you go to your father back then?' she asked. 'When Stone threatened you with this book? Wasn't Prinny worth eating a little humble pie?'

'You know why,' he said. 'Father would have made me marry Clemency. I didn't want to do it.'

'But now you are unhappily engaged, which makes me wonder what has changed. What could have happened to make you so desperate to get away from Stone? That you'd marry a woman you didn't love, just to escape him?'

He gazed at her mutely. Down in the pit, the Dodd-Bellingham brothers and Agnetti were watching them. The Prince gazed across from his box. Only Jonathan Stone was missing.

'Did you know that the magistrate has arrested an innocent man for Lucy's murder?' Caro said. 'Are you going to let him hang? Because I think you know who killed her, Pamela, too.'

'Nobody killed Pamela. Simon told you what happened. Neddy dropped her off in Soho the following morning.' But his voice lacked conviction.

'I don't believe you,' she said. 'I think you went along with something very bad that night. I think that's why you've made peace with your father, and agreed to marry Clemency Howard, because you're lost and you're trying to find a way back. But you won't. Not unless you tell me the truth. I need you to trust me, Octavius. Together we can take on Jonathan Stone.'

Miss Howard was watching them too, the earl and the countess frowning across at them. On stage, Charles Surface whipped aside the screen to reveal Lady Teazle hiding there.

'I was angry when you wouldn't stand by me,' Caro said. 'I tried to convince myself that you could be guilty of murder. But I don't think you'd have tried to kill me. Not when you know that I carry your child. Is it Neddy you're protecting? Or Prinny? If he was the fifth man at the masquerade, then I need to hear it.'

She waited for him to say: 'What fifth man?', but he only rose, buttoning his coat.

'Was Pamela for him?' she persisted. 'Or for Stone? Or for someone else? She told a friend that you used to watch her, that you wanted her.'

He turned sharply. 'She was half my age. Of course I didn't want her.'

Liar, she thought, wondering if she was wrong about his innocence. Might he have tried to kill her, despite the child in her womb?

He stood looking down at her, emotion working its way across his face. 'Pamela is alive and well,' he said. 'Lucy was killed by a passing stranger. Perhaps this man, Von Siegel. I don't know. You have to believe it, Caro. Because if you don't, you will be sorry. Stone will find a way to make you pay. He always does.'

*

Caro left the theatre between the fourth and fifth acts. Drury Lane was choked with carriages, the street a swarm of early leavers and late arrivals. Journalists hovered on the fringes of the crowd, waiting for the Prince to emerge. Theatre spells and other harlots vied for the attention of the departing gentlemen.

A hand gripped her arm and she turned. Lieutenant Dodd-Bellingham. He must have seen her leave the theatre and come after her.

'Don't you want to talk to me too? I was growing used to our little chats. The way you keep returning – like typhus.'

No sign of last night's lazy smile, his blue eyes perfectly frigid. *Simon must have told him that I asked about Somerset,* she thought, *and he's taken it as a threat, just like he did with Lucy.*

A small party of his redcoat friends caught up with him. She recognized Hennessy and Cartwright from last night.

The lieutenant raised his voice. 'You see those scribblers over there?' He nodded at the waiting journalists, who were eyeing them with interest. 'Remember those lists they like to compile?

Ranking the ladies by complexion and grace and so on? You used to top a few of those, didn't you, Mrs Corsham?'

'Neddy,' Cartwright said reprovingly. 'Not very chivalrous.'

'We all get older, lieutenant,' she said. 'Not all of us wiser.'

'*Touché*,' one of the other redcoats offered in half-hearted gallantry.

The lieutenant smiled. 'Hennessy here claims that not a lady in those lists compares favourably to the average doxy in Covent Garden. Whereas Cartwright says that breeding will out. You want to know my own view? The way some ladies behave, it's impossible to tell the difference.'

A ripple of startled laughter ran through the redcoats. The journalists scribbled in their little books, and Caro flushed under their scrutiny.

Hennessy pointed. 'Look, there's Agnetti. Let him be the judge. He's spent long enough looking at them. Ladies, harlots, he's painted them all. Signor Agnetti! Hey, over here!'

The artist, who had just emerged from the theatre, walked over to join them, frowning.

'Settle an argument, will you, Agnetti? Who is the most beautiful woman you've ever painted?'

He studied their eager, pink faces. 'That would be my wife.'

The officers exchanged amused glances. 'Second, then,' Hennessy persisted.

Agnetti's eyes encircled the group, coming to a rest upon Caro, seeming to understand something of the situation. 'I would never demean my sitters by subjecting them to a contest of looks. Mythology teaches us that such presumption tends to end badly. That being said, Mrs Corsham makes a convincing Aphrodite to any man's gaze.' He offered her a stiff bow and walked on.

'Not like Agnetti to play the gallant,' Cartwright observed. 'There now, see, Hennessy, breeding will out.'

'You can't trust Agnetti's judgement,' Hennessy protested, forgetting that he had called for it in the first place. 'Didn't you hear him? His wife wasn't a beauty.'

'Perhaps she was to him,' Caro said, quietly.

The redcoats moved off together, still arguing. 'You can't chalk that one up to breeding,' she heard Hennessy say. 'She's a Craven. City money doesn't count.'

'Stay out of my business,' the lieutenant said, still eyeing her coldly.

'Or what? Am I to be murdered? Like Lucy and Pamela? Or will you try to rape me, like you did poor Miss Willoughby?'

He laughed richly. 'Rape? Is that what she calls it?'

'Yes, and I believe her. A witness saw her leaving the bower in utmost distress.'

'That lamplighter, I suppose? Who is likely to listen to him? Who is likely to listen to Miss Willoughby for that matter? She has a loose reputation and she went willingly with me to the bower. What did she think would happen there? A meeting of prayer? Girls who are loose with their morals cry rape all the time. Not a court in the land would convict me, and you know it.'

PAMELA

25 February 1782

On auction nights, the tableaux house was always packed to the gilded rafters. The competition between the bidders was sport for the spectators in itself. Pamela fiddled nervously with her silver necklace as she watched from the side of the stage, feeling the anticipation in the room. Seven near-naked girls were tending a painted tree of golden apples.

'Behold the hero, Heracles,' George cried.

Peter Jakes squeezed her arse as he pushed past her onto the stage, wearing only a loincloth.

Pamela had spent the day with Mrs Havilland, making preparations. Going over everything, leaving nothing to chance. No mistakes, no displeasure, or no money.

'You have nothing to worry about with me,' Pamela had told her.

'See that I don't.'

Now her calmness deserted her, her hands fluttering, her skin damp. She tried breathing slowly, overwhelmed by this odd threshold on which she stood. A new life beckoned. No more scrubbing floors. No more tears on long cold nights. No old bitch with a silver scratcher to stand between Pamela and her lieutenant.

George gave her a little push. 'Go on, love.'

They cheered as she stood blinking in the stage lamps. Men standing in the aisles, to the sides, pressed in between the tables. She gave her last performance her all, letting them gaze upon her breasts a beat longer than usual, before drawing the tattered garment closed.

Afterwards, the rostrum was carried out, and a large flamboyant gentleman took the stage. He worked by day at James Christie's auction house on Pall Mall, and liked to waggle his eyebrows encouragingly when the bidding fell quiet. Not that there was much chance of that tonight.

'Gentlemen,' the auctioneer said, 'now that you have had the opportunity to admire this first-class piece of goods, I will commence the bidding at a hundred guineas.' He brought his gavel down, and immediately several gentlemen rose to shout their bids. Listening as the amount climbed – 'one hundred and twenty', 'one hundred and fifty' – Pamela studied their faces with trepidation.

Her heart leapt as a flash of scarlet caught her eye. 'One hundred and seventy-five,' Lieutenant Dodd-Bellingham cried.

Their eyes met and he grinned. Somehow he had found the money. Her heart sang, a glorious choir of angels.

But could he afford to keep bidding? Steadily the price kept rising. She willed him on as, one by one, the bidders dropped out. Two hundred guineas. Surely he'd have to drop out now? Unless he'd taken on more debt, just for her?

'Two hundred and ten guineas? You, sir? No? Come now, sirs, a trifling sum.'

The lieutenant raised his arm again, and another bidder threw up his hands. There was only one left against him now: an old man who'd viewed Pamela in private twice before. He had a glass eye and silver furze on his sunken cheeks. To her dismay, he waved his handkerchief. 'Two hundred and twenty.'

'Two hundred and thirty?' the auctioneer asked.

The lieutenant raised his hand again. Pamela prayed to Artemis, Hestia, and all the other virgin goddesses. *I've asked for nothing much before. But let it be him.*

Glass-eye bid two hundred and forty guineas, and a hush fell over the room. Everyone looked at the lieutenant, but he wasn't bidding. Smiling regretfully, he showed Pamela his palms. Her eyes swam hotly, as Glass-eye received the congratulations of the men around him.

'Are you going on, sir? No?' The auctioneer raised his gavel. 'Are you sure?'

The lieutenant wasn't even looking at him. He was gazing across the room at a gentleman with a long, white face and a broken nose. The gentleman nodded and the lieutenant raised his arm once more. 'Two hundred and fifty guineas,' he shouted.

Glass-eye banged the table in frustration, but shook his head at the auctioneer. She could hardly hear the auctioneer's words over the angels' song. 'No, sir? He's out. The soldier has it!' His gavel came down and the room broke into frenzied applause.

Then Mrs Havilland was ushering her off-stage. She twisted to see the lieutenant's face, but he was surrounded by men pounding him on the back. Mrs Havilland told her to wait, and the girls came over to wish her luck, envious of her handsome soldier. She couldn't stop smiling.

One of Mrs Havilland's watchers escorted her to the audience room. To her surprise, the lieutenant was standing alone outside the door. She went up to him, bolder now. 'I hoped it would be you.'

'Alas,' he said, 'your price was well beyond my reach.'

Her smile faded. 'What do you mean?'

The watcher tapped her on the arm. 'He's in there,' he said, gesturing to the audience room.

Angrily, she shook him off. Who was in there? Had the lieutenant been bidding for someone else? His friend, Lord March?

'Not my choice, treasure,' he said. 'But it won't be so bad.'

Like emptying a chamber pot. She wanted to hate him for misleading her, but found she could not.

'But afterwards? When he's . . . had me. We will spend some time together then?'

He gave her an odd look, almost tender, and her heart swelled. 'Yes,' he said, a little distantly. 'I'm sure we will.'

The watcher tapped her again, and she walked angrily into the little red room. Seated inside with Mrs Havilland was a gentleman she didn't recognize. He had a small, elfin face, the skin shiny and unlined, so she couldn't have said if he was thirty or twice that. Dressed impeccably in grey moleskin, a silver wig, a diamond cravat pin. She'd seen worse.

'Good evening,' he said. 'My name is Jonathan Stone.'

Curiosity overcoming her disappointment, she studied him with interest. In the past few weeks, she had learned much about Mr Stone. Mr Agnetti and the girls who sat for him had answered all her questions. About India. About his money. His big house at Muswell Rise. His antiquities. His masquerades. His paintings.

Mrs Havilland poked her hard in the back with her scratcher. *Smile.*

Mr Stone addressed her kindly. 'Are you here of your own free will, Pamela? Nobody has forced you here?'

'Yes,' she said. 'Nobody has forced me.'

He smiled. 'The lieutenant has done well for once. You too, madam.' He rose and kissed Mrs Havilland's hand. Then he turned to Pamela and did the same. 'I will send for you in a few days.'

'You're not taking me home tonight?'

'Soon. Mrs Havilland has said that you can stay here for the time being.'

He gave her one last look of consideration, and Pamela felt a surging sense of power. *I know a secret about you*, she thought. *One you don't even know about yourself.*

CHAPTER FIFTY-FIVE

CHILD VISITED A couple of the nearby livery halls, where he discovered that the Worshipful Company of Fruiterers did not own a hall of their own, which was why they held their meetings and dinners in taverns like the Devil. They did rent offices in the hall belonging to the Worshipful Company of Parish Clerks, but by the time Child had limped across town to Silver Street, the hall was closed for the night. Frustrated, his head pounding, he trudged home.

A letter from Mrs Corsham awaited him there, in which she insisted that he call upon her first thing tomorrow morning to report his progress. Judging by her tone that he could put her off no longer, he dashed off a reply, gave it to his landlord's boy to deliver, and then took his aching body off to bed.

The following morning, his body all mottled with purple bruises, unable to face the walk, he took a hackney carriage to Mayfair. As he walked through Mrs Corsham's morning-room door, her look of reproach was swiftly supplanted by one of concern. 'Mr Child, you are hurt. What has happened?'

She listened, her face drawn, as he told her about Hector's murder and its aftermath.

'That poor boy.' She clutched her necklace, casting an anxious look at her son, who was spinning a top on a patch of parquet.

'He is dead because of me,' Child said. 'Because of our inquiry.'

'No,' Mrs Corsham said. 'We cannot blame ourselves. This is the fault of one man alone. Let's save our anger for him.'

Sombrely, they talked about their discoveries since their last meeting. 'If I'm right,' Child said, 'and Lucy's note about pineapples refers to the gentleman seen riding in that carriage with Kitty, then he might well be the one keeping her. Perhaps he led Lucy to her door?'

'And he might lead us there too.' Mrs Corsham smiled. 'Let us hope your theory is correct.'

She insisted on coming with him to talk to the Fruiterers. Child didn't relish her company, afraid she would let slip some secret that Jonathan Stone might later coax out of him, but she would not be dissuaded.

Not that her company was entirely without advantage. On the ride across town, her comfortable carriage was a sight kinder on his aching bones than a hackney cab. And a short time later, when confronted by the blank face of officialdom in the guise of the Fruiterer's chief clerk, he could not deny that Mrs Corsham at her imperious best elicited results.

'What do you mean your records are confidential, sir? We are talking about a crime, a matter of murder.'

The clerk, who had a face the colour and texture of an old oyster, blanched at her tone. His office was a small, dim room that smelled of tobacco and ink, the Fruiterer's coat of arms painted onto the old oak panelling above their heads. Rather than burden the clerk with the sorry truth – that one of his members was a likely whoremonger consorting with a notorious harlot – they had described the man they sought as a potential witness.

'Forgive me, madam,' the clerk said, 'but my members—'

'Are law-abiding gentlemen who would be quite appalled to think that their clerk had refused to help. Do you want me to return with the Lord Mayor, sir? He has banked with my family for years. As does the Sherriff of London, the Chamberlain, and the Recorder.'

She listed half a dozen other names, important City gentlemen of her acquaintance, until the clerk, looking utterly alarmed, capitulated entirely.

'I am happy to help, madam, but there were over fifty fruiterers at the dinner. I have no knowledge of who came in which carriage.'

'We believe this gentleman to be a grower of pineapples.'

'That is a highly skilled trade. Only about a dozen of our members have tried their hand, I believe.'

'Well, that's a start,' Mrs Corsham said. 'Give us their names, please, sir.'

The clerk rose, looking most unhappy, and went to a filing cabinet. Returning to his desk with a ledger, he perused it for some minutes, pausing occasionally to write a name on a sheet of paper. Eventually, he handed them the list. Fourteen names and addresses, most residing in the countryside outside London, on estates surrounded by their orchards and market gardens.

Mrs Corsham gazed at Child in dismay. 'Why, it will take us the best part of a week to visit them all.'

'The man is around fifty,' Child said. 'Perhaps a little older.'

'That will narrow it down. If you will return my list, madam?'

He made several crossings out, leaving them with eight names.

Child fished the Magdalen card from his pocket, the one he'd found in Lucy's rooms. *50–60 pineapples, 2s 1d.*

'How many pineapples could a fruiterer grow in a year?' he asked. 'Fifty? A hundred?'

'A hundred?' The clerk laughed. 'It takes three years to bring one to fruit, and a grower will lose several for every success. Even a highly skilled gardener would be fortunate to produce more than a dozen specimens in a year.'

Child studied the card again. *50–60*. And they were looking for an older gentleman, rising fifty. If those numbers referred not to the pineapples, but to the gentleman himself, then perhaps the other numbers – *2s 1d* – referred to him too.

'Which of these men have children?' he asked the clerk, in a sudden flash of inspiration. 'I think the gentleman we're looking for has two sons and a daughter.'

Mrs Corsham looked at the card in his hand, making the same leap. 'Oh, very good, Mr Child.'

The clerk made more crossings-out on his list. 'I don't know all the family histories,' he said, 'but I do know that two of these gentlemen are bachelors, and that Mr Collins lost his only son in the American war. I can't speak for the others.'

That left them with five names:

> *Mr James Adams, resident of Camberwell*
> *Sir Andrew Bagnall, resident of Chiswick*
> *Mr Joshua Blacker, resident of Wanstead*
> *Mr Humphrey Sillerton, resident of Clapham*
> *Mr Matthew Henley, resident of Merton*

They thanked the clerk, and descended the stairs to the street.

'It is not so very many places to visit.' Mrs Corsham sighed. 'Though it will take us at least two days, perhaps three. Do you think Kitty was ever sincere about wanting to reform?'

'Lucy must have thought so, or why else would she go looking for her at the Magdalen Hospital? Mrs Rainwood, the matron there, said change for these girls was hard. She said many who tried were tempted back to their old ways.' He stopped, frowning, making a new connection.

'Mr Child?'

'Hector said Kitty had been going to church, over at St Andrew-by-the-Wardrobe, near Blackfriars. That's not her local church. It's quite some distance from Soho.'

'I don't see how that helps us.'

'Hear me out. Mrs Rainwood told me that St Andrew-by-the-Wardrobe is renowned for its evangelical preacher. Did you know that they say sinners can be born again? If Kitty *was* sincere about reform, intending to start anew, then maybe she moved away from London and its temptations? In which case, might she have chosen to live somewhere with an evangelical church?'

Mrs Corsham turned back to their list. 'You're thinking of Clapham?'

'Known for nothing more than its evangelical merchants and the church they built. This Humphrey Sillerton might even be one of them. He wouldn't be the first religious hypocrite. Perhaps Kitty's money ran out? Or he made her an offer she couldn't refuse?'

'It's a leap of logic,' Mrs Corsham said. 'But one I rather like. Let Clapham be our first port of call.'

*

Once they were over London Bridge, the traffic thinned, and Mrs Corsham's coachman whipped the horses to a trot. Beyond the Elephant and Castle tavern on the outskirts of London, the houses grew intermittent and they picked up speed. Great swathes of lavender fields flanked the road to the north. In the distance, Child glimpsed the little fishing village of Battersea on the river.

'Do you think Sillerton is keeping Kitty in Clapham?' Mrs Corsham asked.

'It's possible, but he's probably married and Clapham's a small place. He's unlikely to want her on his doorstep. Perhaps she's in one of the nearby villages? Brixton or Balham?'

'Given the evangelical nature of Clapham, he's hardly likely to be open with us about his peccadilloes. Surely he'll deny ever meeting Kitty?'

'The nature of Clapham is precisely the reason he'll talk to us. Like I said, he's probably married.'

She pursed her lips. 'You mean blackmail?'

'You want to find Kitty, don't you?'

'Yes, I do.'

Some minutes later, they drove into Clapham, a village of handsome brick houses and respectable-looking taverns. They rattled past a rectory, a grammar school, and the remnants of an old church. A new church stood on the edge of the common, a handsome construction with a portico of Doric columns and a bell tower. The common was ringed by large villas, built by the same evangelical merchants who had built the church.

Salvation and sin. Had Kitty sought one and found the other here in Clapham? Child hoped fervently that he was right.

CHAPTER FIFTY-SIX

HUMPHREY SILLERTON'S ORCHARDS and estate lay about a quarter-mile beyond the Clapham common. Waved through the gates by the porter, they turned onto a long drive flanked by acres of peach, pear, plum and apple trees. On the gravel fore-court in front of the red-brick manor house, a groom was preparing a carriage, the vehicle lacquered in red, blue and white diamonds. Child raised his eyebrows at Mrs Corsham, who smiled. This was their man.

A footman emerged from the house to greet them, and Mrs Corsham asked to see Mr Sillerton. Evidently taking her for a wealthy customer, the footman explained that his master was taking tea with his wife in one of his hothouses, and that he would happily escort them there. They followed him through a parterre and a walled garden, where labourers were pruning, watering and raking the paths.

The hothouses were magnificent glass-and-iron construc-tions. Through the glass panes, Child glimpsed figs and oranges, lemons and pomegranates. The pinery was the most magnificent of all: tall as a church, with a stone portico over the entrance in the shape of a pineapple. Inside, it was as humid as a bathhouse. Gravel paths ran between large earthen beds laid with bark. In the centre of each bed was a large, spiny-leafed plant, with a pineapple growing at its centre.

The footman led them along the central aisle to a circular

space at the centre of the pinery. Here, at a marble-topped table, a gentleman and a lady were taking tea. The gentleman rose to greet them, and the footman explained that Mrs Corsham wished to see him on a matter of business.

'Then you are most welcome, madam.' Humphrey Sillerton shook her hand.

A bluff, hearty-looking man, Sillerton was sober in dress, with a round, amiable countenance that conveyed no great cleverness or guile. In Child's experience, such faces belonged to two types of men: those who set great store upon personal honour and trust, and those who lacked these attributes entirely. Given the circumstances that had brought them here and the presence of Sillerton's wife, Child presumed that Sillerton fell into the latter camp.

Mrs Corsham introduced Child as her man of business and Sillerton eyed his bruises curiously.

'A fall from a horse,' Child said.

Sillerton murmured a few words of consolation, then introduced his wife. Pretty, considerably younger than her husband, she wore a cream-and-yellow striped gown and a chaste white bonnet. Child noted a large diamond ring on her finger. Humphrey Sillerton was evidently doing well for himself, spending his money freely on both his wife and his whores.

Mrs Corsham apologized for her lack of appointment. 'This journey was undertaken on something of a whim. I wish to source a supplier of pineapples for my table.'

'Then you have come to the right place, madam,' Sillerton said. 'If you and your man will accompany me, I will give you a tour of the pinery.'

To Child's dismay, the wife accompanied them too. Her presence was going to make their task all the trickier.

'*Ananas Comosus*,' Sillerton declared, drawing their attention to the fruits in the beds. Some were a greenish-yellow in colour, others darkened to amber-gold. 'I grow two varieties here: the Jamaican Queen, and the Black Prince. They are laid in beds of tanner's bark, the heating provided by furnaces. Do you see those Grecian urns? They disguise the chimneys.'

Child glanced at Mrs Corsham. She gave him a look that said *patience*.

'Each fruit costs eighty pounds. Quite a sum, I know, but imagine a pineapple on a silver platter, the centrepiece of your table. A signal to your guests that you are a woman of exquisite taste and affluent means.'

Mrs Corsham smiled. 'I confess all mention of money matters makes my head spin. In the absence of my husband, I prefer to leave such discussions to Mr Child. Perhaps your wife could show me some more of your pineapples, whilst you gentlemen talk?'

'But of course, Mrs Corsham.' Glancing at his wife, Sillerton smiled fondly. 'That is, if you have no objection, my dear?'

'Of course not.' Mrs Sillerton smiled at Caro. 'Do come this way, Mrs Corsham.'

Sillerton watched the women walk away, giving every appearance of a man besotted with his wife. Fleetingly, Child entertained the thought that he might have been wrong. Yet the carriage matched the description, and Sillerton wouldn't be the first man in love with his wife to bed a whore when the opportunity arose. Indeed, his evident feelings for his wife might make it easier to secure his cooperation.

'If eighty pounds is too steep a price,' Sillerton said, 'I also rent pineapples for a guinea a day, though naturally I require a deposit. Mrs Corsham's guests need never know that the pineapple is not her own, though they would, of course, miss out on its glorious flavour. And if a guinea is still too much, I also recommend a man who can carve pineapples out of wood. In the right light, nobody would know that they were not the real thing. But Mrs Corsham, I'm sure, deserves only the best.'

'Mr Sillerton, we did not come here to talk to you about pineapples.'

Confusion reigned on the man's face. 'I don't understand.'

'I am a thief-taker in the employ of Mrs Corsham. We wish to talk to you about a young woman of your acquaintance: Kitty Carefree, a harlot, formerly of Soho, London.'

Sillerton stared at him. 'A prostitute? I have never consorted knowingly with such a person.'

'Come, sir. She was seen riding in your carriage. The pair of you were observed kissing.' He lowered his voice, a little surprised that Sillerton had not done the same. 'If you talk to me in confidence, then there is no need for your wife to learn what you've been up to.'

Sillerton's face had turned the colour of one of his plums. 'How dare you, sir? To come to my house, alleging such a thing?'

The women were walking back towards them now. Child gazed at them in alarm. What was Mrs Corsham thinking? He'd barely begun to put the squeeze on Sillerton.

'Mr Child,' Mrs Corsham cried brightly, as they drew nearer. 'Having examined the pineapples more closely, I believe they would clash with the wallpaper in my dining room. I have dragged you far on a flight of fancy, but I fear I have made a mistake.' She looked at him meaningfully.

Child didn't understand. Mrs Corsham evidently believed that they were wrong. And yet she too had seen the carriage in the drive.

Humphrey Sillerton trembled with the force of his anger. 'You have made a mistake indeed, sir.'

Mrs Sillerton gazed anxiously at her husband. Mrs Corsham

held out her hand, and reluctantly Sillerton shook it. The women curtseyed to one another, and Child bowed, though Sillerton stood stock still. With a snap of his fingers, he summoned his footman, who escorted them out.

'What the devil?' Child said, once they were outside.

'Hush,' Mrs Corsham said. 'It wasn't what we thought.'

'How can you be sure? The carriage looked right to me.'

'Oh, I think it was Humphrey Sillerton that the girl from the Whores' Club saw going into the Devil tavern – and Kitty Carefree whom he was seen kissing on the Strand. I just don't think he knows he was consorting with a prostitute.'

'What do you mean he didn't know? She wasn't kissing him for a tour of the sights.'

'Look at the wife,' Mrs Corsham said, and Child turned.

Through the glass he could see Mrs Sillerton talking solicitously to her husband. A curl of red hair had escaped her bonnet.

'That's her,' Mrs Corsham said. 'Kitty Carefree.'

PAMELA

26 February 1782

Pamela's plan had come to her fully formed, perfect in conception, brilliant in design, like a rose-cut diamond beneath a jeweller's glass. Secrets. They were a currency, Lucy had said. One that Mr Stone was rumoured to deal in himself. It held a pleasing symmetry, Pamela thought.

She longed to put her plan into execution right away, but the constant presence of her watcher complicated matters. She'd hoped that after the auction she'd be the mistress of her own destiny, able to come and go as she pleased. But Mr Stone's odd reticence in wanting to take her virginity meant she was still cooped up in the tableaux house, chafing at the delay.

Later that morning, Lucy came to the tableaux house to see her. She sailed into Pamela's bedroom in a wide-hooped gown of turquoise silk, closing the door on Cecily's curious face. She looked tired and drawn.

'Poor Theresa lost the baby. She almost died.'

Pamela stared at her, aghast. She'd never intended that. 'Is she out of danger?'

'The doctor says she'll live.' Lucy bit her lip. 'But she is jaundiced and shivering and . . .' She put her face in her hands.

Consumed by guilt, Pamela put her arm around her while she cried.

'Forgive me, Seymour,' Lucy said. 'I have been up half the night. Mr Agnetti asked me to tell you not to come today.'

'Is he very sad?'

'He cries,' Lucy said shortly, always lacking sympathy when it came to gentlemen.

Pamela consoled herself with the thought that they'd all be happier eventually. When the lieutenant threw Mrs Agnetti over. When Mrs Agnetti could give her husband the love he deserved.

'Listen,' Lucy said, 'I heard about your auction. I need to talk to you.'

They sat upon her bed, side by side, and Lucy took her hands. 'Kitty told me that you were bought by Mr Stone. There will be a masquerade, she says. She doesn't know why they want a virgin. It isn't normal. I don't think you should go.'

Not go? Her hundred and twenty-five guineas depended on it. And she would owe Mrs Havilland a princely sum for her board and lodging if she did not. She could end up rotting in the Fleet Prison.

'Kitty thinks they are up to something. I don't like it.'

Pamela frowned. 'Who is up to something?'

'Mr Stone. The lieutenant. Their friends.'

'Something involving me?'

'I think so, yes.'

Her frown deepened. 'Kitty says Mr Stone treats his harlots well.'

'Kitty is wrong about a lot of things. Especially men.'

Pamela spoke a little heatedly, not liking the way Lucy was talking. 'Then maybe she's wrong about them being up to something.'

'Listen to me, please.' Lucy's eyes pleaded with hers. 'I don't want you to go.'

Chapter Fifty-Seven

THE CHURCH OF Holy Trinity was cool and bright, light streaming through the arched windows. Child sat next to Mrs Corsham in one of the pews near the organ. The place was empty, apart from an old woman sweeping one of the wooden galleries above, humming 'Soldiers of Christ, Arise'. The church door creaked and they turned. Mrs Sillerton, formerly known as Kitty Carefree, walked slowly down the aisle.

She sat in the pew behind them, drawing back her hood, her face pale, luminescent in its beauty, her red curls neatly pinned. 'I was married in this church not eight weeks ago,' she said. 'I met Mr Sillerton only six weeks before that. He was widowed last year, three children grown and married themselves. I think he was as lonely and lost as I was myself. He says I am a gift from God. I took it as a sign that I was forgiven. And yet, if it was a part of His plan, then why does he torment me so?'

'Because a girl is missing and a woman is dead.' Child didn't need to utter any threats. Kitty's presence here was a sign that she understood it. In Clapham a man might believe that a prostitute could be born again, cleansed of sin – but approving of reform wasn't the same as marrying it.

'I take it you heard about Lucy,' Mrs Corsham said.

Kitty dabbed a square of lace to her eyes. 'I read about it in the newspapers. My poor dear friend. I wish she'd listened to me, but she would not.'

'Lucy came here to see you in Clapham?'

Kitty nodded. 'Twice in two days. The last time I saw her was on the very same day she was killed. I didn't want her here. I wished her to go away, but now I would do anything to bring her back.'

'We need to know everything you told her,' Child said.

She drew a breath. 'I was here in church with Mr Sillerton, and suddenly there she was, sitting across the aisle, staring right at me. At St Andrew-by-the-Wardrobe, the preacher told me I was absolved of my past sins, received into God's grace. I had even started to believe it – believe that I really was Katherine Sillerton. But there was Lucy, come to find me, the only part of my old life that I ever missed.' Her tears were flowing more freely now, and she continued to dab at her eyes ineffectually with the scrap of lace.

'After the service, I saw her again in the churchyard. I made an excuse to Mr Sillerton and he returned to the house alone. "Your husband looks happy," Lucy said, as we walked amongst the graves. "Is he kind to you?" I said he was the best gentleman who ever lived, and she said she was glad of it.'

'How had she found you?'

'I made a terrible mistake.' Her voice rose, still angry at herself. 'After my marriage, in early August, I wrote a letter to my former governess in Hampshire. I had broken off all communication with her after I moved to London, because I was ashamed of my sinful life. But she was the dearest woman I ever met, and I knew she would have worried about me over the years. Now, at last, I had some honourable news to impart. Even so, I took precautions. I gave her no address, providing her with only a few scant details about my new life. Somehow Lucy tracked her down and talked her into letting her read my letter. Those details proved enough for her to find me. She told me I might have been absolved by God, but I had not been absolved by Lucy Loveless. She said she'd come to hear my confession.'

'We need to hear it too,' Mrs Corsham said gently. 'We need to hear about Pamela.'

Kitty twisted the handkerchief in her hands as she spoke. 'She was just another of Agnetti's sitters, a little younger than most, but already bold. Lucy and I took to her. We gave her advice – all the things I wished someone had told me when I was starting out on the town. Mr Stone bought her virginity at auction, and it was all going to happen at one of his masquerades. Pamela was pleased that I was going to be there too. I thought it a little strange – that Mr Stone wanted a virgin. He's not the sort who likes to lord it over a meek, passive girl – he prefers harlots who know tricks, who know their way around. Well, Lucy didn't like the sound of it either. She had a real affection for Pamela – I think she saw in her the daughter she'd lost. We should have listened to her – but the girl would have been a fool to walk away from so much money. Everyone has to lose it sometime – I wish I hadn't told Pamela that, but I did. I said Mr Stone looks after his harlots. And up until then, he always had—' She broke off, weeping again.

'Tell us about the masquerade,' Child said.

'There were four of us from the Whores' Club: myself, Becky, Rosy and Sally. The lieutenant picked us up from my rooms in a hired carriage, and then we collected Pamela from the tableaux house. We rode out to Muswell Rise, everyone giving Pamela their tuppence of advice. She seemed a little nervous, but who wouldn't be? I wept buckets my first time. When we arrived, the lieutenant took us to a bedroom to change our clothes. Mr Stone makes the girls wear white robes and sandals, like the women in Agnetti's paintings. He had a special robe for Pamela, embroidered with silver thread. We went downstairs, where the others were waiting. Four gentlemen, including Mr Stone, all wearing masks.'

'Only four?'

'Yes, at first. Mr Stone, the Dodd-Bellingham brothers and Lord March. His lordship always wore a mask, because he was afraid of his father catching him in scandal. But we always knew that it was him, because his buttons are stamped with the Amberley crest. Outside, the servants gave the gentlemen torches. We walked across the grounds, skirting the woods, to the lake. Outside Stone's bathhouse, across the water, I saw more torches, and guessed that was where we were heading.'

'The little white temple on the edge of the lake?' Mrs Corsham said.

Kitty nodded. 'There is a stone pool in front of the bathhouse, which in summer is filled with water from the lake. Sometimes, during the masquerades, we'd go there to bathe. But this was the dead of winter, the lake half-frozen. The pool had been drained, and I couldn't understand why Mr Stone had taken us there. Now I think he wanted to keep what was to happen away from the servants. Mr Stone knocked on the bathhouse door, and another gentleman opened it from inside. He wore a mask that covered his head: a goat with horns.'

The fifth man. Child exchanged an uneasy glance with Mrs Corsham.

'Something felt wrong,' Kitty said. 'The men were so silent, when normally they're laughing and joking between themselves. I was afraid for Pamela. I wanted to stop it, but what could I say? I think she was afraid too, because when Mr Stone told her to go to the man, she hung back. But one of the others gave her a push, and she walked towards him. The man in the mask looked her over, then they went into the bathhouse together. Mr Stone ordered the rest of us back to the house.'

'Did you know who this fifth man was?'

She shook her head. 'Not then. A banquet had been laid out in the dining room as usual, but no one felt like eating. All the men removed their masks, even Lord March, and Mr Stone tried to raise everyone's spirits. He called for wine, and pulled Becky onto his lap. The lieutenant kissed me, and Sally kissed Lord March. Simon was just sitting there, and Mr Stone told Rosy to attend to him. But Simon said he wasn't in the mood. Normally that would earn him a rebuke from Mr Stone, but that night he let Simon leave without any argument. So Rosy disrobed, and went to join Becky and Mr Stone.

'We weren't at it very long, before I heard Pamela outside, calling my name. A servant came to the door, and whispered something to Mr Stone, and he left the room. The lieutenant told us to stay where we were, and he and Lord March went after Stone. But we heard more shouting and we were worried about Pamela, so Becky and I got dressed and went outside.'

Kitty started crying again, and they waited impatiently, until she composed herself. 'They were all in the forecourt, in the middle of an argument. Lord March was holding Pamela. She was struggling, hysterical, and he was trying to calm her down. The lieutenant grew frustrated and slapped her face, which only made her scream louder. I called out to her, asked what was wrong, and Stone ordered us back inside. Then we saw the reason why.' Her fists clenched on top of the pew. 'The fifth man, the one from the bathhouse, came forward into the light. He had to use a stick to help him walk. He had taken off his mask, and his face, oh his face. It was all riven with sores, and no nose, just a gaping black hole. Those monsters had given Pamela to a man who was dying from the pox.'

CHAPTER FIFTY-EIGHT

CARO STARED AT Kitty, appalled. It couldn't be true. Ambrose had been so ill back in March, barely able to walk. And he'd promised her, hand on heart, that he'd given up his women. He'd even made bleak jokes about losing the inclination. Why would he have asked Stone to find him a virgin?

Kitty seemed to read her incomprehension. 'The tales are as old as time. Intercourse with a virgin cures a man from syphilis. That's why you see them out on the street. Children with rotting faces.' She shuddered. 'There's no truth in it, of course, anyone with half a mind can see it. But when a man is dying, he becomes desperate. Prepared to try anything.'

Caro remembered the parade of physicians and quacks through Ambrose's rooms at the Adelphi. Mercury, arsenic, fumigation. Poultices of wild pansy and China root. He'd even tried to contract malaria, because one quack had told him the fevers would cure him. His desperation as the disease spread. His terror of dying.

'I don't think they wanted to do it,' Kitty said. 'The other gentlemen, I mean. Becky overheard the lieutenant say to Lord March that the man with the pox knew too much about Stone's business. He'd have struggled to find himself a virgin looking like that, so he made Stone do it for him.'

'Why involve the others?' Mr Child's face was expressionless, but his hands were balled into fists. 'Why the other girls? Why have witnesses?'

'To make Pamela feel more at ease, less suspicious,' Kitty said. 'She wasn't supposed to find out. The man intended to tumble her wearing his mask. But somehow she discovered it, and that's when everything went wrong.'

'What happened next?'

'Pamela was screaming at them all, Lord March still holding her, trying to soothe her. The lieutenant slapped her again, and I shouted at him to stop. I think Pamela got scared, because she bit Lord March on the hand. He let her go, and she ran off towards the woods. She can't have been thinking straight, because where would she have expected to go?'

'Did they run after her?'

'Not at first. Mr Stone was more concerned about the man with the pox than about her. He followed the man to his carriage, apologizing. But the poxy scoundrel was angry and he rode away.'

'He left,' Caro said faintly. 'You are certain?'

'Yes, I watched him go, back down the drive. The others were angry. Guilt does that to a man. Mr Stone was worried about the reaction of the man with the pox. Lord March's hand was bleeding, and he looked furious. And the lieutenant was muttering about Pamela, calling her a bloody bitch. The coward was afraid he'd messed things up for Mr Stone.'

'How about his brother?'

'Simon was still off on his walk. Mr Stone said they should split up and look for Pamela. The lieutenant told us to go back inside, but we were angry too – about what they'd done. The men went off after her, towards the woods, and as soon as they were out of sight, Becky and I followed. We got as far as the lake, but I twisted my ankle in the dark and couldn't go on. Becky helped me back to the house and we stayed up all night, waiting for Pamela to return. But she never did. Neither did the gentlemen. Only Simon Dodd-Bellingham. We asked him if he'd seen Pamela, and he said no. It wasn't until after dawn that the other gentlemen returned. They said they hadn't found her, that she must have made her own way back to London.'

'How did they seem?'

'Pale, quiet, but they'd been out all night and it was bitterly cold. Lord March had lost his coat, he was shivering. He and the lieutenant had red mud and straw on their boots – and the lieutenant had spilled something white on his redcoat. Mr Stone gave us girls two hundred guineas apiece, and said we were never to speak of this night again. That if we did, it would mean an end to his masquerades and no one would thank us.' She broke off momentarily. 'How could we have spoken out? Four whores, up against gentlemen like that. They'd have called us liars, destroyed our lives like they destroyed Lucy's.'

'So you took the money?'

She nodded, her eyes closed. 'Lucy called it blood money. But we didn't know anything for certain.'

'You didn't wonder, when you didn't see Pamela again?'

'Of course we wondered. But why would they have killed her? Those men had broken no laws, however evil their intent. And no one would have believed Pamela against their word.' Kitty stared at the cross on the altar, her pale face framed by her tumbling red curls: a Magdalen's penance.

Caro was still struggling to take it all in. How could Ambrose, her kind, amiable brother, have done such a thing?

Mr Child broke in on her thoughts: 'This puts a new complexion upon our inquiry. For one thing, it rules out a carnal motive for Pamela's murder. None of those men would have wanted her – not if she'd just been tumbled by a man afflicted with the pox.'

'Not necessarily,' Caro said faintly, making an effort to gather her thoughts. 'We don't know for certain that things between them ever progressed so far. Pamela might have discovered his syphilis before he was able to take her virginity.'

Was she clinging to false hope? Desperate to believe that whatever else had happened to Pamela that night, this wasn't part of it?

'What other motive could there be aside from carnality?' she said.

Mr Child looked at Kitty. 'Pamela told her friend, Cecily, that she knew a secret that could make her rich. Cecily dismissed it as foolish fancy, but what if Pamela really did know a secret – about one of those men? Perhaps she'd been blackmailing him? And he took the opportunity to silence her out there in those woods?'

Kitty sniffed. 'She was always sneaking around Mr Agnetti's house. Theresa caught her in her bedroom once. And I was convinced one time that she'd been listening at the door.'

'Mrs Agnetti told another of her husband's sitters that Pamela had murdered her baby.'

Kitty's eyes widened. 'Surely not?'

'The truth may matter less than the fact that Theresa believed it. She disappeared on the same day as Pamela. Could there be a connection?'

'With Theresa?' Kitty shook her head. 'I don't see how.'

'We heard there was a rivalry between them, over Lieutenant Dodd-Bellingham.'

'Pamela and Theresa didn't like one another. That much was obvious. I suppose the lieutenant could have been the cause of it. Pamela had a fancy for him, I think. A lot of girls do.'

'Did you know about his amour with Theresa?'

'Lucy and I guessed – sometimes we made excuses for her, when Mr Agnetti seemed suspicious.'

'When was the last time you saw her?'

'The morning of the day she disappeared.'

'How did she seem?'

'Theresa hadn't been well. She was jaundiced, running a fever. I said she shouldn't be going out. But she said Mr Agnetti needed her to take some sketches to Jonathan Stone. Whatever the tensions between them, she was always mindful of her husband's work.'

Caro turned to Mr Child. 'Theresa Agnetti visited Stone's estate on the first of March – only a few hours before Pamela arrived there herself. I wonder what she and Stone discussed?'

'I read in the newspapers that she'd been out that day on errands,' Child said. 'They never said where. Theresa returned home at five o'clock. Her husband was out, but the servants saw her. Then sometime between seven and nine, she slipped out of her house and never returned.'

'Do you know where Theresa could have gone?' Caro asked Kitty. 'Nobody's seen or heard from her in over six months.'

'I've thought for a long time that she was dead. Perhaps she drowned herself, or jumped from a cliff. I can't see how she could have had anything to do with what happened to Pamela. It's those four gentlemen you need to be looking at, not the Agnettis.' Kitty's voice had grown warm, and the old woman in the gallery peered down at them.

'Well, at least we know now that Mr Agnetti isn't a killer,' Child said.

'Mr Agnetti? Of course he isn't,' Kitty said. 'He always treated Pamela well, as he does all his sitters.'

'The lieutenant tried to suggest that Agnetti had beaten

Lucy back in March. I presume, from what you say, that isn't true.'

'Lord no. Not Mr Agnetti.'

'Then who?'

'I don't know. Things between Lucy and I were already fraught by then. I saw her bruises and I asked her what happened, but she wouldn't say.'

'Perhaps the killer was responsible,' Child said. 'Or one of the others was trying to scare her off. They are all complicit in this sorry tale, after all.'

'What happened after you told Lucy your story?' Caro said.

'She told me that I had to go home and write it all down. Not just about Pamela, but about all the gentlemen who came to the Priapus Club. All the names I knew, including the Prince of Wales – especially him. She said she'd be back the following day to collect it. Well, I had no choice, did I? The next day we met here at the church, and I gave her my written account. I asked her what she was going to do with it, and she said she knew who had killed Pamela and that she had proof. She intended to use my testimony to compel the authorities to act.'

'*He knows,*' Caro said. 'Those were Lucy's dying words. Presumably the killer found out that she was poised to unmask him, and decided to kill her.'

'I begged her not to do it,' Kitty said. 'She was exposing us both to danger. Lucy wouldn't listen. She said she knew a woman who might help her, an important lady with powerful connections. Lucy had been to Carlisle House the night before and the pair of them had talked. She said she was meeting the lady again at Vauxhall Gardens that same night, where she'd ask for her help. This woman, you see, was the sister of the man with the pox. He'd been one of Lucy's clients in the past, before he got sick. Lucy had met the sister before, and thought she might have a conscience. She said she'd had the opportunity to be of service to this lady at Carlisle House, and she hoped that the lady might help her in return.' Her gaze met Caro's. 'That was you, wasn't it?'

Images were flashing through Caro's mind. Lucia at Carlisle House, searching the crowd, their whispered conversation in the cloakroom. *Lucy went there looking for me. She wanted to talk to me in private, but then I was sick.*

Would I have helped her? she wondered. *If Lucy hadn't died in my arms? If she'd told me this story about Ambrose, would I have helped her? Or would I have closed ranks, like Mordechai? Protecting the family name? And then Lucy would have had to think of another way. Because she was never giving up. "I am Lucy."*

'Lucy wrote a letter to the Home Secretary in which she claimed she had given your testimony to a friend,' Child said. 'If anything happened to her, then that friend would give it to the newspaper. I take it this wasn't you?'

Kitty stared at him incredulously. 'She'd never have left it with me. I would have burned it. My testimony is a danger – to the Prince, to the killer, and most of all to myself. I knew that it would lead people like you to my door. I wake up every morning afraid that Mr Sillerton will learn of my past.'

'Then where is it?' Child asked gently. 'Can you think?'

'I don't know. Perhaps Lucy was lying. She had few enough friends left.' Kitty closed her eyes, tears seeping through the lids. 'There now, I have told you everything. So leave me in peace, I beg you. I remained silent about Pamela, it is true, and I will live with the guilt for the rest of my life. But in Clapham, here at the church, I can make amends. Even if you do not believe that I deserve happiness, then dear Mr Sillerton does. My love for him is sincere. We hope for children.'

Mr Child, perhaps mindful of his promise to Mrs Rainwood that he wouldn't make life harder for Kitty, met Caro's gaze.

'Enough women's lives have been destroyed by what those gentlemen did that night,' she said. 'And I hope soon we'll have all the testimony we need.'

BOOK FOUR

12–18 SEPTEMBER 1782

CLYTEMNESTRA: 'What ails thee, raising this ado for us?'
SLAVE: 'I say the dead are come to slay the living.'

Aeschylus, the *Oresteia*, 458 BC

CHAPTER FIFTY-NINE

MRS CORSHAM'S SKIN shone with perspiration. She leaned forward suddenly, grabbing her parasol, thrusting it out of the window, rapping frantically upon the carriage roof. They lurched to a halt, and she threw open the door. Child watched, concerned, as she ran to a tree by the side of the road, followed by her anxious footman. He turned away when she started vomiting, but then turned back. Why would Mrs Corsham ever have agreed to meet Lucy in the bowers? What service could Lucy have done her? An inkling began to form in his mind.

Not wanting to explore it further, he thought about Kitty and the other girls. Yes, they had lied, taken blood money. But only because they were scared – afraid of losing their livelihoods by taking on men with the wealth and power to destroy them.

Thinking about that conversation with Kitty, something nagged at him. A discrepancy in her story? Or a detail that jarred with something else that he'd been told? He couldn't quite place it, chasing the thought around in his head, until Mrs Corsham returned to the carriage.

'Forgive me,' she said. 'It must be something I ate.'

'I'm sorry about your brother,' he said.

'It is unconscionable,' she said flatly. 'Whatever the truth about Pamela's death, I hold him accountable.' She stared straight ahead, and he sensed her words did not come easily. 'Ambrose's condition grew much worse after March. And now he is in a prison of his own mind, the place he always feared most. Despite everything we heard today, I still pity him.'

'He is your brother,' Child said, thinking of his wife, Liz, who had adored her brother, Frank.

'If Pamela was murdered out there in those woods,' he continued, 'I wonder if the others helped conceal the crime – buried her body somewhere on Stone's estate. It would explain the red mud and straw on the boots of the lieutenant and Lord March.'

'If we could find Pamela's body, then wouldn't the authorities be forced to act?'

Child thought of the Home Office. 'I wouldn't count on it. Besides, Stone's estate is vast. Where would we start?'

Mrs Corsham sighed. 'Then we must force one of them to confess. I had hoped Lord March might talk to me – I think his conscience is as troubled as Kitty's – but he refused.'

'He might have good reason,' Child said. 'Hector told me that he forgets himself in drink, and has fits of violent rage. I also wonder why he and the lieutenant were arguing over Pamela's necklace. Loredo says it's Indian, by the way. Just a modern trinket.'

Mrs Corsham gazed out across the fields towards the smuggler's haunt of Stockwell. 'I keep thinking about Simon. Why did Mrs Ward change her mind about him? Why was she so desperate to get him out of her house? Why couldn't she tell her husband the truth? I think Simon wronged her deeply. Or more likely, wronged her daughter.' She told him about the children's reaction to the Dodd-Bellingham name.

'You mean the sort of wrong that might break a father's heart? Or ruin a girl's marriage prospects?'

She nodded. 'Simon taught the Ward children Latin. And eighteen months ago, the daughter can't have been much older than Pamela. I think we should speak to Simon again. If one of them is likely to talk, then it's him.'

Child concurred. 'Kitty said that Simon returned to the house that night alone and went to bed. But he could have encountered Pamela earlier, whilst out on his walk. Perhaps she tried to blackmail him about whatever went on at Ward's house?'

'Or perhaps Ambrose never took her virginity and he simply wanted her?'

'He wasn't alone, if he did. Lord March, Lieutenant Dodd-Bellingham – they wanted her too. All that pent-up lust, unable to touch her because of the auction and Mr Stone. Each let off the leash, searching those woods for her alone.'

'Simon knows something about the lieutenant and Somerset, I think,' Mrs Corsham said. 'He claimed Neddy had never visited that county. That part might even be true.' She told him her theory about the three places named Somerset in America. 'From what Ansell Ward said, it seems to relate to a military matter.'

'Another rape? A *crime de guerre*? I could ask around the soldiers' taverns?'

'Simon first,' she said firmly. 'Let's see what he tells us.' She pursed her lips. 'I owe Mr Agnetti an apology, I think. I should have been honest with him from the start. Perhaps if I explain our suspicions fully, he will talk to me more openly about his marriage?'

'That's assuming there's anything useful he can tell us,' Child said. 'From everything we've heard, one fact seems stark enough: there was a lot that Mr Agnetti didn't know about his wife.'

PAMELA

1 March 1782

Mr Agnetti looked terrible, his eyes swollen, his face heavier. He was mourning the loss of his dead child. Pamela thought about offering him words of comfort, but how hollow they would sound. So she just lay there on the altar, thinking of the lieutenant and her plan. Occasionally, she thought about Mrs Agnetti, lying sick upstairs. It made her feel a little sick herself.

Mr Agnetti made no conversation, but nor did he lose himself in his work, as he often did. His movements with the chalk and charcoal were slow and ponderous. Once he drifted off entirely, staring into the distance.

'Mr Agnetti?'

He rose. 'I must check upon Theresa.'

She listened to his tread on the stairs, the knock at the bedroom door. Agnetti turned the handle and knocked again. His tone grew sharper. 'Theresa.' After a little while, he descended the stairs and resumed painting.

Simon Dodd-Bellingham called at eleven, and Mr Agnetti sent her downstairs. Kitty was practising her scales on the harpsichord.

'She's locked him out,' Pamela said. 'Mrs Agnetti.'

'Theresa's probably just asleep. They went out to a ball last night.'

Pamela looked up sharply. 'She's better, then?'

'Not well enough to go out. I told him not to take her. He said she insisted.'

The lieutenant must have been at the ball, Pamela thought. No remorse then. No sign that Theresa was intending to change her ways. It made her feel a little better about everything that had happened.

A short time later, Simon Dodd-Bellingham poked his head round the door. Seeing them, he smiled, and produced two black boxes tied with pink ribbon from his coat pocket. 'My brother asked me to give you these.'

Pamela took her box and untied the ribbon. Rose-petal macarons. And one of those cards: the golden man with the head of a goat.

'When?' Kitty asked.

'Tonight.'

'Not much notice.' Kitty pouted.

'Mr Stone only decided today. We'll pick you up at your rooms at nine, the other girls too.' He turned to Pamela. 'We'll collect you from Mrs Havilland's. Don't be late.'

Trepidation pushed everything else from her mind. But once she had her hundred and twenty-five guineas then she could be free of her watcher, free to put her plan in place. She might even be able to set it in train tonight.

'Might I have a word with you, Pamela, please?' Simon said.

Kitty's gaze followed them curiously, as Pamela accompanied Simon into the hall. To her surprise – because he'd never tried to get her alone before – he went into the drawing room, closing the door behind them. Pamela didn't like that room, despite its elegant furnishings. It was the scene of her rival's trysts. And she didn't like that big painting over the fire, of the girl coupling with the bull.

'Can I ask you something in confidence?' Simon said. 'Could you give this letter to Mrs Agnetti? It needs to be done discreetly – Mr Agnetti mustn't know. Do as I ask, and I'll give you half a crown.'

Pamela's eye fell upon the letter in his hand, recognizing the lieutenant's bold script on the address.

'Why can't your brother give it to her himself?'

'He thought it would be better if I delivered it, but she's sick in bed.'

The lieutenant was breaking things off with her. Pamela smiled. She wouldn't have to face Mrs Agnetti, she could simply push the letter under her door.

'Very well.' She pocketed his coin. 'I will be safe tonight, won't I?'

His face flushed. 'Why wouldn't you be safe?'

'Lucy said she thought that I might not be.'

'Who's Lucy?'

'One of Mr Agnetti's sitters. Well?'

'Of course you'll be safe, I give you my word.' He smiled, showing her his yellow teeth.

Chapter Sixty

Grimmond showed them into the Dodd-Bellingham residence, explaining that Simon Dodd-Bellingham was upstairs, changing his clothes, after a morning in his workshop. 'We are content to wait,' Mrs Corsham said. 'Pray tell him we are here.'

They waited in the drawing room. It would have been grand once, with lofty windows overlooking Bloomsbury Square, and a painted ceiling, now riven with cracks. The furniture was as threadbare as the Indian carpet. Sooty portraits of Dodd-Bellingham ancestors in far more salubrious settings added to the tale of an illustrious line run to seed.

A small crate stood on the tea table and Child peered inside. More of Simon's antiquities: a few pieces of broken pot; what looked like an ancient oil lamp; and a cloth bag of old coins. Child shook a few out, the surfaces scratched and worn, the edges clipped by ancient counterfeiters. Some things never changed.

Between the windows stood an old, worm-eaten bureau. Child's eye fell upon it. 'Watch the door.'

He thought Mrs Corsham might protest, but everything they'd heard from Kitty Carefree had evidently overcome any remaining sensibilities she'd had about what members of the beau monde should and shouldn't do in one another's houses.

Opening the bureau's fall front, he saw that the interior was divided into pigeon holes and drawers. Taking out a sheaf of correspondence, he leafed through it. Several letters addressed to the lieutenant were from women Child presumed to be society matrons, arranging times for him to call upon their daughters. Another letter, apparently from an agent, discussed the financial affairs of several prominent gentlemen. Child presumed these efforts were part of the lieutenant's endeavour to find himself a wealthy wife.

Opening a drawer at random, he examined the clutter inside. A few military badges that looked like campaign mementoes; a wilted daisy chain; a lady's glove. And a pair of enamelled portrait miniatures attached by a blue ribbon. One painting was of Lieutenant Dodd-Bellingham, the other of a lady with a thin white face, wearing an odd turban of blue cloth. In the corner were the artists' initials: T.A. Child beckoned Mrs Corsham over. 'Is that her? Theresa Agnetti?'

'Yes,' she said, studying the portrait. 'This must be the miniature that the lieutenant mentioned. It's true, then. She really was in love with him. The poor woman.'

Putting the portraits back, Child moved on to the next drawer. More correspondence, this time addressed to Simon:

Farthingale Hall
Farthingale
Wiltshire

4 September 1782

Dear Sir,

I take great pleasure in writing to inform you that the statues and other artefacts have now been fitted according to your client's commands and await your inspection.

*Furthermore, the hangings and tapestries for the lady's
bedroom have arrived safely, with no water damage. I
have stored them with the clothes and other articles that
you entrusted to my care, until such time as the house is
ready for habitation. I am confident that your client and
his wife will be delighted with Farthingale Hall in every
respect.*

Your humble servant
John Denning

There were several more letters from John Denning, dating
back to April, when it seemed that Simon's client had purchased
Farthingale Hall. Alongside this correspondence was a roll of
receipts, tied with a ribbon: purchases from upholsterers and
cabinet-makers, and a haberdashery in Newport Alley named
Maison Bertin.

'He's coming,' Mrs Corsham whispered. Child shoved
everything back into the drawer, stepping away.

Simon Dodd-Bellingham greeted them with his usual wary
smile. 'Mrs Corsham. Mr Child. This is a bad time, I am afraid.
I have an appointment at the museum.'

'We'll walk with you,' Mrs Corsham said.

He gave another toothy smile. 'As you wish.'

They turned out of Bloomsbury Square onto Russell Street,
Simon carrying his crate in both hands. The street was domi-
nated by the vast mansion of Bedford House. Through the
railings Child could see footmen in Bedford livery striding
across the gravel, and grooms leading fine stallions through to
the stables.

'We have spoken to a witness who contradicts the story you
told us entirely.' Mrs Corsham was unable to keep the anger

from her tone. 'This witness testifies that you and your friends procured Pamela for my brother, Ambrose, who is afflicted with syphilis. Pamela discovered the deception and an argument ensued. We believe she was murdered by one of you later that night.'

'It is lies,' Simon stammered. 'I deny it.'

He started to say more, but Child cut across him. 'If you refuse to help us, then we will ask ourselves why you continue to lie. We will be forced to look into certain events in your past.'

Simon turned, indignant. 'What events in my past? Speak plainly, sir, or not at all.'

'I had the fortune to pay two visits recently to the home of Ansell Ward,' Mrs Corsham said. 'We discussed your time in his house at some length.'

Simon's laughter sounded a little strained. 'You mean that old story about those wretched figurines? There is no truth in it at all. But Ward got it into his head that I was responsible and there was no shifting it. I've lost a few clients as a result, but fortunately most people like to see evidence when allegations are thrown about. So do your worst, Mrs Corsham. I'll ride it out.'

'We know you are innocent of the theft,' she said. 'The crime was staged, we believe by Mrs Ward.'

Simon gaped at her, in what looked like genuine astonishment.

Child picked up the thread. 'It is not unheard of for a woman or a girl, if they have fallen victim to a crime of an intimate nature, to conceal it from the man who loves them most. You tutored Mrs Ward's daughter, Julia, I believe?'

Simon had turned white. 'How dare you?' he said. 'Withdraw that accusation, sir.'

He took a step towards Child, fists clenched. Child shifted his weight in anticipation of the blow. Notwithstanding the years between them, he thought he could put Simon Dodd-Bellingham on his back, and after everything they'd discovered, he would enjoy every second. Perhaps sensing it, Simon stepped away. 'I have no wish for further discussion with you, sir. Nor you, madam. Leave me alone.'

'I intend to speak to Mrs Ward,' Mrs Corsham called after him. 'Her daughter too. When they hear about the crimes you and your friends committed, I think they will tell me exactly what you got up to in that house.' She listed them on her fingers. 'Giving a young girl, a virgin, to a man with syphilis. Her subsequent murder. The possibility that other girls at those masquerades might be in danger.'

Simon had stopped walking. Now he turned. 'You can say nothing to Miss Ward. You mustn't. This isn't right.'

'Oh, I can, sir, and I will.'

Simon exhaled, sweating but not from the walk. 'It is not what you think,' he said. 'I did not molest Miss Ward. We are in love, and hope one day to be married.'

Mrs Corsham's look of surprise was matched only by Child's own.

Chapter Sixty-One

Montagu House had been sold to the trustees of the British Museum when the Duke of Montagu, like so many other noblemen, had moved west to Mayfair. Now it housed books, fossils and other historical artefacts bequeathed by collectors to a grateful nation. As they crossed the forecourt, Caro listened with a sceptical ear as Simon Dodd-Bellingham told them of his love for Julia Ward.

'I admired her from the moment we first met. Miss Ward has a love of learning, a joyful heart, and a kind nature. Not at all the sort of girl my brother would desire – and all the better for it. Over her studies, we discussed history and philosophy. We'd laugh together. I began to entertain the thought that she might have fonder feelings for me. The day I declared myself to her, I never felt so nervous. Nor so happy to learn that my desires were reciprocated.'

'*Amor magnus doctor est*,' Mr Child said wryly.

Simon glared. 'I might have been her teacher, but there was nothing improper about it. We kissed but once – before fate intervened to part us. Perhaps we would have been parted anyway, even without the theft – what with my debts, and my mother's history. But Miss Ward thought there was a chance that her father could be persuaded. He admired my family name, and despite everything, I am a gentleman. We decided to bide our time, choose the right moment to ask.'

'I think it safe to say that Mrs Ward caught wind of your little romance,' Caro said.

'But Julia's mother liked me,' he exclaimed. 'I thought the theft was just a disastrous turn of fate. Why would Mrs Ward have done such a thing?'

'There's a difference between adopting a man as a charitable endeavour, and welcoming him into your family as a prospective son-in-law.'

Caro could see how it must have gone. Mrs Ward, like all City wives, would have wanted to marry her children to advantage. Given her husband's wealth and connections, her daughter could certainly hope to do a sight better than Simon Dodd-Bellingham. Perhaps Mrs Ward had also thought that her daughter might be able to talk her husband round – just as Caro had talked her own father round when she'd wanted to marry the dashing, yet penniless, Captain Corsham.

They climbed the steps to the central hall with its French murals. Most of the rooms on the ground floor were given over to the library, and Caro glimpsed several scholarly gentlemen at work. They walked up the grand staircase to the first floor, where the antiquities and specimens of natural history were housed.

'Miss Ward never wavered in her love or her belief in my innocence,' Simon said. 'We correspond secretly, using her brother as a go-between. I even bought her a diamond ring with a small inheritance from an aunt, which she wears on a ribbon under her clothes. She chastised me for spending my money unwisely.' He smiled. 'Like many City girls, Miss Ward is practically minded. She refuses to countenance an elopement until I am on a firmer footing. But with my debts . . .' He made a gesture of frustration. 'I tried to revisit my rate of interest with Mr Stone, but he only sent his man, Erasmus Knox, to see me. Somehow he knew about Julia and me.'

'And he threatened to reveal your secret courtship to Julia's father?'

'Mr Ward can hardly bear to hear my name spoken,' Simon said despondently. 'He thinks I betrayed his trust, and to him there is no greater crime than that. He'd marry Julia off in a heartbeat if he knew of our intention. So you see, madam, this is no debauched tale, but rather a story of love divided.'

Child cocked his head. 'I can certainly see why you don't want Miss Ward finding out about your visits to Stone's estate. The masquerades, the girls. It's not exactly *Romeo and Juliet*, is it?'

'I told you the last time we spoke that I had no option but to attend. I took no pleasure in it.'

'Somehow I doubt that Miss Ward would see it like that,' Caro said. 'The price of our silence upon that topic, sir, is your loquaciousness upon the murders of Pamela and Lucy Loveless.'

Simon gestured hopelessly at a man waiting at the end of the corridor. 'My appointment.'

'We'll wait,' Child said.

Simon sighed. 'If Mr Stone finds out that I have talked to you, then he will tell Mr Ward.'

'That's a risk you'll have to take,' Child said. 'But Stone won't find out from us. Not if you tell us the truth.'

Simon stared unhappily at the box of antiquities in his hands. 'Then I have no choice.'

*

While they waited for Simon to return, they wandered the South Sea rooms, admiring carved wooden figures and paintings upon leather scrolls. When Simon caught up with them, he was still carrying his crate. 'They only wanted two of my pots, and none of the coins. All my best pieces go to Mr Stone, at generous prices naturally. He subtracts any profit from my debt. It will be years before I can repay him at this rate.'

Caro's sympathy was in short supply. 'You knew what Stone planned to do with Pamela? That he intended to give her to my brother?'

'I thought it was shocking. We all did, even Neddy. But what else could we do?'

'Warn her not to go?'

'Stone would have called in our debts, had us locked in the Fleet. I'd have lost Miss Ward. But Pamela might never have been infected. I spoke to a physician. He said it was unlikely.'

Seeing no absolution in Caro's face, he started walking. 'I told you the truth last time. I know nothing of any murder. I really did go for a walk. The girls told me what had happened with your brother when I returned, but I just went to bed. In the morning, when I awoke, Neddy and the girls were gone.'

'You expect us to believe that you know nothing about it?'

'It is the truth. I swear it on Miss Ward's life.'

'Tell us about that morning,' Child said. 'Leave nothing out.'

They walked to a small tearoom with a garden and a skittle alley, and a view over the fields to the distant village of Highgate. They sat outside, though it wasn't warm, the breeze cooling their tea.

'All I can tell you is that Mr Stone was not his usual self at breakfast,' Simon said. 'Neither was Lord March. I presumed they felt as guilty about Pamela and your brother as I did myself. As far as I was concerned, Pamela had returned to London along with Neddy and the other girls. When I got home, I did ask him about Pamela, but he didn't want to talk about it. Neither did I, truth be told. I wanted to forget that I'd ever played a part in it. Much later, after Lucy came to see me,

I spoke to Neddy again. I demanded to know if it was true that Pamela had been murdered. He said it wasn't, that she had found a wealthy keeper. I accepted my brother at his word.'

'I saw your brother and Lord March arguing over a silver necklace at Carlisle House,' Caro said. 'It belonged to Pamela.'

Simon shook his head. 'Why would they kill her? It makes no sense.'

Mr Child studied him evenly. 'Theresa Agnetti visited Stone's estate earlier that same day. Do you know anything about that?'

'Yes, I was there, delivering some new pieces for Mr Stone's collection.'

'Do you know what he and Mrs Agnetti discussed?'

'No, she asked to talk to him in private. They went downstairs to his study.'

'Was that usual?'

'No, I suppose it wasn't. Normally, when she came to the house on her husband's business, they talked in front of me. Mr Stone enjoyed her company. They knew one another from their time in India.'

'How did Theresa seem on that last occasion?'

'Calm. I was relieved.'

'Why so?'

'I had taken her a letter from my brother earlier that morning. They had been having an amour behind Mr Agnetti's back, and he wished to end it.'

'How did she react when you gave her the letter?'

'I don't know. She was upstairs in bed. I gave it to Pamela to deliver.'

From Mr Child's expression, Caro knew that he was thinking the same as her. How would that have made Theresa feel?

To have her rival deliver a note of dismissal from the man she loved?

'Do you have any idea where Mrs Agnetti is now?'

'No, I told you before, I hardly knew her.'

'That house in Wiltshire,' Mr Child said. 'Farthingale Hall. Does it belong to Stone?' He registered Simon's look of surprise. 'I read a letter in your bureau.'

He flushed scarlet. 'Those papers are private. A gentleman doesn't read another's correspondence.'

'Then you're out of luck, because I'm no gentleman – as your brother was keen to remind me. That house was purchased in April, not long after these events. Could Stone be keeping Mrs Agnetti there?'

'Mrs Agnetti? What makes you say that?'

'She walked out of her house without any clothes, and you have purchased and sent lady's clothes there, amongst other things.'

'It was just an order Stone had me collect. The house is for one of his mistresses.'

'Have you met her? Could it be Theresa Agnetti?'

He shook his head vigorously. 'Mr Denning, the steward at Farthingale Hall, saw the lady who is to live there. Stone was showing her around the place. He described a very different woman to Theresa Agnetti. Young, full in figure, and very beautiful. Even a charitable man wouldn't describe Mrs Agnetti thus.'

Caro felt all this was a distraction. Mrs Agnetti had loved the lieutenant. He had just broken her heart. She was hardly likely to have lurched into an amour with Mr Stone. Nor, she felt, was Theresa the sort of woman who would tempt Stone, no matter how much he had enjoyed her company.

'Our witness says that when your brother and Lord March

returned to Stone's house, they had red mud and straw on their boots. You are familiar with Stone's estate. Where might it have come from?'

'The stables?'

'They went into the woods, away from the house.'

'I can't think.'

'Try harder,' Child said.

Simon's brow furrowed. 'There is a disused farm on the north side of the estate, beyond the wood. I've seen it from a hilltop: a yard and some buildings. The yard was red, like a wound in the landscape.'

Caro met Child's gaze. 'A disused farm would offer plenty of places to hide a body,' she observed.

Simon shook his head, as if he was still unwilling to believe that Pamela had been murdered.

'I asked you about your brother and Somerset,' Caro said. 'I think you lied to me. Now I want the truth.'

Simon's shoulders slumped. He removed his spectacles and rubbed his eyes. Betraying his brother was evidently coming at a cost.

'Something happened last year,' he said. 'It wasn't long after Neddy had returned from the colonies. A gift was delivered to the house, and Neddy opened it in front of me, thinking it was from one of his women. The box contained a white feather. I thought it was some sort of joke, but Neddy didn't take it well. He threw it on the fire. Then later that day, an ensign who had served with Neddy called at the house. As they were going into the drawing room, I heard Neddy say: "I received a package from Somerset this morning."' Simon spread his hands. 'That's all I know.'

Caro's mind was racing. *A white feather, symbol of cowardice amongst military men.*

'Did you really go for dinner at the Prince of Wales on the night Lucy was murdered?' Mr Child asked.

Blushing, he shook his head. 'I went to Lyme Street, to stand opposite Ward's house. Sometimes Julia comes to her bedroom window, and we look at one another.'

'Did she do so on that night?'

'No, but it brought me great solace just to be near her.'

'Some men will go to great lengths not to lose the woman they love,' Mrs Corsham observed. 'Some are even prepared to kill to prevent it. Pamela told a friend of hers that she knew a secret that could make her rich. One of the possibilities we've been considering is that this secret concerned one of you. That it might even be the motive for her murder.'

'I'd like to think that I'd kill for Miss Ward,' Simon said. 'But how could I possibly have made Pamela rich? I have no money – and neither does Neddy. Thanks to Mr Stone.'

'You never heard Pamela speak of any secret?'

'No,' he said. 'But I only met her a few times.' He closed his eyes. 'That last morning, when I went to the house, when I asked Pamela to deliver my brother's letter, she asked me if she'd be safe at the masquerade. I said she would.' He stared down at his hands. 'Don't think I don't have a conscience. I think of her often – what we did. I blame Mr Stone for that most of all.'

Chapter Sixty-Two

Mrs Corsham's carriage rattled along King's Street and then turned west onto High Holborn. This stretch of the street was lined with lottery shops: barbers offering a chance to win ten pounds with a shave; bootblacks where a man might win a guinea; stalls where threepence bought you a dozen oysters and a chance at a side of ham. Child thought fleetingly of Jonathan Stone, and his own odds of getting out of this mess unscathed.

'We need to find Pamela's body,' Mrs Corsham said. 'You need to take a look around that disused farm.'

'You said the grounds were full of guards and gamekeepers. I'd never get close.'

'Tomorrow is full moon. The night of the masquerade. All the guests will be wearing masks.'

'No,' Child said firmly. 'It's too dangerous.'

'We could dress you up as a gentleman. And we have one of the lieutenant's invitations.'

'Not a chance,' Child said. 'Wherever Pamela is buried, I don't fancy lying next to her.'

They sat for a time in silence, each absorbed by their own thoughts. Halfway down Fleet Street, Mrs Corsham turned to him again, her eyes alight with excitement. 'After the lieutenant received that white feather in the mail, he said he'd just received a package from Somerset. And when Lucy threatened him, she said she was thinking of taking a trip to see Somerset.'

'What of it?' Child said.

'I wonder if he was talking about a place at all? What if he was referring to Somerset, a person?'

A slow smile spread over Child's face. 'If you're right, then this Somerset must be known to both the lieutenant and the ensign. If it was a woman, surely he'd have said Mrs Somerset? So it must be a man. Another soldier?'

'If he served with the lieutenant, then he must be an officer. I remember him telling me that his regiment were redeployed to Jamaica. Only a handful of wounded officers were permitted to return home. The lieutenant was granted leave to accompany them because the King wanted to meet him. You could surely find out if one of them was named Somerset?'

Child nodded. 'Drop me at Charing Cross, and I'll do so now.'

*

Most of the troops stationed in London were billeted in taverns close to the royal palaces, as the English had a natural distrust of soldiers living in permanent barracks. Child wandered the alehouses of Whitehall in search of soldiers who looked easy in drink and conversation. His freedom with his coin attracted the attention of several cadaverous girls with matted hair and soiled clothes – a far cry from the Whores' Club. He waved them away.

Child soon learned from a drunken private that the non-commissioned officers – those who'd come up from the rank and file, rather than gentlemen like the lieutenant – liked to drink in the Griffin on Villiers Street. It took him a few minutes to walk down there.

The tavern wasn't much different from the one he'd just left. Drink, dice, cards, a slightly better class of doxy, and bawdy songs. Child idled around a game of chicken-hazard, occasionally flashing his coin, until someone invited him to join in. The dice were clearly cogged and he bet cautiously, limiting his losses, until enough time had passed for him to drop the name comfortably.

'Did any of you ever come across an officer named Somerset? He served in the colonies, I think.'

'Jack Somerset? Sir Douglas's Foot? Non-commissioned sergeant? Took a ball in the arm at Bound Brook?'

Sir Douglas's Foot was the lieutenant's former regiment. 'That's him. I heard he was back in London now.'

The man who had spoken had a crooked aquiline nose. The other players called him Pitt, because he supposedly resembled the young Chancellor of the Exchequer, though Child couldn't see it. 'That's right. You know the army threw him out?'

'I didn't, no.'

'Bit too fond of this.' Pitt raised his glass. 'But aren't we all?'

Child cast the dice. 'Know where I can find him? Friend of mine owes him six shillings and wants to make good.'

'Last I heard he was living at the Rag Fair. That should tell you everything about how he's faring. He'll be glad of your six shillings.'

Child thanked him, and shortly thereafter, made his excuses and left. He was due to dine with Solomon Loredo and his family at eight, and some of the soldiers' banter had made him realize what a mess he must look. His coat was stained with blood from yesterday's beating, and his chin was bristled. His lodgings were on the way to Loredo's house at St Mary-le-Bow, and he decided to stop off for a wash and a shave. As he walked across town, he dwelled again on his conversation with Kitty Carefree, trying to identify the discrepancy niggling away at him. By the time he reached Holborn, he'd failed to come up with the answer. Keep thinking, he told himself. It'll come to you.

A carriage was idling near the entrance to his court, and as Child passed, the door opened. The larger of the two men who'd accosted him in Soho stepped out. Child turned to run, but the man's scarcely less-large friend was already behind him. He gave Child a gap-toothed grin, and nodded to the interior of the carriage.

'Get in. Mr Stone wants a word.'

CHAPTER SIXTY-THREE

CARO HAD WONDERED whether Mr Agnetti would be at Vauxhall for the exhibition. Yet when she arrived at his house in Leicester Fields, she saw lights in the windows of both his studio and the drawing room. Miles waited in the hall while the manservant showed her upstairs, where she discovered Mr Agnetti painting by candlelight.

He laid down his brush and bowed. 'Mrs Corsham.'

'Forgive my intrusion at this late hour, sir. I need to speak to you in confidence. My thief-taker found Kitty Carefree. I spoke to her.'

Agnetti nodded to his manservant. 'Leave us, please.'

Clearing a sofa of drawings, he invited her to sit, and then pulled up a chair himself. 'Do go on, madam. You mentioned that you had spoken to Kitty? I do hope she is well?'

'First, I wish to apologize,' she said. 'For suspecting you of involvement in Lucy's murder. Kitty told us who the fifth man was. My brother Ambrose.'

'I am so sorry. That must have been hard.'

'Ambrose didn't kill her, I am certain. But his part in this despicable enterprise was almost as bad.' Caro told him the whole story, believing that only candour would earn his trust.

'Appalling,' he said, disgust and distress written large upon his face. 'How could they have done that to a child?' He rose and paced the room. 'Then you truly believe that Pamela is dead? Murdered by the same animal who killed Lucy?'

'Yes, I do. We think Pamela is buried on Stone's estate.' She paused judiciously. 'The reason I have called on you is that it's possible that Theresa played a role in these events. You described a tension between your wife and Pamela, but we think it was much more than that. Someone told us Theresa believed Pamela murdered her baby.'

He sat down heavily and passed a hand across his face. 'How can that be true? You should know that Theresa was not always rational in those last days. There were times when I feared she was losing her mind.'

Caro fought a wave of nausea. 'But if Theresa believed it to be true, and she was not behaving rationally, might that not have given her a reason to harm Pamela? I don't say Theresa killed her, not for a moment, but she visited Stone's estate on the day she later disappeared – the same day Pamela attended that masquerade.'

Agnetti made a bemused gesture. 'I asked her to call on Stone. She took him a contract and some sketches.'

'It seems odd to attend to your business if she'd already made up her mind to leave.'

'As I said, she was not always acting with reason. I believe her decision to leave might have been made in the moment. Why else would she have taken no money? And no clothes?'

'Could you tell me about those last days? What happened between the two of you? I would not ask if I did not believe it to be important.'

His reluctance was etched into every line on his tired face, but he nodded slowly. 'If you truly think it might help your thief-taker catch this beast among men. But allow me first to wash and fetch some wine.'

He was gone some time. Caro wandered the studio, looking at the paintings. Agnetti had worked upon his Clytemnestra, Lucy's face made flesh and blood, breathed back to life by his brush. 'We make progress,' Caro told her softly.

When Agnetti returned, he handed her a glass of wine and she sipped it tentatively. Retaking his seat, he drew a lamp closer.

'To truly understand my wife's actions, you must first hear about our marriage from the beginning.' Agnetti spoke slowly, his mellifluous voice rising and falling with the strain of the telling. 'I first met Theresa at the house of her father, who served as British consul to the Kingdom of Naples. Her family lived on a small estate outside the city limits, and I stayed there while I painted her father's portrait. He was pleased with my work, and he asked me to paint his daughter too. From our first meeting, I could tell that Theresa was a girl of fragile spirit. She barely said a word in our first sittings, mute with shyness, twitching with nerves. But later, as she grew to trust me, I saw the true Theresa: a young woman of learning, with a deep curiosity of the mind, and a fascination for art, philosophy and languages. Yet I sensed a deep sadness within her too.'

He sipped his wine, grimacing, though to Caro's taste it was very fine. 'Theresa was then but twenty-one years old, and yet in the five years since she had set foot on Neapolitan soil, she had never once ventured out into society. I found it curious – this learned young woman, shut up in that villa, with only her parents and their servants and her books. Later, I learned the reason why. Before Theresa had left India, when she was just fifteen years old, she had fallen in love with a gentleman who did not love her back. Distraught by his rejection, she had attempted to commit suicide by cutting her wrists. That's why her father brought the family to Naples – to escape the scandal and restore her to health. Back then, I knew nothing of this. I saw only a timid girl, who had begun to fascinate me.'

He pointed to a painting. 'Do you know the story of Philomela? She was raped by her brother-in-law, who cut out her tongue so she couldn't tell anyone what he had done. The gods transformed her into a nightingale so that she could sing.' He smiled. 'So it was with Theresa in our sittings. I watched her grow in confidence, learned how to make her smile. She would laugh, then stop, surprised at herself. Over a few short weeks, we fell in love. I think her parents had almost given up hope that she would ever marry, and when I asked for her hand, they were almost as happy as I was myself.'

He turned away, his face lost in shadow, the candlelight giving his wine a ruby glow.

'But Theresa was never truly happy. She hid it well, and yet I could tell. The good moments we had – and there were many – could never entirely banish the demons that plagued her. And as we struggled to conceive a child, her troubles only grew. She began drinking more, and became a subject of gossip in Neapolitan society. I hoped that when we moved to England, among her own people, her situation would improve, but she did not adapt to London society either. The ladies, in particular, were not always kind.'

Caro prickled at the condemnation. 'Theresa wasn't always the easiest of companions.'

'No,' Agnetti conceded. 'She had an anger within her too, one that I never truly understood. Sometimes I was myself the recipient of it. But often her rage was directed inwards, at herself. The only people in whose company she ever appeared content were Lucy and Kitty – perhaps because she never felt judged by them. I encouraged the association, because I wanted more than anything for Theresa to be happy. Between she and I, relations only worsened.'

He took another gulp of wine, staring at his paintings. 'We'd argue over her moods, or she'd become upset and break things. Sometimes I grew angry too – this wasn't the way I wanted to live. I tried to give her the love she needed, but I couldn't reach her. In the end, distressed, ashamed, I retreated into my work, and we could go for days without speaking. I consulted physicians, even a mad-doctor, but she was furious at me for even talking to them. I tell you this because it is important that you understand Theresa's character. She loved me, I believe, but she was frightened that she'd lose my love, as she had lost the interest of the man she had loved in India. So she pushed me away before it could happen.'

He leaned forward. 'You asked me before about Lieutenant Dodd-Bellingham. At first, I thought it was merely one of her flirtations. Theresa was often coquettish in public – I am sure you observed it yourself. I think she did it to provoke a reaction, evidence that I still cared. I did care, very much. But I did not wish to encourage such behaviour by responding. I am also one of those men who sometimes struggles to find the right words. I thought if I gave her time and air to breathe, she could find the serenity she sought. Instead, I forced her into the arms of Dodd-Bellingham.'

His voice hardened. 'I thought him a coarse, boorish fellow from the first. He paid many calls to this house on business for Mr Stone, and Theresa dealt with much of my administration, as Miss Willoughby does now. That too was a mistake upon my part. The lieutenant is, I think, the kind of man who looks for vulnerability in a woman.'

'When did you start to suspect about him and Theresa?'

'Over the final few weeks that she resided in this house. But

I told myself that she loved me, that she would never hurt me like that. Then came the night of the Amberley Ball. Theresa had just lost the baby, and I was so very worried about her. She was jaundiced – shivering and sweating, but she demanded to go out, and in the end I didn't have any will left to fight her. At the ball, I lost her in the crowd. I went looking for her, and came out onto the terrace. That was when I saw them – down below, in the privy garden. The lieutenant had my wife bent over a wall, debasing her in the vilest fashion.' He shuddered. 'When he looked up and saw me watching them, he smiled.'

'I'm sorry,' Caro said, recognizing how much it must be costing him to tell her this.

His voice cracked. 'I was so angry. At him, at her, at myself. But mostly at how two people who had once loved one another – who *still* loved one another – could have come to this. For a week I had mourned our dead child, and suddenly I did not even know whether it was mine. Yet I did not shout or beat her. I took no steps towards divorce. I did not call the lieutenant out, or file a suit of criminal conversation. I did nothing. And I think she took that as the greatest betrayal of all. Proof that I didn't love her, that I was indifferent. It all came back to that single fear in her mind.'

Mr Agnetti's distress was written in his hunched posture, his twisted mouth. Caro wondered whether he really believed it, this fiction he had written to console himself. She debated telling Agnetti about his wife's painting – those miniatures were surely a sign of Theresa's deeper feelings for the lieutenant. Maybe it would ease his burden, help him to forget his wife and his pain? But it might simply hurt him further.

'You suppose that Pamela and Theresa were rivals for the lieutenant's affection,' he said. 'Perhaps you are right, and their antipathy was greater than I guessed. But I cannot think you right that she was involved in any murder. My wife was a gentle, kind woman. Not a killer. I think in losing the baby, she simply lost some part of herself. I hope when she finds it again, she will return.'

For all his illusions about his marriage, Caro wondered if this part might be true. The loss of her child, her husband's perceived indifference, her lover's rejection, her turbulent mind – all might have conspired to make Theresa Agnetti believe that there was little worth staying for. Yet Caro wished she could be certain.

'You would take her back?' she asked, thinking of Harry and judgement day. 'Even after everything she's done?'

He gave a sad smile. 'My friends tell me to forget her – that in time I will marry again. But she is still my wife. Whatever she has done, I share a part of that blame, and I refuse to betray her again by losing faith.' He gestured to his bureau, a cascade of correspondence littering the desktop. 'I have written to every hospital and asylum in the kingdom. My agents search for her at home and abroad. To date they have found no trace, but one day they will. She is out there somewhere. I know she is.' His dark eyes bored into her. 'I have been honest with you, Mrs Corsham, and I have one question to ask you in return. Have you come across any indication of Theresa's whereabouts in the course of your inquiry? If so, then I beg you to tell me. I cannot rest until I know that she is safe. I would place no legal restraint upon her to return. I wish only to try to persuade her that things will be different.'

'I'm sorry,' Caro said. 'We have found nothing.'

Seeing his disappointment, she chose her next words carefully. 'Kitty believes that Theresa chose to put an end to her own suffering.'

'She is still alive,' he said fiercely, placing his hand upon his heart. 'I would feel it here, if she was not.'

Chapter Sixty-Four

Back in the private room at the supper house, Jonathan Stone was seated at the table, eating a platter of oysters, Child sitting opposite. Erasmus Knox was standing by the fire.

Child had just given Stone a tale of his movements over the past three days – censored in parts, embroidered in others. Fruitless conversations with whores and taverners. His meeting with Hector – given that the boy was dead, it couldn't do much harm. His beating at the hands of the Home Office. He described Mrs Corsham as distraught, following the episode at the park with her boy. 'Give it a few days, and I think she'll tire of this.'

Stone smiled. 'You wouldn't be lying to me, Mr Child? I explained to you that I had a keen ear for the truth.'

'You know what,' Child said, attempting to bluff it out. 'I don't really care if you don't believe me. Do your worst in Deptford. I'll take my chances in court.' Perhaps Mrs Corsham could buy the judge, after everything they'd been through together. Or her husband could intervene. Stone wasn't the only one with power and connections.

The moneylender regarded him placidly. 'I regret that in those circumstances, Mr Knox here will be forced to pay a visit to Samuel Hardcastle. You are acquainted with his wife, Sophie, I believe? I have no wish to destroy his happiness. Nor that of his wife and children. That I am willing to do so should speak volumes about my intent.'

Child's defiance collapsed like a house of cards in a draught. On one side, Mrs Corsham, who had placed her trust in him. On the other, Sophie, with her happy smile and her lonely heart. Out on the street. Her children disowned and homeless. Because of him.

Stone glanced at Knox. 'Where is Sophie at this time?'

'At the Drury Lane playhouse with her husband,' Knox said. 'A neighbour's watching the children.'

'Sophie has nothing to do with any of this. Please. I've told you everything.'

'I don't believe you.'

Knox addressed Child: 'We have several testimonies from neighbours and tavern-keepers. People who saw you and Sophie together. Kisses. Tender embraces. Her slipping out of your rooms at all hours. I prefer letters in such cases, but sometimes a human account can be just as eloquent.'

Stone studied Child's anguished face. 'Humility is truth. It's time for you to be humble, Mr Child.'

Child only gazed at him mutely.

'Your stubbornness in this matter surprises me,' Stone continued. 'Especially given your circumstances: your late wife, your dead son.'

Child glared, his eyes moistening, everything spinning. 'Don't bring them into it. Just don't.'

He sensed a flicker of movement from Knox, over by the fire, an acknowledgement of the room's shift in tension.

'Your little boy was born simple, isn't that right?' Stone sighed. 'Your wife struggled with it, people say. And you did too. Drinking. Arguing. Staying out all night. And then one day, your wife wandered down to the river, filled her pockets with stones, and tied a larger one around the neck of your little boy. It was three days before they found them.'

'Stop!' Child said. 'I mean it.'

'And where were you all this while? In the whorehouse. I wonder if that's why she decided to do it.'

Child sprang at him, hands clawing. Moments later, when he opened his eyes, he was lying on the floor, and Erasmus Knox's boot was on his throat. Knox pulled him up, righted his chair, and sat him down in it firmly. Stone smiled.

'Given all that, I am surprised you would be quite so cavalier with Sophie's future. Your women don't have much luck, do they, Mr Child?'

Child thought of Sophie performing tricks for soldiers in return for bread money, like those desperate women he'd seen in the soldiers' taverns earlier that night. Then he heard someone talking, in a voice that sounded like his, telling Stone all about Simon and Julia Ward, about the Whores' Club and the puzzle purses, about Miss Willoughby and Somerset. About everything.

Much of it Stone already seemed to know, but occasionally he frowned. When it came to Kitty Carefree, now living in Clapham as Katherine Sillerton, he smiled. 'Very good, Mr Child. Finally, we come to Mrs Corsham. Have you established what she was doing in that bower?'

Child swallowed. 'She was meeting *her*,' he said helplessly. 'Lucy Loveless.'

Stone blinked in surprise. 'You are sure?'

'Mrs Corsham admitted it. She thought Lucy was an Italian contessa, if you recall.'

'That doesn't explain why they would have met in the bowers.'

Child stared down at the table. 'I don't think Lucy wanted

to be seen. Neither did Mrs Corsham. Lucy had offered to help her with some personal trouble.'

Stone leaned forward. 'What kind of personal trouble?'

Child hardly heard him over the roaring in his ears. 'I think she's with child.'

Stone's smile grew very wide indeed. 'And just like that, the truth has set you free.'

PAMELA

1 March 1782

Pamela had never ridden in a carriage before. Nor had she ever been in the countryside. Not that she could see much in the darkness. Black fields on either side, high hedgerows, the silver curve of a river.

The carriage held five girls, as well as the lieutenant and his frog-like brother. Pamela was wedged against the door next to Kitty, whose feathers kept tickling her nose. The lieutenant seemed lost in thought, not smiling much tonight. She imagined the pair of them riding alone in a carriage like this. Her dressed as a lady with jewels and furs, the lieutenant all brushed and handsome in his redcoat.

These thoughts provided welcome distraction from everything she was going to have to do with Mr Stone. Cecily and the girls at the tableaux house had given her all manner of advice. Tricks to keep him happy, to distract him during the act. Mrs Havilland had sat her down in her parlour, and given her a long lecture about what to do and when to do it. Pamela had rolled her eyes, earning her a sharp rebuke. 'This is my livelihood, girl. I'll not have a little scrubber like you ruin my reputation.'

Now her nerves were creeping in. Don't think about it until you're doing it, Cecily had said. Or you're likely to panic.

She smiled at Kitty, who seemed to sense her apprehension and patted her hand. 'You should take rooms in Marylebone or Soho tomorrow, once you have your money. I'll come with you, if you like. When you have a few clients, we'll get you into *Harris's List*. We know all the right people.'

One of the girls smiled at her, though the others were less friendly. Pamela tried to remember their names: Becky, Sally . . . Not that they mattered.

'Then once you're in *Harris's List*,' Kitty went on, 'I can propose you for the Whores' Club.'

'Thank you,' she said. 'But I won't be doing this for very long after tonight.'

The one with dark curly hair, Rosy, arched an eyebrow. 'You won't survive long on the town on a hundred and twenty-five guineas.'

Rosy was jealous of the sum. Pamela could tell. But she didn't know the half of it.

Pamela glanced at the lieutenant, but he was staring out of the window. 'I mean to marry a gentleman,' she said.

'Just like that?' Kitty smiled.

Sally jangled her bracelets. 'You think the men are going to be so cunny-struck, they'll fall over themselves with proposals? Gentlemen don't marry whores. It's all a myth.'

'Sometimes they do,' Kitty said. 'Remember Lavinia Fenton. But it takes time, Pamela. First they have to keep you. Then they need to fall in love. But it's not just a normal falling-in-love, it has to be one so strong it overcomes every other objection: family, friends, public shame.'

Pamela only smiled. Perhaps one day they'd mention her name in the same breath as Lavinia Fenton. *It happens. Remember Pamela Dodd-Bellingham?* Except she wouldn't be Pamela after tonight. And her old name wouldn't do either. She'd choose another, one fit for a gentleman's wife. In London, a girl could always invent herself anew.

She wasn't sure how things worked at the masquerades – whether she'd get the chance to be alone with him tonight. If she did, she intended to put her plan into motion right away. If not, then tomorrow, when she was free of her watcher. She would call on him at his house, and lay out her proposition. And he would agree to everything – because he'd have no choice.

Chapter Sixty-Five

A PACKAGE WAS delivered the following morning. Caro opened it, half expecting to find another puzzle purse. Instead, she found that it contained Agnetti's drawings of Pamela and Lucy, Pamela's necklace and the invitation with the satyr.

Her concern mounting, she read the accompanying letter from Mr Child. He had been taken ill, he said, unable to work any longer on her inquiry. He would return her deposit as soon as he could. A few short lines described his discovery that Lieutenant Dodd-Bellingham had once served with a non-commissioned officer named Jack Somerset – information he hoped she could pass on to his successor. Finally, he'd scrawled a few cursory apologies. Nothing more.

Furious, she read the letter again. She didn't believe a word about his mysterious illness and she wondered if he'd been scared off – by Hector's murder and the beating he'd sustained. He'd seemed well enough yesterday, though – a little distracted perhaps, but fired up by the progress they had made. Had he been bought off by Stone? Or one of the others?

She called for her carriage.

*

At Mr Child's lodgings, she banged upon the door. Then got Miles to bang harder, in case he was asleep. No answer. For a moment, she stood there, uncertain what to do next. She didn't want to hire another thief-taker. Not when they'd come so far together. She wanted Mr Child. I'll come back tonight, she thought. Talk some sense into him then.

*

Returning to her carriage, she instructed Sam to take her to the Rag Fair – the last known address, according to Mr Child's letter, of this soldier, Jack Somerset. Her coachman stared at her, appalled, but he knew better than to argue. They rode south-east, through the City, wending their way down to the Tower, eventually coming to a halt in the shade of its walls on Little Tower Hill. Given the nature of the neighbourhood, Caro opted to wait in the carriage, dispatching a reluctant Miles to make inquiries after Jack Somerset.

All around she saw only crowds and squalor. Shops and stalls selling old furniture, pots and pans, penny-brick loaves, and countless purveyors of second- and third-hand clothes. A man carrying a long stick hung with hats pressed his warty face against the carriage window. Caro draw back sharply and he gave a toothless grin. 'Bicornes, tricornes, continental cocks,' he bellowed, until Sam flicked him with his whip, and he backed off, shouting curses.

Half an hour later, Miles returned, looking disgruntled. 'Only Somerset anyone seems to know is a woman,' he said. 'But I was told she had her brother living with her for a time. It's rough out there, madam.' He showed her his shoes and stockings, caked in mud and excrement. 'Wouldn't it be wiser to wait for Mr Child?'

'No, fetch the steps, please. Help me down.'

Miles and Sam exchanged a glance, and she wondered if they thought she was going mad.

On Rosemary Lane, hawkers of cloth and ribbons sat

cross-legged in the mud, their wares laid out on blankets, narrowing the street to a dense passage of people. Bantering and bargaining, arguing in a cacophony of London and Irish accents, the locals turned to stare as Caro and her bewigged footman strode past.

They proceeded down a succession of filthy lanes and roofed-in courts to a market named Glass House Yard. Thick with crowds, the yard was strung with ropes, groaning under the weight of coats, breeches, shirts, waistcoats, skirts, petticoats and jackets. Ragged urchins were down on the ground, trying on odd shoes and boots, caked in polish to conceal the patches and holes. A few stalls sold older clothes: Tudor doublets and ruffs. A small party of handsome men declaimed Shakespeare to one another, as they tried them on.

They turned into an alley of ancient lodging houses. A woman on a step was swigging gin, her red-faced baby screaming from a box on the ground. Everything stank, especially the cats: stringy creatures that prowled the mounds of rubbish, hunting for scraps. Miles came to a halt by the entrance to a small courtyard squeezed between a low-looking tavern and a butcher's shop. He studied the scrap of paper in his hand. 'I think this is the place.'

The yard was as squalid as its surroundings, carpeted with mouldering straw and dog excrement. A pair of mangy hounds, tied to a post, barked ferociously as they approached.

'Shut your racket, or you'll get my skinning blade,' a woman screamed.

She was squatting on the ground, her blue silk dress torn and patched. Her hair was tousled and wild, tied with ribbons and scraps of fur. She had a sore on her lip and a bloodied knife in her hand.

'You want eyebrows?' she asked. Turning to the dogs: 'Rag, Ribbon, stop that racket.'

On a bloodied cloth in front of her was a dead mouse she was in the act of skinning. A basket by her side held about three dozen more corpses. Muttering to herself, she made a few proficient cuts, removed the corpse from the skin, and tossed it over to the dogs, who devoured it greedily.

'There,' she said, rocking back on her haunches to grin at them. 'Now we can hear ourselves speak. Dark brown like your hair, madam, or something bolder? Red or black? White, even? Yellow's rarer, hence dearer, but not with your colouring, no.'

She gestured to a plank leaning against a wall. Pinned to it were rows of false eyebrows evidently made from mouse fur, in the colours she'd described. Caro swallowed uneasily, thankful that this was one of her good days.

'I'm looking for a man named Jack Somerset,' she said.

'My brother. He's dead. Three months back.'

'I'm sorry.' Disappointment flooded through her. 'Can I talk to you about him?'

'Buy my eyebrows, you can ask me what you like.'

'Why don't I just give you the money for them, and you can keep the eyebrows?'

She squinted suspiciously. 'Why would you do that?'

Caro smiled tightly. 'Call me eccentric.'

'Go on, then,' she said swiftly, as if afraid Caro would change her mind. 'Two shillings.'

Caro nodded at Miles, who stepped forward to give her the coins.

'No need to look like that, fart-catcher,' the woman said, seeing his look of disdain. She extended her bloodied hand to Caro. 'Suzy Somerset.'

Wincing a little, Caro shook it. 'Did you ever hear Jack

speak of a soldier named Edward Dodd-Bellingham?' she said. 'He was a commissioned officer, a lieutenant, in your brother's former regiment.'

'He never stopped bloody talking about him. Probably died cursing his name.'

'They didn't like one another?'

'Jack loathed him. Called him a shitten stink of a son of a whore.' She grinned. 'Wasn't always like that, mind. In the old days, at the start of the war, he thought if you peered down that man's arsehole, you'd spot the sun. He used to write me letters from America. I had the taverner next door read them to me. How Dodd-Bellingham would drink with the men. How the ladies loved him. He had favourites amongst the NCOs, and my Jack was one of them. Said he'd make Jack his steward when he reclaimed his family's country house.'

Suzy moved to sit with the dogs, offering them her bloody hands to lick, squinting up at Caro as she talked. 'Jack had wanted to see America, and take it to the Yankee bastards. But the war didn't go like it was supposed to, and by the winter of '76 they was in some pisspot fort, cut off from their supply lines. Rebel scum all around.'

'Van der Linden's Mill,' Caro said, remembering Ansell Ward's story.

'The camp was freezing, exhausted, men starving to death. Living off tripe soup and flour cakes and dead horses. Jack said some men even ate their own shoes. They welcomed the snow, because at least they could melt it to drink. But their blankets weren't thick enough, nor their coats, nor their gloves. Fingers and toes turned black, men were dying in their own shit from disease. Dropping dead in the snow.'

Listening to her talk, in words she was sure were her

brother's, Caro wondered how many times she had heard him recount the story.

'Jack thought they would all die there, cut off like that, and Dodd-Bellingham agreed. He tried to convince their commanding officer to surrender, but the fool wouldn't do it. The snow was coming in harder, and the foragers had to go further afield to find food. Like ducks on a pond, they were, in sight of the enemy rifles. So one night Dodd-Bellingham called Jack and five others to his hut and told them his plan. At nightfall, they'd take the best horses out of the camp, under cover of darkness. They'd ride south, wait out the winter, then make their way back up to New York. Everyone in the fort would be dead by then, and there'd be no one to give the lie to whatever story they came up with.'

'They were planning to desert?' Caro said. 'I was told the lieutenant led a raiding party that saved the camp.'

Suzy grinned again. 'They came upon an enemy supply train by chance later that night. Saw the fire some distance off, and tethered the horses. Twenty Yankee soldiers sleeping and only two sentries. One had fallen asleep, the other swigging from a bottle. The lieutenant pulled him down from the wagon box, and slit his throat. Then he and his men butchered every one of them as they lay there sleeping, like babes in a bower.'

Caro stared at her appalled. Not English lions, but ravaging wolves. Men who'd broken every rule, every moral, governing combat.

'With a wagon-train full of supplies, the prospects for the fort would look much brighter,' Suzy went on. 'So back they went, wagons and all, hailed as the saviours of their company. When the thaw came, Dodd-Bellingham was feted in New York. It weren't just my Jack who thought he farted sunbeams now. He thought his secret was safe. If any of his men talked, they'd only be tattling on themselves. And why would they want to tell? They all adored him. Until they returned to England, and he and Jack fell out.'

'Go on.'

'Jack had taken a musket ball at Bound Brook. But those blackguards at the War Office didn't want to pay his pension, so they slung him out of the army for drinking on the job. He asked Dodd-Bellingham to intervene, and perhaps the lieutenant tried, but at the end of his trying, there was still no pension. So Jack asked him for a little blunt, just enough to see him through, but the lieutenant said he didn't have none to spare. Well, Jack got mad then. Threatened to tell the War Office about that supply train, said he was prepared to risk a hanging if Dodd-Bellingham would be kicking there next to him. The lieutenant told him to go to hell, so Jack took himself off to Whitehall to have a word.'

'The War Office had an inquiry,' Caro said.

'And decided my Jack was lying through his teeth. They said he was bitter, taking out his resentments on a decorated officer. Jack was raging, but he wasn't giving up. He said once the war was over, he would write to America. The rebels must have found the bodies of the men they'd killed. In the meantime, he wanted to let Dodd-Bellingham know that he hadn't forgotten. Jack used to accost him in the street. He sent him white feathers in the mails. Or he sat opposite him in taverns, just staring. Until I found him dead in his bed three months ago. His heart, they say it was.' She spat on the ground.

'Did anyone else ever come here to talk to Jack about Dodd-Bellingham?'

She nodded. 'Pale fellow. Broken nose. He told Jack he was from the War Office, though he didn't look like it to me. Jack thought they was taking his story seriously at last. But nothing came of it.'

The visitor sounded like Erasmus Knox, Jonathan Stone's man. Stone would surely have the ability to get letters to America, despite the war.

'A lady came too,' Suzy said. 'Only a few weeks back.'

Caro showed her Lucy's picture. 'Is that her?'

Suzy nodded. 'She said she'd see that Dodd-Bellingham paid for his crimes. I told her it weren't my fight, but Jack would have liked it.' She sniffed.

And not long after that visit, Caro thought, Lucy was murdered. By the lieutenant, to protect his secret, after Lucy had threatened him? Perhaps Pamela had learned it too, in the course of her obsession with him? Might she have wanted more from him in return for his silence than he was prepared to give? To be his mistress? Even his wife? Had he killed her to find a way out?

Suzy picked a louse from one of the dogs. 'Dodd-Bellingham's not just a coward. Jack said he's wicked too. None of the men liked what they had to do that night, sticking it to those poor bastards while they slept. But Jack saw the lieutenant's face as he went in with his bayonet. Smiling in the firelight, as if he enjoyed it.'

Chapter Sixty-Six

CARO HADN'T BEEN able to bring herself to come before. Ambrose was sitting in his porter's chair, staring at the objects on the table in front of him. His favourite pocket watch. Adam Smith's *The Wealth of Nations*. The bag of marbles he'd played with as a boy. Things she'd asked the footmen to lay out daily to remind him of himself.

Except who was he? The man in front of her? Laughing, generous Ambrose, ready to forgive any flaw in family or friend? Mordechai had always called him selfish and she'd defended him hotly. But what act could be more selfish, than to risk the life of a young girl to save himself?

She'd tried telling herself that his mind must have been disordered. The Ambrose she loved would never have done it. But perhaps there had always been another Ambrose. The side of a man that mothers, sisters, wives, never got to see.

The door opened and Mordechai entered, holding a copy of *The London Hermes*. Wordlessly, he handed it to her. Her stomach contracted as she read the lines to which he pointed.

So to the further adventures of that intrepid lady, Mrs Wiltshire. We regret to report that in the course of her nocturnal excursions at Vauxhall, Mrs Wiltshire has experienced a slip. Since her tumble, the poor lady has been suffering from a swelling. All eyes now hunt for the clumsy gentleman responsible for this mishap,

Mrs Wiltshire rarely being short of admiring company. Not Captain Wiltshire, certainly, an innocent in all respects, and absent these past three months in France. With his wife out of action, Vauxhall will certainly prove a duller place.

The words blurred before Caro's eyes. She had no doubt that it was Stone's doing. But how could he have guessed? Had Lord March told him? Dizziness overcame her, and she put a hand to her brow.

'Judging by your expression, I needn't ask if it's true,' Mordechai said. 'Harry will divorce you. What choice will he have? His pride will demand it. You'll have to go to the country. Don't even try to change my mind.'

All her worst fears had been realized. Harry the laughing stock of London. No secret trip to Germany was possible now. People would say divorce was his duty – to Gabriel, his son. To remove him from the care of a mother who barely deserved the name. She put a knuckle to her mouth.

Mordechai was still talking, but she hadn't heard a word.

'Pamela,' she said, interrupting him, 'the virgin who disappeared. Stone bought her for Ambrose. He was the fifth man at Muswell Rise. He thought she could cure him of his syphilis. Did you know?'

His face contorted with disgust. 'Of course I didn't know.'

She studied him sceptically. 'But there was something you weren't telling me, when we were here with Cavill-Lawrence. What was it?'

He was silent a moment, staring at her incredulously. 'Duty,' he said eventually. 'Obligation. Some have it. Some don't. Some had it once, but then lost it – like His Majesty the King.'

'How can you say that? Duty is his watchword.'

'Not any longer. His Majesty's spirits have always been

melancholic. The world knows that. But since the defeat of our armies at Yorktown, he has sunk into a malaise. And these peace talks have only made things worse. He sees it as a personal humiliation. In private, he talks of abdication. Cavill-Lawrence thinks that I don't know it, but I do.'

'Stand aside?' Caro cried. 'But he cannot.'

'The Queen has tried to dissuade him, to no avail,' Mordechai went on. 'I understand the letters of abdication have already been drawn up, and any day he may wake up, minded to do it. His ministers pray for a change of heart – they keep all bad news from him, afraid that the smallest disturbance to his mind might be enough.'

'And then Prinny will be King,' Caro said.

Little wonder that Cavill-Lawrence was so concerned about the Priapus Club and these murders. To have a boy-king accede to the throne, embroiled in a scandal like this . . .

'Did Ambrose know?' she asked. 'Back when he made the loan? Did Ambrose know about the abdication? Did Stone?'

'I imagine that's why they did it. They spied an opportunity to ensnare the Prince. But no amount of reward was worth such risk.'

Ambrose would have seen it differently, Caro thought. A grocer's grandson, banker to the King of England. New clients would have followed the Crown, aristocratic owners of the great estates. They'd have been able to pick and choose whom they let through the doors of the Craven Bank.

As for Stone, Caro could guess the nature of the rewards he envisaged. A knighthood? A seat in Parliament? A peerage? And if the Prince – like his father, a mercurial man – ever forgot his obligations to the men who'd lent him money when no one else would, then Jonathan Stone could doubtless remind him of certain scenes he had witnessed during the Prince's nocturnal visits to the Priapus Club.

Forcing herself to look at Ambrose again, she confronted an unpalatable truth. If her brother had been acting in his right mind when he'd made the loan, then he'd also been in his right mind when he'd asked Stone to find him a virgin. If you could call it his right mind, because she could scarcely conceive of anything more wrong.

'Stop hiding his syphilis,' she said. 'Because if the King does have a change of heart, if he ever finds out about the loan, then you need to blame *him*.' She glared at the man in the chair. 'Say his wits were wandering. Say Jonathan Stone took advantage.'

Mordechai's face was expressionless. 'I am astonished that, after everything, you still have the presumption to offer advice that no one has asked to hear. Go home and look to your child, while you still can.'

As Caro descended the stairs of her childhood home, she felt no sense of loss. There was nothing left for her here anymore. In the hall below, she found Louisa weeping.

'Oh, Caro,' she said. 'Why wasn't being a mother, being a wife, ever enough for you?'

Why was it always enough for you? she wanted to say. But she bore her sister-in-law no ill will and submitted to her awkward embrace. Then she called for her cloak and gloves and walked out to her carriage.

On the journey home, watching London pass by, she thought: *Jonathan Stone has finally made a mistake. He should have threatened me with this, not sought to punish me – because if I do one thing more before the roof falls in, let it be this.*

CHAPTER SIXTY-SEVEN

THE HACKNEY CARRIAGE smelled of tobacco and sweat. Caro opened the window, allowing the cool night air to spill inside. She had never travelled in one before and it was not an experience she cared to repeat. The seat was badly sprung, her back jarring at each bump or hole in the road.

After she'd left her brother's house, she'd returned home to read to Gabriel until he fell asleep. Then she'd dressed and gone out to Carlisle House. Her gown was purple and black silk, striped, low in the neck, closely fitted. Her harlot's dress, Harry called it, one of those jokes that wasn't a joke. She wore a little more rouge than usual, dyed ostrich feathers in her hair. At Carlisle House they'd stared, but then they would have stared anyway, after the story in *The London Hermes*.

She had given one of the Carlisle House footmen a message to take to her coachman, Sam, saying that the Henekers had offered to drive her home in their carriage. Then she'd left Carlisle House by the same alley where she'd been attacked by the plague doctor, heading for the rank of hackney carriages further down the street.

They had reached the outskirts of the city, passing the gates to the Foundling Hospital. It made Caro think of Pamela and her necklace. The carriage headed north on the road to Highgate and Muswell Hill.

In the bag at her feet was a volto mask, which would cover

her face entirely. In her panniers were candles and a tinder-box. And in her hand was the satyr invitation that would gain her admittance to the Priapus Club.

*

Torches blazed at the gates to Stone's estate. With no footman to fit the steps, Caro alighted unsteadily from the carriage, landing heavily in the mud. She paid the coachman, and offered him a guinea if he'd wait for her at a tavern they'd passed a quarter-mile back. Putting on her mask, she approached the gates.

A porter emerged from the lodge. On the other side of the gates she could see two groundsmen, each armed with a fowling piece. She passed the porter her invitation, and he looked her over. 'Why didn't you come with the others?'

Remembering that Sir Amos had said that harlots emulated the manners of ladies, she spoke haughtily, in her normal voice. 'I forgot my invitation and had to go back for it.'

Sighing, he unlocked the gate. 'Take her to the bathhouse,' he said to one of the groundsmen. 'Make sure someone vouches for her.'

She had planned to slip away into the woods once she was out of sight of the gates. But the groundsman stayed close to her side, seeming to enjoy her proximity. The house was a blaze of light in the distance, and she glimpsed many carriages drawn up outside. There were more lights across the lake, voices and laughter carrying from the bathhouse. Moonlight shone on the water, reflecting the stars.

A figure was walking towards them, coming up from the house. A well-dressed gentleman in a Pantalone mask with a hook nose and slanted eyes. He carried a bottle of brandy in his pudgy hand.

'Well now,' he said, in a rich Scottish burr, not a voice she recognized. 'Late to the party too, my dear?'

'All the best guests are.' She gave an elegant curtsey.

He stood back, appraising her. 'I'd never have taken you for a harlot. I wish my daughter had half your manners.'

She spoke pertly: 'No, you don't.'

He laughed again, delighted, and offered her his arm. 'Allow me to escort you, madam.'

'You can vouch for her, then, sir?' the groundsman asked.

'We have met before, sir,' she said. 'I was here another time.'

'I thought you seemed familiar,' he said, which made her heart sink. 'Remind me of your name again, my dear?'

'Clara.'

'That was it. Clara.' He slid an arm around her waist, running his palm over her rump, making her squirm. Turning to the groundsman, he spoke peremptorily: 'I'll take her from here.'

The groundsman bowed and headed back towards the gate.

The voices and laughter grew louder as they walked through the woods, towards the bathhouse. Wind stirred the lake and the trees whispered. The Scotchman kept a tight grip upon her waist.

They emerged from the trees, the bathhouse only yards away. Flanking the path that led to it were a pair of stone statues of satyrs coupling with goats. Naked girls were splashing around in the stone bathing pool that Kitty had described, watched by gentlemen in masks from the bank. The girls turned to stare at Caro, evidently wondering who she was. The gentlemen stared harder, and she wondered if they were men of her acquaintance.

You're wearing a mask, she told herself. *There's no reason to suppose they'll recognize you. You just need to keep your nerve, find an opportunity to slip away.*

At the entrance to the bathhouse, they were greeted by clouds of sweet-smelling smoke. Many lamps were lit inside, and it was warm. Gentlemen and harlots were entwined upon daybeds, some masked, some clothed, some not. Candlelight flickered across the bathhouse murals – black copulating figures, like the ones on Simon's urn. Jonathan Stone was on his feet, giving some sort of speech.

'Those who seek true enlightenment should forget the doctrines of the Testament. Everything of value in those pages was stolen from the ancients – and every constraint upon man's freedom was imposed by the Church to increase its power. In ancient times, men had full liberty in love, and they worshipped Priapus, god of generation and destruction. The greatest men of ancient Greece visited the temple courtesans, the Hetaerae, and the act of congress lifted their minds to heights of noble thought and artistic endeavour.'

The men murmured their approval, stroking the cheeks or other parts of their companions. Caro's Scotchman led her to a footman, serving wine from a silver tray. He took two glasses, and she fought the urge to run. The smoke was making her head spin, and it was very hot inside the mask. The Scotchman found a vacant daybed, and beckoned to Caro, pulling her onto his lap.

Simon Dodd-Bellingham was standing against a wall, alone. He met her gaze and she turned away, right into the eyes of Lieutenant Dodd-Bellingham. Clad only in his breeches, a masked, naked woman on either side of him, he grinned. For a moment, she thought he'd recognized her, but then he turned to one of his companions, kissing her long and hard, using his tongue. Candlelight illuminated Stone's face from below, giving him a saturnine glow.

'The life of the libertine is a holy life,' Stone said. 'Intimate congress the act by which life passes between the generations.

The mingling of vital fluids is the true elixir of immortality. Thus man creates life, and becomes as the gods.'

The Scotchman put a finger under Caro's chin, and guided her face to his own. 'Here.' He stuck his thumb into her mouth. Revolted, she resisted the urge to vomit. He thrust deep, her panic rising as she endured the invasion.

The Scotchman withdrew his thumb, replacing it almost immediately with a long silver pipe. She tried to refuse, but he frowned, pushing it into her mouth. Hot and acrid smoke filled her throat. Her lungs burned, as she breathed it in. The room shivered and turned, and her nausea spiked. Coughing, retching, she ran from the bathhouse, pushing her way past another footman coming in through the door. Outside, she lifted her mask enough to vomit.

The gentlemen by the pool laughed, and the girls hooted their derision. Caro wiped her mouth on her sleeve and swiftly pulled her mask back on.

'Your moll's cast up her accounts, Cromby,' one of the poolside revellers called, and she saw with a sinking heart that the Scotchman had followed her outside. 'They see him coming and they just can't help it – up it comes.' More laughter.

Sweat sheathed her skin, her heart thumping against her ribs. The Scotchman walked towards her. 'Come on,' he said, a little crossly. 'Back inside.'

She backed away from him, glancing towards the woods. 'Did you ever play hide-and-go-seek?'

'Of course. As a boy.'

Spreading her arms, she span on the grass, getting closer to the trees with each turn. 'Count to ten,' she said. 'Then come and find me.'

A note of amusement entered his voice. 'And what will I do with you then?'

She ran her hands over her breasts. 'Whatever you like.'

Ducking into the trees with a gust of wild laughter, she ran. Her slippers slid on the mulchy earth, the branches clawing at her skirts. Her breath came in short gasps as she ran harder, desperate to put distance between them. The exertion cleared her head and she cast her gaze around, trying to get her bearings. Simon had said that the disused farm was north of the house, on the far side of the wood.

'Clara,' she heard the Scotchman calling, some distance behind her now. 'I'm coming.'

Pulling off her mask, she ran on, not looking back. The trees were tall and black and primal, and she struggled to make out the gaps between them. Her skirts caught on a branch, and she slipped, turning her ankle. Moonlight barely penetrated the canopy of the trees now, and in other circumstances the darkness might have frightened her. But she was too full of other fears: poacher's traps and Stone's armed keepers and the men from the bathhouse.

Gradually, the trees thinned overhead, until she could see the stars again. She emerged from the woods, at the top of an incline, sloping down to a plain of grass. In the distance, in the moonlight, she made out the deserted farm. It was larger than she'd anticipated: five or six buildings, grouped around a yard. How long would it take to search them all?

Glancing back into the woods, hearing no sound of pursuit behind her, she hurried across the grass. The farmyard, a wide expanse of red mud, as Simon had described, contained a water-trough, a sty, and a dilapidated well. Caro turned, taking a survey of the buildings: an old farmhouse, half fallen down; a large barn in a similar condition; a stable; a couple of outhouses; and some sort of workshop, perhaps a kiln.

The barn first, she decided, walking over to the door. It was bolted from the outside, and she struggled to lift the rusting bar. Eventually it slid upwards with a grating screech. She pushed at the door, then kicked it, until it gave with a rattle. Her hands wouldn't stop shaking, and it took her a long time to light one of her candles.

Inside, it was cold and damp, the roof very high. Birds fluttered in the rafters, and the floor was thick with their droppings. Slowly, she walked around it, looking for any disturbance of earth, or anywhere else a person might conceal a body.

She searched the barn for a good quarter-hour, but found nothing untoward. Returning to the yard, she walked towards the farmhouse. The roof had fallen in, bringing part of a wall down with it. Loose masonry could be dangerous – would they have chosen to enter the building in that condition? Mindful of other dangers, she gazed across the plain, towards the wood, but as she did so, something else caught her eye. A word daubed on the side of the well in white paint, directly onto the bricks and moss: POISON. Hadn't Kitty said that the morning after Pamela disappeared, the lieutenant's redcoat was splashed with what looked like white paint?

She walked over to examine it more closely. The paint looked fresher than anything else around her. The well's cover was wooden and warped, and several large blocks of masonry had been laid on top of it. To discourage anyone from looking inside? Like the warning that the well was poisoned?

She tried to lift one of the blocks of masonry, but it was too heavy. Dragging it to the edge, inch by careful inch, she toppled it off the side, leaping back to avoid her toes being crushed. Turning to the next block, she pulled again. A bead of sweat crawled across her ribs like an insect, and the taste of vomit in her mouth made her want to vomit again.

The second block fell. Her muscles ached, and she had torn

a nail. She toppled the third block – and then the fourth. The wooden cover was riven with cracks, hinged in the centre. With effort, she raised it, lifting it up and over, and then gazed down into the well's black interior. She stood back, covering her face, as a vile, putrid stink rose up to greet her.

Something rotten was down there. Something dead. Fumbling again with her tinder, she lit another candle. Covering her nose with her other hand, she looked again.

About fifteen feet down, the well's bucket hung on a rusting chain. Something was caught on it. She set her candle down and seized the well's handle. It kept sticking as she turned it, the mechanism rusting, but she forced it through the rotations. Slowly, the bucket rose up the well. Caro glimpsed a large piece of cloth, a garment perhaps, saturated with damp and mould. Blue satin, she thought, squinting. Gold embroidery.

As she leaned forward to grab it, she heard a crack in the distance, from the direction of the wood. An animal? A gamekeeper? The Scotchman?

Listening hard, she peered into the darkness. Then she heard a chuckle right behind her, and span around.

Lieutenant Dodd-Bellingham stood there, his redcoat vivid in the darkness.

'I knew it was you.' He smiled.

PAMELA

1 March 1782

So many trees. More even than the Hyde Park. The snow had melted in London, but not out here, clumps of it clinging to the bare branches, like wet fingers in sugar.

Her feet might as well have belonged to someone else for all she could feel. It was insanity to be wearing sandals and robes in winter, but Mr Stone had insisted upon it. The men were wearing masks. Not the kind that gentlemen usually wore to masquerades, but strange, old men's faces with blank holes for the eyes and mouth. The girls wore similar masks – all except Pamela: women's faces, with real human hair glued to the sides, which looked silly on Kitty with her red hair hanging down behind. The expressions of the girls' masks were sad, their mouths open wide in anguish. Pamela shivered, her teeth chattering uncontrollably.

They'd changed at Mr Stone's house, which was larger than all the houses she'd ever lived in put together. That had buoyed her spirits. But now, out here in the woods, all she felt was trepidation. All this to-do with the clothes and the masks – it was downright strange. Why couldn't Stone just take her to a bedroom, tumble her, and be done with it?

It's just another performance, she told herself, one worth a hundred and twenty-five guineas. Not a sum to be sniffed at.

Even when compared to the sum she'd ask for later. Having seen Stone's house, she had considered asking for more. But she wasn't greedy. Nor did she want to push her luck. Three thousand pounds. No more. No less.

Glancing up, she caught the lieutenant watching her through his mask. She gave him a coy little smile, the kind he liked. Lord March was watching her too. Pamela knew it was him, because she'd recognized the buttons on his coat. Mr Stone walked at the front of their procession, carrying a flaming torch and a strange stick, like a beadle's staff. The lieutenant's brother brought up the rear. The men wore their own clothes; naturally, Lucy would have said – why should they freeze their balls off out here?

Flames flickered through the trees up ahead. They emerged from the wood, onto the bank of a lake. Ahead of them was a white building with pillars, like the ones in Agnetti's paintings, torches burning at the door. On either side of the path stood a statue: a horrible man-goat like the one on her invitation, rutting with a nanny-goat, taking her from behind.

Before the bathhouse was a large stone pool, about ten feet by twelve, and ten feet deep. Pamela guessed that in summer it would be filled with water from the lake, but it was empty now, full of twigs and stones and mounds of snow.

'Christ, it's cold,' the lieutenant said.

Pamela didn't like him in that mask. Not fitting with his redcoat at all. She tried to catch his eye again, trying to let him know that whatever happened here tonight, she was still his. But she couldn't tell if he even noticed.

Two of the girls were whispering, and Lord March snapped at them to be quiet. Stone strode up to the door and knocked on it with his staff. More theatre.

The door creaked slowly open, and she glimpsed a man

inside. He was dressed like a gentleman, wearing a mask like the head of a goat. She presumed he was another friend of Mr Stone's.

The man moved forward into the light. He walked with a stick, tall, but hunched, his rich clothes hanging off him.

Mr Stone beckoned to her. 'Come forward, so he can see you.'

She frowned. 'Who is he?'

'Just do as I say. Treat him well. He's paid good money for you.'

This man was to be her first? She didn't remember ever meeting a gentleman who walked with a stick – either at the tableaux house, or at Mr Agnetti's. She could hear the gentleman's breathing beneath his mask, a hoarse, hollow rattle. Old, she thought, with a sinking heart.

'Well?' Stone said to the man.

'You have done well,' he said, in a voice that wheezed. He turned to go back inside, moving with difficulty.

'Follow him,' the lieutenant said, in a thick voice that gave her pause.

She looked around to gauge reactions. But everyone's faces were obscured by those horrible masks.

Someone – the lieutenant? – gave her a little push from behind. *It's just a job, like emptying a chamber pot.* Slowly, she walked forward into the bathhouse, shivering a little as the door closed behind her.

*

The bathhouse was dimly lit, warmed by a brazier. Lewd paintings adorned the walls. In the centre of the room stood a large daybed, piled with pillows and silken sheets. The man in the mask sat down upon it heavily.

'Bolt the door,' he rasped.

As she did so, she remembered Lucy's words unbidden. *No watch. No one to hear you scream.*

But this man didn't seem as if he could do her any harm. Indeed, he seemed exhausted by the smallest exertions. He lay back on the bed, watching her, still wearing the mask.

'What is your name?' he said.

'Pamela. What's yours?'

'I want to see you, Pamela. Disrobe.'

'I want to see you first,' she said. 'Take off your mask.'

'It is not your place to give commands. Do you want me to call Mr Stone back?'

Remembering Mrs Havilland's strict instructions not to make trouble or argue back, she undid the cord at her waist and slid off her robe. In just her stockings and garters, she made a turn for him. The goat-man gave a sharp intake of breath, and thrust his gloved hand inside his breeches.

One hundred and twenty-five guineas, she thought again. For one quick tumble. Except, she saw with dismay, it wasn't going to be quick. The gentleman was trying to get himself primed and failing, working himself a little frantically. Kitty had told her all about that. How a girl needed to be careful when it happened, because a man could get angry – as if the whole world had come to an end, because one gentleman couldn't get a prickstand.

'I could help you with that, if you'd like?' she said.

His head jerked up. 'How would you know what to do?'

She smiled meekly. 'You could show me, sir.'

'No,' he said. 'Stay just where you are.'

The minutes ticked by, as she stood in front of him like a fool. What kind of man paid two hundred and fifty guineas for this?

Finally, for the love of heaven, she saw movement in his breeches. 'Come,' he gasped. 'Quickly. Here.'

She hurried to the daybed, thankful that it was going to be over at last. He pushed her onto her back with great urgency. Unbuttoning his breeches, he made a hash of it because he'd kept his bloody gloves on. Pawing at her legs and her cunny.

'Here, let me,' she said, alarmed that he might touch it. Mrs Havilland had warned her not to take it out before he was ready – but once he was, she had to move swiftly, conceal it beneath the pillow. *The rest can be done as he recovers from the act of love.*

Raising herself a little, she reached round to the back of her thigh. It was tucked into her garter, and carefully, she slid it out.

'Stop moving,' he said, grabbing her hand.

It slipped from her fingers, and rolled off the bed, onto the floor. It didn't break, but kept rolling with a glassy tinkle.

He sat up, alert. 'What was that?'

'Just a bottle of perfume,' she said brightly. 'Come, sir, don't let it distract us.'

But he'd swung his legs off the daybed, supporting himself by the frame. Lucifer's teeth, he was looking for it. Mrs Havilland was going to kill her.

She slid off the bed too, grabbing her robe. But the gentleman was between her and the door. And where would she go? Out here alone in these dark woods.

He bent and picked it up in his gloved hand. Then he removed his mask to take a better look. He had his back to her, and she saw he was nearly bald beneath the mask, black hair clinging to his scalp in clumps. He held it up to the light, and she heard his breathing quicken.

Then he turned his face towards her and she screamed.

Chapter Sixty-Eight

✳

Child hadn't left his rooms since he'd returned home the night before. Normally, gin took him to a place where he could think only of the moment. A Peregrine Child who had no past. No sins. No dead wife and son. No memory, except the slow slide into nothing. But tonight the present was as bad as the past, and the gin wasn't helping.

Mrs Corsham had called twice that day. Solomon Loredo had come too, doubtless wanting to know why Child hadn't shown up for dinner. He'd ignored their knocks, their raised voices, just sitting there, drinking, until they went away. He couldn't bear to think what Stone was doing with the information he'd given him. Couldn't bear to think about Mrs Corsham and her boy.

He poured the dregs of the bottle into his glass and knocked it back. It was the last of his gin. He got unsteadily to his feet, looking around for his coat, finding it on the floor. Shrugging it on, he went to the door, nearly colliding on the darkened landing with a man coming up the stairs.

'Mr Child?' he said. 'I need to talk to you.'

A gentleman's voice, bluff, with a note of strain. Squinting in the gloom, Child took in a wig, a velvet coat, and a froth of cream lace.

'Mr Sillerton?' The Clapham merchant. Pineapples. Kitty's husband.

'My wife, Katherine, has run away, come to London, I think. I need to find her. You spoke to her, didn't you? She went out, and when she came back, she seemed very troubled.'

'I can't help you.' Child tried to push past him, but Sillerton grabbed hold of his coat.

'An anonymous letter came this morning. It said that Katherine, my Katherine, was a prostitute named Kitty Carefree. That was the name of the woman you were looking for. Did you send it?'

'No,' Child said, not wanting this sin laid at his door with all the others. Except it probably *was* his fault. He'd told Stone about Kitty, and Stone must have sent the letter to flush Kitty out.

Sillerton's face was pink and helpless. The happiness he thought he'd found, suddenly snatched away. His new world rocked on its foundations.

'I confronted her and she admitted it,' he said, turning his hat in his hands. 'Words were exchanged – things I can never take back. Please, you have to help me. I must find her.'

Child hesitated, wanting only to run away in search of more drink. But pity stayed his hand. He edged back into his lodgings. 'Come inside.'

They sat at his table amidst the empty gin bottles. In his agitation, Sillerton didn't even seem to notice.

'After our argument, Katherine went upstairs. I should have gone to talk to her, but I was angry. I felt betrayed. After a few hours, I felt calmer, and I went upstairs to find her. But she'd gone, leaving me this letter.' He took a sheaf of papers from his coat pocket. 'She called it her confession. All the things she'd seen and done.' He shook his head. 'Masquerades, so many gentlemen, she even talked of murder. I don't understand it.

Katherine didn't even like the entertainments of the town. She visited London only once in the months I knew her.'

'If it makes any difference,' Child said, 'I think she genuinely loves you.'

Sillerton was silent a moment. 'She said in her letter that her sins were too great. That it was why God had punished her, and taken her happiness. But she is wrong about God. He is merciful, I believe. And if he can forgive, then so can I. I regret my words to Katherine more than anything. These past months have been a blessing – we are trying for a baby. The loss of her – I cannot stand it. I don't care what she was before. I only want her to come home.'

'What makes you think she's returned to London?'

'She said in her letter that she'd gone to the great Gomorrah. She said it was where she deserved to be. It reads as if she isn't in her right mind, and I am fearful of what she might do.'

Child was fearful too, but he didn't share those concerns with Mr Sillerton. The Home Office were still looking for Kitty, and he didn't like to think what they would do if they caught up with her. Which was probably what Stone was counting upon – why he'd chosen to send that letter.

'Please, Mr Child, help me find her.'

He tried to find the words to tell Sillerton 'no'. That he was done with this inquiry, that he could not risk the wrath of Stone. But they wouldn't come. Not when he thought of that poor, frightened woman in the church.

Taking Humphrey Sillerton by the shoulder, murmuring words of assurance, he guided the unhappy merchant to the door. Then he returned to the table, where he primed his flintlock pistol, and headed out into the night to find Kitty Carefree.

CHAPTER SIXTY-NINE

LIEUTENANT DODD-BELLINGHAM SAUNTERED towards Caro.

'Do you know how I knew it was you?' he said. 'Remember those lists the newspapers compile? Complexion, grace, and so on? Well, we gentlemen have lists of our own. Breasts, legs, arse. You won the latter every time. One of the finest sights in London is Caroline Corsham's arse. How did you like playing the whore? I think it suits you rather well.'

She was backing away, across the farmyard, but he kept coming, enjoying the fear on her face.

'What are you going to do? Rape me, like you tried to rape Miss Willoughby?'

He laughed. 'That girl enjoyed every second. You might too.'

'And Pamela? Did she enjoy it? Not much, I think. Is that how she ended up down that well? Because she tried to say no?'

He cocked his head. 'You silly girl. You think you know everything, don't you? I'm minded to drop you down there too.'

She tried to read his expression, to work out if he was bluffing. His cold, blue gaze frightened her. His lip curled in amusement. She remembered what Jack Somerset had told his sister, how when the lieutenant had bayoneted those sleeping soldiers, he'd seemed to enjoy it.

'I've been to see Somerset,' she said. 'Or rather, his sister. I know about Van Der Linden's Mill, what you did to those Yankee soldiers with that supply train.'

He smiled. 'Somerset was a bitter old drunk. His stories were designed to discredit me.'

'But they were true – and Lucy knew it. Did Pamela know it too? Was that why you killed her?'

He ran his tongue along his lower lip. 'Lucy couldn't hurt me. The War Office exonerated me on all counts.'

'But I can,' she said. 'Lucy would have struggled to get a letter to America, but Harry's in Philadelphia now. If anything happens to me tonight, then Mr Child will write to him with Somerset's story.'

'Stone told me he fixed your Mr Child for good. And after those stories in *The London Hermes*, old Harry will think it a blessed relief to be rid of you.'

She backed into the farmhouse wall. Casting her eyes around for a weapon, she picked up the largest stone she could see.

He laughed again. 'What are you going to do with that?'

She threw it as hard as she could, and it struck him in the face. He swore, clutching his jaw, and she ran. But he was on her in a moment, catching her by the waist. He grabbed her wrists in one hand, wiping the blood from his lip with the other. 'You'll pay for that.'

'Cad,' came a voice from the shadows, a rich Scottish burr. 'Damnable bounder. Unhand the harlot, sir. This instant.'

The lieutenant turned, swinging her round, and she saw Cromby staggering towards them, still clutching his bottle. He'd removed his mask, and she saw he was younger than she had imagined. A long, irate face, with high cheekbones and protruding teeth.

'Missy,' he said sternly, 'you led me a merry dance in those woods.' He glanced at the lieutenant. 'I saw her first.'

'This is a private matter, Abercrombie,' the lieutenant said. 'Keep your nose out.'

'The devil I will. First claimed, first served. Stone's rules.'

Abercrombie seized hold of Caro's arm, trying to pull her away from the lieutenant, who jerked her back. 'Get out of here, before I do something I might regret.'

Abercrombie was nearly as tall as the lieutenant, softer, but broader. He took another step towards them, and swung his bottle with force at the lieutenant's head. The lieutenant released Caro, swinging up an arm to defend himself, but he wasn't fast enough. The glass shattered on his skull, blood spilling from a nasty gash. Bellowing, he swung a fist, connecting with Abercrombie's jaw. The Scotchman staggered back, but came at the lieutenant again.

Caro was already several yards away. Pausing by the well, she reached into it and pulled out the sodden, stinking bundle of cloth. Glancing back, she saw that the lieutenant had taken off his coat, and was wrapping it around his arm. Abercrombie came at him again, jabbing with the end of the broken bottle. He feinted, and the lieutenant caught the strike on his coat-wrapped arm. Then he smashed the same elbow into Abercrombie's face. The pair went down in the mud, grappling.

Caro ran on, across the grass, heading north, away from the wood. In the distance were more trees, and she headed for their cover. Ducking beneath branches, stumbling over roots, she did not stop until she reached the stone wall that bordered Muswell Rise. She ran along it for a short time, until she came to a tree that she thought she could climb.

Wedging the putrid bundle under her arm, she clambered to the height of the wall, and swung her legs over it. Sliding down on the other side, she landed awkwardly, dropping her bundle. Retrieving it, her heart pounding, she looked up and down the road for assistance. All was quiet and still, save for a dog barking somewhere on the estate.

She needed to get off the road. Running as fast as she could, she came to a stile, and climbed over it. She found herself in a newly ploughed field, bordered by a high hedgerow shielding it from the road. Striding across the field, she wormed her way through more hedgerows and climbed more fences. Eventually, she spotted a little cluster of lights in the distance. Hornsey, where her hackney coachman was waiting.

CHAPTER SEVENTY

CHILD WENT FIRST to Kitty's former lodgings in Soho and received the sharp end of the African footman's tongue. 'I told you. She left months ago. What are you, simple?'

Next he tried the Whores' Club, where he found the meeting room deserted save for two harlots playing piquet. Both denied having seen Kitty, and he didn't think they were lying.

So Child headed into Covent Garden, asking in every tavern and coffeehouse. The proprietors rolled their eyes, not caring about his urgency.

'Everyone wants Kitty tonight,' one serving maid told him.

'Who else wants her?'

'A pair of gentlemen. Don't know their names.'

'Official sorts? Brown wigs? Don't smile much?'

She nodded. 'You know them, then?'

Child knew them.

At a little after two in the morning, at a hazard-house near Charing Cross, he questioned a party of gentlemen playing able-whackets – hitting one another over the knuckles with knotted handkerchiefs to enormous hilarity. 'Kitty Carefree?' one of them said. 'I thought it was her I saw. She's back on the town, then?'

Child stared at him. 'You've seen her? Tonight?'

'I wasn't sure if it was her or not. That red hair though.' He smiled. 'I'll have to look her up.'

Child resisted the urge to shake him. 'Where? It's important.'

'St James's,' the man said. 'A couple of hours ago now. She passed me on the other side of Charles Street.'

Child took a hackney carriage across town, jumping out at Piccadilly. He scoured the streets of St James's, stopping everyone he passed to ask if they'd seen a beautiful redhead. He even knocked on the door of one of the palatial brothels in St James's Square, but the liveried footmen refused to answer his questions. With his wild eyes and dishevelled appearance, they probably took him for an angry father. His fears heightening, Child headed into the park.

The park-walkers were out in force. Scrawny, lice-ridden creatures, wearing tattered dresses that looked like they'd come from the Rag Fair, they surrounded him as he walked, whispering ribald compliments, anything he wanted for a shilling.

Child repeated his description of Kitty, reaching into his pocket for some coins.

One girl nodded, her eyes on his silver. 'She was selling herself down here, stealing our customers. Poll scratched her eyes – told her to sod off back to Soho.'

'When was this?' Child asked the girl she'd identified as Poll.

Poll shrugged, examining her grimy nails. 'A quarter-hour maybe. She headed that way.'

Towards Westminster. Child handed over the coins and headed on.

He made his way through the misty back alleys between the government offices, emerging onto Whitehall. He stopped to question a tired-looking clerk heading home. 'Yes,' he said. 'I saw her. A real beauty. She was walking towards the bridge.' He peered at Child doubtfully, as if about to break bad news. 'She was with another gentleman.'

Child ran on, his heart hammering, wishing for the vigour of his youth. Up ahead were the Houses of Parliament, silver spires rising in the moonlight. He turned into Bridge Street, the fog thickening as he neared the river. Oil lamps lined the bridge's parapet, disappearing into the fog, like a path to an unearthly realm. Child followed it, stopping as he came to each of the bridge's alcoves. Little boys fished in them by day, and the ladies of pleasure fished from them by night. Coming across a couple kissing, he pulled the woman by the shoulder, so he could see her face.

'Hey,' the man said, indignant. His breeches were unbuttoned, one hand under the woman's skirts. She wasn't Kitty.

Glimpsing another couple up ahead, he ran on. The woman was pulling away from the man, the pair struggling. Beyond them, Child made out the lamps of a carriage.

'Kitty,' he called, his voice carrying over the roar of the river below.

The man turned and, with his free hand, drew a pistol. In the flash as he fired, Child glimpsed Kitty's startled face. He felt a rush of air by his ear as the bullet whistled past him. He drew his own pistol, but the man pulled Kitty in front of him.

The carriage door opened, and another man climbed out. Certain they were the pair who'd given him the beating at the vineyard, Child fired, and heard a crack of splintering wood. The man ducked back inside.

Kitty had pulled away from her assailant again, but Child's pistol needed reloading. Gambling that his opponent was also out of bullets, Child ran full pelt towards him. A woman somewhere behind him screamed 'Murder!'. Perhaps reading the intent in Child's blazing eyes, the man released Kitty and ran to the carriage.

His rage driving him on, Child gave chase, catching Kitty's

assailant just as he reached the carriage door. The man was pulled inside by his friend, but Child grabbed hold of his leg. The carriage moved off, and the man kicked out with his other foot, catching Child in the face. He fell, tumbling onto the cobbles. The carriage door slammed closed, and he watched it drive away.

Retrieving his wig, breathing heavily, Child got to his feet. The woman behind him screamed again and he looked around for Kitty. Hurrying back to the place where he'd last seen her, he stopped in dismay.

Kitty had climbed over the bridge's parapet, and stood gazing down at the roiling waters thirty feet below.

'Please,' Child said. 'Don't do this. It was Mr Sillerton who sent me. He wants you to come home.'

'That man just now, he said I didn't deserve to live. That I was a great sinner. And so I am – my final sin, it is too great.'

'Don't listen to him, Kitty. You are a good person.' He was inches from her now, poised to grab her, haul her back. 'Mr Sillerton loves you. He doesn't care about your sins.'

'Tell him I'm sorry,' she said, and then stepped out into space.

Child moved faster than he'd ever moved in his life, grabbing Kitty by the wrist as she fell, her weight slamming him against the parapet. Below the river churned, the currents fierce and treacherous. Child struggled to hold on, his arm wrenching at the socket. Spray from the river soaked his face. He was half over the parapet himself, afraid her weight might pull him over, but someone on the bridge grabbed his legs.

'I need you to hold on,' he told Kitty. 'Reach up and grab me with your other hand.' He shouted to the people gathering behind him. 'For Christ's sake, pull.'

She gazed at him helpless. Those wide blue eyes.

'Please,' he said. 'I can't hold you for much longer.'

The people behind were hauling him back, inch by agonizing inch. 'Try, Kitty,' he urged, his grip starting to slacken.

Slowly, tentatively, her other hand reached up. 'That's it,' he said. 'You only need to grab hold of me.'

Her fingers were busy. With horror he realized what she was doing, working at the buttons of her glove. Flesh and silk parted with a whisper, and she slid away from him like a woman in a dream.

Child never even saw her hit the water, through his tears of despair.

PAMELA

1 March 1782

The man-monster was dragging Pamela along, back down the path to the house. Every time she looked at him, she fought the urge to scream again. He had sores all over his face, his nose the worst of all, almost eaten away entirely, like the dying, syphilitic beggars she'd seen around Cheapside. He moved slowly, and it was clear from his grimaces how much it pained him to walk. His stick in one hand, gripping her arm in the other. Stick, drag, stick, drag. She could probably push him over in his condition and run, but where would she go? She wanted to return to the house, to see Kitty and the other girls. Kitty surely wouldn't let them hurt her?

Fury surged inside her. Those shitten fucksters would have had her tumble him, a pox-ridden, dying son of a whore. To cure him, she presumed, which was horseshit and anyone with half a brain knew it. Glaring at the diseased man, she consoled herself with the knowledge that the pestilent fuckster would soon be dead. Then she glimpsed the house through the trees, and her anger gave way to fear again.

He dragged her up to the front door and beat on it with his stick. The footman stumbled back when he saw him. 'Dear God.'

'Kitty,' Pamela cried. 'Help me, please.'

'Fetch your master,' the monster wheezed. 'Tell him Ambrose Craven demands an explanation.'

They waited in the hall, watched over by other horrified footmen. Stone came out of one of the rooms, his eyes widening when he saw them, gesturing them back outside. Lieutenant Dodd-Bellingham and Lord March followed them out onto the steps.

Stone spoke lightly. 'Put that nose of yours on, will you, Craven? You're frightening the servants.'

'Do you take me for a chub, you swindling rogue? We had an agreement.'

'What are you talking about, man?'

Pamela was looking at the three of them, gauging their reaction to the man-monster. None of them looked surprised or shocked by his appearance. They had known, she realized. All of them. Even the lieutenant. Her blood was flowing hot, despite the chill night air, her thoughts fizzing and popping, the anger bubbling out of her.

Craven thrust the little vial at Stone, who held it up to the light. His eyes narrowed.

'I knew nothing of this, I swear it.' He turned to the lieutenant. 'You have some explaining to do.'

The lieutenant took the vial. 'The lying little bitch.'

'What is it?' Lord March said.

The lieutenant passed him the vial of blood.

'She's not a virgin,' Stone said.

They were all glaring at her now. How dare they be angry, given everything they'd done? And it was not such a big lie. One tumble with David the second footman hardly counted. Most of Mrs Havilland's girls weren't precisely virgins. Some had sold their maidenheads several times. A few herbs from the quack to tighten them up. A few drops of sheep's blood on the bedsheet, and who need know?

Whereas their lie, these men, their deception by comparison, was so monstrous she could hardly breathe to think of it. Her anger bubbled over, and she screamed at Stone: 'You lousy, lying fuckster. You could have killed me.'

Stone didn't even seem to hear, hurrying after the man with the pox, who was calling for his carriage.

Lord March took her by the shoulders, trying to calm her down, and she lashed out at him. He grabbed her, holding her easily, though she struggled.

Twisting her head, she glared at the lieutenant. 'You gullion son of a whore. You weeping cunny-sore.' She'd see him dead in his grave before she rode around in his carriage. Calmly, he slapped her. She put a hand to her face, momentarily shocked into silence.

Kitty and Becky had come out of the house, and Kitty called out to her. Stone, still talking to the poxy gullion, pointed a finger at them. 'Get back inside.'

'Swiving, lying wretch,' she cried, at no one in particular. 'Bastardly buggering cunts.' Everybody started shouting at once, and the lieutenant slapped her again. Stone was walking back towards her, and she felt afraid again. She sank her teeth into Lord March's hand, tasting blood. Crying out, he released her, and she ran.

CHAPTER SEVENTY-ONE

CHILD KEPT NODDING off. Each time he did, he saw Kitty Carefree falling away from him again – and he would awake with a jerk, like a fever. He wondered if this was the way it was going to be from now on – if she'd join his wife and his son in his dreams.

He was sitting in a chair in Mrs Corsham's drawing room. It was a little before six in the morning. In the hall, he could hear the servants talking about their mistress, speculating about the story in *The London Hermes*. They were worried about their positions – the prospect of the household being broken up when Captain Corsham divorced her. More lives destroyed by Peregrine Child.

He kept remembering Kitty's face. *My final sin, it is too great.*

Amidst his guilt and grief, many disjointed thoughts occurred to him. Kitty's desperation to protect her new life, her one chance of happiness. A happiness that Lucy's actions in pursuing Pamela's murderer risked destroying. And Kitty had known that Lucy would be at Vauxhall Gardens that night, that she had evidence that would unmask the killer.

Humphrey Sillerton had told him that Kitty had only travelled to London on one occasion since he'd met her – which must have been the day he'd attended the dinner at the Devil tavern, August the thirtieth, when Kitty had been seen riding in his carriage on the Strand. August the thirtieth, the same day

Lucy was killed. Where had Kitty gone that night, whilst her husband had been at his dinner? To Vauxhall Gardens? To warn the killer?

Perhaps if he could work out what was still bothering him about Kitty's account that day at the church, it would give him some definitive answers? But it still eluded him – hovering on the edge of his memory, just out of reach.

Pinpoints of dawn light pierced the cracks in the shutters. Child heard a carriage draw up outside, and then voices in the hall. Mrs Corsham entered the room. She was wearing a torn dress, looking almost as awful as Child felt. In her hands was a bundle of foul-smelling cloth.

'What happened?' he said, rising. 'Where have you been?'

'Stone's estate. For the masquerade.'

He stared at her. 'Have you lost your mind?'

'In your absence, Mr Child, I had little choice. I found Pamela, I think. I believe her body is down a well on that disused farm.' She sat down heavily at her tea table.

'I'm sorry,' he said. 'I should have been there.'

'Yes, you should.'

He closed his eyes. 'Kitty Carefree is dead.'

Mrs Corsham listened intently, as he told her what had happened.

'That is a great tragedy. How desperate poor Kitty must have been to do such a thing.' She was silent a moment and then she frowned. 'Mr Stone placed another story about me in the newspapers yesterday. It insinuated that I am with child, and that the father is not Captain Corsham. I'm afraid to say it's true. I thought Lord March must have betrayed me to Stone, but now I wonder. Someone must have told Stone where Kitty was – someone close to our inquiry.'

Child raised a hand. 'Madam—'

'Miles, my footman, has been closer to me than anyone these past few weeks. He must have guessed that I was pregnant. And he was with us in Clapham too. I think he reported it back to Stone – perhaps unwittingly. Cassandra Willoughby has been flirting with him. I thought it rather odd, but it makes sense if she's Stone's spy.'

'Madam, please.' Child raised his voice. 'The spy was not your footman. And Miss Willoughby has nothing to do with any of this. I was the one who betrayed you to Stone.'

She regarded him uncomprehendingly. 'You, Mr Child?'

'I had no choice,' Child said. 'Or rather, I did. But I didn't choose you.' He told her about Stone, the Deptford counterfeiting gang, and Sophie Hardcastle.

'How did you guess?' she asked, looking stunned. 'That I was with child?'

'You hadn't looked well since I met you. And those wretched ginger comfits – my wife ate them constantly when she was carrying our lad. Then I put my mind to the question of what service Lucy might have done you, that you'd meet with her secretly like that, in the bower. And then, when you were sick in front of me, it all added up.'

She spoke coldly. 'Given all that, why are you here?'

'Kitty Carefree left a letter for her husband. She called it her confession.' He took it out to show her. 'It's all here. Everything she told us – and a lot more besides. About Stone's masquerades, all the men she went with – including the Prince. I thought you could use it.'

Mrs Corsham took the letter and read it silently.

'Kitty was ill-used,' she said, when she put it down. 'Not just at the end.' She pointed to the bundle of putrid cloth. 'Take a look at that.'

Child unwrapped the bundle on the table, wincing at the

smell. It was a gentleman's coat of blue satin, embroidered with golden thread, stiff with mould and damp. Darker stains stood out against the others.

'It looks like blood to me.' Mrs Corsham pointed to one of the embellished gold buttons. 'That's the Amberley crest. I remember this coat. It belonged to Lord March.' She rose from the table. 'I am going to wash and change and then I am going to Amberley House. The only question that remains, Mr Child, is: are you with me?'

Chapter Seventy-Two

THE ONLY TIME the Strand ever fell silent was in the lull between the night's revellers departing Covent Garden, and the arrival of the morning shoppers. In that hour, the street seemed to draw breath. Caro took a moment in the carriage to collect her courage and her thoughts. Then she alighted from the vehicle, leaving Mr Child inside. This conversation was one she wanted to have alone.

At the gate of Amberley House, the blue-liveried footmen listened to her request, and then invited her to wait inside while they conveyed her note to Lord March. One of them accompanied her into the house. A bewildering mix of styles and stone, the mansion had irregular wings jutting at angles, halls both old and new, several gardens and a chapel of stained glass.

They walked through a baronial hall, lined with suits of Amberley armour, worn by Lord March's ancestors at Agincourt, Naseby and Bosworth Field. Their portraits gazed down at her from the stone walls. *Interloper*, she imagined them saying. *City people*.

The footman went to deliver her message, and returned some minutes later. 'Lord March will see you, madam.'

He escorted her down a corridor to a small chamber overlooking the privy garden – that same location where Mr Agnetti had witnessed Lieutenant Dodd-Bellingham's seduction of his wife. Lord March was sitting in a carved wooden chair, a watery light softening his ashen face. A scent of herbs drifted through the open window, along with porters' cries from the private waterstairs on the river.

Caro waited until the footman had withdrawn. 'I've seen the well with my own eyes,' she said. 'I found your coat down there, covered in Pamela's blood.'

His voice caught. 'Stone is protected,' he said. 'So are we. Whatever you think you can prove, you can't.'

'Prinny is protected,' she said. 'And if the price of protecting him is to throw the four of you to the wolves, they will do it in a heartbeat and not lose sleep. I have the means to make that happen. I have the last testimony of Kitty Carefree.'

'You think the word of a dead whore will count against mine? Against Neddy's? Look around you. I am an Amberley. That still counts.'

'And I am a Craven,' Caro said. 'The City is not without power – and Stone has enemies there. I'll have the backing of men like Ansell Ward.'

He held her gaze for a long time. 'What do you want?'

'First, to know what happened. I know that Ambrose was the fifth man. You offered him a fifteen-year old virgin, Octavius, a human sacrifice. How could you do it?'

He laughed bitterly. 'She wasn't a virgin. Ironic, isn't it? That's how it all went wrong. She had a vial of blood and your brother found it.'

Which was why they were so angry, Caro thought, played for fools by a slip of a girl. All that guilt about what they were doing – for nothing.

'Did my brother—' She drew a breath. 'Was it consummated between them?'

'Stone said not. Ambrose found the vial, and brought her back to the house.'

'Did Stone get Ambrose another girl?' In that moment, this was more important to her than anything.

'He was supposed to, but Ambrose took to his bed and stopped speaking. Stone told me later that he thought that night had finished him off.'

Because of his guilt and shame, his hatred for the thing he'd become.

'Tell me what happened after Pamela ran off.'

He gazed out at the river, at a passing coal barge, some birds in flight. 'Stone said we had to find her, to buy her off. We were to tell her that he'd make no complaint to Mrs Havilland – she could even keep her money – in exchange for her silence. We'd broken no laws, but it wouldn't look good, and he didn't want the girl making trouble. She'd run off into the woods, and so we split up to look for her. Stone told me to go to the bathhouse in case she'd gone back there.'

He paused, remembering. 'I'd been drinking all day. Didn't want to face it, I suppose. The girl. Your brother. It wasn't right.' His voice rose in anger. 'But I had no choice. You must understand that, Caro. Stone had us all in a vice. It wasn't our fault.'

Caro's voice was cold. 'Go on.'

'By the time I reached the bathhouse, my head was spinning. My hand hurt where she'd bitten me – I was bleeding a little. It was so damn cold, and I wanted to rest. The bathhouse was warm. The girl wasn't there. So I lay down on the daybed, and fell asleep. I don't remember anything else until morning.'

He exhaled slowly, shuddering slightly. 'I smelled it first. The blood. A lot of it. On my coat, on my hands, sticky. Far too much to be from the cut on my hand. At first I thought I'd had a nosebleed, but there was no blood on my face. I had a necklace in my hand, and I recognized it as the girl's. I went outside to the lake. Dawn was breaking. That's when I saw her.'

He stared at a tapestry on the wall, a unicorn and a girl. 'The water had been drained from Stone's pool for the winter. She was lying naked in the bottom of it, and her face it was all . . .' He broke off. 'She had been so beautiful, Caro. But there was so much blood. Unrecognizable. I just stared. I don't know how long for. Then Stone and Neddy were there, asking what the hell I'd done. I had no answer for them. I still don't. I can't remember.' His eyes were wet, and his hands shook, as he gazed at them. 'I wanted her, you see. She had this way of looking at a man.'

'So you raped and killed her?'

He shook his head. 'It doesn't sound like something I'd do. But sometimes I do things and I don't remember.'

'So Stone told you and Neddy to get rid of the body.'

'He said no one could ever know I'd done it. That his enemies would make him pay the price of my crime. That I'd hang for it. Neddy is a loyal friend, and he'd never have crossed Stone. And I – I couldn't face the hangman's rope.'

'Why were you and Neddy arguing over her necklace in that alley?'

'We were worried about your inquiry. Neddy said we should use the necklace to implicate Agnetti in the murders. He never liked the man. I don't know why. I refused to do it.'

Caro's hands dropped to the child in her belly, trying to think clearly.

'I'll marry you,' Lord March said suddenly, snapping her out of it. 'That's what you wanted me to say, wasn't it, when you told me about the baby?'

'And you refused.'

'I'm not refusing now.' He looked into her eyes. 'Father will disinherit me. A Craven, in the House of Amberley. But your child would have a father, and he cannot take my title. Even

Mordechai would forgive a scandal for an earldom in the family. We won't starve.'

The price of silence. Marriage to a murderer. Security for her child. Survival. Society would forgive a countess married into the House of Amberley.

'When did Stone tell you that Ambrose never debauched Pamela?' she asked.

He blinked. 'We're back to that? At breakfast the following day.'

'Then, that night, you didn't know? When you raped her?'

He frowned. 'No. I remember feeling worried for the girl. That she might catch his disease.'

'Then why would you rape her? As far as you were concerned, she had just been poxed. You would have endangered yourself.'

'I don't know. I wasn't in my right mind, I suppose.'

Caro was thinking hard again. 'Did you attack me in the alley at Carlisle House?'

'No,' he said. 'I told you. I could never hurt you, Caro. And I didn't take Gabriel.'

'Did you kill Lucy?'

'No. I hoped her murder had nothing to do with any of this. Later, I wondered if Neddy or Stone had done it to protect us.'

'What happened to the vial of blood? The one Pamela had – that my brother found?'

'Neddy gave it to me, I think. I put it in my pocket.'

He didn't do it, Caro thought. But the killer wanted everyone to think he did.

She tried to think through the implications. But first she had a decision to make. Marrying an innocent man who believed himself guilty was a very different prospect to marrying a murderer.

For a moment she hovered on the cusp between two lives. To allow the real killer to escape the consequences of his actions, in return for escaping the consequences of her own. It was tempting. But then she remembered the puzzle purses and the threat to Gabriel. The hard iron of the horse's hooves outside Carlisle House. Pamela, Lucy, Hector. Everything the killer had done. Her anger sharpened, diamond-bright, cold as a blade.

CHAPTER SEVENTY-THREE

BACK IN THE carriage, Caro described the scene at the bath-house to Mr Child.

Pamela in the empty bathing pool, naked, her face beaten to a pulp. Lord March in the bathhouse, covered in blood, the necklace in his hand.

'I saw the pool when I went to the masquerade,' she said. 'It's very deep. Difficult, perhaps impossible, for the killer to have got the girl out of it alone – not without covering himself in blood. It would have been harder still to bury her in the dead of night without a shovel. Perhaps the killer thought that the others would involve the authorities? Or perhaps he had another reason for wanting everyone to think that Lord March had done it? If Stone was responsible, say, the others would surely have gone to the authorities? They all hated him. But the Dodd-Bellingham brothers would protect Lord March. He was their friend.'

'So the killer created a tableau,' Child said. 'Let us call it *The Murderous Lord*.'

'I think so. He used the blood from Pamela's vial to stain Lord March's hands and coat.' Caro hadn't bothered to explain her reasoning to Lord March. Let him live with his guilt a little longer. She'd simply told him that she'd think about his pro-posal, and had left him sitting there.

'Does that mean you don't think that Pamela was really raped?'

'I'm not sure. She was angry, and rightly so. Swearing at them, threatening them. What if she encountered one of them out there in the woods and went further with her threats?'

'You mean her secret? Could she have been talking about the lieutenant's massacre? Or Simon and Julia Ward?'

'Except neither one of them has money. So I don't see how either secret could have made her rich.'

'Then perhaps she knew something about Stone?'

'But what? It still feels like we're missing something.'

Child concurred. 'We may not yet have sufficient evidence to arrest the guilty man, but we can at least get an innocent man out of prison.'

*

Two hours later, they were seated around the desk of Sir Amos Fox. Between Child and Mrs Corsham sat Nicholas Cavill-Lawrence of the Home Office. Laid out on the magistrate's desk were Pamela's necklace, the puzzle purses, the knife that Child had found at Vauxhall, and the drawings of Pamela and Lucy.

Earlier, they had called at the Home Office. Mrs Corsham had gone in to see Cavill-Lawrence alone, while Child waited in an anteroom, watched over by a gentleman with a grim face and a suspicious eye. More official sorts, like the men responsible for the assaults on himself and Nelly Diver, for the death of Kitty Carefree, and most probably the murder of Moll Silversleeves. But some battles were too big to fight – Mrs Corsham had convinced him of that. Child consoled himself by returning the man's steady glare.

He didn't know what Mrs Corsham had said to Cavill-Lawrence, but he could imagine: *'We have the signed confession of Kitty Carefree, who died on Westminster Bridge after an attempted abduction by two of your agents. Everything is in her account: the masquerades, Prinny, a murdered virgin, a syphilitic banker, an illegal loan. It doesn't take much to draw the lines between them. You desire to protect Prinny. I desire that the murderer be punished. Let us find a way to give each of us what we want.'*

Whatever Mrs Corsham had said, it had elicited results. Cavill-Lawrence was giving Sir Amos instructions.

'I want the Jew, Von Siegel, released. He is innocent of any crime.'

Sir Amos scratched an irritated pink patch on his neck. 'But you said . . .'

'I know what I said. Now I say this.'

Ever the obedient servant, Sir Amos rose and left the room, presumably to speak to one of his Runners.

When he returned, Cavill-Lawrence resumed: 'You are to take a detachment of Bow Street Runners to Muswell Rise. There's a dead doxy down a well, if they haven't already moved her. Lord March has confirmed to Mrs Corsham that the girl was murdered. You will question Jonathan Stone and the Dodd-Bellingham brothers. One of them will talk, if they're facing a hanging.'

'Maybe only the murderer knows who did it,' Child pointed out. 'What if they all deny it?'

'They obstructed justice,' Mrs Corsham said. 'That's a crime in itself.'

'You want me to hang them all?' Sir Amos said.

Child had had worse ideas.

Orin Black arrived moments later, bringing Ezra Von Siegel with him. The lamplighter's face was mottled with bruises, and he carried himself awkwardly. God knows what they had done to him to elicit that confession. Child gave Orin a hard look.

Sir Amos pointed to the drawing of Pamela. 'Information has come to light that the murderer of Lucy Loveless also killed this young girl. You were not a guest at the house of Jonathan Stone on the first of March, I take it?'

Von Siegel looked bewildered. 'Please, who is Jonathan Stone?'

Sir Amos nodded. 'We must therefore conclude that you could not have killed Lucy Loveless. Find his effects for him, will you, Black?'

Von Siegel stared at them in amazement. 'You let me go?'

'I just said so, didn't I?' Sir Amos scribbled on a piece of paper and signed it angrily.

Von Siegel looked down at the picture of Lucy, blinking back tears. He pointed to the necklace. 'I did not know.' He closed his eyes. '*Aleha hashalom.*'

'What witchcraft is that?' Cavill-Lawrence said. 'Some Israelite curse?'

Von Siegel's face was very solemn. 'Prayer for dead Jewish girl.'

Child looked at him sharply. 'This necklace is Jewish?'

'*Hamsa.* Meant to bring luck, to bring protection. But not to her.'

'The necklace didn't belong to Lucy,' Child said. 'It belonged to this girl, Pamela.' He pointed to the drawing, frowning, his thoughts running ahead of him. 'She said her father gave it to her mother.'

Child picked up the necklace and stared at it, his thoughts starting to clear. Pamela's secret that could make her rich. The tableau with Lord March. *Lucy knew who killed Pamela and she said she had proof.*

He looked up and met Mrs Corsham's eye. 'I know who killed them.'

*

Mrs Corsham rode in the magistrate's carriage, together with Nicholas Cavill-Lawrence. Child was relegated to the second vehicle, which carried a contingent of Bow Street Runners. He and Orin still hadn't spoken, but Child eyed him occasionally, feeling uneasy. Before they had left Bow Street, Sir Amos had taken Orin to one side for a whispered conversation in the hall. Child was still wondering what they had talked about.

The carriages gathered speed, and soon they were at the gates of Muswell Rise. Even Stone's armed guards weren't prepared to argue with Sir Amos Fox waving a warrant in high dudgeon. The porter unlocked the gates, and they proceeded down the drive. Stone's butler came out to meet them, but Sir Amos pushed past him.

'Where is your master?'

'Upstairs in his gallery,' the butler said. 'Sir, I ask you to wait . . .'

But Sir Amos, ever eager to curry favour with the Home Office, charged ahead. Child and Mrs Corsham hurried up the stairs in his wake. They burst into Stone's gallery, followed by Nicholas Cavill-Lawrence and the Bow Street men.

Lieutenant Dodd-Bellingham and his brother were carrying a statue of a naked woman to one of the plinths. The lieutenant sported a cut to his left eye and a swollen lip. Stone and Erasmus Knox were conferring by a window. They all turned as one.

'What is the meaning of this?' Stone said.

Child pointed. 'What are you waiting for? Arrest him.'

PAMELA

1 March 1782

Pamela ran through the woods.

Trees caught at her robe and scratched at her hands. She'd already lost one of her sandals, and stones cut into her foot. She needed to get away from this place, to get away from those shitten bastard fucksters. If she could find a wall, she could climb it. Walk back to London.

She paused for breath, listening for sounds of pursuit. Wind moaned through the trees and she shivered, bitterly cold. Her eyes were streaming, her nose running. She'd not last out here the night, that was for sure.

The knowledge spurred her on, her feet flying over the ground as she struggled to think sensibly through the force of her rage. She rounded a bend in the path and nearly ran into him.

'Pamela,' Simon said. 'What are you doing out here all by yourself?' He smiled reassuringly, and her rage erupted again.

'You knew, didn't you?' she said. 'About that man with the pox. When you promised me that I'd be safe. You knew.'

'I couldn't say anything because of Stone,' he stammered. 'None of us could. We didn't want any part in it, but we owe Stone money and . . .'

As she listened to his excuses, all her senses seemed to infuse with her rage: a black cloud in front of her eyes, a roaring in her ears, she could smell it like a bonfire, taste and touch her fury.

'Liar.' Remembering her fear, she wanted him to feel it too. 'Maybe I'll tell Mr Stone what you've been up to.'

He frowned. 'What are you talking about?'

'I knew you from before,' she said. 'I was a maid at the house in Cheapside by St Mary-le-Bow. You used to come often to see my master. I realized who you were when I saw you buying those clothes in *Maison Bertin*. You weren't wearing your glasses.' She smiled. 'I used to listen at keyholes. I heard you plotting with my old master. And now I'm going to tell Mr Stone.'

She watched his expression change, the fear creeping into his soul. 'Pamela,' he said. 'No. Please. Wait.'

'What do you think he'll do when he finds out? I hope you hang.'

'Please,' he said again, casting an anxious gaze around. 'Calm down, why don't you? Let's talk about this.'

She raised her voice over the wind. 'Simon Dodd-Bellingham is a liar. A cheat and a thief and a liar.' She laughed, hearing the shrillness in her own voice.

The blow took her by surprise, coming in the midst of his pleas. Not a slap like his brother had given her, but a fist. She fell to the ground, touched a hand to her nose, and tasted blood. The fuckster. She hadn't known he had it in him.

He stood, looking down at her, nursing his hand. Fear rolled in again. She scrambled to her feet and ran, back towards the house. She could hear him coming after her, crashing through the trees. Heavy in foot, not sleek like his brother, but she was tiring. Glimpsing the lake between the trees, she changed course, heading for the bathhouse. It had a bolt inside the door. She could hole up there until Kitty, or Stone, or one of the others came to find her.

The lake was smooth as glass against the deeper black of the night sky. Pamela picked up her pace, hearing Simon's feet thudding across the grass and the rasp of his breath. Only yards to the bathhouse door now. Her feet flew over the grass . . . into nothingness.

She fell, hitting stone, ten feet down. A crack as she landed. A sharp pain seared through her arm. She'd fallen into Stone's empty bathing pool. Cradling her arm, whimpering a little, she looked up and saw Simon standing on the edge.

She spoke very fast, through her gasps of pain, telling him that she was just joking. That she wouldn't tell Stone, she wouldn't ever tell a soul. That she'd only intended to ask for some of his money, just three thousand pounds, enough to clear the lieutenant's debts. But she didn't want to marry his brother any more, so he could keep it.

Simon jumped down into the pool. Pamela was crying now, pleading, but he wasn't listening. She put a hand to her necklace – her father's only gift to her mother, other than an unwanted baby – the *hamsa* that was supposed to offer her protection.

Simon was casting around for something. He bent, and when he straightened, he had a large stone in his hand. He walked towards her.

'*Elohim ya'azor–li,*' she whispered, trying to grasp the old prayers she'd learned in the little orphanage attached to the synagogue. All the ancient words she'd tried to forget.

They died on her lips as she watched the stone fall.

Chapter Seventy-Four

✳

SIR AMOS DREW his pistol and fired. Simon dived behind one of Stone's plinths, and the bullet took the head off a statue. Child rounded on the magistrate. 'Put it away. We want him alive.'

The Bow Street Runners had drawn their weapons too. Child remembered Sir Amos's whispered conversation with Orin Black in the hall. They don't want a trial, he thought. Nothing that can harm Prinny. They want Simon dead.

'Simon?' his brother cried, bewildered.

Simon was running for the door. One of the Bow Street Runners levelled his pistol, but Child barged into him as he took the shot, and the bullet went wide. Simon went through the door, knocking over a large urn in his haste. Child ran after him, glimpsing Jonathan Stone's anguished face. Simon had closed the door and was trying to lock it, but Child kicked it open, half falling into Stone's library. Simon grabbed a poker from the fireplace, and swung it at Child, forcing him back. Then he ran through another door, and Child pounded after him – onto the galleried landing surrounding the entrance hall and stairs.

Orin and another Bow Street Runner were at the top of the stairs now, cutting off Simon's escape. He ran in the opposite direction, along the landing, knocking over a startled housemaid with a pile of bedsheets. He opened a door, looked inside, then ran on to the next and threw it open. Child, hard on his heels, presumed he was seeking the servants' staircase. Another pistol shot rang out, then another. The Bow Street Runners were firing from the other side of the landing. Child lowered his head as bullets crashed into the elaborate plasterwork around them.

Simon pulled on the final door, but it was locked. He kicked it, but it wouldn't give. His escape cut off, he turned, facing Child.

'Surrender to me,' Child said. 'If you don't, they will shoot you dead.' There were questions he wanted to ask him. Parts of this puzzle that still didn't add up.

Dimly, he could hear Orin Black remonstrating with his fellow Runners, instructing them not to fire, in case they hit him. *Deptford till we die*, Child thought bitterly.

'Don't give them what they want,' he said to Simon. 'In a trial, you can bring Stone down with you.'

Simon turned his head from side to side, still seeking escape. 'My brother will be implicated. He disposed of Pamela's body.'

'You're worried about *him*?' Child said. 'Don't shoot,' he screamed at the Runners. 'You've got nowhere left to go, man.'

But as it turned out, Simon did. He pushed past Child, placing a hand on the mahogany balustrade, and vaulted over it. He landed in the entrance hall, fifteen feet below, falling forward onto his face, his glasses skittering across the floor.

As he staggered to his feet, Orin levelled his pistol. Child's cry was drowned out by the shot. Simon staggered a few paces and then fell backwards onto the floor, blood pooling on the marble tiles around him.

Chapter Seventy-Five

Lieutenant Dodd-Bellingham knelt by his brother's side, weeping. Child stared hard at Orin, who was taking congratulations from the Bow Street Runners. Mrs Corsham hurried up to Child, and placed a hand on his arm. 'Thank heaven you are unhurt.'

Cavill-Lawrence emerged from the gallery, and peered down at Simon. Seeing there was nothing to be done for him, he grunted his satisfaction. Child and Mrs Corsham followed him back into the gallery. Jonathan Stone was on his knees, collecting the pieces of one of his pots, looking stricken.

He glanced up as they entered. 'Simon killed Pamela?' He sounded astonished. 'I thought it was Lord March.'

'Simon made it look that way,' Child said. 'Principally, I think, because he didn't want anyone – especially you – asking why he might have killed her.'

'I'm asking that now. What reason did he have?'

Everyone looked at Child expectantly. The others had heard a garbled explanation earlier at the magistrate's, but they plainly wanted to hear more.

'Pass me your ring,' Child said to Stone.

'I beg your pardon.'

'Your ring.'

Stone slid it off his finger, and Child took the ring to the window, holding it up to the light. He examined the garnet carved with the head of a woman, and on the reverse, the head of a goat. The gold setting, he noticed now, held a slight coppery sheen. You'd probably never notice it, unless you were looking for it.

'It's pinchbeck over brass,' he said. 'I believe the lieutenant said you paid forty guineas apiece for those rings. And much more for this, the original. I suspect they're all fakes. I think Lucy realized after she stole the lieutenant's ring to trick Moll Silversleeves. After all, she was familiar with frauds like this.'

He thought of Nelly and Lucy, all those years ago, in the Sun tavern on Milk Street. *We had a forty-guinea gold ring what I'd napped off a client, and we looked for a certain sort of gentleman: the confident, crafty sort who'd take advantage of a trusting lady. Lucy made out she didn't know the ring's true value – offered it for sale at ten guineas. She did all the talking, I made the switch. Gentleman takes his gold ring home to celebrate his cunning, only to find he's paid ten guineas for pinchbeck and polish.*

'Lucy said she knew who the killer was,' Child went on. 'She said she had proof of his guilt. I think she was talking about that ring. It's why she took it to the bower, to show Mrs Corsham.'

Stone shook his head. 'Are you saying that Simon sold me a fake knowingly?'

Child was stirring the pottery shards of a broken lamp with his foot. It had been decorated with orgiastic scenes like the urn in Simon's workshop. He recalled Simon saying that Stone paid extra for such pieces. Picking up the broken base of the lamp, Child ran his thumb around the edge, feeling a line of glue. He showed it to Stone.

'I'm guessing the base was from an older piece, with a newly fired top – painted by Simon. He turned a genuine piece bought for shillings into something much more valuable that would suit your tastes.'

A large wad of paper was wedged into the lamp's base, presumably to balance it on one side. Child pulled it out and smoothed the papers on Stone's table. Lottery tickets, dated 1781.

'My guess is pretty much everything in your collection is a fake of one kind or another. Broken statues joined together, as he was doing in his yard when Mrs Corsham and I spoke to him for the first time. Pinchbeck jewellery. Counterfeit coins. I should have guessed when I saw the barrel of nails in his workshop. It's an old trick with fraudulent coins, as Mr Stone knows. Simon was uncomfortable with us just being there, but I put that down to the murders. Here is Lucy's proof. It's all around us.'

Stone stared at the lottery tickets in dismay. 'But my collection is worth over fifty thousand pounds.'

'I'd guess a good proportion of that has gone into Simon's pocket. You thought you were bleeding him dry, buying pieces from him on the cheap, because he owed you money he couldn't repay. But in truth, he wasn't your creature, you were his. I imagine he was squirrelling the money away in secret, ready for the day when he'd come into a mystery inheritance and settle his debts. Tell me, do you have a new house in Wiltshire? Farthingale Manor?'

Stone shook his head.

'Simon said you did. I even considered the possibility that you were keeping Theresa Agnetti there. But I think the manor was bought by him, intended for a different lady entirely: Julia Ward. He said she was willing to elope with him, if he improved his finances.'

'But I have studied antiquity,' Stone said plaintively, casting his gaze around the gallery. 'It cannot be true.'

'I only guessed when I discovered that Pamela was Jewish,' Child went on. 'Her necklace was the key to it all. Pamela told a friend that her father had given it to her mother. I imagine he was poor, and abandoned her mother when she fell pregnant. But Solomon Loredo, himself a Jew, told me that the necklace was Indian in origin. I had to ask myself why he would lie.'

Solomon Loredo – who had taken enormous pains to emphasize Simon's honesty at every turn. He had concealed from Child the story about Ansell Ward and the figurines, presumably because the fabricated theft hit rather too close to the mark for his liking.

'I think Solomon Loredo made that ring, Stone's so-called original. And probably most of the other jewellery here too. Like Simon, Loredo had once owed money to Stone. He described it to me as the worst time in his life. This was their revenge. Loredo told me that Simon had been to his house by St Mary-le-Bow on Cheapside. They probably plotted the whole enterprise there. I think that's where Pamela met him for the first time.'

Child had thought it all through in the carriage. 'Pamela was raised in a Jewish orphanage, I imagine. Like their Christian counterparts, they train their female charges for service. Loredo told me he'd struggled to keep a maidservant as they kept getting their heads turned by prostitution.' *Even good Jewish girls are tempted.* 'I think Pamela was one of his housemaids. We know she used to listen at doors. She must have recognized Simon, done a little research, and worked out that Stone was the man they were swindling. Perhaps she tried to blackmail Simon. We know she entertained dreams of marrying the lieutenant, and he had debts. Or maybe she threatened to tell Stone, because she was angry about Ambrose Craven and his syphilis. Either way, Simon couldn't take the risk of Stone finding out, and so he killed her.'

'That poor child,' Mrs Corsham said. 'Embroiled in all these deceptions of men. She deserved better from her life. And, God knows, from her death.'

CHAPTER SEVENTY-SIX

THEY CONVENED IN Stone's palatial dining room, overlooked by a giant Agnetti canvas of the wooden horse being rolled into Troy. Caro sat next to Mr Child, opposite the magistrate and Cavill-Lawrence. Jonathan Stone was not invited to this part of the meeting.

'It is hard to believe,' Caro said. 'Simon Dodd-Bellingham being so bold as to murder Lucy in the bower. To attack me at Carlisle House. To pay a woman to steal my son. To kill poor Hector.'

'I know,' Child said. 'I wanted to ask him about it all.' He glared at Cavill-Lawrence, who looked entirely unrepentant.

'I suppose desperation can drive a man to great lengths,' Caro said. 'Simon could have been hanged for his crimes, so he killed to protect himself. He must have worked out that Lucy was on to him, and decided to silence her.'

'I keep wondering if Kitty told him,' Child said. 'I wanted to ask him about that too.'

'Well, Simon has faced the ultimate justice now,' Cavill-Lawrence said. 'Can we agree that this matter is now at an end?'

Caro frowned. 'Jonathan Stone concealed a murder. As did the lieutenant and Lord March.'

'Do you really want this to go to court?' Cavill-Lawrence raised his startling eyebrows. 'All that family laundry aired?

Ambrose, illegal loans. Stone will drag everyone into this, I promise you that.'

Caro was silent a moment. She didn't want Prinny mired in scandal, especially if it would unleash the King's wrath on the Craven Bank. Her brother prosecuted, Louisa and her children in the poorhouse.

'I don't want Stone to walk away from this unscathed.'

'Oh, Stone will get his desserts eventually, I promise you that.' Cavill-Lawrence spoke with cold dispassion, but she knew he was thinking about his Prince.

'Those rumours about Lieutenant Dodd-Bellingham,' she said. 'The Somerset allegations, the massacre at Van der Linden's Mill. They're true. I want them properly investigated.'

Cavill-Lawrence grunted. 'Of course they're true. The War Office looked into it. Their inquiry supported Somerset's account in every respect.'

'Then why is the lieutenant to be awarded the Order of the Bath?'

The answer came to her in the ensuing silence. *Because the King likes to recount the story. Because they are keeping all bad news from him. They worry that the smallest disappointment might prompt his abdication. Expose his brave English lion as a killer and a coward and it might be enough.*

'Well,' Cavill-Lawrence said. 'Are we agreed?'

'I don't want Solomon Loredo punished,' Child said. 'He was only trying to take revenge on Stone. I don't think he knew for certain that Simon had killed Pamela. He was simply afraid that their forgeries would be discovered.'

'We can hardly try Loredo without all the rest of this coming out,' Cavill-Lawrence said.

'I'm more worried about Stone seeking revenge. Not just on Loredo. On me. On my friends.' *On Sophie.*

'I will make it plain to Mr Stone that there is to be no retribution,' Cavill-Lawrence said. 'Under the circumstances, it is a small enough price for him to pay.'

Child bowed his head, then looked at Caro. 'You are the client, madam.'

'Very well,' Caro said reluctantly. 'But on one condition. I wish to ask Mr Stone a question, and I want you to compel him to answer.'

Cavill-Lawrence nodded to Sir Amos. 'Bring him in.'

*

Jonathan Stone sat at the head of the table, unsmiling for once.

'On the first of March,' Caro said, 'the day Pamela died, Theresa Agnetti called at this house to see you. You spoke to her in private. I'd like to know what you discussed.'

Stone looked a little surprised by the question. 'She told me that she desired to leave her husband. The marriage was unhappy, she said, and she wished to start again, under a new name. She asked me for a loan of five hundred pounds and I agreed.'

Caro gazed at him sceptically. 'Such a loan would be unenforceable. Any debt in Theresa's name would have been her husband's liability. But once she left him, he would have ceased to be legally accountable. And if she'd moved away, changed her name, then how would you find her if she reneged on the repayments?'

'I trusted her,' Stone replied. 'Theresa Agnetti was my friend.'

'Your *friend*,' Caro said, her voice rich with sarcasm.

'You don't believe that a man and a woman can ever be friends? Mrs Agnetti is an intelligent woman, and an interesting conversationalist. I enjoyed her company much more than

I ever did her husband's. I also had some sympathy for her predicament. I am, as you know, a great believer in the freedom of women. I did not think Mrs Agnetti should be condemned to an unhappy life because of one simple mistake in her youth.'

'Did she mention Pamela to you at all?' Child said.

'No. Why would she?'

'They didn't get on. Never mind. It was a theory we had.'

'Did you ever hear from Mrs Agnetti again?' Caro said.

'Every month I receive a repayment by post. She is much happier now, or so she tells me.'

'Can you tell us where she is?'

'I'm afraid not. She has never said.'

Caro exchanged a rueful glance with Mr Child. All that wasted effort looking into the Agnettis. Caro wondered if she should tell Mr Agnetti that his wife was alive and well. Would it make his burden easier to bear, or harder?

Stone looked around the table. 'Will that be all?'

Gazing at the man who had ruined her reputation, who would leave her son without a mother, Caro's voice tightened. 'Your philosophy is a fraud, sir. Women's freedom, equality in pleasure. Would those women come to your masquerades and submit to the whims of you and your friends, if they were rich?'

'Perhaps,' Stone said. 'I assure you they enjoy themselves, Mrs Corsham.'

'Do they?' Caro said. 'Or do they simply have their own line in fakery? From what I have witnessed, Mr Stone, you're a credulous man.'

*

Outside, by the magistrate's carriage, Caro smiled at Mr Child. 'Will you return to the house with me? We need to discuss the settlement of your account.'

'I'm surprised there's anything to discuss. I betrayed you, madam.'

'You were in a bind,' Caro said. 'And you only hastened this scandal along. I think it would have come to this anyway. Captain Corsham's pride would have stood in the way of any solution. So please, Mr Child, I insist.'

He inclined his head. 'Can it wait until tomorrow?'

'You are very eager to refuse my money, sir.'

'I thought I'd look for Kitty's body. Someone also needs to tell Humphrey Sillerton that his wife is dead.'

The girl's suicide had affected him badly, she could tell. His brow furrowed.

'What is it?' she asked.

'Just something that's been troubling me these last few days. Something Kitty said when we saw her at the church. Something that doesn't quite add up. But I cannot think what it is.' He shook his head. 'It will come to me.'

Cavill-Lawrence was waiting impatiently in the carriage. Caro took her leave of Mr Child, and a footman assisted her into the vehicle. Sir Amos was on the steps of Stone's house, talking to one of his Runners. Two more of them were carrying the corpse of Simon Dodd-Bellingham from the house.

'I believe you have something for me?' Cavill-Lawrence said.

Reaching into her panniers, Caro handed him Kitty's letter. As he went to put it away in his frock coat, she laid a hand on his arm.

'Stop keeping things from His Majesty,' she said. 'Stop protecting him from bad news. Remind him of his obligations, of his duty. Before you destroy that letter, you should give it to him to read. Tell him that his son needs time to grow up.'

CHAPTER SEVENTY-SEVEN

AFTER THAT, THERE was nothing left to do except to go home.

Caro sat for hours that afternoon, playing with Gabriel in the drawing room, making battalions of lead soldiers and forts from cushions. He picked one up to show her: 'Papa.'

She smiled at him. 'He'll be home soon.'

But not too soon, she hoped, hugging him tight. She wondered if they'd take the other child from her too, the one growing in her womb, and decided they probably would. She blinked back tears.

It might not be for ever, she thought. Ladies had returned from disgrace before, after a few years, when hearts had softened and scandal died. There was Lady Sarah Bunbury, who'd fallen pregnant by her lover, and was exiled for years to a country cottage. Now, occasionally, Lady Sarah could be seen out on the town with her new husband.

Perhaps one day they'll let me see Gabriel again. Or perhaps he'll seek me out, when he's fully grown.

Or perhaps he'll hate me.

'Mama, can we catch the mouse again?'

'Of course we can,' she said, rising, taking his hand. 'We can lay traps!'

*

Later, when Gabriel was in bed, she sat in the drawing room, off her food again, trying to read Aeschylus and failing. London society would be out in force tonight, for the Prince's visit to Vauxhall Gardens. Her enemies would be delighting in her fall. They would be talking about her now, stories breeding stories. Soon every man she'd ever spoken to would be cited as one of her lovers.

Tears pricked her eyes. She knelt to tidy away the lead soldiers. They reminded her of Ansell Ward: *A la bataille!*

Whatever they do to me next, she thought, Caroline Corsham does not hide herself away. She called for Pomfret. 'Have the carriage made ready, please.'

He gazed at her, concerned. 'Where are you going, madam?'

'To Vauxhall Gardens.'

*

Caro wore the burgundy satin and matching feathers. Let them stare, she thought. Yet as she walked through the gates of the gardens, and the faces turned towards her, her courage almost failed her. But she kept walking, preceded by Miles, her chin aloft, as if oblivious to the laughter.

On the Grand Walk, she encountered the Henekers, strolling together under the stars. She embraced Lottie warmly, pretending not to notice the other woman's stiffness in her arms. 'I am so glad to run into you,' Caro said. 'I have the most astonishing story to tell you about Lieutenant Dodd-Bellingham.'

'That his brother is dead?' Lottie said. 'A thief? A murderer? We heard.'

Her excited tone suggested that the beau monde would not mourn these facts. Simon, after all, was never really one of them.

'This is something else,' Caro said. 'I guarantee you'll like it.'

Despite all Lottie's natural instinct to eschew her company, it was enough to make her twitch. 'You must say more.'

Caro threaded an arm through hers, smiling brightly at Lottie's husband. 'Let me tell you on the way to the Rotunda.'

*

Once in the Rotunda, the Henekers swiftly and strategically abandoned her. The beau monde had arranged themselves in concentric circles of influence around Prinny, the sun at their centre, in a bright yellow frock coat weighed down by badges and medallions. Lord March was by his side, with Clemency Howard on his arm. He offered Caro a hesitant smile, which she didn't return. Prinny followed his gaze, and when he saw Caro, he scowled. She wondered if he knew about Kitty's confession — if Cavill-Lawrence had taken her advice and shown it to his father. I've made an enemy there, she thought.

All around, she could hear her name repeated in whispers. Like a firing squad, she thought. Only I get to see their faces. To see who it delights, who it saddens, and who is afraid they might be next.

Lieutenant Dodd-Bellingham wore a black armband and looked a little subdued, surrounded by solicitous heiresses. Caro walked directly up to him, breaking every rule regarding propriety. The heiresses looked at her in outrage.

'Van der Linden's Mill,' she murmured in the lieutenant's ear. 'We never got to finish our conversation.'

He stepped away from the heiresses a pace or two. 'Haven't you heard? I am to be promoted to lieutenant colonel. The King's confirmed the Order of the Bath. They'll not touch me now, whatever evidence you think you can find.'

Caro looked up at his arrogant face, his cut lip, his duelling scar. 'You may wear your grand cross star,' she said. 'Bathe in the gentlemen's adulation. But the women will know.'

'What are you talking about?'

'Van der Linden's Mill. I told Lottie Heneker the truth.' She looked across the Rotunda, where Lottie was whispering excitedly in the Duchess of Shropshire's ear. 'Every woman who hears that story will believe it – not least because we've always found it a struggle to believe in your heroism in the first place. Your heiresses will doubtless hear it too. You'll probably convince one of them to marry you, regardless, but she will wake up next to you every morning, and remember that her husband is a coward.'

Scowling, he turned his back on her, sparking a fresh round of murmurs. All around her, people did the same. Adrift on a tide of outrage, abandoned by people she'd known and liked, her eyes pricked as she pushed her way through to the door.

One lone figure blocked her path. Jacobus Agnetti. She waited for him to turn away too, but he bowed, kissing her hand.

Gratefully, she returned his smile. 'To have the Prince here is a great coup,' she said. 'You must be very proud.'

He raised his eyebrows. 'His Highness does not look at the paintings. And the crowds only look at him. Miss Willoughby hopes he will commission a portrait. We shall see.' His expression grew more sombre. 'I heard about Simon Dodd-Bellingham. I can hardly believe it.'

'I will acquaint you with the story another time. It will do your reputation no good to stand here talking to me.'

He smiled again. 'There are many things about which I care, but my reputation has never been one of them. I am happy to talk to you, Mrs Corsham, at any time.'

Caro studied his face: his tired eyes, his hair streaked with grey like an old badger. She'd already decided to say nothing about his wife. 'I do not anticipate that I shall be in London for very much longer. But I wondered if I might change your mind about painting my portrait before I leave town?'

He bowed again. 'It would be an honour.'

'Then I shall call on you,' she said. 'Perhaps tomorrow.'

He looked past her, to the watching beau monde, to Prinny and his admirers. 'We could start tonight, if you prefer. I find I tire of this company.'

She laughed. 'Walk out on your public, on the Prince? That would certainly cement your reputation for breaking convention.'

'And yours for public scandal.' He offered her his arm. 'What do you say?'

Smiling at his audacity, she slipped her arm though his. The crowds parted before them, her name and Mr Agnetti's rising like an echo. Together they walked out of the Rotunda, into the moonlit night.

Chapter Seventy-Eight

Child visited the riverside taverns where the watermen drank, asking if anyone had heard about the body of a pretty redhead being pulled from the river. The alleys were dank and dripping, the taverns choked with cheap tobacco. Eventually, an ancient bearded waterman nodded slowly at Child's questions, and told him to try the dead-house south of the Strand.

The wharves stank of sea-coal and shit, but as Child descended the steps to the dead-house, the river's aromas warred with a riper, sweeter smell. Grimacing, Child knocked on the door, and explained his purpose to the beadle on duty.

The dead-house was about fifteen feet square, each wall lined with slate shelves containing cadavers pulled from the river. The beadle walked to one of the shelves and held up his lantern. Child gazed down at Kitty's pale face. He'd hoped she'd look at peace, all her sins washed away by the tides. But her wide blue eyes seemed to stare into some private horror. Child reached out a hand and gently closed them.

There had been so much he'd wanted to ask her, just as he'd wanted to ask Simon Dodd-Bellingham. Those questions nagged at him now.

'Is she your daughter?' the beadle asked, with a trace of sympathy.

'No,' Child said. 'Just a girl I used to know.'

He walked out of the dead-house, carrying the stink of the

place with him, and decided to head up to the taverns on the Strand. He was halfway up Villiers Street, when it came to him. The thing that had been troubling him for days – ever since their conversation with Kitty. Turning around, he headed back towards the river.

*

Child hired a waterman to row him across the Thames, alighting on the south bank at King's Arms Stairs. He walked south, past darkened meadows and silent orchards, until he reached St George's Fields and the Magdalen Hospital.

He knocked at the door several times before someone came. The porter eyed him sullenly. 'We're closed.'

Child begged an audience with the matron, Hester Rainwood. 'It concerns the welfare of a prostitute she was concerned about. I think she'd like to know.'

The porter told him to wait outside. He returned after several minutes and nodded at Child. 'She says I'm to show you up.'

Child followed him through the darkened quadrant, the place silent and still, the inmates asleep. Mrs Rainwood received him in her study again. He had evidently interrupted her reading, for a volume lay on the desk, next to a large fruitcake and a teapot. Child glanced at spine of the book: the plays of Sophocles.

Mrs Rainwood's lead-white countenance was creased with concern. 'Do you bring news of Kitty Carefree, Mr Child?'

'I'm sorry to tell you that she's dead.'

Her face crumpled. Child studied her carefully, still not entirely certain that he was right.

'Before she died,' he said, 'Kitty told me something that's been puzzling me. She said Stone paid her and the other girls at the masquerade two hundred guineas apiece for their silence. Lucy knew this; she called it blood money. It was enough for Kitty to be able to set herself up quite comfortably in Clapham. Whereas the women you help at the Magdalen are poor, in need of charity. So I asked myself why Lucy would have come looking for her here.'

Mrs Rainwood examined him uneasily. 'Forgive me, sir, but I don't know what you are saying.'

'Kitty told me that in early August, she wrote to her former governess. She said Lucy talked this woman into showing her the letter. Lucy wrote the details from that letter down on a card she picked up here at the Magdalen. *Fifty to sixty pineapples, two s, one d.*' Child pointed to the stack of identical cards on the edge of Mrs Rainwood's desk. 'And early August was when Lucy came here to see you.'

Mrs Rainwood set down her teacup and Child noted the rattle.

'I don't think Kitty wrote to her former governess,' he said. 'I think she wrote to you. I think you showed that letter to Lucy that day she came here to see you. And I think the reason she came was because you were her friend, Theresa Agnetti.'

Child studied her face again, recalling his brief glance at the miniature Theresa had painted of herself and Lieutenant Dodd-Bellingham. Her gloved hands. Her mask of lead-white paint.

The girl at the Whores' Club had said that Theresa's skin had yellowed when she'd lost the baby. Theresa had been stick-thin then, but with effort – Child's eye fell upon the fruit cake – a woman could gain a lot of weight in half a year.

'Please,' she said. 'I have burnt it. I swear it.'

'Kitty's testimony?' he said. 'Lucy gave it to you to look after?'

She nodded, biting her lip.

'She told you that if anything happened to her, you were to give that testimony to the newspapers. Why didn't you?'

Her words were very faint. 'Because I was afraid.'

He could see the truth in it, the fear creeping out of her into the room. He thought she might be the most frightened person he'd ever seen.

'Simon could surely not have found you here? And once the newspapers had Kitty's account, you could be no further threat to him? I don't understand. Why were you so afraid?'

She placed one hand upon the other to stop it trembling. 'Because I married a monster, Mr Child.'

CHAPTER SEVENTY-NINE

MR AGNETTI SKETCHED Caro by candlelight, while she told him about Simon Dodd-Bellingham and his motive for murder.

'I always thought Simon the best of them,' he said, when she had finished. 'It is a struggle to believe that he killed Pamela. And Lucy too.'

'And a young boy named Hector.' Caro sighed. 'It was a strange life that Simon led. A gentleman's son, but illegitimate. Part of a great family, but not part of it. In society, but poor.'

'You say he loved this girl, Julia Ward? And was afraid of losing her?'

'Yes, I think he did it all for her.'

Agnetti nodded soberly. 'Love and money are powerful motives for murder. When the two are combined . . .'

'At least it is over now. Justice, of a sort, has been done.'

'But at great cost,' Agnetti said. 'Not least to yourself. What do you intend to do now?'

'Wait for my husband to return. Confront my fate.'

He looked up from his sketch. 'If ever you need a refuge in a storm, then my door stands open. This is already a house of scandal – what's one more sinner?'

She smiled. 'Thank you, Mr Agnetti. It is good to know that I have a friend.'

Laying down his chalk, he flexed his hand. 'I need to rest. Would you like some wine?'

She smiled her assent. The servants had been in bed when they'd arrived at the house, and Agnetti had seen no reason to rouse them. Caro presumed that Miss Willoughby must be in bed too, for there was no sign of her.

'It may take me a little while to hunt down the key to the cellar. If you would like to look at the paintings, then please do.'

Listening to his footsteps descend the stairs, she walked to the window. It was lively in Leicester Fields, parties of drunks wandering from tavern to tavern. She'd told Miles to wait outside by the carriage with Sam in case there was trouble. Yet the revellers seemed in happy enough spirits, bellowing bawdy songs.

Caro crossed the room to study Agnetti's giant canvas. It was nearly finished. Lucy's ghostly face, her howl of accusation. Orestes kneeling, hands to his head, punished for his crimes by the Furies, the daughters of Night.

She found herself thinking about mothers and children. Pamela, abandoned by hers, raised in an orphanage. Lucy, sold into carnal servitude when she was twelve years old. Lucy's child, Olivia, starved to death by her wet-nurse. Mr Agnetti, raised by his father's whores.

And Gabriel.

I should not be here, she thought. *I should be at home with my son in case he wakes, in case he needs me. For if I am not there for him now, how will he know that I ever was?*

Going to the door, she hurried downstairs to find Mr Agnetti. There was no sign of him in the hall, but one of the doors stood ajar, a lamp lit inside. Pushing it open, she found herself in Agnetti's dining room. On the table were two glasses of claret. Perhaps Mr Agnetti was in the water closet? She decided to wait for him there until he returned.

On the table was a half-finished watercolour painting, and

next to it a box of paints with Cassandra Willoughby's initials burnt into the wood. It was a scene from Leicester Fields, the piazza bustling with street hawkers and artists. Caro frowned. The painted figures bore a marked resemblance to those on the puzzle purses.

Looking up from the painting, she hesitated, confused. Across the room was a china cupboard, the doors standing open. Its shelves were filled with crockery and glassware, as one would expect. Yet something odd had caught her eye.

Walking over to the cupboard, Caro put her hand up to the hole. About two inches square, it had been cut into the back of one of the shelves, at eye-level. A shaft of light was shining through it, which was what she had seen. Pressing her face up to the hole, Caro realized that she could see right into Agnetti's panelled drawing room.

Cassandra Willoughby was seated on the sofa, her dress unlaced, her breasts exposed. Miles was standing over her, lacing up his breeches. He reached down to fondle her nipple and smiled.

'I'd better be getting back to the carriage,' her footman said. 'If Mrs Corsham catches me here, there'll be hell to pay.'

She barely looked at him. 'As you wish.'

Caro's throat was dry. She looked again, her mind racing. Had someone been here watching them? Mr Agnetti?

Miss Willoughby was showing Miles to the door. He murmured something to her, and she shook her head. They disappeared from view, and she heard the front door close. Then Miss Willoughby returned to the sofa and stared right at her, a look of despair that confused her even more.

'There,' she said. 'I have done it. Are you happy now?' Putting her head in her hands, she started to weep.

Many thoughts occurred to Caro at once. Ezra Von Siegel's

account of Miss Willoughby's distress, when he'd seen her fleeing the bower after her encounter with Lieutenant Dodd-Bellingham. The lieutenant's denials that he had tried to rape her, which Caro had presumed to be a lie. Now she wondered. Could Mr Agnetti have *made* Miss Willoughby do it? The thought was shocking, incomprehensible, but she couldn't deny the evidence of her eyes. Had he forced her to endure a similar violation just now, at the hands of Miles? If the lieutenant had been as oblivious as Miles to the role he had played in this obscene tableau, then it would explain his laughter when she'd confronted him with Miss Willoughby's allegation.

Caro stood frozen, watching the girl weep. Agnetti had told her that the lieutenant looked for vulnerability in a woman and preyed upon it. She wondered now if, in truth, he was describing himself.

She needed to leave this house, to speak to Mr Child, to ascertain if there was a connection between the scene she'd just witnessed and the puzzle purses and Lucy's murder. Stepping away from the cupboard, she froze. Agnetti was standing in the doorway.

He spoke calmly. 'You should not be in here.'

'No,' she said, smiling brightly, as if to deny what they both knew she had seen. 'That was what I was coming to tell you. I am leaving now.'

He didn't move, blocking the door. Miss Willoughby appeared behind him in the hall, presumably having heard their voices.

'Run and fetch Miles,' Caro cried out to her. 'Quickly. Go now. I'll never let him do any of these things to you ever again.'

Miss Willoughby glanced at Agnetti. He placed a hand on her shoulder.

'My love,' he said. 'I think we have to kill her.'

CHAPTER EIGHTY

THE LAMP CAST a yellow light onto Theresa Agnetti's lead-white skin. She spoke softly, but the fear hadn't left her. Child could see it in her eyes, could smell it on her, could feel it in every corner of that room.

'To understand what happened,' she said, 'you need first to understand the child I was. I was never strong like Lucy. Nor bold like Pamela. Nor brave like Kitty. As a girl, I lost myself in books, forever nervous when people spoke to me, which they seldom did. But one day, when I was fifteen, still living in India, a younger friend of my father's paid me attention. He was handsome and amusing, and he knew so much about the world. An attachment formed, and he led me to believe that we would be married. When he announced his engagement to another lady, I tried to kill myself.' She turned her wrist to show him an old scar.

'Fearing a scandal if we remained in India, my father moved the family to Naples. There I lived an isolated life for several years, until the day Jacobus Agnetti came to paint my portrait. I didn't like him at first. He told me that I was not beautiful enough to suit one of the principal goddesses, that he would paint me as Hestia, goddess of the home. For many weeks I sat for him, hearing not one kind word from his lips, until one day he complimented my eyes.' She smiled faintly. 'Women are strange creatures, Mr Child. A kind man can offer us compliments and we think less of him for it – we ask ourselves if his judgement is in doubt. Whereas a man spartan with his praise makes us feel as if we have earned it – and to crave more, like scraps tossed to a hungry dog. Jacobus and I began to talk while he painted – about myths and their meaning, about the classics and the philosophers. He said I was the most learned young woman that he had ever met. I began to look forward to his visits. It felt as if I had been sleeping for many years and was just waking up. I had never been happier before or since, than the day he asked Father for my hand.'

She was still smiling now at the memory. Then her smile faded, as she gazed through Child into her past.

'Jacobus says that when he paints you, he sees into your soul. All your hopes, your fears, your dreams. And he saw precisely how to turn me to his advantage. I think he knew I was broken inside, and a woman like that was what he wanted. Because he thought I was weak, and I'd never leave him, as his mother did. No matter what he did to me.' She drew a shuddering breath. 'I was happy for the first three months. Jacobus bought me presents – he said I was his world. When he smiled at me, it was like stepping into the Neapolitan sun. The first time he spoke harshly to me, I was so shocked. I had said the wrong thing to a potential client at a dinner and he was angry. I apologized, I wept, and he said that he forgave me. I thought it was an aberration, not the Jacobus I knew. But I soon discovered that the kind Jacobus had never existed.'

Child listened, in mounting horror, as Theresa described her life with Jacobus Agnetti.

'He was always kind and solicitous to me in public. People who knew us called him the perfect husband. But when our front door closed, I could not do anything right. Our house was not well kept enough. My gowns were not the right fashion. I embarrassed him. He accused me of flirting with other men, though I only had eyes for Jacobus. He would withdraw to his studio, and refuse to speak to me for days. Sometimes he would break one of my favourite things and call it a punishment. If I tried to speak to him about philosophy or the classics, he scorned my ideas and called me stupid. Sometimes, in the midst of a tirade, he would extinguish every lamp in the room and order me to sit there in the dark until he returned. If I made a friend, then Jacobus would say cruel things about her. He would force me to cancel my engagements at the last minute so they'd be vexed at me. I lost more friends than I could count, and soon I stopped trying to make them. I made excuses for him to myself: his work, my shortcomings, his lack of the success he craved, my failure to conceive. I thought if I could only make him happy as I had before, then it would all stop.

'For several years we lived in Naples, until Jacobus decided that England was a brighter prospect for his work. We moved away from my family, and the few remaining friends I had. I thought that things might get better, but they only got worse. Jacobus filled the house with prostitutes, aware that it would cause me humiliation in polite society. He would praise their looks in front of me, and compare them to mine to my detriment. He said I was fat, and so I lost weight, so much I could scarcely stand without feeling faint. I was forced to converse with his sitters as equals. Jacobus made me serve them tea and chocolate, as though I was their servant. Sometimes he gave them presents: my favourite books, or ornaments that I loved. Some of them laughed at me. I heard them. But mostly they were kind. And the irony of it all was that Lucy and Kitty became the dearest friends I ever had.'

Tears rolled down her cheeks, making tracks through the paint. 'After we had been in London for about six months,

Jacobus became fixated upon getting a commission from the Duke of Shropshire. We attended a dinner at Shropshire House, and he told me to be sure to pay His Grace attention, to court his favour. Afterwards, as I'd feared he would, he accused me of flirting. It was an argument that we'd had many times before, but this time, he said that if I was going to act like a whore, then I might as well go through with it. At least that way, we might get a commission. I told him that was neither kind, nor funny – but soon I realized that he was serious. Jacobus said that if I loved him, then I would do it. That grotesque old man—' She broke off. 'I refused, naturally. That night he forced me to my knees in our bedroom and cut off my hair.'

Child had never wanted a drink more in his life. He wanted to walk out of that room, to think of anything, even his own deficiencies as a husband, except this. But he had forced Mrs Agnetti to open this box, and he had to gaze into it.

'In the end,' she said, 'I ran out of ways to say no. I thought if I did it, then he'd be appalled at himself and things might change. How could he want his wife to go with another man? But he wasn't appalled, he was pleased. And soon there was another commission, another potential client whom he wanted me to satisfy. Sometimes they rejected me, and Jacobus would laugh at my humiliation. But most of the time, they were only too happy to take what was on offer – which wasn't everything. Jacobus said I could not couple with them as a husband and wife do – he was desperate for a child and if I fell pregnant, he wanted to know that it was his. So he had me do terrible, degrading things, the things his sitters did to please a man. And afterwards, he would leave me little notes inside my books, or underneath my pillow, calling me whore. The only way I could please him again would be to tell him about the things that I had done, and soon I came to realize that it was not about his paintings or his prospects at all. He simply enjoyed it. Later, he made me do it at home, so he could watch.'

'But his sitters speak so kindly of him,' Child said, still unable to comprehend. 'At the Whores' Club they only sang his praises.'

'A man can be kind to prostitutes and also torment his wife.' She wiped her eyes, but the tears kept falling. 'My resistance, in the hands of Jacobus, was a block of marble, and him the sculptor. One day you say yes to something that you do not want to do, because he is your husband and you only want to make him smile. But there is always another ask, another piece of marble chipped away, until one day there you are, a living statue, and you do not even recognize yourself. Jacobus liked my lovers to think that he was a cuckold, but secretly he was their master, able to give and take away this thing they wanted by his command. He chose them carefully, each designed to humiliate me further. Ugly men, cruel men, servants and tradesmen. He knew I despised Lieutenant Dodd-Bellingham for the way he treated women, so he made me pursue him. I drank most of the time. Sometimes I thought I was going mad. Perhaps I was.'

'Why didn't you leave him sooner?' Child said.

'You think it is as easy as that? I had no money of my own. And Jacobus told me that if I ever left him, he would hunt me down and kill me. And for a long time, I still loved him, despite everything. Sometimes the clouds would roll away for an hour, and he would be kind or sorry, and the sun would shine again. But those clouds,' she stared at the lamp, 'they always came back. And in all that time, over all those years, the only person who ever guessed was Lucy Loveless.'

'Lucy knew.' Child could see there was a leap he should be making.

'She told me that Jacobus had no troubles large enough to

justify what he was doing. She said I had to leave him. Sometimes I could see the sense in it. But I still loved him – or at least, I thought I did. And I was afraid – of what I would do, of where I would go, and most of all, I was afraid of him. So I stayed, and then, to my surprise, I fell pregnant. Jacobus was so happy – and I was too. I had wanted a child so very much, and I thought if anything would content him then it would be fatherhood. But Lucy said it would tie me to him forever, that he would pass his darkness onto our child. She gave me a bottle of pennyroyal and many times I thought about taking it. But I couldn't bring myself to kill my own baby. I think I would still be with Jacobus now, were it not for that girl, Pamela.'

'I was told you disliked one another,' Child said.

'I hated her,' she said emphatically. 'Jacobus engineered it. He would tell me every day over breakfast how young she was, how beautiful. He said maybe he'd put me in the country, and take her for his mistress. I was so jealous – but now, here at the Magdalen, the clouds are gone, and I can think clearly. I don't think his sitters really interested him in that way. Those women were their own masters. A transaction freely entered into, the terms understood by both parties, would have held little attraction. For him it was all about love: the price of it, the cost. His heart so blackened, he could only believe he was loved through my defilement. But back then, I believed he wanted Pamela, that they were already lovers. I knew she hated me too. The looks she gave me.'

'It was Lieutenant Dodd-Bellingham she wanted. Not your husband.'

'I know that now. Lucy told me. Pamela put the pennyroyal in my wine, we suspected, because she thought my child was the lieutenant's. I had a very severe reaction to it, and almost died. Jacobus was furious about the baby. He said it was my fault. He made us go out to a ball, when I was still weak from the miscarriage and the pennyroyal. I could barely stand, shivering and jaundiced. But he didn't care, he just wanted to punish me. That night he made me debase myself in the garden with the lieutenant while he watched – the most vile thing he'd had me do yet. I knew then that I had to leave before he killed me, or I killed myself. So the next day I went to Mr Stone's house on my husband's business, and asked him for money. If I'd had to, I would have placed my life in his hands, told him everything. But it was enough for Mr Stone to know that I wanted to leave my husband. People speak ill of him; I understand why. But that day Jonathan Stone saved my life.

'I left that same evening, taking nothing but the clothes I was wearing, which I later burned. I stayed for a time at a quiet lodging house in the village of Kensington under an assumed name. I called myself Hester Rainwood, a former governess, of good family, of limited means. But my money would have soon run out, and I needed to find work. When I saw the advertisement for the position here at the Magdalen, I applied for the post. One of Lucy's clients gave Hester Rainwood a letter of reference. Lord knows what she told him. I thought I could help these women, as Lucy had helped me. Jacobus beat Lucy badly, trying to make her say where I was – but she insisted she didn't know, and in the end he believed her.'

Theresa looked around the little room, as if amazed at how far she had come. 'I remain here within these walls, lest I ever meet anyone who thinks they recognize Theresa Agnetti. My skin is perfectly yellow from the pennyroyal, so I hide behind my mask. I eat what I like, I read what I like. I am content with my lot, such as it is.' She frowned. 'But there is another girl living in my old house now and I am afraid for her.'

Child thought of Cassandra Willoughby: her cropped hair,

her fragility, her distress after her visit to the bowers with Lieutenant Dodd-Bellingham. Agnetti's cold fury with her that day at the Rotunda.

'I mourn Lucy so deeply,' Mrs Agnetti said. 'I wanted to do as she asked – to give Kitty's testimony to the newspapers, but I was afraid that if I did, Jacobus would find me. He is still looking for me, you see. He employs agents, writes letters. And if he tracks me down, there is no doubt in my mind that he'll kill me.'

Child shook his head, trying to clear it so he could think. 'How did Kitty know to send the letter to you here?'

'Lucy confided in her. Poor Kitty was so distressed to learn the truth about Mr Agnetti. She wrote to tell me about her marriage, said I wasn't to worry about her any longer. I never should have shown Lucy, but I felt bad about Pamela. Lucy had convinced me that she'd been murdered.'

'Why did you tell me about her distinctive carriage and the evangelical church? You wanted me to find her?'

'You said she was in danger. Kitty came here to see me in that carriage on the day Lucy was killed. Lucy had brought me Kitty's testimony only an hour earlier. Had they encountered one another and talked, I wonder if things would have been different. Kitty was angry with me for telling Lucy. I tried to calm her down, but she was so agitated. She said people would come looking for her, that she might be forced to give evidence in a trial.'

'Did Kitty know the rest?' Child asked, his voice rising in urgency. 'About the pennyroyal? That Lucy gave it to you? That she helped you to get away? Did Kitty know?'

'Yes,' Mrs Agnetti said. 'Kitty was our friend. She knew everything.'

Child remembered Orin Black's description of the bower.

Mad or bad, a real frenzy. He recalled his own words, on that first day of his inquiry: *Maybe the killer had just found something out about Lucy that he didn't like.*

Kitty didn't go to Vauxhall Gardens to see Simon Dodd-Bellingham, he thought. She went to see Jacobus Agnetti. To tell him that Lucy Loveless had helped his wife to murder his child. *He knows.*

Child rose from the table. 'Oh Christ,' he said.

CHAPTER EIGHTY-ONE

CARO AND AGNETTI stared at one another. Cassandra Willoughby gazed up at him silently. It was the same with Theresa, Caro thought, recalling her odd and awkward flirtations. What did Agnetti do to his women that they submitted to his will like this?

'You killed Lucy,' she said to him, not quite understanding, but certain of it. 'You killed Hector. You tried to kill me.'

How confident he must have been. How brazen to invite her here. Forcing Miss Willoughby to seduce her footman, to serve his wicked compulsion. A celebration of his cunning in getting away with murder.

Then there was Cassandra herself. Her namesake in antiquity had told the truth and had not been believed, whereas the woman in front of her had lied and lied again, in thrall to the man she loved. 'You painted the puzzle purses,' Caro said to her. 'And you took my son from the park.'

Agnetti turned. 'You sent her paintings? Why the devil would you do that?'

Miss Willoughby stammered: 'I wanted to scare her. I was worried for you, Jacobus.'

For a moment, as he glowered at the girl, Caro glimpsed the beating heart of his rage, before he seemed to recall the problem at hand.

'Fetch one of my canvas knives,' he said.

Miss Willoughby departed obediently. Caro's heart was thumping, her mouth filling with acid.

'You would kill me with my carriage outside, and your servants asleep upstairs? The world saw me walk out of Vauxhall on your arm. How will you explain my disappearance?'

Miss Willoughby returned. Wordlessly, she handed Agnetti the knife, the handle tied with red string, like the one that had killed Lucy. Agnetti ran his thumb along the edge.

'There will be no murder,' he said. 'Only a tragic act of suicide. All London knows of your shame. The fate that awaits you when your husband returns. You are simply sparing your husband and son the shame of divorce. We will say that I was painting you upstairs, and went to fetch some wine. When I returned, you were not there, and I presumed you'd gone home. By the time Miss Willoughby discovered you lying here in the dining room, your wrists slashed, it was too late.'

Caro screamed, hoping that the servants at the top of the house might hear her, or it would bring Miles running in from the carriage outside. A few seconds was all she managed before Agnetti's hand closed around her throat, forcing her backwards, up against the wall. He squeezed, smiling, enjoying her distress. Blackness began to creep over her vision, when he released her suddenly, dropping her to the floor.

'I am with child,' Caro said weakly. 'You would murder a baby too?'

'A child conceived in sin,' he said. 'Your whoring will not save you now.'

He crouched down beside her, knife in hand, and she kicked him in the chest. He fell sideways, and she tried to get up, but Miss Willoughby pushed her down. Agnetti grabbed her with his free hand, and she struggled, clawing and scratching. *If I am to die,* she thought, *let there be evidence of a struggle, evidence of murder.*

Agnetti grunted, and passed the knife to Miss Willoughby. 'I cannot hold her with one hand. You'll have to do the cutting.'

'The way he treats you,' Caro said, as Agnetti pinned her down, kneeling on one of her arms so she gasped in pain. 'Those things he makes you do. That isn't love. It is cruelty. It is inhuman. It is wrong.'

Agnetti seized her other hand, wrenching it round. Miss Willoughby frowned at the knife.

'Why did you really send those puzzle purses?' Caro said desperately. 'They were evidence that an artist was involved in these crimes, evidence that might have led us to this house. I think some part of you wanted all this to stop.'

But Miss Willoughby knelt, readying the knife. Caro struggled, but Agnetti was too strong.

'He used to do these things to his wife too,' she said. 'That's why Theresa left him. Did he tell you he is still looking for her? He has agents hunting for her, he's writing letters. Either he wants her back, or he wants her dead. Is that truly a man worthy of your love?'

Miss Willoughby rocked back on her heels. 'Jacobus?'

'She is lying,' he said shortly. 'There is only you. Now cut her wrist.'

'If you do this,' Caro said to Agnetti, 'you'll never find Theresa. Only I know where she is. The truth will die with me.'

He studied her face. 'You are lying.'

'Can you be certain?'

The knife cut into her, and she cried out. But Agnetti pushed Miss Willoughby roughly away.

Blood rolled down her arm. Agnetti put his face up to hers. 'How do you know?'

She smiled through the pain. 'Kitty told me.'

'Kitty said she didn't know.'

'She was lying.'

He placed his hand on her throat again. 'Tell me where she is.'

She laughed. 'No. Never.'

He hit her in the face and the explosion of pain silenced her. He drew his arm back and hit her again.

Miss Willoughby tugged at his arm. 'Jacobus, no. There will be bruises.'

He turned on her. 'You will speak when you're spoken to.' His grip on Caro's throat tightened. 'Where is she? Tell me and this will stop. Otherwise we will keep going until you do.'

Again he hit her. Blood filled her mouth. He lifted her hand. 'Tell me where she is, or I'll break your fingers.'

Except the sentence did not end like it should, but in a strangled gasp. Agnetti dropped Caro's hand. A trickle of blood ran down his chin. Miss Willoughby pulled the knife from his back and stared at it a moment. Then she plunged it into him again.

Agnetti slumped to the side, and Miss Willoughby withdrew the knife as he fell. She knelt beside him and plunged the blade into him again and again and again, until Caro managed to crawl to her side, and gently prised the knife from her hands. Then she took the girl in her arms and held her while she wept.

CHAPTER EIGHTY-TWO

CHILD CALLED UPON Mrs Corsham the following afternoon. Her ginger footman, looking a little chastened, showed him into her morning room. She was seated in an armchair, her feet upon a settle, covered in a blanket. Sunlight streamed through the open windows, casting an unforgiving light upon her bruises. Child had arrived at Agnetti's house in the aftermath of the bloodshed last night, where he had witnessed Mrs Corsham at her most imperious, after a hapless Bow Street Runner had attempted to arrest Miss Willoughby for the artist's murder.

'Don't look like that,' Mrs Corsham told him now. 'The doctor says nothing is broken. I will heal.'

He cleared his throat awkwardly. 'And the baby?'

'Oh, it lives, I am certain. Truly, I think this child will survive anything. Tell me, please, how is Miss Willoughby?'

'In the care of Mrs Hester Rainwood at the Magdalen Hospital.' He gave her a pointed glance.

'That is the name she chooses to continue living by? If she came forward, she would inherit her husband's estate – be a wealthy woman.'

'She chooses not to. If anyone will know how to help Miss Willoughby, then it is her.'

'I am glad of it,' Mrs Corsham said. 'When I think of everything those women have been through. Perhaps you could give her some glad news. My brother and Nicholas Cavill-Lawrence called to see me earlier. I told them that if there was any attempt to prosecute Miss Willoughby for Agnetti's murder, then I would give evidence in court on her behalf. The prospect did not please them. Tell her there will be no trial.'

'I'm on my way to see Humphrey Sillerton,' Child said. 'To inform him of his wife's death. He won't take it well, I think.'

'A sad business.' She sighed. 'I still struggle to believe that Kitty plotted to kill her dearest friend. And to use Agnetti to do it – given everything she knew.'

'She was desperate. Prepared to do anything to protect her new life.'

'In the wrong hands a secret is a weapon,' Mrs Corsham murmured. Then she pointed to a purse lying on the tea table. 'Your commission, Mr Child. I have also written to Mr Stone, and settled your debt with him. I didn't want you ending up in the Fleet Prison.'

Child felt himself blushing. 'You didn't need to do that, madam. Especially after everything I did.'

She held up a hand to silence him. 'You are going to be in the newspapers, I'm told. Two murderers caught in one day. Your skills as a thief-taker will be in demand.'

Child took the purse, weighing it in his hand. Everything he'd prayed for. If only he felt like he deserved it.

'Well, then.' He held out his hand and she shook it. '*Palmam qui meruit ferat.*'

'I'm afraid I don't know that one, Mr Child.'

'It means, we got the bastards – didn't we?'

She smiled, wincing a little at the pain it caused her. 'So we did.'

*

Three days later, Caro sat in her drawing room, reading. She had just put Gabriel to bed, dusk drawing in. Miles pulled the curtains and lit the lamps. Her bruises looked worse today, turning purple and yellow, but she felt better in herself and thought she might eat. As she contemplated what dish might sit most easily in her stomach, she heard the clatter of a carriage outside. Someone rapped at the front door, and she heard voices in the hall. A moment later, the drawing room door opened, and she stared at the man in the redcoat who filled the frame.

'Oh,' she said faintly. 'Harry.'

Her husband had lost a little weight – sea travel often had that effect upon a man. His soft brown eyes studied her face. 'I heard about what happened. Thank God it wasn't worse.'

But there was no tenderness in his eyes, and from his face she knew he'd heard the rest of the story too.

'Cavill-Lawrence said you were in America,' she said. 'That you would be there for several months more.'

'My reception in Philadelphia was warmer than we anticipated,' he said. 'Things were concluded rather sooner than we thought.'

'Then we will have peace?'

'I hope so.'

But not in this house, his expression said.

Walking to the console, he poured himself a glass of Madeira. He stayed there, drinking it, looking at her steadily – as if he'd preferred it when there had been an ocean between them.

'Is it true?' he said, at last. 'Are you with child?'

'Yes,' she said. 'I'm sorry.'

'Who is the father?' he asked. 'Lieutenant Dodd-Bellingham? Jacobus Agnetti?'

'Neither of them,' she said.

'Who then, Lord March?'

She hesitated, uncertain whether the truth or a lie would serve her best. His question was one she'd wrestled with herself, counting days and dates. It had been so hot back in July. Lord March there and not there – as she knew now, courting Clemency Howard. Night after night, she'd taken herself off to Carlisle House, seeking diversion. And one night she'd met a man who'd made her laugh, a Polish composer with a pointed beard and a wicked smile.

Now, here on judgement day, she opted for the truth – not because she thought it could save her, but because she felt too weary to lie any more.

'I don't know.'

The disgust on his face hurt her – as only he had ever had the power to do. He drained his glass and set it down. 'Let us discuss it in the morning. I am tired.'

She listened to him mounting the stairs, and then sat there for a long time. Eventually, she rose and went to the mirror over the console. Her bruises would fade, but the lines would only multiply – and no journalist ever made a list about those. She thought of Lucy's plan for her retirement: a plot of land in Hampstead on which to build houses. Lucy, who'd made her own way in an unkind world since she was twelve years old.

There will be a plan, she told herself. I just haven't thought of it yet. Let tomorrow bring what it will bring. I am Caro.

Historical Note

Those who read my first novel, *Blood and Sugar*, will already have been familiar with Caroline Corsham. I loved Caro as a character, and wanted to give her more scenes than the plot in that first book justified. Instead, I decided to give her a book of her own.

I took enormous pleasure in researching Caro's London. Jerry White's *London in the Eighteenth Century* (2012), Amanda Vickery's *The Gentleman's Daughter: Women's Lives in Georgian England* (2003), and Hannah Grieg's *The Beau Monde: Fashionable Society in Georgian London* (2013) are all excellent books for those wishing to learn more. *The Beau Monde* includes a chapter on those ladies who transgressed the boundaries of polite society by having adulterous relationships or illegitimate children. Some, like Georgiana, Duchess of Devonshire, were aided by their husbands to conceal their pregnancies, travelling abroad to give birth in secret. Others, like Lady Sarah Bunbury, Elizabeth, Countess of Derby, and the original 'Caro', Lady Caroline Lamb, were ostracized from polite society, forced to live lonely lives in the countryside or abroad. Others still, like the former Duchess of Grafton, managed to survive divorce by marrying a gentleman of sufficient social standing – in her case, the Earl of Upper Ossory – to overcome society's disapproval.

The stories about Caro in *The London Hermes* are based on those in contemporary scandal sheets, such as *The British Apollo*,

The Tatler and *The Female Tatler*. David Coke's *Vauxhall Gardens: A History* (2011) is a picturesque guide to the famous pleasure garden. Avril Hart and Susan North's *Historical Fashion in Detail: The 17th and 18th Centuries* (1998) and Susan North's *18th-Century Fashion in Detail* (2018) include beautiful photographs of the fashions of the beau monde.

The sex trade was a huge part of the Georgian economy, and according to one estimate, one in five female Londoners had participated in prostitution at some point in their lives. Hallie Rubenhold's *The Covent Garden Ladies* (2005) and Dan Cruickshank's *The Secret History of Georgian London* (2010) are both fascinating books, and provided me with much inspiration for both character and plot. The Whores' Club really existed, as did virgin auctions, tableaux performances and *Harris's List*. The fictional entries in *Harris's List* for Lucy Loveless and Kitty Carefree include some phrases and a poem that I have culled from original listings of long-dead prostitutes.

The Priapus Club drew much inspiration from both the Society of Dilettanti and the Medmenham Friars, or Hell-Fire Club. Both clubs professed an interest in ancient Greece and Rome, using their studies to justify and intellectualise sex with prostitutes. *The Secret History of Georgian London* has two interesting chapters on these clubs, which include sections on the Georgian passion for classically inspired architecture, landscape gardens and art. Other useful books were Evelyn Lord's *The Hell-Fire Clubs* (2008) and Geoffrey Ashe's *The Hell-Fire Clubs* (1974).

Once I had pinned down this part of the plot, the theme of ancient Greece and the classical world (a subject of fascination both to the Georgians and to myself since childhood) took on a life of its own. The collecting of antiquities was a passion for many Georgian gentlemen, and to see such a collection in situ

I recommend the quite wonderful Sir John Soane Museum in London. Both amateur enthusiasts and professional antiquarians often carried out 'restorations' on their antiquities that make the modern reader wince, and created an environment that was ripe for exploitation by fraudsters. Mark Jones's *Fake? The Art of Deception* (1990) provides a compelling history of archaeological fraud, dating back to the Middle Ages. The lottery tickets in the ancient oil lamp and the use of a barrel of nails to age counterfeit coins are real examples of eighteenth-century frauds taken from Jones's book.

Joshua Reynolds painted two portraits of the Dilettanti Club, on which Agnetti's painting of the Priapus Club is based. Reynolds also painted many of the leading prostitutes of his day, causing much speculation as to the precise nature of his relationships with his 'muses'. Again, Cruickshank's *The Secret History of Georgian London* has an excellent chapter on Reynolds, which explores his love of painting his clients and his muses in classically inspired scenes.

A second theme of the book, that of artifice and concealment, also arose quite naturally from the plot, and led me to many entertaining aspects of Georgian life: con-tricks like Lucy's Ring Game; masks and masquerades; the Puss and Mew; illegal boxing matches; false eyebrows of mouse fur; and fake pineapples. I even spent a very enjoyable afternoon making puzzle purses with my nieces.

Other plot lines grew out of this theme: a virgin auction, where the virgin wasn't really a virgin; a desperate man trying to conceal his syphilis; a staged burglary; a staged murder. Jacobus Agnetti is perhaps the ultimate example of concealment in the book: a man capable of great charm and also grotesque cruelty. Abusive relationships are as old as time, and it is not hard to find eighteenth-century examples of such marriages. A friend who works with the victims of domestic violence also recommended Sandra Horley's *Power and Control: Why Charming Men Can Make Dangerous Lovers* (2002), which was an informative and sobering read.

Lieutenant Dodd-Bellingham is loosely based on the wonderfully named Banastre Tarleton, a former rake turned hero of the American war. An evocative painting by Reynolds of Tarleton in action hangs in the National Gallery. At the Battle of Waxhaws, Tarleton's forces slaughtered a large number of American soldiers trying to surrender under a white flag. To the Americans, his name thereafter became a byword for war crimes and butchery. Tarleton's long-time amour, the actress Mary Robinson (or 'Perdita', as she was more widely known) had previously been the lover of the seventeen-year-old Prince of Wales, who had offered her twenty thousand pounds to become his mistress. Perdita was painted by many of the leading artists of the day, including Reynolds, Gainsborough and Romney.

Jonathan Stone is loosely based on John King, a famous eighteenth-century moneylender, who brokered loans for those wishing to lend above the legal interest rate of 5 per cent. To do so, he had to work his way into the circles of the beau monde, entertaining regularly, and thoroughly researching the backgrounds of potential aristocratic debtors. King was said to be another of Perdita's lovers, and is also alleged to have tried to blackmail her, threatening to reveal compromising letters between her and the Prince of Wales.

The libidinous appetites of 'Prinny' – heir to the throne, later the Prince Regent and King George IV – have been depicted in countless books, films and TV programmes. Just as famous as his love of women was his love of profligate living and consequent debts. By 1787, these had reached such astronomical levels that Parliament was forced to act, voting to provide the extraordinary sum of £161,000 to settle with the Prince's creditors – on condition that he never got into debt again. To nobody's surprise at all, by 1795, Prinny's debts amounted to £630,000. Saul David's *Prince of Pleasure* (1998) has several chapters on Prinny's early life.

King George III's depression at the loss of the American colonies is equally well documented. In March 1782, immediately prior to the Paris peace talks, he went so far as to draw up letters of abdication addressed to Parliament and his son. No decisive evidence has ever emerged to explain why he changed his mind.

Acknowledgements

For a writer, so much depends upon the team around them, and I am fortunate to be supported by the very best in the business. Thank you firstly to Antony Topping, who is by turns shrewd, calm, insightful, imaginative and funny – everything a writer needs in an agent. Thanks too to everyone at Greene & Heaton, especially Kate Rizzo.

My editor, Maria Rejt, is warm and wise, and I could not wish for a better champion of my books and my writing. Indeed, the whole team at Mantle and Pan Macmillan are a marvel, both in their love of books and knowing what to do with them. Thanks in particular to Josie Humber, Alice Gray, Rosie Wilson, Kate Tolley, Ami Smithson (who makes my books look so beautiful) and to Stuart Dwyer and his team, who magic them into the shops.

Many brilliant experts in their field answered my annoying questions as I was writing this book . . . Hallie Rubenhold, who knows everything there is to know about sex in the eighteenth century; Dr Kate Adams, who answered countless medical questions about syphilis and pennyroyal; Dan Fox and Alexander Goldberg, who fielded all my obscure questions about eighteenth-century Judaica; Robbie MacNiven and Stephen Brumwell, who helped me commit a war crime; Jessica Asato, who recommended some terrifying books on coercive control; and the Facebook mothers' collective, who told this childless author more about the symptoms of pregnancy than I ever wanted to know. Needless to say, any mistakes in the book are mine, not theirs.

Thanks also to Glenn Parry for the pineapples, Julia Bye for the German, Dad for the Puss and Mew, Adrian for Henry's wives, Rebecca F. John for Rag and Ribbon, and Imogen Robertson and Fay Young for novel clinic.

The love and support of the writing community has been a revelation to me, and I am so fortunate to have made so many new friends. Thanks especially to David Headley and everyone at Goldsboro Books; to the all-conquering Ladykillers, who murder – martinis in hand – so very effortlessly; and to Colin Scott, who is always there to say YAY and FTS. It would be a lie to say this book couldn't have been written without them, but I would have had a lot less fun along the way.

The excitement and support of my old friends and family as I embarked on this new career means more than I can ever put into words. In particular, a loving thank you to my brother, Luke, mainly because he will be annoyed if I leave him out. The day I spent making puzzle purses with my sister-in-law, Gemma, and my nieces, Holly and Lyla, was a particular highlight amidst the wrestles of writing this book.

Daughters of Night is dedicated to my dad, teller of stories, slayer of monsters. In 1982, when I was six years old, Dad went away to Greece for months, to appear in Peter Hall's production of the *Oresteia*. I didn't want him to go, and to cheer me up we made a scrapbook about the play – a wholesome tale of sex, revenge and murder – and I think of this book as the flowering of that seed of interest. Nearly forty years on, Dad is still always there for me, even when he's on the other side of the world. I love him so very much.

Acknowledgements

Finally, the biggest thank you goes, as ever, to my husband, Adrian. His love and pride mean the world to me, his support is given every day. I can't write it all down here, as it would fill volumes, but truly I married the best of men.

Reading Group Questions

1. How well did the book portray the nightlife of eighteenth-century London? Could you picture the entertainments of the beau monde? And the world of the sex trade? Where and how did those two worlds meet? How did the latter imitate the former?

2. In Caro and Agnetti's first meeting, they debate the rights and wrongs of the Georgian sex trade. Did you have sympathy with either point of view? How similar was their argument to today's debates about prostitution?

3. In what ways did the book portray the eighteenth-century's obsession with the classical world of Greece and Rome? Why do you think the author chose the four quotes from the *Oresteia* to begin each part of the novel?

4. Artifice and concealment are a second theme of the book. Can you think of examples from the plot? Or from characters? Or in the background details? Can you think of similar examples from contemporary society? Do you think we are we more or less concerned with appearance today?

5. Did you like Caro as a character? Did you sympathize with her predicament? How did the book make you feel about the double standards that existed for women and

men in the eighteenth century when it came to sex and adultery? What do you think Harry's decision will be about Caro and his marriage?

6. What did you think about the power of money, commerce and debt in eighteenth-century society? How did you feel about the choices that Peregrine Child made in the book? Did he retain your sympathy as a character?

7. Did Pamela's story help you understand why women were drawn to prostitution? Did her choices change the way you felt about her as a victim? How reliable was she as a narrator?

8. How well did the three narrative strands in the story mesh together? Did Pamela's story in the past help you better understand the murder inquiry in the present? Did you enjoy the contrast between Caro and Child's distinct spheres of investigation?

9. How did you feel about the way the book portrayed relations between women and men in the eighteenth century? Were there differences and similarities to today's society?

10. How did you feel about the character of Jacobus Agnetti? Did your opinion of him change throughout the book? How big a surprise was the revelation about the Agnetti marriage at the end of the book?

Loved *Daughters of Night?* Discover Laura
Shepherd-Robinson's first novel, *Blood & Sugar* . . .

Waterstones Thriller of the month and winner of the
Historical Writers' Association Debut Crown

June, 1781. An unidentified body hangs upon a hook at Deptford
Dock – horribly tortured and branded with a slaver's mark.

Some days later, Captain Harry Corsham – a war hero embarking
upon a promising parliamentary career – is visited by the sister
of an old friend. Her brother, passionate abolitionist Tad Archer,
had been about to expose a secret that he believed could cause
irreparable damage to the British slaving industry. He'd said
people were trying to kill him, and now he is missing . . .

To discover what happened to Tad, Harry is forced to pick up
the threads of his friend's investigation, delving into the heart
of the conspiracy Tad had unearthed. His investigation will
threaten his political prospects, his family's happiness, and
force a reckoning with his past, risking the revelation of
secrets that have the power to destroy him.

And that is only if he can survive the mortal dangers
awaiting him in Deptford . . .

An extract follows here . . .

PROLOGUE

Deptford Dock, June 1781

The fog hung thick and low over the Thames. It rolled in off the water and along the quays, filling the squalid courts and dock-side alleys of lower Deptford. The local name for a fog like this was the Devil's Breath. It stank of the river's foul miasma.

Now and then the fog lifted, and Nathaniel Grimshaw caught a glimpse of the Guineamen anchored out on Deptford Reach: spectral lines of mast and rigging against the dawn sky. His greatcoat was heavy with damp and his horsehair wig smelled of wet animal. He had been pacing in that spot for nearly half an hour. Each time he pivoted, Jago growled. The dog's black fur stood up in spikes and his eyes shone like tiny yellow fog-lamps in the gloom.

Nathaniel could hear the fishermen talking, and he could taste their tobacco on the wind. He wanted a pipe himself, but he wasn't sure he could hold it down. He didn't know how they could stand there, in such close proximity. A figure loomed out of the mist, and Jago growled again, though he quietened when he recognized the stocky, square frame of the Deptford magis-trate, Peregrine Child. A pair of bleary eyes peered at Nathaniel between the wet folds of the magistrate's long wig of office. 'Where is it, lad?'

Nathaniel led him through the fog to the wall that divided

the Public Dock from the Navy Yard. The fishermen parted to let them through, each man turning to observe Child's reaction.

On the quayside stood a ten-foot pole topped by a riveted iron hook, where the fishermen liked to hang their largest catches. Lately it had displayed a shark that had washed up here last month. Now the shark was gone and in its place hung a man. He was naked, turning on a rope in the wind, secured under the arms, with his hands tied behind him. Nathaniel didn't like blood and there was a lot of it – dried on the dead man's chest and back, smeared across his thighs, in his ears, in his nose, in his mouth. He had seen murdered men before – washed up on the mudflats, or dumped in the dockside alleys where he worked as a nightwatchman. None of them had prepared him for this. This one was more than a corpse. He was a spectacle, like the boneless man at the Greenwich Fair.

Steeling himself, he studied the man again. He was about thirty years of age, very thin, with long black hair. His eyes wide open, staring accusingly. His lips were pulled back in a frozen rictus, white skin stretched taut over angled cheekbones. Beneath the first mouth was a second: a gaping, scarlet maw where the throat had been slashed.

Child stepped forward, his face inches from the body. 'Jesu.'

He was staring at a spot just above the dead man's left nipple. The lines seared into the pale, hairless skin were smooth and deep. The flesh around them was puckered and blistered. From where he stood, Nathaniel could just make out the design: a crescent moon on its side surmounted by a crown.

'It's a slave brand,' he said. 'Someone's marked him like a Negro.'

'I know what it is.' Child stepped back, still staring at the body.